Superior Collision
Book Five
Crossing Forces

SUPERIOR COLLISION

CROSSING FORCES BOOK FIVE

USA TODAY BESTSELLING AUTHOR

C. A. SZAREK

Superior Collision
C.A. Szarek
Crossing Forces Book Five

Paper Dragon Publishing
North Richland Hills, TX

eBook ISBN: 978-1-941151-31-0
Paperback ISBN: 978-1-941151-32-7
Published in the United States of America

Second eBook Edition: January, 2018
Second Print Edition: January, 2018

Other Books by C.A. Szarek

<u>Crossing Forces—Romantic Suspense</u>

Collision Force (Book One)
Cole in Her Stocking (A Crossing Forces Christmas)—*FREE read!*
Chance Collision (Book Two)
Calculated Collision (Book Three)
Collision Control (Book Four)
Superior Collision (Book Five)
Incendiary Collision (Book Six)—*Coming soon!*

<u>The King's Riders—Epic Fantasy Romance</u>

Sword's Call (Book One)—*Also in Audio!*
Love's Call (Book Two)—*Also in Audio!*
Rogue's Call (Book Three)—*Also in Audio!*
Fate's Call (A Novella from the World of the King's Riders)—*Also in Audio!*

<u>Highland Secrets—Historical Fantasy/Time Travel</u>

The Tartan MP3 Player (Book One)
The Fae Ring (Book Two)
The Parchment Scroll (Book Three)
Highlander's Portrait (A Highland Secrets Story)—*Coming soon to Audio!*
Highland Valentine (A Highland Secrets

Story)—*only .99*
The Princess and The Laird (A Highland Secrets Prequel)

<u>Highland Treasures—Historical Fantasy/Time Travel</u>

Highland Oath (Book One)—*Coming January 2018!*
Highland Essence (Book Two)—*Coming soon!*

<u>Anthologies</u>

Deep in the Hearts of Texas—*FREE read!*
    Story: Promise (A Crossing Forces Companion)

Crossing Forces

Small Town Texas doesn't always mean small time crime.

Welcome to Antioch, population fifty thousand.

With a police department full of detectives and officers who are good at what they do, throw in the occasional FBI agent, and the bad guy doesn't have a shot, no matter how big the crime.

They work together and fight together. Relationships will be forged and changed along the twists and turns.

When fate intervenes, love and happiness can be found in unlikely places.

Dedication

This one's for my father-in-law, Chip. We didn't expect to lose you in 2016, but I'm glad we got to say goodbye. It always blew my mind that you read my books, and that you loved this series as much as I do.

I remember you telling me I made you blush! But then again, you always made me laugh.

I'm sorry you didn't get to read this one, I'm sure you would've liked Taylor and Shannon.

Here's to hoping there are bookstores (or libraries) in Heaven! I'll always miss you, Dad.

Chapter One

"**Y**ou have *got* to be kidding me!" Taylor glared at the little paper monster under the driver's side windshield wiper of her government-issue black Dodge Charger.

It had the indecency of flapping in the winter breeze. Like it was waving—or laughing.

"A freaking parking ticket."

Scratch that.

Another freaking parking ticket. She hated to admit it, even in her own head.

It was obvious from one look at her car that she was FBI—which was exactly *why* the meter maid hated her. And, a little voice whispered, *exactly* why Taylor continued parking in the same spot outside her building in downtown Dallas anyway.

She shook her head at her pride and stubbornness. When working a case, it helped. When she was trying to prove a point she was *obviously* losing, it didn't. Besides, breaking the rules wasn't her at all. She needed to pay the two tickets—before they turned into something worse than just a fine.

"I'd never hear the end of it around the office."

John would've laughed.

She jerked, her hand shaking as she reached for the thermal paper.

Stop. Right. Now.

She'd forbidden herself from saying his name since she'd found out who'd killed him, several months ago.

Taylor would get justice for her fiancé—and former partner—but she'd decided to move on. To stop mourning him and do things like she always had. Like she'd been trained to do.

Get justice for him because it was right, and not out of some sense of revenge.

Because the latter wasn't only wrong, it wasn't *her*, either.

She'd let the need for vengeance drive her for months, and had nearly killed the wrong man. Something she couldn't have rectified if he'd died.

Guilt haunted her, even now.

Joe Pompa and what'd happened in that safe house in Antioch, Texas consumed her nightmares. Made her second-guess herself, too.

Taylor sucked in a breath and pushed the memories away.

Things to do.

She glared at the ticket one last time before she got in the car.

In about an hour, she had a meeting with the federal prosecutor on her case, Ross Catrone.

"Guess I'd better go to Muni Court instead." She whipped the stupid ticket toward the passenger seat, and snarled when it floated to the floor.

It was laughing at her again.

The ten minute drive turned into twenty, due to the lunchtime traffic downtown. She cussed the whole way.

Her day was shit—had been even *before* the new ticket.

Negativity was her new friend, and she couldn't seem to shake it. Her boss, Matthias Baker, had called her into his office first thing that morning to have the *partner* talk again.

How many times did she have to tell him she didn't want a new partner?

Didn't *need* one, either.

Taylor sighed and drummed her fingers on the steering wheel as she waited for a massive Ford truck to move so she could park.

When she'd left the office, Baker had hollered that they weren't done.

She groaned when she saw the waiting line to the window clerks. Everyone else had had the same idea of paying their tickets at lunchtime, too.

Taylor waited. And waited. At this rate, she'd be late for her meeting and starving.

She forced her hand down at her side so she wouldn't stalk her watch anymore. Couldn't stop tapping her leg while she waited. The ticket rustled in her palm.

OCD much?

The shout of "Next!" was forever away.

The clerk smiled in the '*hurry, I'm busy*' way as she slid the new ticket in the little slot.

"Can I see your ID, please?"

Her FBI badge was closest, so she held it up to the bulletproof glass.

The woman's overdrawn eyebrows rose, then her eyes moved from Taylor to her photo and back. She looked down at the ticket, typed something into her computer then looked up. "Ah. You got this today. I'm sorry, ma'am—"

"Special Agent." Taylor tried not to bark.

The clerk didn't even look a little contrite. She narrowed her eyes. "I'm sorry, *Special Agent*. As I was trying to say, if you just received this today, you need to give the court time for processing before you can pay it. It can take up to two weeks."

Two weeks? Seriously? So inefficient.

"Wish I woulda known that," she muttered.

"It states it on the ticket, ma'am."

Touché.

She sighed and bit back her retort. Didn't need to take her bad day out on the poor court clerk, even if the woman's customer service skills needed a tweak. Taylor took the offending thermal paper back when the clerk passed it to her. "Can I pay the old one?"

"Yes, ma'am. Do you have the citation?"

"No, I'm sorry, I don't."

The woman threw her a look that said, *'really?'* Or maybe, *'you should know better'.* That penciled eyebrow was arched as high as possible, and the clerk's mouth was a hard line that shouted her patience with Taylor had come and gone.

It went downhill from there.

"Sixty-eight freaking dollars? *Seriously?*"

Since she'd have to go back for the other ticket later, it was really sixty-eight times two.

She grumbled all the way to the car. Glanced at her watch again when her stomach screamed.

Food or Catrone?

Not that she really had any news to share. Had tried to cancel the meeting, but the stubborn man had insisted on them keeping the appointment so Taylor could *'update'* him.

That'd better not be code for trying to ask me out again.

He could hound her about anything but *that.*

She'd chased Carter Bennett—the bastard who'd killed her fiancé—to Oklahoma and back. There were rumors he'd headed out to California again, where he'd killed two of his own crew, but he hadn't turned up, despite all the eyes she had looking out.

She needed him to hit a car train or something. If she

could prove he was working again—stealing high dollar rides and fencing them—he'd be a hell of a lot easier to track. Even a single stolen Hummer would be helpful.

Taylor shook her head. Upholding the law was supposed to be her thing. Not wishing for someone to break it.

Maybe she should call Eddie Vasquez again. See if the LA-based agent had any new info. But the guy was pretty good about calling her, so he would've already if he had something, right?

She tapped the steering wheel then stopped when she caught the action. Nervous tics weren't her deal, despite the few she'd caught herself doing lately.

Taylor refused to let this case rule her.

She would rule *it*.

Get Carter Bennett.

The judge's gavel came down hard twice.

Shannon tried not to groan from his seat. His knee bobbed up and down until he put his hand on his leg. The polyester fabric of his dress uniform class A's scratched his palm.

He hadn't been called to testify yet.

Hated coming into Dallas for DWI trials, but it had to be done. The only alternative was not to haul idiots in for driving drunk.

That wasn't an alternative at all.

He owed his sister more than that.

This particular piece of scum was looking at real time. During his third DWI, and he'd caused a bad accident. Three people hurt, one killed.

Shannon had been first on scene. He'd recognized the asshole, too. Had arrested the guy on DWI number two a year before.

This one was worse than the second. He'd never forget that sight, in front of the CVS on Main Street. The drunk's POS Buick—circa 1980s—had been twisted up *inside* the hood of a late model minivan.

His heart had hit his combat boots when he'd heard the screaming toddler in the back seat. He'd rushed to the van and called for an ambulance even before backup had made scene.

Then he'd seen the little girl crying right beside her brother. Both kids were under five, and their car seats had saved them from serious injury.

Their mother had survived the accident with a collapsed lung and broken bones, but her best friend, a woman way too young to die, had not. The deceased wasn't much older than Shannon's sister had been.

The loser driver had been charged with Intoxication Manslaughter this time.

Too bad the first two DWIs, and their accompanying jail time, hadn't been deterrent enough to keep him from getting behind the wheel the third time. God knew how many times he'd made it home without getting caught.

"We'll recess until one," Judge Newton announced. The older man knocked his gavel twice.

Shannon wasn't the only one to groan.

The trial had only started that morning, and it already felt like weeks. There was no way it was going to be a one-and-done kind of trip into Dallas.

Nikki, his boss's assistant, had booked his hotel for a week, but it'd likely take longer than that. They were playing it by ear, but he definitely wanted to go home to Antioch on the weekend. Wanted to see his mom and Cailey, even if only for a day or two. Being stuck at trial wasn't his idea of taking time away from work. He'd rather be on shift, in his patrol car.

He glanced at his watch. It was almost noon anyway, so a lunch break couldn't hurt.

Onlookers started to rise and file out.

Shannon stood, resisting the urge to stretch. When he was about to go, the prosecutor called his name. He closed the distance to her, trying not to show his irritation at the way the morning had gone.

Veronica Wesley had been the assistant district attorney on a few of his cases. She was competent and seasoned, but the pretty thirty-something attorney wasn't as good as Nate Crane.

Damn, Shannon missed the guy. Brother to one of APD's finest, Detective Pete Crane, Nate had up and moved to New York City a few years ago to be an ADA there. He'd married an FBI agent, to boot.

The prosecutor smiled, and he forced one in return. Her blue eyes were friendly. "Sorry about the long morning, Sergeant."

He shrugged. "It happens."

"I was sure they'd take a deal, but Barry wouldn't hear of it. He's confident his case is airtight." She tucked a strand of blonde hair behind her ear. It'd escaped her curly updo.

Shannon studied her.

Was she nervous? Or was it something else?

Barry Whitmore, the defense attorney, was no better than an ambulance chaser, but he was too polite to point it out.

"Airtight? Against our case?" he asked.

She shifted in her stilettos. Her gray pinstriped skirt suit drew his attention. It stopped just above her knees. Her blazer was tight, and the pink blouse she wore beneath revealed cleavage. Her outfit was just the right combination of sexy and professional, but Veronica Wesley wasn't his type.

"Our case is just as tight," she said finally.

"Good."

The prosecutor didn't say anything.

"Is there an issue?" Shannon asked.

Her brow furrowed, but she shook her head. "No, just expect it to be long and drawn-out."

He nodded, but didn't like the look on her face. "Why didn't he want to take a plea?"

Was she trying to imply that he or APD had done did something procedurally wrong?

She hadn't mentioned any concerns in their pretrial conference.

As much as Shannon might've wanted to, neither he nor his guys had laid an inappropriate hand on the piece of scum on scene, or afterward when he'd been booked.

"Because we're proceeding on Intox Manslaughter. The deal was more years than they'd agree to."

He crossed his arms over his chest and scoffed. "Please. It's no less than he deserves. It'd be murder, if I had a say."

Ms. Wesley nodded. "I don't disagree. A DWI Three on its own is bad enough."

"I don't care how long it takes, as long as he goes to prison. It won't give Jenny Kinkaid her life back, or return her to her family, but it's closure for them."

"You sound like you speak from experience, Sergeant Crowley."

He grunted. "Yeah. My sister. Same sitch. She was only twenty-three and left a two-year-old for my mom to raise." Shannon didn't like talking about his sister. Eleven years ago felt fresh, especially when he had to deal with a drunk at trial.

The prosecutor's gaze was sympathetic. "I'm sorry."

"It was a long time ago, but it's why I'm all for keeping drunks off the road."

"Well, as long as you crossed your *t's* and dotted your *i's*, we'll be fine. Your reports are great, as is the video footage. We'll be fine." She seemed to relax with every word. Her shoulders loosened and she smiled again.

"By the book, Ms. Wesley. Like always."

"Sounds good, Sergeant." Her expression was pleased. "Are you going to grab lunch?"

"Yes." Shannon glanced at his watch. "We have an hour."

"There are lots of places within walking distance."

"Thanks."

Her tongue darted out, moistening her bottom lip, highlighting her pink lipstick. Blue eyes locked onto his.

He paused, waiting for her to speak.

"Do you have a place in mind?" the prosecutor asked.

Shannon tried not to blink.

Is she asking to come with?

Ms. Wesley answered by looking him up and down.

Wow. Didn't see that coming.

He smiled and reached for his cellphone. "I have to make a call, but I'll see you after lunch, Ms. Wesley." Feigning busyness was easier than letting her down. No one liked to be rejected. Besides, if she was into him, it wasn't professional. That didn't work for him.

Disappointment darted across her face, but she schooled her expression fast and gave a curt nod. "Be ready, I'm going to call you to the stand when we reconvene."

"You got it."

Chapter Two

The scent of Italian food teased her nose even before Taylor made a fist to knock on Ross Catrone's office door. Her stomach rolled over and growled.

Well, it was more like curses at this point. She hadn't eaten anything except a protein shake circa six a.m. after a two mile run on her treadmill.

"Come in."

The federal prosecutor wore a wide smile when she slipped inside and shut the door. He had a takeout container in front of him—lasagna by the looks of it—and her stomach demanded she stake a claim.

She cleared her throat. "Looks like this is a bad time—"

"Not at all, have a seat. And some lunch." Catrone reached into a white paper bag with green and red writing on it. He slid a Styrofoam container toward her.

"For me?"

"Sure. Thought it'd be rude to set a lunchtime meeting and not feed you. Hope you haven't eaten. Sorry I didn't wait, I was starving."

"Ah. Thanks." Taylor took one of the chairs in front of his desk. Her suspicious nature made her arch an eyebrow as she perched on the edge of the seat.

The man took one look at her and laughed. His dark eyes twinkled. "Go on, Special Agent. I don't consider this a date. No worries."

She didn't relax in her seat. Nor did she reach for the food, even though her stomach was threatening to digest itself. "Why did you want to see me?"

"Ah, cutting to the chase?"

"Yes, sir. No use wasting time."

The prosecutor *tsked* and sliced into thick layers of pasta and meat with plastic-ware. "Life's too short to be so uptight, Carrigan. Relax. Let a man buy you lunch once in a while." His gaze was hooded as he took a bite.

Taylor sucked back a sigh, or maybe a groan. "Look, I appreciate the sentiment—"

Catrone laughed. "I'm not asking you out." He grinned. "Won't make that mistake again. It might put me in physical peril." When he winked, she gave in to her desire to smirk.

She crossed her arms over her chest. "What did you want to see me about?" she repeated, choosing not to remark on his jibe. Might get too specific about what *parts* of him were in peril. Not exactly politically correct.

Not that Catrone would, but she'd hate to have the tables turned and give him fuel for a sexual harassment claim.

"Just wanted to check in. We haven't chatted in some time."

"Not much to tell. No new sign of Bennett. We still haven't found Rowdy Vargas—dead or alive."

"Hmmm, it's been too long for Bennett to have not made a move."

"You're tellin' me." Taylor tried to keep her frustration under wraps. She gave in to temptation and opened the Styrofoam container he'd presented to her. The delicious scent of garlic and marinara sauce hit her senses and she swallowed a moan.

"Hope you like lasagna. It's my favorite, so I was goin' on faith." He winked again and she wanted to roll her eyes.

"I do. Thank you."

"Still so formal, Carrigan." His words were wrapped in amusement.

She ignored him and took a bite. Flavor burst on her tongue. The perfect combination of sweet red sauce, melty cheese, ground beef and soft noodles. She held back her delight. The lasagna was awesome.

"So, what's your next move?" Catrone asked.

Taylor refocused on him instead of her delicious lunch. Didn't want to admit she was open to suggestions—or that she was so stuck. "I've gone over all the reports a dozen times. I've got everyone on the lookout from California to Oklahoma. Bennett has no family. Neither does Vargas, so there wasn't anyone to seek out and question."

"What about Joe Pompa?"

Her heart skipped. "What about him?"

"Have you reached out to him lately?"

I wouldn't be able to look him in the eye.

"No. I don't think he's relevant to the case at the moment. He's in Texarkana awaiting trial."

"But you did interview him?"

No.

"He gave several statements, yes."

Catrone tilted his head to one side. "You didn't speak to him personally?"

No, but I read all the reports.

Taylor cleared her throat and forced her eyes to remain locked with the prosecutor's. "I didn't find it necessary, after I reviewed his statements and the final reports. And, of course, our entire FBI file, as well as what Antioch PD submitted. Detectives Lucas and Manning were very thorough."

"Hmmm..."

"If you have something to say, just say it."

He paused with his fork partway to his mouth. Averted his gaze, but only for a second. "I've never known you to be a coward."

"Excuse me?" She fought a wince when her inquiry broke, instead of sounding like the demand she'd been going for.

Catrone sighed and met her dead-on. "Look, I know what happened in Antioch, and I'd like to think I know you pretty well—"

"You don't. And the rest isn't any of your business."

His handsome face softened and Taylor glared.

She didn't want to know what he had to say next, and she regretted the defensive bark.

No one knew how Joe Pompa haunted her, and *that* wasn't about to change.

"Carrigan, I'm not telling you how to run your investigation—"

"Then don't. I know what I'm doing."

"All I'm saying," he went on as if she hadn't interrupted, "is don't leave any stone unturned. Pompa might be able to help. He's been on his feet for a few months now. Seeing what he might know couldn't hurt."

"I don't need him. I need to get Bennett."

The prosecutor threw his paper napkin over his empty food container and reclined in his leather chair. He sighed, and studied her until she wanted to squirm. "You're letting this eat at you."

Taylor rose and schooled her expression. "We're done here. Thanks for lunch, and I'll keep you posted on anything new."

"Carrigan, wait—"

She didn't.

Taylor grabbed her half-eaten lasagna only because her stomach was still rumbling. Pride demanded she leave it, but hunger won this round. She closed the container with as much grace as she could manage, and didn't spare

Catrone a parting glance.

Before she could reach for the door, it swung open. She heard a feminine exclamation at the same time warm tomato sauce hit her neck and slid down her chest, noodles and chunks of meat following before the Styrofoam hit the floor.

The container split, lasagna went flying. Like a bomb, red sauce-spatter was left in its wake, dotting her shoes and the pale tile. Probably her pants, too, but they were black and it didn't show.

"Oh my God! I'm so sorry!" Wide light blue eyes were frantic when Taylor looked up. Margot, Catrone's assistant, wore a mortified expression and pink cheeks.

It didn't make her feel any better.

She bit back an expletive and assessed the carnage to her white silk blouse. "Accidents happen," she muttered.

Catrone was on his feet and around his desk in seconds, with a roll of paper towels in hand. "Here, I always keep these around for emergencies."

Taylor looked at her shirt, then the floor. "Looks like a murder scene."

He tore off a few paper towels and handed the wad over. "Who's the victim? You or the lasagna?" The prosecutor was amused, but his young blonde assistant looked even more horrified.

Taylor smirked. "Not sure, since I *was* going to eat it." She gestured to her ruined fine silk. "Maybe my shirt."

"I'm so sorry!" Margot covered her face with the file folders in her grip. "I'll get it cleaned for you and buy you more food."

"That's not necessary. Don't worry about it."

The younger woman—girl, really, she couldn't' be twenty-five—didn't look convinced, but her boss threw her a nod and she seemed to relax.

Taylor tried to escape, but Margot continually apologized. She ignored the assistant and said her goodbyes, dashing out before the building day porter had made it to the office after Catrone's call about the mess.

She sighed when her detour to the restroom did nothing to save her top. Buttoning her blazer didn't cover up the glaring red-orange stain, either. It lined her collar and covered her chest.

Taylor glanced at her watch. She was going to have to go home and change before she headed back to the office.

My day is even shittier than before.

Grumbling about wasting time—something she despised—she dug for her car keys and trotted to the parking spot she'd been lucky enough to snag right outside the building. Still time left on her meter, so there was no parking ticket to greet her.

Thank God.

Someone called her name before she could push the button on her fob to open the Charger's door.

Taylor glanced over her shoulder, intending a dismissal for whoever was about to bother her, but stopped in her tracks.

A dark-haired uniformed cop jogged toward her, small paper bag in hand. He wore a friendly smile that made her belly flutter, but she promptly ignored that.

She also ignored the urge to cover her tomato-sauce-stained shirt with both hands.

"Special Agent Carrigan, it's good to see you."

She met unusually colored amber eyes and had to swallow hard.

Taylor had met Sergeant Shannon Crowley from Antioch Police Department when she'd been working her case—chasing Joe Pompa—with Detective Cole Lucas and

Pompa's brother, Detective Jared Manning, five months before.

He'd been the one to debrief her—and confiscate her weapon—after the shooting.

"Nice to see you, too, Sergeant." She cleared her throat and straightened her shoulders, but *really* wanted to flee to her car.

His smile widened and her knees wobbled a little.

What's wrong with me?

Her face warmed and she fought the urge to lean on the Charger. "What brings you to Dallas?"

Sergeant Crowley studied her before answering. "Trial."

Taylor fidgeted. "Ah. How's it going?"

"Just started today but it's going to be a long one. DWI Three and Intoxication Manslaughter."

"Oh wow." She couldn't look away from his eyes. Or his high cheekbones. Full mouth. Dark hair that was just a tad too long, in need of a good cut. That didn't matter— it gave him a charming air. Fit well with his smile and tall muscular frame. His shoulders were broad and she remembered what it felt like to be up against his side.

In the protection of his strong grip.

He'd put his arm around her when she'd needed it, and hadn't judged her for falling apart.

She'd been drawn to him then. Thankful in a way she could never repay. Because she'd been in crisis, of course.

No other reason.

Crowley was speaking, but Taylor didn't process anything, just watched his lips moving.

Seeing him for the first time darted into her mind. She'd been meeting her temporary partner, Detective Jared Manning, also for the first time, at a bar in Antioch called *McAuley's*.

The sergeant had held the door open. He'd been wearing tight jeans he'd had no issue filling out, and a brown leather jacket.

"Agent Carrigan?"

She jumped. He'd been waiting for her to speak and she'd been staring.

Like an idiot.

"Are you okay?"

Taylor forced a nod and wanted to glare. He was hot even when he was concerned. "Just having a hell of a day." She gestured to her stained shirt, then cursed.

Nothing like pointing it out.

Her neck burned. She shut down unfamiliar embarrassment by chanting her father's mantra.

Emotion is weak.

"Sorry to hear that."

Damn, he looks so genuinely bothered for me.

"Not your fault."

Sergeant Crowley nodded and lifted the paper bag. "Well, I need to eat and get back. We're only recessed until one."

"It was nice to see you again."

"You too."

He smiled, and Taylor had to swallow. Again.

She threw him a nod and turned to open the car door. "Good luck with the rest of your trial."

"Hey, listen."

She paused and glanced over her shoulder.

"I'll be in town all this week, maybe into next. Wanna get together? You can tell me all about your bad day over dinner tonight."

She froze. Her mouth opened, but no words exited. Her heart sped up and she shut down the urge to say yes.

Dammit.

"Actually—" she finally managed, but couldn't turn back to him.

His expression fell and she felt like a piece of shit for some reason.

Taylor cleared her throat for the hundredth time that morning. "I'm really mired in a case right now, so I can't. But maybe I'll run into you again before you leave town."

He nodded, but he was already backing away from her car.

Lasagna churned like cement in her stomach and her movements were jerky as she lumbered into the Charger and started it. She forced her eyes away from the handsome uniformed cop. Drove away, not returning his parting wave because it made her feel like an even bigger idiot.

Taylor chastised herself on the drive back to her apartment.

Her reaction to him was...an inconvenience. She was reading into things that weren't there, in herself *and* in the sergeant.

He'd comforted her in a time of need, and walked her through what'd happened with Joe Pompa in that Antioch safe house. He'd been nothing if not professional when he'd taken her statement and had kept her distracted from what she'd done. Kept her calm and factual.

Sergeant Shannon Crowley had been doing his job.

Nothing more.

Nothing less.

Chapter Three

"**F**uck you." Carter slammed the receiver down into the cradle and rammed his hand through his messy hair. That made his shoulder ache, and he cursed even more.

His months-old bullet wound was all but healed, but it still took a bite out of him when he moved too fast, or stretched his biceps out. He'd dug out the bullet himself, and hadn't that been a big-ass piece of craptacular cake, topped with shit-flavored icing.

One of Bubba's bimbos had stitched him up, and given him a blow job to *'make him feel better'*. Well, he'd been distracted from his arm, for damn sure.

"Hey! What the hell did my phone do to you?" Bubba's voice held laughter, and his rotund belly shook. His gray wife-beater had sweat stains under the arms, like the large man had run a mile.

Yeah. Right.

Maybe he'd come from playing with the same chick who'd serviced him. That was more likely. Guy wouldn't know an exercise if it bit him in the ass.

Bubba yanked his black sweatpants up, something he did constantly.

Good thing, too. Carter didn't need to see a set of sweaty balls that weren't his own. Especially if they'd just been used.

"Who has a real phone anymore anyway?" he snapped and glared.

"You're welcome for using it." Dark eyes flashed and all traces of amusement were gone. Bubba's bald head was creased, just like his brow.

"Sorry," he made himself murmur.

His friend finally relaxed, and took a seat on the ratty couch across from him. "What's up?"

"Grady said no."

"Ah, shit. I thought for sure the slimy bastard would agree. Especially since there was money involved."

"*'Not for all the money in the fucking world,'* he said. He said his crew is out, too." Carter swore some more—and left out the part where Grady had called him a ratty traitor.

Fuck Grady O'Malley, anyway.

Desperation ate at his stomach.

He needed to get the hell out of LA. He'd already stayed here too long, with the hope of finding Rowdy. Had no money and he needed some income so he could really disappear.

There'd been no sign of his former teammate, and so far, sure as hell no chance of making any dough.

Fuck. Fuckity fuck fuck.

He dragged his hand down his face and tried not to stomp his good foot like a two-year-old. Needed a plan, and he needed it fast.

"So, what's your next move?"

Carter tried to tamp down his immediate ire at the guy who'd been doing him a favor by letting him crash at his place.

Was his old friend trying to be helpful, or being nosy for another reason?

True, he'd always fenced their stolen rides, and therefore, took a cut, so his success was Bubba's...

But was there more in that look?

He watched the big man carefully before he answered.

Quit being a paranoid freak.

"You askin' 'cause you got an idea?" Carter said

slowly.

An overly beefy shoulder went up with a half-shrug, and he shook his head. "Just askin'."

He couldn't help the string of curses that left his mouth. "I need to get the fuck out of here."

"Nah, you're fine here."

"Fine? Sure I am. I'm fucking broke."

"I told you I'd cover you. Besides, you need to lay low. No one knows you're here, and it needs to stay that way, right?"

Yeah, Bubba had floated him some money, but Carter *hated* owing people anything. It usually bit him in the ass. But now...he needed to make nice and seem grateful. "Yeah, and I appreciate it." He forced a nod, then a smile.

The fence's keen gaze didn't waver, but the big guy seemed to relax a tad. He leaned into the back of the couch that'd been Carter's bed for the last few weeks. It'd seen better days, like most of the furniture in Bubba's house. The guy sure didn't flaunt the money he had.

Too bad the condition of the damn sofa contributed to the ache in Carter's back and the constant pain radiating down his bad leg.

"I need a big hit. I need..." He cursed again, and dragged his hand down his face. Stubble scratched his palm, but he didn't see shaving in his near future. He'd have to give a shit for that, and he didn't.

"I know, man. Sorry Grady didn't work out."

"Fuck Grady." He would've worked with the asshole, had the crew leader been willing. "Do you know anyone else?"

Bubba shook his bald head, his expression screaming regret. "Not in Cali."

Carter perked up. "So? I don't care *where*. I'll go.

Like you said, you'd cover me. Where?"

"I can make a few calls. Maybe to a buddy out in Arizona, but it's a longshot. He's been burned by the laws, and doesn't trust easily."

"Even if you vouch for me?"

He shrugged. "I can give it a go, but no promises."

"Awesome." He rocked on the end of the maroon recliner, from eagerness as much as to try to alleviate the ache in his leg and lower back. Probably should stretch, but then he might pace, and he didn't want his nerves to show.

"I'll see what I can do." Bubba grabbed the phone from the table and started dialing.

Carter muttered thanks, his mind spinning a mile a minute. There were too many unknowns he'd need to figure out ASAP—not just Bubba's old friend.

In LA, he knew the train schedule, the tracks, the lines, even when the big manufacturers shipped. He'd have to learn it all for wherever he landed—and fast as shit, if it was to work.

He'd negotiate as low a cut as he could with the crew, too. Then he'd get Bubba to fence the rides. As soon as he had enough money, he could disappear for a while. Rowdy was a thorn in his side, yeah, but he'd have to figure that out.

The FBI was still hot on his ass, and he needed to stay hidden for a while, until things died down. Then he could hunt Rowdy. He'd always hated outliers, and his former teammate had already escaped his wrath.

It *wouldn't* happen again.

Carter had shot his old friend, but he didn't think the injury had been severe enough—or that he was that lucky—to have killed Eric 'Rowdy' Vargas.

Nah, the asshat was out there, *somewhere.*

He didn't know what idiot FBI agent was on his tail, either. It pained him to admit.

At least one of the agents on his case was a female named Taylor Carrigan. That info was thanks to her dead BFF, the guy they'd all known as John Donovan—whose real name had turned out to be Murray. He'd been FBI, too. He hadn't even had to torture the bastard too much for a tell-all on Agent Carrigan.

Pussy.

She was out of the Dallas office, and the lead investigator. John had been undercover to bust them.

What was worse was Joe Pompa, old crew leader and former older-brother figure, had betrayed them all, because the fucker had *known* John was a fed in their midst.

Carter had done what he'd needed to then.

Traitors.

His whole crew had turned out to be traitors. They weren't really the only family he'd ever known.

Doesn't matter now.

He'd gotten them. Killed Rick and Mac right there at Joe's old place in LA, after he'd discovered they were only with him to watch him. They were really Team Joe—and had been reporting back to the guy, even though he'd been on the run.

Rowdy's loyalties also had lain with Joe.

He'd gotten away that night, but Carter had hunted their leader and the two others that had fled with the traitor, all the way to Texas.

He'd taken care of Bran and Moose, too.

Bubba setting the receiver in the phone's shallow cradle caught his attention.

"Well?" he prompted when his friend said *nada.*

"I left a message."

"A message?" Carter cursed—for the hundredth time that day.

"It's just how these things work. No worries, he always calls me back."

"When?"

The big man cocked his head to one side. "Soon. Patience, my friend."

He growled. "Don't fucking tell me to be patient. This is important."

Bubba narrowed his beady eyes. "I know. Back off, or I might decide not to help you anymore." The attitude was almost unknown from the fence.

Carter reared back—and put his own ass in check. "Sorry, dude. I'm...stressed."

"I know. Just chill. He'll call."

He forced a long exhale and refrained from more four-letter words.

"You're fine where you are. No one knows you're here, and we're keepin' it that way. You can breathe easy, man."

Yeah right, was his first instinct, but he nodded. Couldn't call Bubba an idiot and expect to keep his place on the ratty couch.

It might be a piece of shit, but it *was* a place to sleep, and right now, needed, as much as he hated to admit.

Chapter Four

"**S**o you really like it here?" Shannon eyed his friend and former partner with skepticism.

In lieu of sitting alone in his hotel room, he'd called Mark Rodriguez on the off-chance his buddy had a free evening. Turned out the guy was working, but like he'd said, he had to eat.

They'd met in a Chinese restaurant in Mark's patrol district. According to his buddy, all the local cops vouched for the place.

It was a hole in the wall with only about six tables but Shannon had no complaints about his sesame chicken dinner. The ambiance was nice, too. A great date spot, with Asian tapestries on every wall and low lighting. Even sported paper lanterns hanging above each table.

Mark laughed, and leaned back in his chair. "Yeah, actually. Why, you worried about me?"

"Well, I actually miss your ass."

"Aww, partner." His dark eyes twinkled and his mustache twitched with his grin.

His friend was happy; Shannon could see it.

That was great, but he genuinely missed working with him. They'd been partners for three years before he'd made sergeant.

He flashed a grin back, and gestured to his friend's uniform, and the new sergeant stripes on his sleeve. "Looks good on ya, I gotta say."

"Thanks." Mark ducked eye contact and reached for his soda, a classic move for him, unable to take a compliment. "I miss Antioch, but I love being a sarge."

"I knew you had it in you. Are the guys of Dallas PD treating you right?"

"Oh yeah, a great bunch of guys. And gals."

Something in his friend's tone made Shannon pause. "Gals? As in, one in particular?"

Mark shook his head but his goofy smile gave him away. "Maybe."

"Maybe?" He laughed.

"Well, it's new. She's a detective."

"A detective. Can you handle that?"

His buddy threw back his head and laughed. "I'm sure as hell gonna try."

"Good luck, for real. I hope to meet her soon."

"If all goes well, you will, sooner than later. You know I have to bring her home to meet my mom."

He chuckled and nodded. His old partner was close to his mother, not unlike Shannon with his own. She lived in Antioch, where Mark had been born and raised.

"Speaking of, you know she already has us married off."

"I bet. Expecting grandbabies, no doubt. Shoulda held back the news a bit. It's hard to date a cop, man."

Mark sobered. "I know. When it's them, everyone says, *'It's different this time.'* I want to believe that."

"I hope it is."

"Me too, she's great. What about you?"

"Me? Nah, no one special." Shannon shook his head.

"Damn shame, with that face of yours."

He growled and his friend laughed again. He still hadn't lived down the time he'd gotten hit on by a buxom brunette on a traffic stop a few years back.

The woman had been handsy as well as the verbal come-on, and he'd threatened to arrest her. She'd offered to *persuade* him well enough that he wouldn't write her a speeding ticket.

Mark had snagged the dash cam video, and it'd made

the rounds at the PD.

The woman had said he had the face of an angel. Of course, the nickname had stuck. Every time they got a new hire, the story was somehow revived and all the guys had a laugh at Shannon's expense.

"Still say she was high," Shannon said.

Mark chuckled again and shook his head. "We shoulda never stopped calling you Angel."

Movement by the door caught his eye, and a petite fair-haired woman entered the restaurant, going straight to the checkout counter.

The retort died on his tongue.

She was dressed in dark slacks and a matching blazer. The outline of the gun at her waist was visible to the trained eye.

Shannon glanced at his watch. It was almost eight. "Working late, Agent Carrigan?" he called.

She didn't smile when she turned, and he found himself wishing for even a slight curve of her full mouth.

Disappointment settled low and he tried to shake it off.

Recognition softened her features a tad, making her even prettier, but it didn't satisfy him.

What did you expect?

She'd shot down his dinner invitation that afternoon.

The hostess brought her order, already bagged and ready to go. The *beep beep* of the buttons on the cash register were audible from where Shannon sat with his friend.

He couldn't tear his eyes away from the petite FBI agent who looked impeccable despite the time of day.

The first time he'd met Special Agent Taylor Carrigan had been at *McAuley's*, the local cop bar in Antioch. He'd held the door open and told her where she could find Detective Jared Manning. Hadn't said more than a few words to her, but her demeanor had screamed *uptight,* from her strawberry-blonde hair in its librarian bun down to her shiny black loafers.

That image hadn't changed when he'd seen her in action at a crime scene, either. He'd been first on scene at the double murder that had to do with the case she was working, and she'd been a demanding, impatient investigator wanting to do everything herself, including not wanting to wait for the Crime Scene Unit before breaching the scene.

Manning had confirmed what a pain she was, but it hadn't dimmed Shannon's interest.

When he'd taken her statement after a shooting incident a few weeks later—where Manning's biological brother had ended up with a bullet in his head—he'd seen something in Carrigan that'd solidified his draw to her.

Vulnerability under her toughness.

She'd snapped and tried to push him away, but he'd kept her calm and drawn her to him, giving in to the odd urge to touch her.

Shannon had tucked her into his side and walked her to his cruiser. He'd regretted releasing her then. Had wanted to hold her, though Agent Carrigan would've never allowed that.

He'd thought about her often in the following months, and seeing her outside the federal court house that afternoon had been welcome. He'd always liked a challenge.

Which was probably why he'd asked her out.

He found himself disappointed again when the *ching* sounded and the cashier closed the register's drawer with a *click.*

Carrigan hadn't spoken, and would probably leave

just like that.

So much for her saying she hoped to run into me again.

His stomach jumped when she did the opposite, and headed to his table.

"Nice to see you again, Sergeant." Still no smile, despite the pleasant tone. Her hazel eyes glowed almost gold in the dim light of the hanging lantern.

Damn, she's gorgeous.

Mark cleared his throat and Shannon jolted in his seat—and reached for his manners.

"Mark, this is Special Agent Carrigan, you remember her from that case in Antioch a few months back?"

"Yeah, I think it was right before I left." His buddy stood, and threw his hand out to the FBI agent. "Mark Rodriguez."

The petite FBI agent shook his old partner's hand and finally smiled.

He was jealous as hell it wasn't for him.

"Nice to see you again. A sergeant as well, I see."

"Yeah, for a few months at DPD now." The radio on Mark's hip screamed.

"Officer needs assistance. Officer needs assistance..."

"Shit, looks like I gotta go."

"Damn, sounds like it," Shannon said. "Be safe. Hope all is well."

The guy slapped him on the back. "You know it, brother. Good to see ya. Call me and we'll get together again before you leave." His friend keyed up his mic to answer the call, then he dropped a twenty dollar bill on the table. He was gone before Shannon could tell him dinner was supposed to be on him.

Agent Carrigan's shifting from foot to foot next to

him caught his attention. "Hope everything's okay," she said.

"I'm sure it will be. Rodriguez is a hell of a cop. I kinda want to rush out there with him." He made eye contact with her and smiled. "Sit with me. I'll call the waitress to clear the table."

"That's probably not a good idea."

"Why not? I'm still eating, and you have to eat." He gestured to her paper-bagged order. "You can tell me about that bad day. Although, I hope it improved."

Carrigan made a face and shook her head. "It didn't. By much."

"Oh? I'm sorry to hear that."

She stared at him for a few seconds before speaking, and he wanted to squirm. "You are, aren't you?"

"What?" Shannon reared back, studying her.

"Genuinely upset I had a bad day."

He blinked. Didn't know what to say.

Did she have an issue with good manners?

"Uh..."

"Forget it. I'm sorry. I...should go."

His hand shot out of its own accord and landed on her wrist. "If you want to make it up to me, stay. Take a load off and eat what you ordered."

Her body screamed hesitation, but she didn't pull away. Her gaze darted to where his hand enclosed her wrist.

His eyes followed suit, then Shannon couldn't look away from where they were joined—or help the wish they were joined in a different, more intimate manner.

Her bones were so delicate in his large hand, and Carrigan's skin was so soft. Without thought, he stroked her smooth flesh with his thumb.

The FBI agent jumped and tugged free.

But she sat down, instead of running away.

They locked eyes. "Sorry," tumbled out from both of them at the same time.

Carrigan fidgeted on the chair, her cheeks pink.

He never would've pegged her for a blusher, but Shannon couldn't look away. He didn't want her to call him on staring, so he cleared his throat and looked down at his dinner. "This place has awesome sesame chicken." He forced himself to reach for his chopsticks.

"They have awesome everything. I always come here when I'm in the mood for Chinese. It's my favorite place in the city." She put her bag on the table and took two containers out of it. "You have good taste, I got the same thing."

Breathing a tiny internal sigh of relief, he leaned back and smiled. Reached for his soda and took a sip. "Want something to drink?"

"No, I don't drink when I eat. Takes up too much room in your stomach." She didn't look at him when answering. Carrigan opened the takeout chopsticks and snapped them apart.

"Ah. Never thought much about it."

She shrugged. "Not many people do."

"Not many health nuts pick that meal off the Chinese menu." Shannon gestured to her open container. She'd already dug in and taken a bite of seed-and-sauce-covered chicken.

"Not a health nut. I'll run it off."

"Not much to run off, Special Agent. You're a hundred pounds soaking wet."

Finally, she cracked a smile and his heart honest-to-God shuddered. He chided himself. The smile had definitely made the small tease worth it.

"Well, thanks. I'm not crazy about it, but I do try to

stay healthy. Besides, I like to run. It gives me time to think."

"Healthy works for me. I hit the gym a few times a week."

"What's your drug of choice?" Carrigan asked as she took another bite.

"I like to lift."

"Cardio?"

"I vary my routine." Shannon wouldn't admit how much he liked Zumba. If the guys at work discovered it, he'd never hear the end of it. Right up there with *Angel,* the unwanted nickname.

Not that Carrigan would tell anyone, but he couldn't confess that what most considered a feminine exercise style was right up his alley.

She stared, as if she didn't believe him.

"All right, I have a secret." The words tumbled out, unbidden.

"Oh?" The FBI agent appeared to be genuinely interested. Her hazel eyes became keen, and she pitched forward in her chair, hovering over her dinner, chopsticks in hand.

He sighed. Had put his foot in his mouth, and now he was going to have to see it through. Shannon dropped his gaze and shifted on the padded seat. "I like Zumba."

Dead silence greeted his ears, and when he got the balls to look at her, the Carrigan's expression was implacable.

"Go ahead. Ridicule away," he muttered, and gestured. He shoveled chicken past his lips and savored the smooth flavor, despite the unwanted spotlight.

She shook her head, but her mouth twitched. She looked down at the Chinese takeout container, then reached for the other one, opening white rice. Without a word.

He found himself craving her laugh, even though it'd be at his expense.

"Zumba can certainly make one break a sweat," she said finally. Amusement wrapped her statement, despite her unchanged demeanor.

"There it is."

"What?" Her eyes widened.

Shannon's stomach jumped; she was even more beautiful. He hadn't figured her for a person who could—or would—play innocent. "I'm a big boy, I'll survive a tease or two."

Carrigan grinned and his breath caught. The small flash of white teeth and the wide curve of her full mouth lit up her face. She looked young, gorgeous, and could definitely pull off the innocence she'd been going for moments before.

Damn, he couldn't breathe.

He wanted her.

More than he'd wanted any other woman...ever.

"So, I suppose..." The smile was still firmly in place, even as she put a spoon into the rice container. Like she was pretending she hadn't trailed off.

"You suppose what?" His inquiry came out fragmented, so he cleared his throat.

"Two things, actually." She held up two fingers.

"What's that?"

"You don't work out anywhere *near* the police department, and you have the rhythm required for Zumba."

Shannon laughed. "True on both accounts. I used to competitive dance when I was a kid. Ballroom, salsa and some swing."

"Dance?" Carrigan arched a fair eyebrow.

"Yeah, with my mom, actually."

"Hmmm, you're quite different, Sergeant."

"Shannon."

Carrigan stilled, and her smile fell off a bit. "*Sergeant* is fine for me, if you don't mind."

I do.

He couldn't tell her that. Didn't want to shut her down any more. *Needed* her smile. "Okay. But I'm more than my rank at work. And...if by *different*, you mean gay, I'm not."

The FBI agent laughed.

It sounded startled, like it was rusty, unused.

He grinned; couldn't help it.

"I certainly didn't mean to imply I thought you were gay." Her eyes trailed his upper body, and his heart sped into overdrive.

Could she be as interested in him as he was in her?

Carrigan averted her gaze much too soon, as if she realized what she'd been doing. She cleared her throat and tucked a nonexistent strand of her hair behind her ear.

Shannon's words had packed bags and taken a hike. His mouth went dry. He wanted to assure her; she could look at him *all* she desired. Could kiss him too, if she felt the same yearning. Do a hell of a lot more than kiss him, actually.

He cleared his throat for the hundredth time, because it distracted him, kept him in his seat. He resisted the urge to grab her across the table and kiss her senseless.

Shannon shook himself, and ended up dropping his chopsticks.

"You okay, Sergeant?" Carrigan's eyes were back in his direction.

"Yup. Just a bit clumsy, I guess." He forced a smile,

and ordered himself to relax. Reached for the bamboo utensils and took his last bite of chicken.

"Didn't think dancers werc clumsy."

He froze.

Is she teasing me?

He could say so many things to that. Hit on her. Give her a one-liner about how he'd love to show her his moves.

Just act natural.

In other words, *not* like he wanted her so badly he could come out of his skin. Or in his jeans.

Shannon widened his smile. "Oh, once in a while I struggle with my natural grace."

"What a pity." She grinned again.

His heart took off. If she didn't stop looking at him like that, how much she appealed to him wouldn't be a secret much longer. He'd do something stupid, like give in to the desire to taste her mouth. He chuckled and shook his head. "Yeah, well, I guess a guy can't have it all."

Carrigan echoed his headshake. "Guess not."

Not that he knew her well, but this was the most relaxed he'd ever seen the FBI agent. He was thoroughly enjoying their time together and dreading when she'd walk away from him.

"How'd your trial go for the rest of the day?" she asked, tugging him from his thoughts.

"Frustrating. The prosecutor and defense attorney acted like squabbling children. I've never seen Judge Newton's face so red or seen him slam the gavel down so many times, and I've been in his court for a dozen cases."

"I hate trials that drag. Same for cases, too. Hate wasting time." She scrunched her nose and stabbed a piece of chicken as if it'd offended her.

She wouldn't appreciate if Shannon told her she was adorable, but he wanted to. "Speaking of your case?"

Carrigan sighed, her frustration was palpable. "Yes and no. I know who, just not where they are right now."

"Ah. Anything I can do to help?"

She stared for a good fifteen seconds before she opened her mouth. "You're so genuine all the damn time." Her voice dropped, and she touched her cheek. Looked away.

The touch of vulnerability was so opposite of what he knew about the FBI agent.

Shannon wanted more of that. "Should I apologize?" He kept his query light and tried not to let the curiosity about what she'd been getting at leak into his tone.

Her cheeks flamed for the second time—or was it the third?—since she'd taken a seat at his table.

He was pleased. Probably more than he should be.

Carrigan shook her head but avoided his gaze. "Oh, no. Just not something I'm used to in my—our—line of work."

He smirked. "Yeah, I know what you mean. Sad, but I guess it's how it is these days."

She finally spared him a glance, but her expression was far away. Then she sighed again. "This case is killing me, but I don't think there's anything you can do to help, unfortunately. Unless you happen to know the whereabouts of one Carter Bennett or Eric 'Rowdy' Vargas."

"I remember the names. Isn't Bennett the guy who shot up the old trailer park in Antioch and left two warm ones?"

"Yeah. The other guy used to run with his car theft crew."

He nodded. "Yeah, I remember from briefing."

One corner of Carrigan's mouth shot up. "That was a long time ago."

Shannon tapped his forehead. "Great memory."

Her mouth relaxed into a smile.

He found himself craving more.

Down, boy.

"Never a bad thing in a cop, Sergeant."

"Nope. So I'm told."

"Anyway, when Bennett fled Texas, he was spotted once in Oklahoma, maybe in Nevada, and then not again. We have suspicions he headed to Los Angeles, but there's been no sign of him in months."

"He was injured in Antioch at the shooting, right?"

"We suspect, yes. Blood was found in the car he ditched."

"What if he died?"

The FBI agent shook her head and her denial was whiplash fast. "No way. He's lying low. We got his cash stash, so he's gonna have to make a move sooner or later." She was hard, so sure. "Besides, no one reported finding his body."

Shannon didn't doubt her words—or her instincts. He'd seen her in action. Despite her non-procedural demands on scene that night, Carrigan was a damn good investigator. "You'll find him. You'll get him."

Her lips softened again, and eased into a slight up-curve. "Thanks. Appreciate that."

"I mean it. And if I can do anything to help, I'm all yours." He wanted to reach out, squeeze her hand, but didn't.

She stared silently again until his heart stuttered.

Finally, she nodded and took a bite of rice.

Chapter Five

Taylor groaned and cursed. She fisted her sheets and threw her head back into her pillow in lieu of giving in to the urge to glance at the blue glow of the numbers on her alarm clock.

She should probably turn it backwards, like she had to when bouts of insomnia hit her from time to time.

Otherwise, she'd watch the clock, stare as the hours passed and obsess about lack of sleep.

Like now.

Tonight didn't need to turn into that kind of night, despite...everything.

Amber eyes were haunting her.

Oh, and the dimple in his right cheek.

She hadn't been able to stop thinking about Sergeant Shannon Crowley since she'd gotten home from her late dinner with him.

They'd stayed at *Hakka Wu*, her favorite Chinese place, until the kitchen had closed. They'd exchanged cellphone numbers, and he'd told her he hoped to see her again before leaving Dallas.

She regretted that he hadn't asked her out, like he had that afternoon when they'd run into each other near the court house.

Taylor had found herself wanting more than the parting wave and smile the sergeant had offered.

Wait. No.

'Wanting' was too strong a word.

She'd had a nice evening with a man she barely knew, and had enjoyed herself. Had felt like a normal human being for the first time in a long time.

End of story.

Right?

"It's not like it was a date." Nor would she *want* a date with the Antioch PD sergeant.

Taylor didn't date.

She and John hadn't really dated. They'd worked together. Made a great team. The rest had...fallen into place.

Partners. Friends. Lovers. More.

It hadn't been planned.

She remembered the first time John had told her he loved her. It'd slipped out. They'd been on a stakeout, actually. Before he'd gone under with Joe Pompa's crew.

He'd apologized. Then he'd taken it back, and kissed her like she'd wished he would've done so many times in the months before.

They'd slept together for the first time that night.

John had asked her to marry him only about two weeks later.

She hadn't even realized she'd loved him until then. But she *had* loved him.

Pain inched up from her stomach.

Taylor crushed her eyes shut as John's brown eyes replaced the sergeant's unusual whiskey-colored ones in her mind.

I can't take thinking of...John.

She'd moved past the crippling devastation. She'd blocked the memories—good and bad—especially of his normally olive complexion being so pallid when she'd ID'd his body at the morgue.

Taylor couldn't let hurt and loss debilitate her like it had when Baker had called her in to tell her John had been murdered. Couldn't handle it again. Feeling like *that*, and letting the emotion take her over. Lead her.

It'd spiraled out of control. What'd resulted was revenge, pure and simple. She'd shot the wrong man.

Emotion is weak.

"Emotion is weak," she said the phrase when thinking it wasn't enough. Cleared her throat when her voice cracked, even though she was alone in her apartment's big bedroom.

Maybe she should call her dad in the morning. He'd put her in check even if she didn't tell him a thing—which she wouldn't. Just hearing his stern tenor, his sterile questions about how her life was going, would remind her of what she'd always known.

Getting close to people gets you burned.

Crushed in the worst way possible.

She wouldn't do it again. Ever.

Taylor turned over for the fifth time. She needed to get some sleep. Needed to be clear-headed when she went in to the office the next day. Had to get somewhere on the case.

She'd call Eddie. First thing.

Avoid her boss at all costs, since he was determined to continue the *'new partner'* discussion. Irritation over the argument that morning with Baker flared and she made a fist. She sat up and knocked her head into her headboard a few times.

She gave in to the urge to glance at the clock. It glared *3:23* in bright blue.

Taylor closed her eyes again. She was going to hunker down into her covers, but it wasn't worth it. Sleep wasn't happening.

Throwing her plain gray comforter back, she slid her legs off the bed, avoiding the other side.

Where John used to sleep.

"Oh, God. Just stop. Now." Her commands jarred

her. Bounced off high ceilings.

She shook her head and stood, reaching for her lamp. She needed to run. Would hit the treadmill until she tired, then maybe she could catch a few hours before she had to face Baker and another argument her boss wouldn't win.

Taylor *wouldn't* think of a certain Antioch Police Department sergeant.

Carter tugged the hood of his jacket over his head and scrunched his shoulders as he limped his way into the convenience store. His spine tingled, as it always did when he was on his feet too much, and the old bullet wound in his right biceps screamed a protest as he adjusted his gait.

No one really knew him here, but he never could tell where the eyes might be, and he couldn't afford to get recognized.

He needed a fucking beer, and he was tired of Bubba's too-jovial personality. Didn't *anything* get under the big man's skin?

It was killer waiting to see if the guy's contact in Arizona would help him out or not. He'd already made Bubba reach out two times. It was waiting-game time, and Carter couldn't be a demanding little bitch—any more than he already had been, anyway.

He hadn't heard anything about the FBI, or even the local cops in a while, which was good, but that was only because he was smart and they couldn't find his ass.

God knew where his old crew leader, Joe, was now. It pained him to admit it, but he didn't know if he'd hit him the night they'd unloaded big weapons at each other in Texas.

Dead or in custody—Carter hadn't heard, or been

able to dig up. If the feds had Joe, they were keeping things quiet. Or he'd yet to run across the right source.

The store's doorbell chimed a welcome and he ignored the clerk's friendly greeting. Hobbled to the bank of refrigerators and scanned the alcoholic beverages.

His lower back was killing him. White-hot pain radiated up into his hip from his bum leg—it'd been a mess from birth. No amount of braces or surgery had been able to relieve him of a permalimp. Carter could run if forced, but his body never liked it. Always got revenge the next day.

He selected the cheapest forty that only half-tasted like shit and made his way to the counter with it. Slammed it down.

The pretty little thing working the register couldn't be more than eighteen. A redhead like he liked them, too. Her hair was up in a ponytail. Just the thing for a guy to grab onto. Tight shirt, big boobs, nice ass in tight jeans.

He gave her an obvious onceover.

Her eyes widened—at his aggression, Carter guessed, but he didn't feel like mustering a smile to make her feel better.

Wasn't trying to get laid.

"Will that be all?" she asked.

He took a bit of satisfaction from the way her inquiry shook. Didn't feel much like speaking, so he nodded. Grabbed a twenty from his pocket, cursing the fact he'd had to *borrow* it from Bubba.

The no-money thing got him all riled up again and he scowled.

The girl paused in reaching for the bill. "Something wrong?"

"No." He shoved the money at her, sans an apology.

She hammered the buttons on the register and

yanked his receipt free before it was done printing.

Carter admired her rush to get rid of him. Scaring the little girl was probably going to be the highlight of his evening.

He didn't like the way she was eyeing him. Like she was trying to memorize what he was wearing.

She put his change on the counter, as if she couldn't bear that their hands might brush.

He flashed a half-smile and fisted his beer. Tipped the fat bottle to her and made a quick exit, limp and all. "How rude," he whispered when he made it to the parking lot. "She didn't even tell me to have a good night." He grinned, cracked open his forty and gulped from it.

Getting drunk was tempting, but he still had work to do.

Carter slipped into the jalopy Bubba had given him to drive and cranked the key. The old engine roared to life with only one chug.

He put the cap on the beer and slid it under the passenger seat. Last thing he needed was to get pulled over by LAPD and get into trouble over an open container.

Not to mention the illegal weapon or three he had on his person, and in the car.

If Bubba's man in Arizona didn't work out, he had a few contacts in New Mexico—thanks to his old boss Joe—he could reach out to on his own. Maybe he could put a crew together to hit a train there, but their loyalty to Joe was going to be an issue, which was why he hadn't called them in the first place.

One or two rides wouldn't cut it. He needed a large number of high dollar rollers so he could get gone.

As long as word of his little bumble hadn't spread there, he might have a shot. For some reason, no one wanted to trust him after he'd whacked Mac and Rick.

He'd just been cleaning up after traitors, what was the big deal?

No one would cross him, and he'd proved it. They were all a bunch of pussies, including Grady fucking O'Malley.

It was a shame Rowdy—the fucker—was so sharp, too. He'd disappeared a few times over the years, whenever the law was on to them, and he was good at it.

Carter had never discovered where he went, but he would. Vargas' days were numbered.

Joe probably knew, but it wasn't like Carter could interrogate his old boss.

The shitty trailer he'd found them in popped into his head. He'd started shooting. Joe and Moose had returned fire.

He was sorry about Bran. She'd always been a quiet little thing. But Joe loved her, so she had to go, even if they'd had a little spat and broken up before the John-shit had hit the fan.

Seeing the crew leader hold her while she died had been satisfaction enough, though. Well, it could've been better.

They could've died together.

Carter left the parking lot and headed back toward Bubba's place. He needed to hurry so he could nurse that beer.

Drunk was about the only way he wouldn't pound the big guy's face in. Maybe.

The burner phone in his pocket screamed for his attention before he'd made two turns. He dug it out and slammed his thumb on the button to answer, cursing the fact he hadn't bothered with a smart phone. This one was old school. "Yeah?"

"Where you at?" Bubba had an excited edge that

made Carter sit taller in the driver seat.

"On my way back." He flexed his free hand on the steering wheel and clenched his jaw.

"Got good news."

His heart skipped and he tightened his grip on the small cellphone, pressing it to his ear until pain bit back. "Yeah?"

"Get your ass back here. I got a call from Arizona."

Chapter Six

owdy rolled over on the mattress and it cushioned his weight instead of digging into his sore side. The squeak of real bed springs made him sigh into actual pillows.

Then he remembered.

Sat up with a gasp.

"Jesus, relax."

Ordering his heart to calm, he tried to smile for Camille.

The look on his former foster sister's face told him it hadn't worked. Her forehead was creased, marring her mocha skin. Her dark, kinky curls danced around her shoulders as she shook her head. "Someone really worked you over, huh?"

He hadn't told her *why* he'd shown up on her doorstep or why he'd had two barely healed holes in his body. "Cami, like I told you before. It's safer if you don't know."

"So you say. But your damn nightmares keep me up at night, big brother."

Big brother.

No one had called him that in years.

He sank back into the pillows with a sigh, tucking his hands behind his head. "How can you even hear me? You're down the hall."

"My apartment isn't that big." Cami sat on the edge of the bed. She patted his sweatpants-clad leg. "Just tell me, Eric. You look like you need to talk."

"I can't. And I need to go. Staying here is too dangerous for you. I'll head out in the morning."

It'd already been three weeks. Rowdy had lain low in California for as long as he'd been able to—almost two months—but when his wounds hadn't gotten better, and he'd only got sicker, he'd bought a bus ticket and headed to his sister—against his better judgment.

He couldn't have gone to the hospital, and he hadn't risked more than a night or two couch surfing. Besides, as soon as they'd heard about his crew, they'd kicked him out anyway. Everybody knew Carter was a vindictive little asshole, and nobody wanted to be a target—like him.

Carter could find him at any moment, even if no one knew about Cami. No one, except Joe Pompa, and it was a good bet his old boss was as dead as the rest of their crew.

At Carter's hand.

The fucker.

"I don't want you to go. We're family."

He sat up and cupped the side of his sister's face. Caressed her soft skin and reveled at the beautiful woman the awkward biracial kid who'd constantly complained about her hair had grown into.

Her leaf-green eyes shone with unshed tears, and just about ripped out his heart.

They might not be blood, but they *were* family.

Which was why he'd walked away from her years ago.

Rowdy was a fuckup who couldn't stay out of trouble with the law, and she'd aged out of the system and made something of herself.

"We'll *always* be family, Dr. Bonner."

Cami smiled.

Somehow, that made him feel worse. He was grateful she'd reopened his messed-up wounds, got the bullets out, stitched him properly and got him antibiotics, but that only meant he'd put her medical license in danger, too.

He'd always be a selfish fuck.

She threw her arms around him and hugged him tight.

Rowdy rubbed her back for a moment, like he had when they were kids and she'd woken from a nightmare. They'd met when she'd been four to his nine. A tiny little thing with dark skin and huge emerald eyes.

She'd been the reason he'd stuck around at placement after placement. They'd been in the same foster homes a few times, but even when he'd eventually do something stupid and get booted to the curb, he'd always kept in touch with Cami.

His caseworker had lectured him time and again, citing that she was a positive in his life, and if he didn't get it together—which he never had—he wouldn't be allowed contact with her. He'd run away at seventeen, anyway.

Then when he was nineteen, he'd met Joe Pompa. The guy had taken him in, given him a family. And a job.

Rowdy was damn good at stealing cars. On the big scale, from trucks and trains. Made a shit-ton of money, too. Most of which was in two duffels under the bed he was currently on.

When he left, half of it was staying, even if his sister didn't know it yet. She could use it for her school loans.

He'd intentionally lost touch with Cami when he'd joined Joe's crew. She'd been on the fast track to medical school, and he was just a good thief. She didn't need illegal shit in her life.

"You don't have to go. No one knows you're here. It's safe." Cami leaned back and stared hard, like she was trying to memorize his face.

It won't be safe for long.

He couldn't tell her that. Didn't want to freak her out,

and knowing his sister, she'd be pissed and want to protect him.

"I do have to go. But I'll see you again."

Rowdy didn't contemplate that he didn't know *where* to go.

Nowhere was *safe*.

"Mommy, I can't sleep."

His gaze shot to a little boy with messy dark hair and green eyes to match his mother.

Devon rubbed his face with a small fist and fought a yawn. His superhero pajamas had a blue cape attached to the shoulders of the red shirt. He stood in the doorway of the guestroom, his shadow thrown out in the dim light of the hallway behind him. Kind of looked like he was flying, actually.

"C'mere, little man," Rowdy said. He winced when his side didn't like the shifting on the bed, nor him opening his arms for his sister's six-year-old kid.

Cami's ex wasn't in the picture—much. He was a doctor, too. Evidently there wasn't a prerequisite that doctors weren't assholes. At least he provided for his son, but she complained the guy missed more visitations than he saw the boy.

He kinda wanted to beat his face in for that alone, not to mention the fact that Doc Asshole had cheated on his sister and crushed her heart.

Devon flashed a wide-awake smile and scrambled up to him. Snuggled close, resting his head on Rowdy's shoulder.

I really need to go.

Cami wasn't the only one in danger.

Guilt was a constant that wouldn't leave him be. It was justified. If anything happened to either of them, it would *kill* him.

"What's wrong, Dev?" Cami rubbed her son's arm.

"Nothin'. I needed Uncle Eric."

Rowdy and Cami exchanged a look.

Annnnnnd more guilt took a chunk out of him. Right from his heart. Chewed on him and came back for more.

He was going to break the *kid's* heart when he left, and by the looks of it, his sister's, too. No amount of money in the world would fix it.

But he'd rather have them hurt and pissed if it meant *alive.*

If Cami knew the danger of Carter Bennett, she'd probably kick his ass for bringing it to her home, but maybe not. She'd probably grab a pitchfork and fight, because he was family, and growing up like they had...family meant the world to her. Was one of the many reasons his ass was in her guestroom in her modest apartment in Phoenix.

"Tell me a story, Uncle Eric!"

He looked down into the emerald eyes that sucked him right back to childhood. The kid in his arms might be a boy, but all he could see was Cami, and the first time she'd climbed on his lap with tears running down her cheeks. A four-year-old that didn't understand why her mommy wasn't coming for her.

Shit. I'm truly fucked.

"How about you go back to bed, little man?" Cami's question was wrapped in amusement. "It's late, and I don't want to hear you complainin' when I wake you up early for school." She made monster noises and tickled his tummy.

According to his sister, his little nephew was exceling in his kindergarten class.

Devon giggled and shook his head. "Noooooo, Mommy. I can't go back to sleep without a story."

Cami rolled her eyes and grinned when Rowdy caught her gaze.

To see her happy stole his breath and made his chest ache for a reason other than finally healing bullet wounds.

"How about a *short* story?" he asked.

"Yay!" Devon pumped his little arm.

"Would that be all right, Mommy?" Rowdy asked, batting his eyes at his sister and going for innocence.

Cami snorted and crossed her arms over her chest. "I guess so."

"Tell me a good one, Uncle Eric!"

He made some quick shit up about a little boy who could fly, but it worked.

His sister laughed, Devon giggled, and soon his nephew was asleep in his arms.

Too bad the truth of watching them both, seeing their innocence, was killing him. Rowdy needed to get the hell gone, before he got them hurt...or worse.

He blew out a breath when Cami gathered her son to take him to his room, and dreaded her promise to be right back. It wasn't like he could sneak out, but still...

"Hey," she whispered, holding up the doorframe to his room a few minutes later. Her arms were crossed over her chest, and her head was cocked to one side.

"Hey," he returned. Didn't like the calculating look on her face.

"You're great with Devon," Cami said, closing the distance between them and taking her former seat on the bed.

"I had a lot of practice with this little girl I knew once." Rowdy tugged on one of her kinky curls until she flashed a smile.

Too bad it had a sad edge he didn't like.

"I wish you'd stay. It'd be good for him to have you

around."

He snorted. "Right, like he needs a criminal in his life, around all the time."

She frowned. "It'd be good for me, too." This was barely a whisper, and made the guilt come right back up.

"Cami, you know I never flew straight."

His sister sighed and broke their eye contact. "That doesn't matter. It never has. And besides, it seems, whatever it was—" She held her hand up when he protested. "I'm not digging for info, just trying to make a point. It seems to me like that part of your life is over, because it ended badly." Cami gestured to his side, the worse of his two wounds.

It's going to be worse. Final. When Carter kills my ass.

Rowdy couldn't say that. He cleared his throat. "I *am* done with what I was doing, and who I was doing it for. But I don't know anything else."

"But you can."

"Can what?"

Her eyes were imploring. "Fly straight, as you put it. You came here, got away from it—them. Keep it that way, don't go back. Put it *all* behind you, Eric. Make a life in Phoenix like I did. Get a job. I know people who have connections and don't ask a lot of questions."

He laughed. "I thought you wanted me to fly straight."

She smacked his chest and mock-glared. "I'm not talking about anything illegal, ass. I mean a mechanic shop or something. You know your way around cars, always have. I know a guy who knows a guy who has a shop where they supe them up, like racers or something. You know, like *Fast and Furious* stuff."

Rowdy sighed. "Cami—"

"Please, Eric."

He crushed his eyes shut and ordered his breathing to regulate. Lying to her was going to kill him, but he couldn't promise her a damn thing.

Not until Carter was out of the picture.

He met her gaze when he had the balls to do so, and nodded. Couldn't find his voice.

The smile that lit her face made him feel guilty as hell, but he didn't look away, because she'd call him on his bullshit.

"Okay. I'll call my friend in the morning, and see if his friend has a place for you. He kinda owes me one, so I'm sure it'll work out. You can stay here until you're on your feet and you can afford to get your own place. I'm gonna love having you around, and so is Devon!" Cami threw her arms around his neck and smacked a loud kiss on his cheek.

Rowdy didn't correct her on the money issue. He had over four hundred thousand dollars in cold hard cash under the bed. Had been saving for years, not to mention he'd snatched Rick's money when he'd fled Cali from Carter.

He swallowed and hid his face against his sister's neck for a moment. Just held her, because he didn't want her to catch on he was lying his ass off to please her.

She'd flay him open, not to mention how her disappointment would slay him.

Cami radiated hope and love, and smelled like sunshine.

I'm going to hell for sure.

When she pulled back, she patted his cheek. "I know you'll tell me everything when you're ready to talk, but this is a start, big brother, and I'm so happy. Tomorrow's a new day."

It sure is.
Tomorrow, Rowdy would be gone.

Chapter Seven

Dread gripped her stomach and yanked it into a tight ball when Taylor saw the unfamiliar figure sitting in the chair in front of her boss's desk.

Their deep voices melded as she approached the open door.

Relax. Breathe.

Matthias Baker, her boss of three years, looked up, making eye contact with her even before she stepped into his office.

"You wanted to see me?" She cursed the croak in her inquiry and cleared her throat.

Instead of answering, Baker gestured for her to enter, since she continued to hover barely inside the doorframe. Didn't want to go in.

Her boss's gaze was hard, and perhaps a little triumphant.

She tried not to narrow her eyes. They'd have words, later.

Taylor did her best to plaster on a pleasant expression as the man in the chair stood when Baker did. She gave him a onceover.

Young. Blond. Good-looking. Tall and broad. Build somewhere between swimmer and linebacker.

"Carrigan, meet Alec Holman, your new partner."

The reason Baker had called her to his office had been obvious from the moment she'd spotted the younger man's outline through the glass wall.

Her gut twisted even more.

When the guy smiled, he looked twelve.

"Jesus. Fresh from Quantico?" She put out her hand

to accept his offered shake and ignored the glare she could feel over her shoulder.

The kid's smile fell. "No, ma'am."

"Don't call me *'ma'am.'*"

"I'm sorry, ma—Agent Carrigan." Her new *partner* blushed and shifted in his shiny black loafers. He wore dark pants not too different from her own. His shirt was a long-sleeved powder blue button-down, and his tie navy. He didn't have a jacket on. At least his gun was holstered correctly at his waist.

Taylor smirked and crossed her arms over her chest.

"Carrigan." Her name was all warning, but she ignored Baker when he came around from his desk and closed the door. The dirty look he sent her way had her squaring her shoulders and schooling her expression.

She should probably try to play nice with the kid, at least until they were released from the boss' office.

"Holman's a transfer." Baker returned to his seat.

Holman sat, too, but Taylor hesitated, then decided to remain standing. Didn't want to encourage a long chat. She had work to do. A case to solve. Carter Bennett to bag.

She cleared her throat again and leveled her gaze on the new guy.

His eyes were blue, a deep hue she should've found pleasant. Was her favorite color, after all.

Instead, she was annoyed. "So, what kind of experience do you have?"

Her boss glared harder.

Taylor stopped herself from demanding what his problem was. Didn't she have a right to know what her *new partner* had going for him?

She had to work with the kid, after all. Baker didn't.

"I worked on the Special Investigations Task Force out of LA for two years. Born and raised in Dallas, so when

the opportunity to work at home came up, I jumped on it."
His voice was deep, making him seem older than his
appearance.

Bet your mommy is pleased.

"I'm looking forward to working with you." He
smiled again. Didn't look any older than before.

Well that's one of us.

She forced a nod. "You know Eddie Vasquez?"

"Yes, I worked with him."

Taylor perked up. Maybe he knew something about
her case that she didn't. Maybe he *could* help.

Baker looked pleased. He reclined in his chair,
unusually silent as he watched them interact.

"I'm familiar with your case," the kid went on. "Was
undercover with Eddie's main contact. A CI named
Brandon Martinez, but everyone calls him Bubba."

"Yeah, I know of him." She parked on the corner of
her boss's desk instead of sitting next to Holman.
"Undercover, huh? What did you learn?"

"I didn't find out where Rowdy Vargas is, if that's
what you're digging for, but I was with them a few months.
Didn't run into Carter Bennett, just helped them hit a few
car trains. Last I knew, Bubba doesn't know where Vargas
or Bennett are, or if they're together."

"Helped them?" She arched an eyebrow.

The kid's blue gaze burned, and he seemed a few
years older. "I'm good with computers. Bubba hooked me
up with a crew Bennett used to run with before he joined
Joe Pompa's. Their tech had gotten picked up, and
sentenced to five-to-ten. Took me a while to get them to
trust me, but I passed their test bust. We got the whole
crew after the second train, but they haven't seen or heard
from Bennett since he killed his crew. Their leader knew
what he did. Said he was a thief, not a murderer, so he had

no intention of playing nice if Bennett reached out. Unfortunately, he didn't get a chance to try, because we busted them."

Taylor sighed. "I need to find the bastard."

"We will find him." Holman nodded.

She paused.

How could Holman seem so invested in her case already?

"Well, seems like you two have work to do." Baker was too pleased for her liking, but she held back her scowl—for now.

"Uh, Holman, can you give me a moment?" She straightened from the desk and tried to smile for the kid.

"Sure." He stood and nodded.

"Uh, if you ask Jay—Agent Palumbo"—Taylor pointed—"at his desk over there, he can show you to my— *our* office."

Holman nodded. He was smart enough to close the door when he left.

"Carrigan, I don't want to hear it." Her boss joined his hands and rested them across his torso. His posture was too casual for an argument.

He'd made up his mind.

Which means I'm screwed.

She lowered herself to the chair. Perched on the edge, because she wouldn't be staying long. "Did I do something wrong?"

Baker laughed. "That's your opener? What's your angle?"

"Did I do something wrong?" Taylor repeated.

"You know the answer to that."

"Then why am I being punished?"

He laughed again, and shook his head. "Punished? You think assistance for your case is punishment?"

"I work better alone."

"Bullshit."

The next instant they both thought of John.

Something passed through Baker's dark eyes and he averted his gaze. He cleared his throat before looking back at her.

It just about killed her.

Taylor bit down, locking her jaw so she wouldn't tell him to go to hell. "Obviously, you ambushed me with Holman for a reason."

"You're lucky I called you in. I could've shown him to your office first thing. Before you got in."

They both knew that would've made her a human grenade in his office before the clock struck a quarter after eight.

Baker leaned forward, his expression unreadable. "I'm gonna level with you."

"That so?"

"This is *it* for you."

"What?"

"You work with Holman. He goes everywhere you go. I mean *everywhere*. Hold your hand in the restroom if necessary. Or you're off this case."

She tamped down her instant rage and fought the urge to rush to her feet. The back legs of the chair came off the carpet as she pitched forward even more. "This is *my* case."

"For now." He narrowed his eyes, daring.

"That wasn't our agreement," she bit the words out through clenched teeth and flexed her hands. Taylor planted her fists on her lap and tried to ignore the anger threatening to overtake her.

Emotion is weak.

Her father's gravelly voice played on a loop in her

head. If she closed her eyes, she could see him in full uniform, while standing at attention in front of him as if *she* was the one in the Navy.

"I told you when I let you do this, our agreement could change at any time. It's all been dependent on what I think you can handle. We both know you're too close to this. I've let you go it alone long enough."

"I can do this. I *am* doing this."

Baker sighed. "I know you are, but something's changed after Antioch. I'm worried about you."

Taylor's heart stuttered and she tried to ignore it. Banished Joe Pompa's bloody face and crumpled form on that kitchen floor when the memory popped up. If she uttered a denial, her boss would call her on it. "Shrink cleared me."

"I know."

She wanted to assure him she wasn't headed down the revenge path. She'd get Carter Bennett the right way, and get justice for John. Wanted to remind him the situation had been ruled a good shoot. Joe Pompa hadn't died.

She said nothing. Didn't want her boss to have an inkling of the guilt that was still killing her.

"Taylor—"

"Matthias—"

They stared at each other after playing the rare first-name game. He broke eye contact first, giving another sigh.

"I'm okay. I can do this, and I don't need Holman. This case is mine."

"Holman is nonnegotiable." This was hard, a command that made her angry all over again.

"I don't need some baby agent following me around like a lost puppy."

Baker smirked. "Buy a collar and a leash, because he's a keeper."

She couldn't even crack a smile. "So that's it? This is an ultimatum?"

"Call it what you want. Now go get acquainted with your new partner. Show him around the office and introduce him to everyone. Get him up to speed on what's been, and what's next."

Rage melted into defeat and she tried not to let her shoulders slump. Baker wasn't going to give in. Not this time. Losing didn't taste right in her mouth. "I have a case to solve, I don't have time for that," Taylor grumbled.

Amusement darted across her boss' face and he quirked a half-smile. "I've never seen you pout before, Carrigan."

She growled. "I don't pout."

He grinned. "Leave the door open so you're not tempted to slam it on your way out."

She narrowed her eyes at the dismissal and wanted to flip him off, but didn't. She *really* didn't like losing.

Taylor stalked to her office, glaring at the maintenance man who was mounting a nameplate outside her open office door.

He scurried out of her way so she could enter the room, but not before she saw what it'd said.

The top line stated *Taylor Carrigan, Special Agent* but underneath was etched, *Alec Holman, Special Agent.*

She growled and made a fist. "The jerk had this planned for today."

"I'm sorry, what was that?" Holman glanced over his shoulder from what used to be John's chair. He wore a friendly smile she wanted nothing to do with.

Emotion rushed up, and she flashed back to a man with much darker hair, greeting her with a similar smile and sitting in the same place.

Taylor had finally gotten the balls to clean out his work area and empty his desk a month or two before. Since she'd taken his things home, the office had been forlorn.

Baker had been smart enough not to challenge her need to do so herself. He hadn't pressured her, but she'd heard the whispers of fellow agents about her *shrine* to John, so she'd gotten it all out of the office. She could still grieve in private.

She barely looked at John's side of the room, if she could help it. Hadn't even managed to turn the calendar to the proper month, but Holman must've, because it was correct now.

Taylor forced a breath and called herself on her weakness, then straightened her shoulders and shook her head for her *new partner*. The two words still left a bitter taste in her mouth. "Nothing. Talking to myself."

"Ah. I do that from time to time, too." The smile never left, despite the fact she'd neglected to offer one in return.

"I bet you do." She looked away before he could answer, but he didn't. Swallowing a sigh, she tugged her chair away from her desk and took a seat. Reached for her mouse and woke her computer up.

She'd entered her login information and opened her email; was starting to read one of the several demanding her attention when Holman cleared his throat. She rolled her eyes and refused to turn to him.

"What now?" he asked.

"What d'you mean?" She glanced over her shoulder, spotting the half a dozen brown boxes in the corner of John's—Holman's—side of the room.

Damn, that's gonna take getting used to.

They were perpendicular to the two filing cabinets in the corner, as if they belonged, but they hadn't been there yesterday.

Case info. *All* the reports, files and perhaps a piece of evidence or two.

Baker must've ordered them, because she only kept the latest stuff in her office. Would venture down to the file room if she needed to look something up. Tried to avoid John's reports from his time inside Pompa's crew unless absolutely necessary.

Those six boxes contained her life.

At least, since she'd lost John.

Taylor turned back to her computer. She threw a nod toward the boxes, but didn't look at Holman. "You might wanna get to reading." She wasn't about to hold her new partner's hand. He'd have to figure it out on his own.

"I already have."

She whirled her chair around, abandoning her email for the second time. So her new partner was an overachiever?

Taylor ignored the little reminder in the back of her head that whispered that was probably a good thing. "You have?"

Holman nodded. "I was briefed yesterday. Already looked through the case as a whole." He pointed to the boxes. "I have a bit of a photographic memory, so..." Holman shrugged and his cheeks reddened.

She resisted the urge to roll her eyes again. "So, what do you think our next move is?"

"Ross Catrone is the prosecutor, right?"

"Yes." She wanted to snap at him for answering a question with a question.

"And you had a meeting with him yesterday?"

She arched an eyebrow. "Keeping tabs on me?"

Had Baker given her a partner or a spy?

He shook his head. "No, it's just that, I was here when you were there."

Taylor clenched her jaw. Hadn't seen him at the office yesterday, but she'd only spent an hour or two in. The rest of the day, she'd run a few things down that had ended up being a waste of time.

Not too different from this morning so far. Go figure.

Come to think of it, Baker had left her alone all day yesterday, even after their argument in the morning.

How convenient.

New boy must've come in right after she'd stormed out.

"So, how'd it go?" Holman prompted.

"It didn't." She wasn't about to tell him about the lasagna incident. Or about Sergeant Shannon Crowley. Taylor stilled when the handsome uniform cop from Antioch popped into her mind.

Where did that come from?

She'd had a nice evening with him, even if by accident. But she wasn't allowed to think about him. It had no purpose.

"It didn't?" Holman's question jolted her and he shot her a funny look.

She shifted in her chair. "Right. Didn't have much to share. I need to find Rowdy Vargas. He's the key to finding Bennett. I feel it in my gut."

"I don't disagree." He looked thoughtful for a moment, then reached for a gray folder on his desk.

There were two casefiles there, and one was open. It had to be Carter Bennett's—she'd recognize his blond head from his picture at any distance.

Holman thumbed through the other one, and leveled

her with a serious gaze. "Joe Pompa."

"What?" Taylor's heart skipped and she cleared her throat.

He flashed a photograph paperclipped to the inside of the file.

She avoided the dark eyes staring out at her—and the guilt that curled up to her throat. Started to shake her head, then stopped herself and ordered her gut to unclench. To no avail.

Her new partner glanced down at the file, then back up at her. "Pompa is the next move."

No.

"How so?" she croaked.

"He's the key to finding Rowdy Vargas."

"How? He's in prison. Awaiting trial in Texarkana."

Holman gave her a long look that called her protest weak, even if he didn't say it. "We won't know if he's heard anything new unless we go talk to him."

I was afraid you'd say that.

Chapter Eight

"So, how we doin' this?" Carter looked at the five men scattered around the makeshift table of stacked milk-crates with rough panels of wood resting across their uneven tops.

Plans, stolen train manifests and maps lay on top of the wood.

A few laptops were perched at the end of the setup, along with a police scanner. Various other electronics weren't far, including listening devices.

All the equipment was high tech, more so than he'd seen the likes of before. They'd put money into their equipment and intel—not so much their table.

The techy stuff, Bran, from his old crew, would've drooled over.

The scanner was on, but the chatter sounded more like a buzz, since the volume was low. Every once in a while he'd catch a word or two, or a shout.

The sprawling warehouse they were in was full of enough cars to make Jay Leno jealous, but they were all suped up modern hotrods, no classics in sight. Mostly Japanese in make, with the occasional American muscle car, but nothing like Carter's favorite 1963 Charger.

Kai March, Bubba's old friend and the crew leader, was half Asian, and seemed to be a collector as much as he was a thief.

Too bad he was an asshole, too.

"First of all, you'll remember your place," the leader growled. Kai's spiked hair was three colors—bright hues of green, purple and pink. He had nose rings and ear gauges, and a smattering of other piercings all over his face, and up the curve of his ears.

Carter presented his palms, high and flat. "Hey, I was just askin'. Not trying to run the show, believe me."

Someone snorted and he wanted to stab the guy to his right, but he plastered on a pleasant—grateful— expression.

"I'm doin' Bubba a favor, and I have no idea why he vouched for your traitor-ass. I know all about you, Carter Bennett."

Perfect, because I don't know jack about you.

That bugged him, actually, because gathering intel and making plans had always been his strong suit.

There was a muttering of agreement among the other crew members, except the blond computer geek.

That guy—Carter couldn't remember his damn name—didn't look up from the laptops' screens. His fingers were flying a mile a minute over one of the keyboards, but he kept glancing at the other screen, too. Multitasking.

"Hey, this is business, man," he told Kai—whose dark eyes were still locked onto him. They both ignored the rest of the crew. "Just a little business, then I'll be outta your hair. I don't want any trouble, just some rides and some dough. Then I'll get gone."

They'd talked money already, and Carter hadn't gotten his way.

Kai and his boys were getting way more than he'd wanted to allow, but it was the price of working with a traitor—or so the crew leader had said.

They had all the power, so it wasn't like he had much of a choice. Couldn't hit a train on his own.

At least they were knowledgeable about the routes, carriers and such. The plan was for a massive order of Hummers.

Not his first choice, but they'd have to do. He would've preferred something higher dollar, but Kai had told him he already had a buyer.

A local guy, which meant Bubba wouldn't get a cut.

Carter would have to go with the flow—as much as he *hated* that idea. Had a feeling, because of *him*, Bubba now owed this asshole a favor, and had probably paid him off to take Carter on.

The big guy had had him deliver a package to the dickhead, and even though he hadn't asked questions, or opened it, his gut said it was money.

Just more shit for him to pay back later.

Dammit.

But he had to respect Bubba for having his back when no one else would touch him.

Kai smirked and crossed his arms over a broad chest. He was tall and solid, like a linebacker.

No one he'd want to tangle with in a physical fight.

Dressed in all black leather, too. Considered himself some sort of badass, no doubt. "Okay, listen up," the leader said, as if Carter hadn't asked his question moments before. "We do this like always."

He wanted to roll his eyes. That was the kind of opener Joe Pompa used to do.

"We got five semis lined up to take the rides away, so we'll get as many as we can. This'll be a big job, and a lot of money is at stake. We need to be fast as hell. In and out, and no one gets hurt."

The guy started lecturing about being reckless in the next breath, and it was almost like Carter had been transported back in time.

Joe always used to impart that little nugget of wisdom to their crew, as well.

Too bad the Arizonan asshole stared at *him* directly,

as if he'd be his crew's downfall. Hell, Kai probably believed that shit, anyway.

Fuck him.

He didn't say that out loud, of course. Still had to be cool, and play for team *thanks-for-doing-me-a-favor*. But he wasn't about to bow down and lick anyone's balls. He had skills, too.

Carter paid attention, asked questions when necessary, and threw visual daggers at the crew members who snorted and snickered like little girls every time he opened his mouth.

Their leader consistently wore a smirk he wanted to wipe off his face—using his fists, or the butt of his Heckler and Koch forty.

"So, we're all set, three weeks from tomorrow. Any questions?" Kai's eyes swept his audience, and didn't land on Carter for once.

Like he wouldn't have given a crap if he had a genuine inquiry.

"Wait. Three weeks? Why so long? According to your plans, there's a shipment tomorrow night." Carter pointed to one of the manifests on the table.

"I said three weeks, traitor."

"Three weeks it is," one of the crew said, beaming when he threw him a glare.

Kai's assholes fell into line right behind him. All backing his word like it was law, nodding one-by-one.

"I'm just asking why, is all."

"I don't recall giving you that kind of permission." Kai arched a pierced eyebrow, his gaze full of challenge.

Carter swallowed back the one hundred and five curses he wanted to spit out at the bastard.

Who the fuck does this guy think he is?

"Oh, look, California traitor is angry. His face's all

red," another of the assholes said. He crossed his arms over his chest and grinned. He was short and stocky, with sandy hair and bad taste in clothes, if his ripped T-shirt and skinny jeans were any indication. He had a tattoo on his throat, to make it look like someone had cut his jugular.

It looked scary authentic, and didn't go with the smirk he wore. It did work with the dare in his expression, but only if Carter could make that tat real.

His temper exploded and he took a step forward. Clenching his fists at his sides wasn't working anymore.

Asshole Number Three just stared back, making no moves.

When another one of them, Asshole Number Two—the first to verbally agree with Kai's plan—stepped forward, the leader threw a hand up to stop his advance.

So they wanted to see what Carter was made of, did they?

There might be something wrong with one of his legs, but his fists worked just fine, as Asshole Number Three was about to find out. After that, he'd take on Asshole Number Two, and even Kai if the guy wanted to play.

"Our intel is better for the shipment in three weeks. We weren't able to confirm the contents of tomorrow's shipment. Sometimes hacked manifests are wrong, and it's not worth the risk. The engineer for the train next time is on our payroll, too. He'll overlook a few things. Also, a that timeline was first-available on the trucks and trailers." The computer geek at the end of the table broke the tense silence, and shrugged when all eyes darted to him. "He asked a valid question."

Kai frowned, but no one spoke.

"Thanks," Carter forced out, throwing blondie a nod.

"I was only asking." He wouldn't call the geek an ally, but at least he wasn't an asshat like the rest of his crew.

The guy nodded, and didn't look the least bit ruffled at the look his leader pointed in his direction. Maybe he was used to Kai being a giant dick.

"Anything else?" he asked. Looked at the tech, not Kai.

"You're *need-to-know*, California traitor," Kai growled. "And you got all the info necessary in that category. You ain't special."

"I want to look at the schematics, again. And the manifest for the train."

"Why?" The leader stepped forward, only inches away, but between him and the table with the plans he wanted another look at.

"Look, no matter how you feel about me, it's not my first day. I can't count how many times I've done this. I know what I'm fucking doing." He tried to keep his statements even, and not give in to the anger rising all over again.

He'd been Joe's number two, but he wasn't going to say Pompa's name aloud here, especially if they knew what he'd done, like Kai had barked earlier.

Maybe they'd known Joe. Sucked for him, really, because everyone who'd known Joe Pompa had a tendency to like him.

Carter hadn't just *liked* him, he'd revered the bastard. To his own detriment, of course.

"So does my crew. And we don't require *your* input. We're not green at this, either." Kai gestured to the cars behind them in the warehouse.

Great, he *really* needed someone that kept trophies.

Not only was Kai an asshole, he was a fool.

"Fine," Carter ground out. There wasn't any use for

him to speak his mind. It hadn't worked well so far.

"We're done for tonight."

He narrowed his eyes when the tall asshole indicated the door.

"You're dismissed, traitor," Kai spat.

The snickers from the assholes in the peanut gallery boiled Carter's blood.

His palm itched to grab his H & K from his waistband and exercise his trigger finger. Perhaps he *should* remind these bastards what he was capable of.

"Have a good week, or three." Asshole Number Three gestured, as if he was tipping an invisible hat.

He had a gesture for him all right, but he made a fist and glued it to his side instead of flipping the guy the bird—or punching him in the face.

Or grabbing his forty.

He forced his eyes on to Kai's and went for a pleasant expression. "When do we meet up again?"

The crew all lived in the warehouse, but it was obvious *he* wasn't welcome.

He'd seen their living area, the corridor that led to their individual rooms, and their chillin' area, complete with couches, recliners, a huge TV and every game console known to man. Females were scarce—if the mess was any indication—but they probably had their pussy come and go, not unlike at Bubba's place.

Carter had to admire their closeness. They were family.

Like *his* crew had been before Joe had betrayed them all, over John and the FBI.

The fucker. Applied to them both, actually.

"I'll call you. *If* I need to," Kai said.

He bit back his smartass reply, telling himself for the thousandth time to play nice. Humiliation didn't feel right, but it was better for him to clamp it shut for now and go. He and Bubba needed to have a talk.

One of the assholes yelled, "Enjoy Phoenix!" and that was answered by a few laughs that made anger roll over Carter again.

He buried his hand in his jeans pocket, gripping his car keys until the metal bit into his skin.

Don't say a word.

He chanted the sentence as he made his way to leave the warehouse.

If even *one* of the assholes had the balls to say *anything* about his limp, his H & K would get the workout it'd begged for.

Carter almost wished one of them would open his big, fat mouth.

Chapter Nine

Taylor stared at her cellphone as if it had the plague. Didn't reach for it.

She'd been putting off *the call* since she'd fled the office at five. Early for her to call it a day, but she'd wanted to get away from Holman.

He was sharp and had great ideas. If she gave him a real chance, he could—and *would*—help her get Bennett.

She hated it. Wanted to do things on her own. For John.

They had a plan to meet up at six a.m. for the trek to interview Joe Pompa at the federal prison four hours away, in Texarkana.

She didn't want to go.

Taylor had paced in her apartment when sitting on the couch watching the news hadn't distracted her from her case. She'd shoved down leftover Chinese just because her stomach wouldn't shut the hell up until she fed it.

Then she'd dug out her laptop and read a few reports—again.

The folder on her desktop labeled '*Antioch PD*' had taunted her even though she hadn't gone anywhere near clicking on it. Didn't need a reminder of Pompa, no matter how a review of Detectives Lucas' and Manning's statements and reports might help her impending trip.

She really should've at least looked at the docs from the trailer park, where two members of Pompa's crew had been killed by Bennett. Taylor had been on scene, of course, working with the two detectives from the small city.

They'd arrived shortly after the shooting. What they hadn't known at the time was that Pompa had gotten away.

Detective Jared Manning had known. Pompa was his brother—they'd been estranged, but blood was thicker than water. The detective had harbored him in a safe house.

She closed her eyes. Refused to think about how she'd followed Manning for weeks, ultimately confronting his partner, Cole Lucas, only to have her concerns fall on deaf ears. The former FBI agent had refused to believe his partner capable of wrongdoing.

Taylor shook herself from Antioch and that night, when she'd rushed into the safe house and found Pompa with her two detectives. Didn't need to read reports or statements. It was etched into her memory forever.

A split-second *wrong* decision. Damaged to three people's lives.

Jared Manning would hate her for the rest of his life, even though his brother hadn't died.

Joe Pompa had survived, but had had to learn to walk again. Was still in therapy and would be for a while.

Taylor struggled daily with the guilt. The bad dreams at night. She checked on him regularly, with the prison doctors now, and with the hospital before that. Manning probably had no idea—and she wanted it that way.

Pompa had taken a shot at her, so the APD had ruled it a good shoot.

She hadn't been legally liable. Didn't matter.

Her gut—and her heart—knew she'd been in the wrong.

The man had been trying to flee, shooting the gun high above her head for a distraction, not to kill her.

She'd pulled the trigger anyway. Had to live with it now.

Her cellphone rang, vibrating and screaming her

ringtone. It danced down the coffee table until she made a grab and swiped her thumb across the touch screen.

She hadn't recognized the number—it wasn't in her contacts—but it had the local area code. "Carrigan."

"Hi."

Even with one word, the familiar male voice washed over Taylor and she shifted on the edge of her brown microfiber couch. "Sergeant Crowley?" She'd written his number down last night, but hadn't put it in her phone.

"Yeah."

Why is Shannon Crowley calling me?

She didn't know what to say.

"Are you there?"

She cleared her throat and adjusted the phone against her ear. "Yes. How can I help you?"

He laughed.

It caught her off guard. She stood, rocking on the balls of her feet, and fighting for balance. "What's funny?" Taylor winced at the snap in her tone.

"You. After last night, you're so formal with me."

The knock on her apartment's door made her jump.

She glanced at her phone then at the door. The sergeant's speech had echoed, as if he was in a hallway.

He can't be—

"Gonna let me in?"

She swallowed. Twice. Glanced down at her clothes. Blue yoga pants and a gray FBI tee from her Quantico days—it was faded, oversized and comfy. Bare feet and her hair down. She wasn't fit for public consumption.

Taylor ended the call and tossed her cell to the couch, jogging to the door. She wrenched it open, fully intending to tell her uninvited guest to go the hell away.

Words dissolved when they made eye contact.

Sergeant Crowley smiled and held up a brown paper

bag. "Thought if I bribed you with sweets, you might invite me in."

Her gaze trailed his tall muscular frame and she had to swallow again. He wore a brown leather jacket. He'd had it on last night, too, at *Hakka Wu*.

The jacket was open, and a black, pec-hugging T-shirt peeked out, tucked into tight dark jeans. He sported an etched oval belt buckle and cowboy boots. Only missing a Stetson, but it didn't dim his appeal.

Crowley was...*gorgeous*. Even with his messy, needs-a-trim dark hair.

She scowled. "How did you find out where I live?"

"Lucky guess?" He shrugged, flashing a mischievous grin that did funny things to her insides.

Taylor tilted her head and ignored the zing of awareness when his eyes raked her body. She fidgeted and wanted to run. Resisted the urge to tug her shirt down. Felt naked. "Tell me who helped you invade my privacy, so I can plan their death."

He laughed and shook his head. "I have no intention of invading your privacy. I thought—"

"You thought *what*?" she snapped.

The handsome cop's expression sobered. "I'm sorry. Had a good time with you last night, is all."

She missed his smile already and sent the sentiment to hell. Taylor reached for her irritation, but had trouble holding on tight. She *should* be nicer to him. "So you show up unannounced at my apartment?" No way was she going to admit that she'd enjoyed dinner with him, too.

"Yeah. I guess when you say it like that, it's..."

"Stalkery?" she retorted.

Crowley blinked and shook his head. "No, I mean..." He looked forlorn, like she'd shot his puppy.

Guilt bit at her. She cursed under her breath and

gestured for him to come in. She really didn't have a reason to be a bitch.

Surprise lit those beautiful amber eyes but he shut his mouth and slid into her apartment.

The sergeant put the bag on her coffee table and shoved his hands into his jeans pockets.

Taylor shut the door and stayed by it even after she'd clicked her deadbolt in place. She was paralyzed at the sight of the guy in her living room.

The space was neither huge, nor tiny, but with him standing by her couch, it seemed smaller, and all the oxygen had dissipated.

The low volume of the TV filled the awkward silence, and she couldn't make her bare feet close the distance between them.

His broad shoulders were scrunched, and somehow his level of discomfort made her feel a tad better.

She blew out a breath. "Are you staying, or what?"

"Depends." Crowley looked around her living room before his gaze settled back on her.

"Depends on what?"

"If you want me to. If you're going to hover by the door all night in your own place, I might as well go."

She wanted to close her eyes, but didn't. Tremors chased each other down her spine and Taylor fought a full body shudder. Hated being on edge in her own apartment. Hated it more that he'd noticed. "What's in the bag?"

Again, surprise darted across his handsome face. "Cheesecake."

Dammit.

Her favorite. The Italian flag and little chef logo printed on the brown paper told her it was from *Mario's*, an awesome little mom and pop Italian bakery around the corner from her building. Also her favorite.

Double dammit.

"I'll get some plates."

He didn't say anything but his full mouth rippled in a tease of a smile that left her wanting more.

She cursed herself all the way to her small kitchen, where she yanked her cupboard door open and whipped two small dishes out. Taylor grabbed two forks and some paper towels, pulling on the roll so hard it kept spinning after she'd gotten what she needed.

The sergeant hadn't moved from the same spot, but he'd slipped out of his jacket. It rested on the back of her couch. Crowley rubbed his thighs, and she felt his nerves. "I'm sorry I showed up. I didn't mean to upset you. I just...wanted to see you." He looked at her dead on, and his eyes were mesmerizing.

Her heart jumped. "It's okay. Sorry I yelled at you."

"I kinda expected it." He smirked, revealing just a hint of the dimple in his right cheek.

She felt herself smiling, instead of getting angry. "Not sure what to say to that."

His big shoulders loosened. "I suppose I should've expected a gun."

Their gazes shot to her Glock, lying holstered on the coffee table, at the same time. "I guess I could've taken that approach. Would you have left?"

Crowley shook his head and grinned. "Nah."

Taylor laughed. For some reason, the pressure in her chest lessened and she blew out a breath. She relaxed into her couch, and leaned over to set the plates and silverware down before she reached for the paper bag.

The man not five feet from her hadn't moved an inch.

"You can sit, you know. I won't bite."

He shifted in his cowboy boots before he finally offered a curt nod and slid onto the couch next to her.

"You look nice, by the way."

She scoffed and spared him a glance. "Right."

Crowley's expression was open and honest, and she wanted to abandon the quest for her favorite dessert and scoot closer.

She didn't.

"I mean it." His weight shifted her body when he moved forward on the couch. "I've only seen you in slacks and a blazer. I like when you look...relaxed. Your hair is beautiful."

Heat crested the back of her neck and scorched her cheeks. Taylor kept her hands busy by opening the two individually packaged pieces of cheesecake. She glanced at him. "Thanks," she muttered. "You look nice out of uniform, too, Sergeant."

"Can you call me Shannon?" His plea was low, and that amber gaze intoxicating.

Their hands bumped when they reached for a fork at the same time.

She yanked hers back, then felt stupid. Fought the urge to crush her eyes shut. She didn't answer—couldn't. "Thanks for the cheesecake. I love *Mario's*." The words fell out, fragmented and shaky.

He handed her a fork. "You're welcome, Taylor."

Her name—with a slight emphasis—jolted her and she averted her gaze.

Had to, or she might do something stupid, like whisper his name when she was leaning in to kiss him. The idea had her jumping to her feet. "I'll get us something to drink. Make some coffee or something. Sound good?"

Shannon blew out a breath and threw his head back

into the plush brown fabric of the couch he should most definitely not be on.

She hadn't even waited for him to answer before disappearing around the corner into the kitchen.

What the hell are you doing?

He'd ambushed her.

It'd gone better than expected. His gaze brushed the gun only about three or four feet from him.

Much better than a bullet in your ass.

Mark hadn't asked too many questions when he'd helped chase down her address, but his dark gaze had been too knowing.

Shannon sighed and closed his eyes. Pushing her had gotten him nowhere. He'd wanted to kiss her. Especially when she'd licked her lips nervously and leaned toward him.

She'd seemed on board, until he'd said her first name. *That* had made her run.

From the moment he'd laid eyes on her, his dick had ached.

She looked so...innocent with her hair down. The strawberry-blonde waves fell down her back and around her shoulders, begging him to run his fingers through them. Freckles he hadn't noticed before were strewn across her nose. Her loose T-shirt contradicted the blue yoga pants that hugged her perfect ass and thighs. He wanted his hands there, too.

The surprise dessert with Special Agent Taylor Carrigan was only going to get him blue balls.

Shannon had been obsessed with her all day, when he should've been paying attention at trial.

Too bad it's all one-sided. I should just go.

The cheesecakes sat on the plates Taylor had placed them on, each had a fork resting next to them, and a paper towel tucked neatly beside. She'd even folded the paper bag flat.

Also on the coffee table, on the other side of her gun, mail was stacked, despite the fact it'd been opened. A pen lay next to a pad of paper near the envelopes, both also orderly.

Shannon smirked.

She was a neat freak to the core.

The couch had a matching oversized stuffed chair to the left, with an ottoman sitting flush to it. A dark wood entertainment center took up most of the wall in front of him, with a flat screen TV that had to be about fifty inches.

There were a few paintings on the walls, but nothing personal. Random art landscape scenes with the occasional farm house in the distance.

The only framed photo made his gut tighten.

It was on the entertainment center. Taylor and a dark-haired man sat for the camera, her in front of him, and his arms around her. The smile on her face was like none he'd ever seen, and he felt guilty as hell hoping for one like that for him.

Damn, I really should go.

"How do you like your coffee?"

Shannon jumped and bit back a curse. He found her standing right inside the room, two steaming mugs in her hands.

"Sorry I startled you."

"No worries. Was in my own little world." He forced a smile.

Taylor studied him until he squirmed.

Shannon scrambled to his feet. "I'll help you. No need for you to get it for me."

She nodded and he followed her into a galley kitchen that was just as neat as her living room. Small appliances were lined up on the counters, the double stainless-steel sink in the middle.

There was a table with two chairs against the far wall, and the only thing on its surface, a full napkin holder, as well as salt and pepper shakers. They were perfectly centered, as were the chairs on either side of the table.

"Sugar's in that cupboard." She pointed above the sinks as she poured flavored coffee creamer in her black mug. It sported the FBI logo.

He retrieved the sweetener and put some in his mug. Liked her proximity, and wanted to move closer, to feel the heat coming off her body. "You like things clean and neat."

Taylor nodded. "My dad's career Navy. Kinda rubs off when you grow up that way."

"Ah. My dad was Army."

"Was?"

"He's gone now, since I was a kid, actually. It's just Mom and my niece, Cailey."

They made their way back into the living room, falling into normal conversation.

Shannon talked about his mother, and how he'd become the man of the house at seventeen, when a heart attack had taken his dad. Then how he'd lost his sister to a drunk driver and was helping his mom raise his niece. He talked about Cails a lot, actually. The kid was his heart.

She was sassy and thirteen now, and he adored hanging out with her, even if she always knew everything.

The FBI agent didn't offer much conversation about herself, but he let it slide, and reveled in each smile she flashed.

He basked in the few laughs she gave and smiled back when she slung a smartass remark. He didn't mind sharing himself and his life in Antioch, or his past.

"I have a new partner," Taylor said.

"Oh yeah?"

She made a face and Shannon wanted to kiss her.

He didn't want to ruin the open conversation, so he leaned away and took a sip of coffee. The cheesecake was long gone. "How's that going for you?" he asked when she didn't remark.

"It was just today, so I'm not sure. I don't want a partner."

"Ah, so it wasn't your choice?"

She shook her head. Her hazel eyes clouded and darted to that picture on top of her entertainment center.

His gut ached all over again. He regretted his question.

She obviously missed her fiancé and he couldn't compete with a dead guy. Knowledge of Taylor's past was a double-edged sword.

The night he'd taken her statement after she'd shot Manning's brother, she'd been open about her case, and who John Murray had been to her.

At the time, it hadn't mattered.

Why is now different?

"Well, hopefully you'll sort it out. Working with someone's better than being alone." Shannon wanted to reassure her. Kiss her. Hold her. He clutched his coffee mug instead. With both hands.

She still avoided his gaze, but gave a slight nod. "It'll be fine." Her tone was unsure, not something he was familiar with, coming from her. "He's young, a kid, really, only twenty-seven, and a transfer from LA, but he grew up in Dallas."

"Twenty-seven is a kid?" He forced words out— scrambling to keep conversation normal. "Like you're so much older than that."

Taylor arched a fair eyebrow. "Isn't it rude to ask a lady how old she is?"

He chuckled. "I didn't."

"I'm thirty-four, if you must know." One corner of her mouth lifted.

"Hey, I didn't ask!" Shannon laughed again, feeling some of the tension dissipate. "And you don't look your age. So, you and your new partner probably both look like kids."

"Well..."

"Well what?" He cocked his head to one side.

"How old are you?"

"Thirty-two." If he'd known her better, and the tension wasn't there, he might tease her about cradle robbing.

She wasn't into him, so it didn't matter. He ignored how his gut sank a little.

"His name's Alec Holman. My new partner, I mean." When her eyes met his again, her vulnerability was palpable. "Thanks for the cheesecake."

His stomach did a back-flip. "You already thanked me." He put his mug on the table, and ordered himself to keep his fingers joined in his lap.

She blushed, making those freckles stand out, but didn't look away. "I mean, thanks for coming over tonight. Even if you weren't invited."

He smiled and brushed hair back from her face. Couldn't help it. She looked sweet and innocent and he burned for her. His cock twitched. "Thanks for not shooting me."

The slight curve of her luscious mouth made his heartbeat kick up. "Too messy."

Shannon chuckled. "Good thing."

Taylor sat sideways, facing him on her couch, one

knee bent on the cushion between them. It prevented him from getting as close as he wanted to, but that was probably a positive.

Do not kiss her.

He cleared his throat. "Well, I'm glad you let me stay. I've had a nice evening with you again. Better than last night."

"Yeah, me too." She stilled, as if she didn't like what she'd just said. Straightened her shoulders. Looked at the clock on her cable box, avoided his eyes. "Well, it's getting late, and I need to get up early to run this cheesecake off."

He sucked back a sigh. She'd retreated again. Expected, maybe, but it had a bite he didn't want to admit. "You're probably right." Shannon rubbed his thighs then pushed to his feet.

I want to stay.

She looked up for a moment, then took the hand he offered her and stood next to him.

Touching her, even just her slender fingers in his, was a bad idea, lighting his body up like a pinball machine, so he released her for both their sakes.

She smiled, and it had a shy edge that gave him hope.

"Will you call me before you leave town?"

"Sure." Shannon ordered himself not to read into it, and reached for his jacket.

"Maybe we can do dinner again. On purpose this time."

"Sounds great."

Taylor's smile widened. "I'll even let you pick the place."

"Nah, you live here, it'll be better if you do. Your favorite, whatever." He swung into his jacket, although the last thing he wanted to do was hurry his exit.

"Okay, Shannon."

He froze. His heart stuttered.

Their gazes collided.

Her lips parted and Shannon's resolve shattered.

He slid a hand into her hair and settled it at the back of her neck. Tugged her forward and dipped down, pausing at the last second to allow her to pull away.

She didn't.

His stomach and his cock jumped at the same time. He pressed his mouth to hers. Still, she didn't tug away, or fight when he deepened the kiss.

Soft and sweet, he tasted flavored coffee and cheesecake, and something that was just Taylor.

She moved into his kiss, but didn't throw her arms around his middle or his neck, so he held back, forcing his body to still. Letting her lead. Didn't pull her into his arms like he wanted to either, but it didn't matter. He was granite in his jeans and throbbing for her.

Shannon pulled away on a pant before he grabbed her up, threw her over his shoulder and high-tailed it to her bedroom. He wouldn't pressure her.

Her hazel eyes were heavy lidded and hazy, passion-filled.

He swallowed a groan and contented himself with caressing her cheek, brushing back that incredible hair. The strawberry-blonde waves were as soft as her skin. "I'll call you."

Taylor nodded but it was the barest thing, like she was unaware of...everything.

Whaddya know.

He'd kissed her senseless, and it wasn't even the best in his arsenal. Shannon smiled and forced his feet to the door.

Chapter Ten

Taylor watched the door, as if he'd step back through at any second.

Her heart thundered in her ears and there was an ache between her legs she hadn't felt in so long, she'd forgotten what desire was like.

She stood there a good five minutes. Replaying the sergeant's exit.

Shannon had kissed her.

She'd let him.

Worse, she'd kissed him back. Her body had responded, leaving her pulsing. Leaving her wishing he'd stayed.

Guilt rose up and bit her when her eyes skimmed the picture of her and John on top of the TV. She'd lost him over a year ago, but it still felt fresh.

Didn't it?

What the hell am I thinking?

John wasn't the only lover she'd ever had, but he was the only man she'd ever loved. The one she'd imagined being with for the rest of her life.

She wasn't ready for...intimacy yet, even if it was only just sex.

No matter how glorious the man's mouth moving over hers had been. Or how it'd made her crave more, his arms around her.

The heat coming off his body had seeped through his tight cotton tee, but Taylor hadn't wrapped herself around him. She'd felt his arousal, too.

Shannon hadn't pulled her to him, as if he could sense she'd feel...trapped.

Would she have?

She shook herself and swallowed.

More guilt surfaced when Taylor glanced at the remnants of dessert and coffee. She didn't regret spending the evening with the sergeant.

He'd made her laugh. Had shared himself with her in a way she hadn't reciprocated, but he hadn't hounded her, or pressured her to talk about...*anything.*

What did Shannon Crowley want from her? More than the obvious?

He'd treated her like a person he'd wanted to get to know. No one had really shown genuine interest in her since—

Her phone dinged.

She glanced over her shoulder, but didn't spot it. Cursed when she remembered seeing it last, when she'd let Shannon in. Taylor knelt on the couch and dug it out from between the cushions. She swiped her thumb across the screen to read the message.

Back at my hotel. Have a good night.

She smiled—couldn't help it—and avoided glancing toward the picture of her and John. Added Shannon's number into her contacts and labeled him *APD*. Then she frowned. Still hadn't called Jared Manning.

Taylor sighed and collapsed into the couch. It wasn't quite nine p.m. She needed to call the detective. "It's kinda late, isn't it?" she whispered, then shook her head.

Don't rationalize, just get it done.

She distracted herself by answering Shannon's text.

Thanks. You, too.

She waited a few minutes, but the sergeant didn't send a message back.

Taylor had tried to buy enough time.

Get it done.

She sucked in a breath, then another. Thumbed through the vast list of names and numbers in her phone until she found the right one, and hit the green circle.

It only rang two times.

"Manning."

She recalled his deep voice as if they'd worked together yesterday.

The memory that piqued most was him shouting, cursing, after she'd almost killed his brother.

Words abandoned her, and all the good feelings from spending the evening with Shannon evaporated.

Pressure descended and threatened to cave her chest in.

"Hello?"

Taylor jolted. "Uh, sorry. It's Carrigan."

Silence. Nothing less than she'd expected.

"What do you need, Special Agent?"

Surprise washed over her at the forced politeness.

Definitely more than expected.

"I need your brother's help." Silence greeted her again, lasting so long she finally winced.

A bitter laugh sounded and she grimaced, even though he couldn't see her.

Never mind.

The obligatory southern manners couldn't last.

Nothing less than she deserved.

"Why the *hell* did you call me?" Manning's inquiry was a mixture of command and incredulous. "You know where he's at. You know how to go about it."

"I called, because—" Taylor swallowed when her

voice cracked. Because she felt guilty as hell, but she'd die before she'd admit that. "Professional courtesy," she finally pushed out.

The detective laughed again, a harsh bark. "Thanks for waiting until he learned how to walk again. Sure he'll appreciate that. Oh, he has a limp. One of his hands doesn't work right. Because of you."

She crushed her eyes shut, thanking God she was alone, but wishing for Shannon at the same time. Didn't take the time to question that. "Jared..." she whispered.

Taylor had already apologized.

She couldn't—*wouldn't*—tell him what she'd done was eating her up from the inside out. Or about her nightmares of watching his brother hit the kitchen floor in the safe house like a sick movie in slow-mo.

All the blood.

Again, she was met with silence.

A tear rolled down her cheek and she swiped it away.

Emotion is weak.

Taylor sucked in a breath. "I just thought you should know."

"Yeah. Well, thanks." Manning's sarcasm made more unwanted emotion well up.

Her chest ached and it was hard to breathe. She'd known he'd hate her forever, but *hearing* it was different.

It almost...hurt.

Why do you care?

But she did. Even if she couldn't make sense of it.

"How are things? I heard you got married. Congrats." She hoped she sounded even, as normal, as she'd been going for.

The detective chuckled. "We've never chatted casually, and we're not about to start. Don't pretend you give a shit about me or my life. Do me a favor. Lose my number."

Taylor reared back as if he'd slapped her. Tried to reach for anger, but she couldn't. Didn't blame Manning for how he felt, or how he talked to her.

The detective relieved her of the need to answer. "Hope my brother gives you what you need, Special Agent. Have a good night."

Then he was gone.

Her head reeled.

She never should've reached out to him.

"What were you thinking?" she whispered. Her scold reverberated in her head.

Maybe she'd wanted Manning to assuage some of the guilt...the hurt.

No one but Taylor could do that, even if she couldn't let it go.

The psychiatrist her boss had made her see had urged her to forgive herself so she could move on.

Yeah. Right.

In the end, she'd said what she'd needed to say to be cleared for duty. That didn't make it true, but the shrink had been convinced enough.

Baker hadn't, but Taylor had gotten her way, persuading him she was okay.

She paced her living room, a hard back-and-forth until the burn of the carpet stung the bottoms of her feet. Shot a glance to her phone and was torn between tossing it and grabbing for it.

Shannon's amber eyes popped into her head and she groaned, reaching for the cell with a hand that didn't feel like hers. Her fingers shook as she found his number fast. Pounded the green circle before she could change her mind.

It rang three, then four times.

Her stomach twisted and disappointment crashed over her after the fifth ring, when his voicemail message sounded.

She hung up.

They'd spent the evening together, why did she need to call him the same night?

Taylor headed to her room, phone still in hand. She should just hop in the shower and call it an early night.

No need to reread reports she'd properly avoided. Or delve into others that would make her feel worthless. She'd just end up obsessing more about the morning's trip...and Manning's failed call.

The cell vibrated in her hand. The ringtone made her shriek even though she'd heard it a million times.

Her heart hit overdrive, and she hastily swiped at the screen. Had to do it twice—she missed the first time. "Hello?" Damn, she sounded out of breath.

"Everything okay?" Shannon asked by way of greeting.

Taylor swallowed. *No.* "Yeah."

"Good. Sorry I missed your call, I was in the shower."

She sucked back a groan when visions of him standing in her living room in that tight black shirt and those snug jeans—hugging his ass and thighs—popped into her head.

If he looked that good with clothes *on*, she didn't need naked fodder to contemplate.

Especially with her body's reaction to one little kiss.

"It's okay." She winced as her words came out on a croak.

There was a pause.

She made it to her bedroom, closed the door and fought the urge to lean into it. Or slide down it until her yoga pants hit the carpet.

"Are you sure you're all right?"

"I'm good."

Liar, liar.

She was a mess—Joe Pompa, Jared Manning, her case, and *him* all churning her mind. Her head and her eyes went all syphon on her. Taylor braced her free hand on the wall next to her bed so she wouldn't keel over.

Shannon gave a little sigh and she pictured him stretched out on a bed that wasn't hers.

Naked.

Thick biceps. Pecs, abs, hard thighs...

Her stomach fluttered and she hollered at herself not to go there.

"I had a great time tonight." The smile was evident in his sentence.

Just like that, her body loosened and she felt lighter. Was able to breathe easier, too. Taylor focused. "Me too. Really. Thanks." She straightened from the wall and sat on the side of the bed she always slept on.

Imagined Shannon on the other side, then screamed at herself for it.

"I'm glad you called," he said.

"I'm glad you called me back."

"Always."

She believed him. Her stomach fluttered and her pulse picked up.

He started talking, like he had when he'd been at her place. About anything and everything, his mom, his niece, his day at court and the frustrating trial. All things he hadn't said before, giving her more insight into what she already knew.

Shannon Crowley was a great guy.

She concentrated on his words, relaxing into her comforter and pillows. Taylor closed her eyes and let his deep voice wash over her.

It didn't matter what he was saying. It mattered that he wasn't pressuring *her* to say anything back.

She laughed at a funny story he told about a traffic stop a few years back, and an unwanted nickname from his partner. Made worse by the bunch of cops he worked with. "Should I start calling you Angel?"

Shannon growled, and she grinned.

"Is that a no?"

"I can't believe I told you that. I can't believe I told you I'm into the girliest exercise ever, either."

Taylor laughed again. "What can I say, people always spill their guts to me." She gripped her phone tight to her ear and felt...great.

He chuckled. "I don't doubt it. You're good at your job." He took a breath. "You should laugh more often, Special Agent. I like the sound of it."

Her heart skipped and she sucked air, too. "Thanks," she whispered, but it had a breathless edge she didn't like.

What was this man doing to her?

She should hang up.

Now.

Instinct told her losing control was bad.

Shannon Crowley was tempting, and she didn't need *tempting* in her life, especially not right now.

Chapter Eleven

"Just do me a favor and stay in the car." Taylor tried not to glare or bark at Holman.

The *last* thing she wanted to do was make a long drive to interview a man she couldn't look in the eye. The forced tagalong made it worse, even if it was his idea.

Maybe *that* was the worst thing of all.

"I need coffee," she muttered.

"Will it make you nicer?"

She paused, her hand still on the Charger's handle. She smirked and met his gaze. "So, look who's a smartass? We might get along after all."

Holman arched a fair eyebrow. "Really? I see you as more stiff and proper than sarcastic."

Taylor blinked.

What the hell?

Basically, his words were the polite way of saying she had a stick up her ass. Nothing she hadn't heard before. Although, she certainly hadn't seen her new partner as a guy with balls who could speak his mind when she was in bitch-mode.

She smiled, slowly. Then got out of the car without another word.

Holman's laughter accompanied as she headed toward the convenience store's double glass doors.

If the kid could keep her on her toes, maybe she wouldn't have to plot his demise more than once or twice a week.

The cappuccino machine called her name. Taylor threw the clerk a nod when the man greeted her.

He was cashing out a trucker-looking guy who winked when she walked by.

They had a four hour drive to Texarkana, and she wanted to get there and get back, so she'd ordered Holman to meet her at six. The kid had complied, looking sharp and smelling annoyingly good.

Not as good as Shannon had last night.

She shuddered and forbade herself from further thought of the sergeant.

It didn't work.

Taylor had *more* than enjoyed spending the evening with him, not to mention talking to him on the phone until almost ten. She'd showered and obsessed about the shower *he'd* mentioned, and had had naughty thoughts about kissing him in her shower, touching him.

Shannon touching her back.

Things that could never happen.

He was obviously interested in her in a way she couldn't handle.

She'd have to shut him down gently. Never should've asked him to dinner. Shouldn't have called him, either.

Taylor sighed. It wasn't something she'd be fond of doing, but she'd have to. Wasn't about to hop in bed with him, no matter what her hormones wanted her to do.

What she'd had with John, she'd never have again.

What am I even thinking?

She'd spent one evening—two if she counted the accidental dinner—with the man.

He'd kissed her, not asked her to marry him.

She'd run an extra mile on the treadmill that morning to try to forget about the previous two nights, but it hadn't worked for shit.

Shannon Crowley's amber eyes and charming dimple wouldn't stop haunting her.

Taylor cursed as she plucked a container from the rack.

The bell above the door sounded once more, but she didn't look up from the liquid salvation filling her twenty-four ounce cup. The scent of French Vanilla enveloped her senses and her mouth watered. *Totally* looking forward to the first sip.

"Give me all the money! Hurry, man!"

She released the button on the cappuccino machine. Backed up and whirled around, ducking behind a rack of sweets. Couldn't see the counter from where she was in the back of the store, but she was confident *they* couldn't see her, either.

"Seriously, this isn't a water gun, get moving."A hooded figure wearing all black waved a small revolver around.

It looked to be a snub-nosed thirty-eight caliber. Or maybe a twenty-two.

A holdup before seven a.m.? Really? So much for my French Vanilla.

The poor clerk shoved money into a plastic bag from his own counter while the robber ranted.

The doorbell sounded and Taylor cursed again.

More people were the last thing this situation needed.

"Get out! Now! Or I'll shoot your ass!" The robber waved his gun at the would-be shopper. "If you call the cops, I'll find you and kill you!"

A feminine shriek sounded with the door's bell again, as she no doubt made a hurried exit.

Taylor scanned the aisles she could see.

No one else seemed to be in the store.

Good.

She drew her Glock from her waistband holster,

holding her breath as the leather creaked and the *snap* of the strap resounded in her ears.

"Hurry! You're taking too long. What're you reaching for? Don't move! I'll shoot you!"

Oh God, don't be a hero, she ordered the clerk, praying he didn't have a gun under the counter.

"N-n-nothing, man!" The clerk's hands flew up. He dropped the bag of money to the floor behind the counter.

Whether on purpose or by accident, it gave Taylor the chance she needed.

The thug cursed and jumped over the red Formica top after his prize.

The clerk backed up, keeping his palms up. His eyes widened when he saw her.

She pressed her index finger into her lips and shook her head. Then she raised her forty. "Federal Agent! Come out slowly, and drop the gun!"

Of course, the thug stayed low, popping his gun up and taking a wild shot.

She dove to the floor, cursing. Her ears rang from the loud burst of the small weapon. She slid behind the nearest display.

He took another shot and a window shattered.

Sirens sounded in the distance.

The runner had probably called 9-1-1.

Or maybe Holman had.

The clerk was nowhere in sight. He'd probably slipped down the hallway and into the back. Hopefully he had a way out of the building from there.

Taylor's phone was vibrating wildly in her right pocket, but she ignored it. Flexed her hands on the grip of her gun. "We don't have to do this the hard way," she yelled.

Another gunshot was the only answer.

Three down, two to go.

Unless he had another weapon, the small revolver should only have two more bullets. Hopefully he didn't have extra ammo or a speed loader.

"Come on out, so we can talk," she urged.

"Yeah, right, bitch. So you can shoot me?"

"No one has to get hurt here." She moved forward, her guard—and her gun—held high. Wasn't going to get anywhere yelling around the corner, and was betting, maybe praying, the guy only had two more shots.

"What the fuck are you doing?" the robber yelled, popping to his feet and hopping over the counter. He aimed the revolver at Taylor's chest.

"Put the gun down. This doesn't have to go down like this." She swallowed and tried to remain as even as she could. Hadn't been on the wrong side of a gun barrel since *that night.*

Unwanted memories ambushed her. Joe Pompa yelling, waving around his brother's forty-caliber Sig, while he had Manning pinned to his chest, using him as a human shield.

No. Focus.

She couldn't afford distraction. Had a gun in her face.

"Freeze! FBI!"

The gunman startled at Holman's voice, but didn't take more than a half-second to recover. He charged Taylor, putting his knee into her stomach.

Pain rushed up, air breached her lips, and she fought against doubling over. Her Glock went flying.

Before she could blink, metal bit at her temple and a strong arm seized her chest.

The bastard was tall, and she was only five-one. His arm was like a vise, holding her so hard she couldn't breathe. Her arms were pinned to her sides, to boot.

Holman cursed. "Let her go!"

"I'll kill her."

"No, you won't."

Unfamiliar panic flipped her stomach. The longer she couldn't catch her breath, the more her head spun. Taylor blinked to clear her vision. Moisture burned the corners of her eyes and she gasped for air.

Get it together. Now.

She never lost her cool in a stressful situation.

"I *will* kill her." To illustrate his point, he ground the revolver's short barrel into her cheek.

She struggled, but he held her tighter. "If you have a shot, take it," she pushed out to her partner.

Sirens wailed, not far off now.

"You bitches called the cops," the thug barked.

Taylor winced when spittle hit her face. Tried to lean away from the gun's muzzle, but the man jerked her against him. It put more compression on her aching chest, and she had to pant to get any air.

"You shot the window out, they were gonna come anyway. Think this through. The longer you have her, the worse this is going to be. Let her go, we can work this out."

"I'll just kill you both and it'll be fine for me." With each word, the guy squeezed her. His forearm inched up, until he held her across the throat. His large hand clamped down over her shoulder, pinning her to him.

She had to cough to breathe. Her face was hot, scorching. Taylor could smell the guy's sweat and feel his overheated body through her jacket.

He was so strong—probably on something, even though his speech wasn't slurred, or his movements unsure.

"How you doin', partner?" Holman asked, but his

eyes stayed trained on her captor.

"Could stand here all day," she croaked.

Her partner smirked.

The rush of booted feet made her wince.

Cops would just freak the robber out even more.

"Police! Freeze!"

A few uniformed members of Dallas' finest entered the store the same way Holman had—through the large broken window. One aimed at her and the bad guy, and the other aimed at her partner.

The robber started to scream, pressing the revolver into Taylor's temple so hard pain bit back. She had to blink through the pressure to see anything.

"I'll kill her right now. I'll shoot all you fucking pigs!"

"FBI!" Holman shouted, but he didn't move. "He's got my partner. I got this, back off."

She wiggled, trying to take advantage of the hollering cops and her captor's movements. Tried to make space between them.

He cursed and slammed her backwards.

Her head bounced off his shoulder. It made her head spin, her vision dance. She tightened all her muscles. *Refused* to pass out.

"Stop moving, bitch, or it's over."

"You heard what the man said, back off, guys," one of the officers yelled, but the cops didn't leave. They retreated, still aiming at Taylor and her captor. Some hovered just inside the store, and a few others right outside the broken window.

The distance calmed the thug, but he smacked his lips and screamed obscenities. Kept moving his gun back and forth, holding it on her, then her partner, only to start the cycle over. The more his arm jerked, the more he jolted them around.

"Carrigan, hold tight. I got this." Holman was unmovable. A machine.

Her heart thundered, and it had little to do with the robber's iron grip.

He was asking her to trust him.

Right here. Right now.

Could she?

Taylor gasped as her captor took a step back, made her stumble, and once again his forearm took her breath, the agony constricting her throat and blackening her vision for a few seconds. She locked gazes with Holman. Would've nodded if she could.

"Now!" She and her partner shouted at the same time.

The robber squealed when the gunshot from Holman's forty rang in her ears, blocking out all other sound with the strength of the *boom*.

All she could hear was a high-pitched tone that took all her attention.

The arm around her disappeared and she fell to her knees, her arms pin-wheeling for anything to steady her but only cutting through air. Pain shot into her thighs and she braced herself on the floor, on all fours.

Cops shouted and boots rushed passed her.

"He's down, hit in the shoulder!" one of the DPD cops yelled. He kicked the shiny revolver away from the robber.

"Ambulance on the way," another answered.

A hand appeared in her line of vision.

Taylor looked up, into her new partner's very blue eyes. Then she slid her hand into his much larger one, and let him pull her to her feet.

When her legs wobbled, he gripped her upper arm.

She let him stabilize her, since she had to cough to

regulate her breathing. The burning in her chest and lungs hadn't let up.

"Are you all right?" Holman demanded.

She nodded, and rubbed her throat.

His gun was holstered at his side, but she'd missed him doing it. He reached out, tilting her chin up. "You're probably going to bruise."

Taylor tugged away, but it was too fast and made her head spin. She wanted to snap, '*Don't touch me,*' but she didn't. "I'm fine," she barked.

"There's my partner."

She glared up at his ghost of a smile, but from his expression, he didn't give a shit.

Chaos ensued—cops and medics coming and going, and bystanders filling the parking lot. The clerk was back from wherever he'd been.

A few moments later, a guy pulled into the parking lot demanding to know what'd happened and shouting that he was the owner of the store until the cops at the perimeter let him through.

Two detectives arrived and asked her and Holman to give a statement.

Two ambulanced made scene.

The robber got loaded up into the one on the right. He was bitching and moaning about his shoulder and declaring to sue the FBI.

"Yeah, yeah, shut up." The cop who climbed inside scowled as he took a seat next to the gurney.

One of the medics slammed the doors shut, shaking his head.

Taylor glanced at her watch and stood beside Holman as he spoke to the detective who'd already grilled her.

Soon, the female investigator thanked them, gave

them her card and said she'd be in touch.

Taylor was about to head back to her Charger when she remembered her cappuccino. "I'll be right back!" She dashed into the store, grabbed a new cup and started the process over.

They'd have to go back to the office now. No way Baker wouldn't bench Holman for a few days to conference with DPD on the investigation. He'd have to turn his weapon in, too.

The Dallas detectives had smartly deferred to the FBI, but she would've been fine with them handling things. Had bigger fish to fry.

It was almost nine by now, but she still needed caffeine.

Stupid situation was going to put her behind on what she needed to do for her case, but she'd try to persuade Baker to let her work without Holman. Maybe she'd get a few days reprieve from her new partner.

Doubtful.

Her boss had been pretty clear yesterday, as much as Taylor hated to admit it. She was supposed to go *everywhere* with Holman.

If she had to camp out at the office, she wouldn't allow Baker to put her on administrative leave, too.

It shouldn't be a long-drawn-out thing anyway. Along with her, five or six Dallas uniforms had witnessed the shooting. That should help expedite things. Not to mention the store video surveillance.

She hoped to God it'd been recording.

On her way out, she slapped a five dollar bill on the counter next to the register, ignoring the cops who gave her funny looks.

When she got back to the Charger, Holman was glaring, arms crossed over his broad chest as he leaned on the car.

"What?" she asked. Taylor shrugged and took a sip of heavenly French Vanilla. Flavor exploded on her tongue and she closed her eyes, inhaling her cappuccino's scent.

"You should've texted me. Or just called 9-1-1. I was right *here*. No reason to handle it on your own." Her partner's disapproval didn't sit right on his handsome face. It made him look older—and irritated her.

"Are you really telling me what to do, Holman?"

"I know I'm new to the Dallas office, but I'm your *partner*. I'm here to help."

She parked her quick retort. He *had* helped her. Saved her ass, really.

No *way* was she actually going to *admit* that.

Not now. Not ever.

"I had the situation handled."

Holman straightened. Stared her down, and Taylor hated that he had a good foot on her in height. "Right."

"It turned quickly. Could've happened to anyone."

He narrowed those blue eyes. "Bet you're glad I was here, then, huh?"

She sighed. Didn't want to fight. If their boss let him work at the office instead of sending him home, maybe they could get somewhere on the case.

Texarkana was out, at least for a few days—or more, depending on what Baker decided to do with Holman. That, she wouldn't do alone. Wouldn't argue the point at all—didn't want to go, let alone face Joe Pompa by *herself*.

Coward.

She fought a wince.

Bottom line, she really owed Holman one. Even if she couldn't tell him. "Yes. Thank you."

He reared back, as if that was the last thing he'd

expected to hear. His arms fell to his sides and his broad shoulders relaxed. "You're welcome."

Taylor gave a curt nod.

"Paramedics wanna check you out." He thumbed toward the open ambulance and two hovering medics.

"Nah. I'm good. You call Baker?"

"Yeah."

"What'd he say about you shooting someone on day two?" She smirked.

"He said to cooperate with DPD, and to come back to the office, of course. No doubt I'll be out for a few days." He frowned. "Baker was concerned about *you*. I am, too. What happened in there? Really?"

"What d'you mean?" Taylor frowned, too. Playing dumb was the way to go. Wasn't about to tell him about her little flashback when the robber first put his gun in her face.

It was over. Done.

I'm fine.

"He wants us back right away, I'm assuming?"

"Yes, as long as Dallas is done with us. You know the routine, gotta turn my weapon in. DPD'll be in touch. They're only cutting us loose so fast because we're FBI. I'm sure Baker'll have someone liaise."

"Probably so."

Holman nodded. "Carrigan, I saw the look on your face right before he grabbed you—"

"I already said thank you, what more do you want?" she snapped.

"I want you to trust me."

She stilled and looked up at him. Taylor uttered the truth; couldn't help it. "I do."

He blew out a breath and his face relaxed. "Good. I know we're new, you and I, but I really want to be your partner."

His slight emphasis on the word for the second time made her want to snarl, but she didn't. "According to Baker, you are. Mission accomplished."

"Baker isn't who I'm concerned with."

She let it slide and sipped cappuccino.

"Hey, the boss said one more thing." Holman's smile could only be called smartass.

"What?" Taylor groaned, but knew what he'd say before he opened his mouth.

"You can't go back to the office unless the paramedics check you out. I'm supposed to text him a picture as proof."

"Jesus. Don't expect me to smile."

His laughter followed as she stomped toward the ambulance.

Chapter Twelve

Holman insisted on driving back to the office, and, since she owed him one, Taylor didn't argue about it—much.

She replayed the holdup in her head, and promptly ignored her conscience piping up that she'd been reckless.

Should've called Holman, I had time.

Her neck was sore, and the medics agreed with her partner.

She'd have a nice bruise to show for her efforts, but nothing that'd kill her or leave permanent damage. If it was bad, she'd just slap makeup on it to avoid questions.

The asshole robber had kneed her in the stomach. Probably have a bruise there, too, but at least no one would see it. It wasn't sore at the moment, but maybe adrenaline was still taking care of that.

Last thing Taylor needed was for word to spread around the office about how she'd gotten her latest *badge of honor*. Holman's version would no doubt be worse than hers.

The pain of the holdup wasn't only her soon-to-be black and blue throat. DPD detectives had reminded them before they'd left; they'd be contacted soon with more on the investigation. Even if the FBI led, they'd still have to deal with Dallas PD, too.

Oh, I just can't wait.

They'd just better be quick about so it didn't impede *her* investigation.

She didn't say anything as Holman parked her duty car and they headed into the building.

"See you in a bit. Gonna see what the boss wants me

to do," he said.

She nodded and went to their office. Taylor sank into her chair with a sigh. She'd cleared her calendar for the day trip to Texarkana, had focused solely on mentally preparing for Joe Pompa.

Now what?

First, she needed to let the prison know they weren't coming. That was just a quick call to the warden's office. Taylor let them know they'd be out soon, but didn't elaborate on the reason for delay.

The woman who'd answered the phone didn't ask, either. Taylor told her they'd call again before showing up.

She hung up, staring at the FBI logo wallpaper on the desktop of her PC and swallowed a sigh. Might as well start typing up a statement of the holdup in an accurate timeline of the events—Baker would ask her for a formal report eventually.

Holman would have to do one, too. She wanted to be prepared for the internal investigation that would follow. She could share it with DPD. Maybe it would help expedite both ends.

She started typing, her fingers flying over the keyboard as she wrote the events of the morning. Ignored her neck when it gave a throb instead of giving in to the urge to rub it, or study the injury in the mirror she kept in her drawer.

Don't think about it.

Taylor let her eyes slip closed and replayed everything like it was a scene she'd been sent to assess, instead of a situation she'd been involved in.

She saw the robber—Donnie Simmons—pop up from behind the counter and put the small stainless steel revolver in her face.

A shudder shot down her spine.

She released her mouse and shook her hands out. Hadn't been thinking about Simmons shooting her—she'd been seeing Joe Pompa.

That could've gotten her killed, whether or not her partner had shown up to play hero.

Dammit, Taylor.

She released a slow breath and flexed her fingers over her keyboard. Needed to finish up and convince herself she wasn't traumatized.

The phone on her desk rang and she cursed her instant startle. One glance at caller-ID told her it was Baker. "Yes, sir?"

"Come see me, if you don't mind."

"Sure." She hung up and made her way to her boss' office.

"Carrigan, have a seat." He gestured without looking up from whatever was on his computer screen.

"What's up?" It was odd for him to be so formal, then not acknowledge her until she took a seat.

"I wanted to get your take on what happened this morning."

"Ah. I was writing up a statement right now. Who're you putting on it?"

"Probably Palumbo. Brief him shortly."

"Sounds good."

Silence fell and Baker's dark eyes appraised her until Taylor wanted to squirm.

"Well?" he prompted.

"Oh, right. I could just finish my report—" She thumbed over her shoulder, toward her office.

He gave her a long look.

"All right."

She started with the approximate time they'd pulled into the convenience store parking lot.

He was quiet while she retold the holdup in its entirety, but his too-keen gaze didn't waver, as if he was trying to find fault in what she was saying.

Unless it's something else. Like he's trying to determine if something's wrong with me.

She wanted to glare, but didn't.

"Well, seems pretty straightforward."

Taylor nodded. "I think so, too."

"Palumbo shouldn't have issue with a fast close-out. Holman will be off a few days, and I want you both to see Dr. Wong," her boss said.

"Excuse me?" she snapped. "No. Just. No."

Baker dragged his hand down his face. "You won't fight me on this. It's nothing personal. It's procedure when agents are victims of a crime. Same as when you fire your weapon. Bottom line."

"I was not the *victim* of a crime."

"Your neck says otherwise." He pointed. "True or false, someone held a gun to your temple today? And choked you?"

Her hands flew up, but she stopped herself short of covering bruising that was *obviously* already visible. Tugged on her shirt collar, and refused the wince at the twinge of discomfort that answered. Taylor didn't want to confirm her boss' question. "I'm fine."

"You're always fine."

She nodded. "Right."

Baker sighed and shook his head. "You're gonna see the doc. It's nonnegotiable."

"Or what?"

He leveled her with a glare as dark as his eyes. "Admin leave, but not a few days like your partner. A week. You'll stay home, too. No casework. No email. No calling to check in. *Suspension.*"

Taylor would never abide a mar like that on her record.

Besides, disobeying a direct order went against her programming, as much as she didn't like it. As much as she despised psychiatrists. She sucked back a groan. "One session, and I work no matter what he says."

"Three, and you only work if he clears you."

"No."

"Yes." Her boss didn't often raise his voice, no matter how hard his tone.

This time, she was close to pushing him to a yell, if the tic in his cheek was any indication. "Matthias—"

"Not gonna happen, *Taylor*. Get what you can done with Holman benched."

She groaned. "Can he not work from the office?"

"No, he'll be off." Baker arched an eyebrow. "You mean, you're not rejoicing being on your own for a few more days?"

"Either way is fine with me." Taylor resisted a sigh and avoided his gaze.

His mouth rippled as if he was fighting a smile.

Considering she'd pissed him off only moments before, she'd take it as an improvement.

"Glad to hear you don't mind having a partner again."

"Didn't say that," she muttered.

"I made your first appointment with Dr. Wong. It's at three today."

Oh, God.

"Can't I get a break at all? What's wrong with tomorrow?" she grumbled.

"If you don't show up, you can stay home tomorrow. And the next day, and the next day—"

"I get it. I'll be there."

"He's willing to come here, if you need him to."
Again, Baker wore a ghost of a smile.

"Uh, no. I'll go to him. Office in the same place?"

"Yes."

Taylor stood, tugging her jacket straight.

"Have a good afternoon, Carrigan." Her boss smiled, but there was too much *'I-won-and-you-didn't'* in it.

She narrowed her eyes. "You, too."

"Don't forget to make your second appointment," he said brightly. "The quicker you do three, the quicker you're back to work. *If* the good doctor agrees."

Jesus Christ.

She stomped back to her office.

Holman wasn't back from downstairs yet, and she was glad to be alone, if only for a little while longer. Taylor had no doubt her new partner would pop his head in before he left. He'd probably need to say goodbye.

She rolled her eyes.

She'd just finished her holdup statement when her phone dinged in her pocket. She griped as she dug it out.

Surprise, and perhaps a little pleasure, rolled over her when she saw who the text was from.

How're you today? Plans for tonight?

Taylor swallowed and stared. What should she say to Shannon?

Her stomach gave a little tremor. She *had* asked him out to dinner. Should she mention the offer and see if he was game?

I shouldn't.

She patted her hair, even though it was still in its tight chignon. Took a deep breath, then called herself an idiot.

Who needed to compose themselves before sending a text message?

Taylor ran her thumb over the touch screen, since it'd gone dark with her hedging. She formed a message and hit *send* before she lost her nerve.

I'm fine, and you? Should be out of the office about five. What were you thinking?

She crushed her eyes shut and called herself every name in the book.

His answer was fast.

I'm better now that I've heard from you. How about I meet you at your place? We can decide what to do then.

She swallowed. Then smiled.

Okay.

Shannon's answer was a simple '*See you later*', but for some reason her heart sped up.

What am I doing?

He'd calmed her last night, and Taylor hated to admit she could use another evening of that.

She didn't want to think about—or *talk* about—that kiss, and she wouldn't let something like that happen again, so what harm was a little dinner?

"Okay, so I'm out."

Holman's appearance made her jump.

Her knee slammed into the side of her desk. She cursed.

"Oh, sorry. I didn't mean to scare you." Her partner slipped into the room, his expression tight with remorse.

"It's fine." She rubbed the throbbing spot through her dark slacks.

Great, now I'll have three bruises from today.

Since *when* did she startle so damn easily?

"Are you all right?" Holman asked.

"Yes. Just finished my formal statement."

"Good. I'll do mine, then I'm out. Baker told me to go home."

Taylor nodded. "I know, he told me."

"Will you go to Texarkana without me?"

Hell no.

"No, I already called. I'll wait for you to get back. Hope Palumbo will be quick about things."

Holman sat in his chair and woke his computer up. "Me too. I want to interview Pompa and get on with this case."

She didn't answer. Pretended to be busy on her PC, even though she watched him from the corner of her eye.

"Not looking forward to meeting Doc Wong." Her partner broke the ensuing silence.

"Yeah, I have to go, too."

He swiveled his seat to face her. "Really?"

Taylor narrowed her eyes. "Yes." Tried to tell him with her glare she had *nothing* more to say about that.

Holman got the message and turned back to his report.

Not even ten minutes later, he'd powered down his machine. He offered Taylor a wave from the doorway. "Get a lot done while I'm gone."

"Sure hope so."

"Don't solve it, though, I wanna feel needed and all that." He flashed a smartass smile.

She smirked. "Afraid I'll steal your thunder?"

Her partner shrugged and grinned. "I guess. Take it

easy.”

"You, too." Taylor watched him go. She shook her head, but couldn't help the slight curve of her lips. Maybe the new guy wasn't so bad, after all.

Chapter Thirteen

Shannon whistled as he jogged down the courthouse steps.

The afternoon had gone surprisingly fast. Rather smoothly, too, even though the stupid defense attorney had grilled him as if he'd been the one driving drunk.

Things were moving quicker than he'd anticipated. The charges would probably go to the jury tomorrow or the next day.

He might be home by the weekend, and not have to come back Monday.

When he'd pulled into Dallas, he'd wanted the trial to conclude in a few days, but now...

Taylor.

A week in the city wouldn't be enough. Or two weeks.

Not after last night.

He'd hedged all morning about reaching out to her, even if it was only one little text message. When Judge Newton had called a short recess, he'd caved. Had wanted to see if she'd answer him.

Shannon had half-expected her to turn him down, which was why he'd been casual in his probing. Shock had rolled over him when Taylor had agreed he could come back to her place. He hadn't had to play the *'you-were-the-one-who-asked-me-out'* card, but he might've. He was driven to see her again.

He hopped in his truck and tried not to be frustrated over the backed-up parking garage. It was going to take forever to get down the ramp and out of the place. The whole court house and surrounding buildings must've emptied at the same time.

The drive to his hotel was short in theory, but not in five p.m. downtown Dallas traffic. His left leg bounced up and down, his boot tapping in time with the random song on the radio he was only half paying attention to.

Shannon drummed his fingers on the steering wheel and swung his gaze around, but his Tundra was stuck for now. He'd been able to back out of his spot, but hadn't gotten much farther than a few feet down the narrow aisle.

He was antsy, not just because of the thick line of vehicles in front of him.

What was it about Taylor Carrigan? And what was happening between them?

They should talk about the kiss, but she wouldn't want to, his gut told him. He wanted to kiss her again—hell, he wanted to spend the evening in her bedroom exploring *way* more than just her mouth, but he wouldn't push her.

He squirmed on the bench seat and chided himself to pay attention to the road he'd *finally* been able to pull out on.

His tires screeched when he tore into the hotel's parking lot and he slammed the shifter into *park*. Shannon dashed into the building with no second thought to his Tundra's poor transmission and hammered on the elevator button, ignoring the few odd looks he got. \

He was in full uniform, so he cleared his throat and straightened.

Don't wanna be described as a crazy cop.

He glanced around for the stairs because it was taking too long, but when he was about to head toward the door with the little plaque on the wall, the elevator finally *dinged.*

C'mon, he chanted as the mirrored double doors opened too slowly. Only ingrained manners made

Shannon allow the older couple who'd been waiting before him to step on the elevator first.

His heart and stomach jumped at the same time.

Calm the hell down.

He wasn't running to a scene or answering a call. A glance at his watch told him he wasn't even that late—it was only five-thirty-six. There shouldn't be any urgency. He hadn't checked in with Taylor yet, so there was no reason to freak out.

She'd said she'd leave her office around five, so she was probably just getting home, too.

Shannon wouldn't be tardy for their...date?

Was that what was going on?

Was he *dating* Taylor?

He shook his head. "Don't put a label on it," he whispered.

The elevator doors opened and he jumped. It wasn't his floor, yet he'd been ready to rush out into the waiting corridor.

I'm hopeless.

The older man threw him a nod as he helped his wife off on the next floor, and Shannon returned the gesture and told them to have a nice evening.

The little slice of forced civility calmed him. He drummed his fingertips on the support rail while he waited for the elevator to take him two floors up, to the fifth.

Finally he was in front of his suite, swiping his keycard. The little green light couldn't flash fast enough.

He wanted his uniform off. Wanted to rush back to his truck and be at her apartment *now*. Like he was a high school kid meeting a girl for their first evening unchaperoned.

Jesus, something is wrong with me.

Shannon glanced at the full-length mirror on the sliding closet door. He could read the insistence on his face and forced deep breath number one hundred and one for the last hour—or maybe it was just the previous fifteen minutes.

The gun belt came off first, then his shirt. He ditched the rest of his clothing fast, and didn't bother picking them up from where they lay on the patterned commercial carpet.

Good thing polyester doesn't wrinkle.

He shoved his legs into jeans and strapped his backup gun to his ankle. He never went anywhere unarmed. The small Sig nestled right above his cowboy boot.

Shannon paused in front of the mirror again, surveying his civilian clothing. He'd chosen dark jeans and a collared gray polo shirt, because he didn't know where she'd pick for dinner, and he wanted to look sort-of nice.

He shook his head at himself as his stomach flipped. *It's not a freakin' first date.*

He was amped up, and in more than one way. Not only did he want to talk about that kiss, he wanted a repeat.

He'd have to let Taylor lead in that regard, but he was on edge. Should probably take advice from that old comedy movie where the lead guy jacked off before his date with the heroine, minus the hijinks that followed, of course.

Nah...he'd never done that in his life.

Shannon could keep his hands to himself where the FBI agent was concerned, right?

He grabbed his cell and fired off a quick message.

On my way.

His heartrate picked up as he waited for her answer, which was one word—*Okay*—a few seconds later.

Couldn't get back to his truck fast enough. He did a repeat of his hotel parking lot job when he finally got to Taylor's building, throwing his Tundra into *park* without a backward glance—though he did remember to lock it. Didn't pay the meter, but it was after six so he shouldn't get a parking ticket.

Shannon took the stairs two at a time and finally, *finally,* made a fist to knock on her door. Wasn't left standing there more than a few moments, thank God.

"Hi." Her greeting was almost shy, but she looked him in the eye.

His body hummed. Wanted to snatch her to him, take her mouth, but Taylor wouldn't appreciate that kind of hello. He screamed at himself to relax, and smiled. "Hi."

There was a pause, and they stared at each other.

Her hazel eyes drew him in, with their rich mix of greens and browns, and he couldn't look away. The glowing light of her living room behind her surrounded her petite form like an aura, bringing his attention to her freckles.

Somehow, she was a mix of innocence and vixen.

"Uh," she whispered, breaking the spell. "Are you gonna come in?"

He nodded and swallowed, because speaking was a no-go.

She slid out of his way, and Shannon wanted to tell her she didn't have to go so far.

He was dying to touch her.

Kiss her.

Taylor looked up at him, tapping both hands on

jeans-clad thighs before shoving her fingertips in her pockets, as if she'd realized what she'd been doing.

He let his eyes rove her body. The dark denim was snug, outlining muscular legs, shapely hips and a slender waist. He craved a view from behind, to check out her ass. Her tight yoga pants last night had already told him it was fantastic. Form-fitting jeans were even better.

She wore a pale pink sweater, with a slight V-neck, and it was tight, too, hugging her breasts. The fabric looked soft, beckoning exploration. Her hair cascaded around her shoulders in loose natural waves his fingers itched to touch.

Damn, she's hot.

Taylor looked perfect, feminine. So opposite of what he was used to with her. She'd been hiding a fantastic body that spoke of the workout routine she'd told him about.

It fed his fantasies.

"I've never seen you in jeans," Shannon blurted.

She touched her cheek, and tucked a strawberry-blonde wave behind her ear. He wanted to groan when her tongue darted out to moisten her bottom lip. "Uh, thanks."

"You look great."

"So do you." Her cheeks went pink, brightening every freckle, but something about that made his tension loosen.

Taylor was just as nervous as he was.

Is that good or bad?

He smiled. "Thanks." Shannon made his feet close the distance between them. "Are you hungry?"

Taylor nodded.

He was, too.

Just not for food.

She swallowed and he ordered himself not to kiss her throat.

A dark spot there made his gaze still. At first he thought it was a smudge, but there was a matching mark on the other side.

What the hell?

Shannon cupped her face and tilted her chin up, his libido vanishing while he focused on what looked like deep bruising.

She uttered a protest, but he maintained his grip.

Shannon's sudden hold on her chin made her still, but he wasn't hurting her. He tilted back and forth gently, and Taylor's gut tightened.

"What the hell happened to your neck?"

She sucked back a groan. "Nothing." Tried to pull away but he didn't release her. If anything, his grip firmed. She grabbed both his wrists, but that didn't force him to let her go, either.

Those whiskey-colored eyes studied her bruises, then met her gaze. "Doesn't look like nothing."

"Long story."

He arched a dark eyebrow. "I got all night."

Do you?

Her heart tripped for a different reason than having to tell him about the holdup and how she'd received a black and blue throat.

What did she want from Shannon Crowley? And what did *he* want from her?

"Well?" he prompted. This was a growl.

A demand that should've irked, but it didn't.

Taylor sighed. "I'd rather not talk about."

Shannon's brow furrowed and he shook his head.

His thumb gently stroked her discolored skin.

She ignored the shiver that shot down her spine. She'd inspected the angry marks when she'd gotten home from work. It looked *bad*. Much worse than it felt.

"Taylor, it looks like someone tried to choke you. This wasn't here yesterday. Tell me what the hell happened today."

"Someone tried to choke me." She tried to keep her voice dry, sarcastic, because she couldn't handle the touch of caring in his hard tone. Her tummy wobbled, along with her knees.

"Who?" The look he sported was like none Taylor had ever seen from him. His handsome face was tight, threatening. Like he had murder on his mind.

For my sake.

Her heart fluttered and she had to swallow—again. "I'm...fine." She cursed her crack.

Damn, why hadn't she taken time to put makeup on the bruises before he'd come over?

She opened and closed her hands on his wrists, and she couldn't look away from the angry concern in his eyes.

"I guess we can stand here all night until you tell me what happened." Shannon finally released her, but he crossed his arms over his chest and glared.

Taylor couldn't help but notice how the movement flexed his muscled forearms—his thick biceps strained against his short-sleeved polo shirt and the gray material stretched across his pecs.

She unwillingly remembered what it'd been like to be pressed into that chest the night before.

Of their own accord, her eyes trailed his frame. The shirt was tucked in, hinting at his abs. Same tight jeans from the night before hugging his muscular thighs. He was wearing cowboy boots again, too.

"Taylor." Her name was all warning.

She jumped. He probably thought her hesitation was because she didn't want to tell him—which was true—but that was better than getting caught ogling him. Taylor wasn't fond of *either* idea. A sigh broke from her lips. "I guess if you have to know—"

"I do."

Regaining a tiny bit of composure, she managed a smirk. "I was going to say, we might as well sit. I told you it was a long story."

Shannon nodded.

She tried to scoot away from him on her couch, but he prevented it, tugging her closer. Taylor didn't fight him. Instead, she launched into what'd happened.

He listened with quiet intensity, like he'd have to write a report on it.

That was a tad distracting, but not as much as her hyperawareness of his body touching hers. They were thigh to thigh, and nearly hip-to-hip. She felt his body heat, sensed his muscles and wanted to focus on that, not *The Adventures of Donnie Simmons.*

She had to fight the urge to climb on his lap and slide her arms around his neck. Taste his mouth like she had last night. Taylor shivered and rubbed her arm. The fine-woven fabric of her sweater was ultra-soft beneath her palm.

"Are you okay?" Shannon demanded when she'd finished.

"Yeah." She nodded to reinforce the word, but the sergeant looked skeptical.

"You sure?"

She squirmed under his appraising gaze. Unfortunately, the movement didn't relieve her nerves. It just rubbed their bodies together, making her want more.

Taylor tried to move away, to no avail.

His large hand clamped on her chin again, so he could get another look at her bruising. "Taylor, this looks bad."

She tilted her head, and it made the swollen skin throb. Bit her bottom lip to keep from gasping. Didn't want to admit she was in discomfort—he'd probably rush her to the ER. "It's fine. Doesn't hurt unless I touch it. It's not as bad as it looks. The paramedics said it's okay."

"I want to beat the shit out of that asshole for putting his hands on you," Shannon growled.

Why does he care so much?

He took a breath and released her, but didn't look away.

Taylor forced words out. "My partner saved my ass. And the guy got shot, so he got his. He's looking at time when he's better, no worries."

"Thank God your partner was there."

Heat kissed her cheeks. She didn't need to hear that crap again, or be reminded of the guilt she felt for being reckless, but she wasn't about to admit *that* to Shannon, either.

She hadn't told him about her mandated meetings with Dr. Wong, or about the torture she'd survived during session one that afternoon. She'd only managed a reprieve for the next day—her second appointment was the day after that, at nine a.m. sharp.

Taylor had convinced the doc she could work in the morning, but she was essentially on light duty until her time with him was complete, and she wouldn't be allowed to leave the office.

Of course, Baker was on board with that. She'd argued again, and he'd won. *Again.*

She was so desperate to avoid being trapped, she

almost wanted to tackle Texarkana on her own. Her boss wouldn't allow that, either.

"What's wrong?"

"Nothing. Why?"

"You're scowling."

"Oh, sorry." She jolted, and ended up bumping shoulders with Shannon.

He slid an arm around her and drew her closer.

Somehow she didn't—couldn't—argue. Taylor sank into his warmth. She fought for a sense of normalcy when the picture of her and John caught her attention.

She closed her eyes when guilt crept up from the pit of her stomach and rested her head against Shannon's shoulder, hiding her face instead of obeying her mental command to move away.

It felt good to be held by someone.

He felt good.

His lips brushed her temple and she squeezed her eyes tighter.

Why do I feel like crying?

Taylor struggled for a distraction, and cleared her throat so she could speak. She forced her head to lift, and met his eyes. "You didn't tell me about your day."

Shannon gave a half-smile, but his gaze slid to her lips. He dipped his head down, and she met his mouth with hers.

She should've leaned away, but she didn't.

The kiss was soft and gentle at first, a question, but when she let him in, and his tongue brushed hers, he delved deeper, kissing her harder. More insistently.

Unlike last night, he pulled her into him until Taylor sat on his lap, plastered to his hard chest.

He groaned, and she answered with a moan when things became urgent.

She clutched at him, snaking her arms around his neck and burying her fingers in his dark hair. *Soft.* His hair was so soft.

Their tongues danced and dueled, their lips tangled and fused, and his teeth nipped, but it didn't hurt.

Desire settled low and hot, until she had to wiggle to appease the empty ache between her legs.

He shifted her closer, and Taylor felt his erection against her hip.

Shannon's hands swallowed her waist and inched up her back, caressing as he went. It was soothing but arousing at the same time.

He spread kisses along her jaw line, and his stubble teased her skin, made her burn for more. The farther he moved away, the more it made her miss his lips on hers, so she cupped his cheeks and tugged until he gave her his mouth again.

That kiss lasted so long, Taylor had to pull away to breathe.

They panted against each other, then he resumed his exploration of the underside of her throat with insistent nips and licks.

She yelped when he brushed her bruises with too much pressure.

Shannon froze and their eyes locked. "I'm so sorry, I forgot."

Taylor shook her head as the pain cleared her hazy desire and she came back into her brain. Her body still throbbed all over, for more.

For *him.*

Then she remembered John and bit back a whimper.

I shouldn't have done this.

"It's...okay... We..."

"Got carried away," Shannon finished.

She bit her bottom lip. Confusion, desire and guilt swirled around her head, and she avoided glancing at the picture that was too close for comfort.

Taylor looked down. Her body was running hot, her blood boiling for a man other than her fiancé.

Passion—that felt good, familiar and unfamiliar all at the same time. It made her want more, but want to push Shannon away at the same time.

"Taylor." His whisper drew her gaze, against her will.

"What?" she croaked and tried not to wince.

"I'm sorry I hurt your neck, but I'm not sorry I kissed you."

She closed her eyes and sucked in a breath, ignoring the sight of his kiss-swollen lips, mussed hair, and the way his breath hitched, as if he was affected by her as she was by him.

Irresistible.

Taylor wanted Shannon.

The confession resulted in more guilt seizing her gut. *John.*

Shannon wasn't her fiancé.

"I just... I'm sorry, I can't do this." She slid off his lap, locking her knees when they wobbled—she'd almost landed right back on top of him. Her legs didn't want to hold her up, and her whole form screamed a protest when she broke their physical contact.

Shannon shot out a hand to steady her and she hated that she yearned for that small touch—and more.

Disappointment darkened his amber gaze, and his full mouth was turned down at the corners, but he nodded as he looked up at her. "Do you want me to go?"

Taylor hedged, rocking back and forth on her feet. "No," she whispered finally. "I meant it when I asked you to dinner."

Why did I say that?

It *would* be better if he left.

She couldn't let him go just yet. Taylor trembled and called herself every name in the book.

Shannon didn't say anything for a long moment, just studied her until she squirmed. He stood and blew out an audible breath. "Okay."

"Good." She forced the answer past her lips, because she had to say *something*. "You can tell me about your day over dinner." She reached for normal with both hands, but seeing this man for the third night in a row was as far from *normal* as things got.

Why can't I tell him to leave?

"You got it." Finally he smiled, but she didn't like the touch of sadness in it.

His dimple was missing, and that was worse than a glare.

Chapter Fourteen

R owdy gave the guy two grand in cash—five hundred bucks more than he'd asked—and snatched the keys to the shit-brown 1992 Ford F-150 he'd just bought from an ad in the classifieds.

Who knew people still took out ads in the actual newspaper?

"Thanks, man."

"We'll have to go transfer the title." The older man smiled. "I think the office is open until five." He glanced at his watch, then pushed up his glasses. The wind made his comb-over flap.

"I'm not worried about it."

"But—"

"Thanks again." He gave the guy a half-salute and hefted his duffel over one shoulder. Didn't give a shit about the plates or the title.

As soon as he was out of sight, he was going to ditch the current plates and steal some off another car, anyway. Wasn't like he could tell the old man that.

Rowdy also didn't give a shit that the truck had been sitting in a garage for a while. The guy said he'd cleaned it up to sell it after his father had died. A mechanic had cleared it, and the owner had given him a stack of maintenance proof he couldn't have cared less about, either.

As long as the thing got him gone without breaking down, he was good. He couldn't do anything on the up and up.

His name—legal or otherwise—couldn't be *anywhere.*

He wrenched the door open and tossed his bag on the passenger side of the bench seat of the old pickup.

The guy was watching him and his gut tightened.

Shoulda stolen a car, actually.

He shrugged and hiked his ass into his new ride. Pretended he didn't care if the truck's former owner memorized what he was wearing, or was suspicious of his motives and disregard of sticking around to make the sale legal.

The engine roared to life at the same time the burner phone in his pocket started ringing. Only Cami had the number.

His heart skipped a beat and Rowdy dug his cell out, answering with a swipe of his thumb across the screen. "Cami? What's wrong?" He backed out of the driveway slowly and made his way down the residential street without another glance at his truck's former owner.

He was only screwed if the old man called the police.

His sister sniffled and alarm washed over him.

She couldn't know he'd snuck away from her place after she and Devon had left that morning, could she?

It was too early, not even lunch time.

He'd wanted to be gone already, but it'd taken more time than planned to find a car he'd wanted to buy. Rowdy had considered a small car lot, but the paperwork involved—even paying with cash—wasn't something he'd wanted to mess with.

A private seller had been less risky, even if he wasn't as confident now, given the look the old man had given him.

"Tyrone is an asshole, as per usual." Her voice broke.

"What did he do?"

"It's a half-day, early release at school, and he was supposed to pick Devon up."

"Lemme guess, he called and said he couldn't."

"Right. Gave me some line of BS about a luncheon with hospital execs he just *had* to go to. Was super apologetic, like he always is."

"I'm sorry, Cam."

What else could he say?

She was so bitter, and now his nephew was going to be disappointed, too.

"I didn't tell Devon, so that's my only saving grace. I'm sick of Tyrone crushing him."

"Speaking of crush, his face under my fist isn't a bad idea."

"I know. Sometimes, like now, I want to let you bash him a few times." Cami paused. "Eric, I…"

"What is it?"

"I'm in a pinch. I can't leave the hospital."

Rowdy slammed his eyes shut at the next stop sign. What came next wasn't a mystery.

"Can you go pick Devon up? I can't leave here until at least three, and that's only if I sneak out, I'm on rotation, and…"

"Cami." Her name came out a sigh.

"I already called the school," she whispered. "Told them my brother was coming for my son."

"Cami." This time her name was meant to be all warning, but he fizzled out. He didn't want to let her down like her loser ex had. But she'd probably given them his *name*. He'd need ID.

Shit.

"Please, Eric. I'll meet you guys at home as soon as I can. This was supposed to be Tyrone's night, and this coming weekend, but like I said, little man doesn't know that, so we can do something fun together. Pizza for dinner, maybe? A movie? Oh! And you can tell me how your interview went at the shop."

Right.

The interview she'd pulled strings to get him, and he hadn't shown up to.

Shit.

He was going to have to lie some more. Too bad it would only take a phone call or two for her to figure out he hadn't gone.

Fuck.

Rowdy ran his hands over his head and swallowed. He'd shaved his head that morning, so the feeling was unfamiliar.

He was so fucked, and he was dragging Cami and Devon down with him.

Just what he'd wanted to avoid.

"All right." The acquiescence came out cracked. He prayed she wouldn't notice.

"Thanks, big brother. I mean it. See? I love having you around. Dev will love hanging with you this afternoon."

He sucked back another sigh. "I'll love hanging with him, too. Someone has to teach him to do guy stuff."

His sister's laughter only made him feel guiltier. "I love you, Eric."

"Me too. What's the name of the school? And I'm gonna need the address."

Carter cursed as he slammed on the brakes at the red light. The tires screeched and he wanted to order everyone that gave him a second look to fuck off.

That bastard Kai and his crew.

Who the fuck did he think he was, humiliating him like that?

For the *second* time, since he'd been summoned by the asshole for meeting number two, since they'd gotten more intel from whoever Kai knew on the inside of the train company. So much for the '*see ya around*' he'd received when he'd left the first meeting.

He didn't give a fuck that the information was helpful, and the new meet-up not only necessary, but smart. Carter would never give Kai any credit, even in his own head.

The bastard crew leader still hadn't required his input, so he'd listened to him talk, put up with BS from the peanut gallery, and left.

Couldn't even take revenge, at least not at the moment.

Wasn't worth calling Bubba to bitch either, although he'd planned on it before he'd stopped to think. He wasn't a pussy, and he *would* smash the chink's face in if he got the chance. After they were done hitting that train, of course.

Almost three weeks.

Carter just needed to lay low until then.

One night's hard work, and he'd take his cut and go. Or...he could take it *all* and leave Kai and his crew in their stupid warehouse to rot. Never to thieve again. Like sprayed bullets and blood spatter.

A favor to society, really. Arizona, and luxury car owners everywhere, should thank him. Not to mention the authorities—they wouldn't have to worry about arresting Kai and his guys, either.

He chuckled and flexed his hands on the steering wheel of the POS Buick.

The other plan still in play, of course, was finding Rowdy Vargas and taking out his old crewmate. He'd get him, too.

Carter put the window down—had to do it old school style, since the beater had power *nothing*. His injured arm burned by the time he was done, but he took in cool air that was only going to get more frigid by evening.

Something told him to glance to his left.

A massive apartment high-rise dominated the city block.

Movement caught his eye.

He saw a kid first. Holding the hand of a man who looked...familiar.

A horn blared from behind him and he jumped. The seatbelt tightened and restricted his shifting. His shoulder screamed a protest. "Fuck you!" he mumbled, but hit the gas pedal, making a hasty left turn that just caused more horns, all for him.

He didn't give a shit about who he'd cut off.

Pulling around the corner gave him a better look at the guy.

Carter parked behind a car on the side of the road and sucked in a breath.

No. Shit.

The man and boy continued across the sizable front lot to the entrance of the building, seemingly caught up in conversation. Never looked away from the kid once. Even carried a small blue backpack on one shoulder and had a huge black duffel bag in his right hand, while the boy hung on his left.

He'd bet money the big bag was full of—well, money.

Cold hard cash that could help his cause. When he was done here, of course. On the other hand, it didn't matter if he had all the dough in the world; he'd still take Rowdy's money, too.

"My, my, Rowdy, aren't we getting reckless?"

The guy used to be observant. Right now, all the

man's attention was on the kid.

"Out in the open, like nothing's doing."

An older man met them when they'd reached the building, and opened things up for them before going on his way.

Didn't seem like they talked much before disappearing inside.

Who the hell's the kid?

Did his old friend have a secret family or some shit? A son? In the same city he happened to be in?

Maybe Karma was real, after all. Or fate, or some shit.

Well, not that it really mattered.

Things were suddenly looking up for Carter.

Now he had something to do with his *'extra'* time.

He smiled slowly and patted the gun in his waistband.

Chapter Fifteen

Texarkana finally happened the following Tuesday. They didn't talk much on the drive, and Taylor was glad Holman didn't push her. They were behind schedule because of her forced, third and final trip to the shrink.

Unfortunately, that left the day with the makings of being long and arduous. Worse than anticipated.

Her second appointment had consumed her Friday. Not seeing Shannon that night had made it worse, but damned if she'd admit *that*.

The sessions' dialogue could be interchanged, and Taylor had practiced telling the stupid doctor what he wanted to hear. Even pretended his questions didn't reverberate in her mind and she didn't contemplate *valid* answers hours after their time together had ended.

She didn't want to see—or even think about—Doc Wong again.

Ever.

Victim, my ass.

She was fine. If she heard '*and how did that make you feel?*' one more time, she was gonna scream.

Then again, he *had* agreed Taylor was fit for duty, so she should rein in that horse. Should probably thank him, too.

Her thoughts turned to what was to come, and she was able to discard the holdup, the shrink, even her Antioch sergeant.

The trauma of having to see Joe Pompa, look him in the eye, speak to him...

It was all so much bigger than a stupid punk kid holding a gun to her head.

Or the man whose kiss curled her toes.

She had a major case of the jitters even before she pulled the Charger into the prison's parking lot, but it only worsened when they checked in, did the required admin stuff, and locked up their weapons.

Temporary or not, she felt naked without her Glock. Jumpy, no matter how she screamed at herself to take a breath and sit still. Taylor fought full body shudders as she followed Holman and a correctional officer down the wide hallway.

Her chants of *'everything will be fine'* went unheeded.

They were shown to an interview room to wait for Pompa, and from the look on Holman's face, he was dying to ask her what was up.

Damn good thing he didn't.

She might've killed him with her bare hands.

The door opened, and Taylor clutched her fingers together, pinning them to her lap to stop the shaking she didn't want to acknowledge. Her heart was at a full canter and she had to consciously slow her breathing.

Pompa looked a hell of a lot like his younger brother, even wearing an orange jumpsuit with a five o'clock shadow and shaved-bald head, much shorter than it was when she'd...known him.

She couldn't see the half dozen or so tattoos that covered his torso, but she spotted dark ink on his left forearm. Couldn't make out the design, though, and didn't have the guts to take a better look.

Taylor tried not to wince as the COs shuffled him into the private room.

One waited at the door, while the other, a large dark-skinned man, clamped a huge hand on Pompa's right biceps.

She avoided the round scar on the prisoner's head, above his ear. If she could've gotten away with it, she wouldn't have looked at him all.

He didn't have cuffs on his hands or feet—it was a minimum security federal facility after all—but he wouldn't have been able to walk that way, anyway. Pompa leaned heavily on a cane, and his left arm shook, as if it would fail supporting his weight at any moment.

Air breached his lips as he sat heavily in the chair across the metal table. It scooted back as it accepted his weight and gave a *screech* that bowed Taylor's tongue with its sharpness.

Holman, seated beside her, cleared his throat.

She screamed at herself to get it together.

Pompa glared up at the oversized guard who'd assisted him. "You can let go of my arm."

The CO nodded, but waited until he'd redistributed his weight by straightening in the chair. Finally, he released him.

Guilt burned, causing a bad taste in the back of her mouth. It was her fault he couldn't even seat himself without assistance.

"I'll be right outside," the officer said to her partner.

"What'm I gonna do, jump them?" Pompa muttered, but he had a bitter edge that made her wince.

Taylor swallowed and sat taller.

"I'm Special Agent Holman, and I suppose—"

"Got a new man, Agent Carrigan?" he asked, looking at his and disregarding Holman's attempted introduction.

She tried to ignore his dark gaze. Wished the other side of the table was really the other side of the room, or the other side of the prison. She cleared her throat. "Agent Holman and I just have a few questions for you."

"Ain't like I don't got the time." A mixture of

resentment and amusement coated his statement. He arched a dark eyebrow. "But why now?"

"Has Rowdy Vargas attempted to contact you?" Holman dove right in.

Pompa looked at her partner, then back at her. "Is this guy for real? Did you miss the fact that I'm in *prison*?"

"We'd appreciate if you'd answer, Mr. Pompa," Taylor said. "We all know thick walls and bars don't keep everything out."

"Unbelievable." He shook his head. "Why the fuck should I tell *you* anything?" He looked directly at her.

"Because if Carter Bennett finds your friend before we do, he's dead." She kept her voice low and even, and tried to ignore the hard look in those dark eyes.

The prisoner threw his head back and let out a laugh that didn't sound too different from his brother's on the phone the other night. "You still haven't found that bastard?"

"With your help, maybe we can," Holman said.

"Right." Pompa leveled Taylor with another long look that made her want to squirm. Hadn't acknowledged her partner at all. "This is fucking crazy."

Taylor and Holman stayed still and silent, letting Pompa work out whatever he needed to.

She prayed they'd get something from him.

Anything.

"I shot him."

Holman spared her a glance, then looked back at Pompa.

"I know you did," she said. "I was there that night. And we found a car he'd boosted and dumped a few days later. Bennett's blood was found in it."

"Maybe the bastard's dead."

"Doubtful," Holman answered.

Pompa dragged his hand down his face and rubbed his shorn hair. It made an audible scratching sound. "I doubt it, too. The asshole's lucky for some fucking reason." Concern crossed his expression and Taylor felt his desperation even before he spoke again. "How do you even know Rowdy's alive?"

"We don't," Holman said.

She put her hand on the table and leaned in. "My gut says he is. Just like it tells me Bennett's hiding and waiting. He wants Vargas as bad as we do, but for different reasons."

Emotion hardened the man's handsome face. "I want him dead, not in prison. He took *everything* from me." He didn't have to say he was referring to Brandelyn Willis, Taylor *knew*.

Willis, the tech queen of their crew, had been Pompa's lover. She'd died in the old trailer park in Antioch.

Taylor had felt bad when she'd seen the young woman's body. Not for Pompa, but for the life stolen because of her taste in men.

"Then tell us something. Anything that can help us find Vargas," Holman urged. "Or Bennett. Any detail."

"Carter has friends in LA. I think he'd take his coward ass out there," Pompa said.

She let him talk. Wasn't about to reveal California had been a no-go.

He went on to mention a few key players the FBI was already on to, not in her case, but Eddie's.

"What about Vargas? Where would he go?" she asked.

"Rowdy's always been the best at disappearing. Not even I know all his hidey-holes."

Disappointment crashed over her, but she tried to

fight through it and ordered herself to sit still.

"Has he reached out to you?" Holman asked.

"Hell no. Probably has no idea where I am. Maybe thinks I'm dead. Thought y'all wanted it that way." Pompa gestured them collectively. "I'm sure you looked into Rowdy's background..."

"Of course," her partner said.

"His story is similar to yours. Foster care, repeated running away, drugs, eventually aged out of the system, et cetera," Taylor said.

"Bullshit. Rowdy was never on drugs." Pompa glared and made a cutting gesture with his right hand. "I got him away from that shit before he got sucked in by the dealers, too."

Her eyes were glued there, because his fingers weren't sitting right. They had an unnatural curl inward, as if from lack of use. Muscle atrophy.

As soon as Pompa noticed, he yanked back and put the hand on his lap. Didn't say anything, but the corner of his mouth shot up in a snarl. "You missed something," he barked.

Taylor jumped, and forced her eyes to his face.

He didn't continue.

"What did we miss?" Holman prompted.

"Rowdy has a foster sister. A few years younger than him. Name's Cami and she lives somewhere in Arizona, Nevada or New Mexico, but that's all I know. He lived in all three states as a kid. Not sure about her, though."

"Last name?" Taylor cleared her throat again, when her words came out in a croak.

"Dunno. You're the mighty FBI, guess you'll have to figure it out."

"Rowdy would go to her?" Holman asked.

Pompa looked at Taylor, not her partner. "I don't

think he'd want to drag trouble to her door, but Carter doesn't know about her, so maybe."

"Arizona, Nevada or New Mexico? Can't narrow it more than that?" she asked.

He shook his head. "No. Rowdy protected her info at all costs. The only reason he told me about her was because he found out about Jared. The rest of our crew never knew that. It was a secret, between him and me."

She tried not to wince when he said Manning's first name but something must've shown in her face, because Pompa's stare didn't waver, but he lost a little of his hard edge.

Like he felt bad for her.

That should've pissed her off, but it just kicked up the guilt swirling in her gut.

"You should know, I don't blame you."

Taylor wanted to look away. Close her eyes. Stand up. *Leave.*

Anything to avoid the dark eyes compelling her to meet them dead-on.

She sucked in a breath. The mood went from hopeful—when Pompa had shared knowledge about Vargas' foster sister—to desperate. She just wanted this over, and she definitely didn't want to talk about *that night.*

Holman shot her a glance, then looked back at Pompa. "Okay, I think we're done here. Thanks for the info. Hopefully we can find Cami. Then your friend. They'll both need to be protected from Bennett."

Great, 'cause I so need my partner to notice me falling apart.

Pompa once again didn't acknowledge Holman. "You did what you thought you needed to do. I get that. I wasn't exactly innocent."

Emotion smacked her in the chest and she fought for composure. The urge to flee—one she was *very* unfamiliar with—was overwhelming. It was hard to breathe.

She flashed back to that night, but instead of seeing a bloody Pompa lying on the safe house kitchen floor, for some reason she remembered Shannon's arm around her at the hospital, then him kissing her before dinner the other night.

Focusing on the sergeant helped clear her head, if only a little.

Normally, her mixed feelings about Shannon twisted her up, but she needed it—needed *him*—right now.

Taylor straightened her shoulders and pushed out painful breaths. "For what it's worth, I'm sorry." She meant it. Didn't look away from Pompa. Some of the pressure lifted from her chest.

Shock washed over her when all he offered was a curt nod.

For the first time, Pompa looked at Holman—really looked at him. "I know you."

"I don't think you do." He shook his head.

"I do. You were in LA, last year. Riding with Taz's crew. You were his tech guy." He frowned. "Son of a bitch. You were undercover. *Fuck.* No wonder John introduced us that night."

Holman didn't say anything, but she blanched at the mention of her fiancé.

Finally, her new partner spoke. "I remember that night."

"I remember Taz's crew all got busted right after that," Pompa bit out. "You sly SOB. John would've made it so we were next, but we went to Oklahoma..."

Taylor fought the urge to close her eyes.

John was killed in Oklahoma.

Pompa pegged her with another compelling stare. "I always liked John, even after I found out he was FBI. He was a good dude. I'm sorry Carter killed him. I was gonna turn myself in with him, save my crew. I didn't get the chance."

To hear his candor and sincerity just about slayed her, even if the information had been shared with her before, at least the part about his plans to turn himself in.

His brother had ranted about it after she'd shot him.

Holman rose, saving her. He pounded on the locked door, calling for the guards.

Taylor's head reeled and her pulse pounded in her ears until her temples ached.

The big guard helped Pompa to his feet and handed him his cane.

The man she'd shot gave her one more look before he let the CO lead him away. "I hope you find Rowdy and keep him safe from Carter. But I won't weep if you kill Carter. A dark cell is too good for his traitor ass."

"Hey, you okay?"

Taylor jumped. "I'm fine," she snapped, no matter he'd sounded genuinely concerned.

Joe Pompa had let her off the hook. Told her he didn't blame her.

So why didn't she feel better?

Because I was still wrong.

Maybe she felt worse.

Even Pompa thought she'd acted in defense of her life—survival mode of any trained law enforcement officer.

"Is the holdup freaking you out now that you've had time to think about it? Decompress? It's only been a few days..." Holman said.

She jolted again, but wanted to thank him for interrupting her headfuck. "No. I'm fine," she repeated. Didn't want to add a polite '*thanks*' to the end of her statement, but she should.

Wasn't about to remind him of her three trips to Shrinkville, either. With her luck, Holman would want to compare notes from his own appointments with Doc Wong.

"Pompa, then? I can imagine it might be off-putting to sit face-to-face with, let alone question, someone you shot."

You have no idea.

"What kind of twenty-seven-year-old guy uses the phrase '*off-putting*'?" she barked.

Her partner stilled. Flexed his hands on the steering wheel of her Charger. Then he sighed and looked away.

Taylor was going to yell at him to be easy on her car, but guilt bit at her. She was all over the place, but it was really an overreaction. To push him away, when he'd been showing he gave a crap about her wellbeing, and all she could do was be a bitch.

Holman had saved her ass—literally—and he'd been great with Pompa, so she *should* show him some respect.

She couldn't manage to push '*I'm sorry*' past her lips.

Her cellphone dinged and she clung to the distraction. Looked away from the man she owed an apology or three to. Not to mention her life.

Can I see you tonight?

The simple message had her smiling, despite her challenging day.

She felt Holman's eyes on her but didn't look away

from Shannon's message.

"Hmmm," he said.

"What?" she growled.

"Must be good."

"Excuse me?" Taylor frowned.

"Never saw you smile before." His statement was conversational, as if she hadn't been a huge jerk a few seconds before.

She was torn between amusement and irritation. "Since you haven't known me for very long, I'd say it's not *all* that odd."

He harrumphed.

She ignored him *and* the little flutter in her stomach when she looked back at her phone's screen. Shannon's question needed an answer.

Taylor should say no, stick to what she'd decided. She'd been thinking—well, obsessing—about it since she'd seen him.

Damn, last Thursday night and their dinner at her fave Italian place felt like a lifetime ago.

After the botched interaction in her living room, they'd managed to have a great evening, except for the *'what is this between us?'* conversation that'd stumbled out.

Discomfort times two, even over delicious lasagna. She'd even admitted she enjoyed his company—and that he calmed her.

Out loud. To him.

While Shannon had grinned, she'd wanted to melt into the chair.

She'd have to talk to him. Tell him where she was at. Despite his interest, and their smoldering kisses, she wasn't looking for the same thing he was.

At dinner, he'd told her no pressure, they wouldn't

label it, but his expression had spoken differently. Had spoken of...*more.*

Taylor couldn't handle it.

They'd seen each other almost every night last week. Then yesterday, he'd met his Dallas cop friend for dinner instead of coming over, and she'd worked late.

Still, they'd texted before they'd both gone to bed, and she'd missed him. Hadn't confessed it, though.

His case had gone to the jury yesterday, so she expected Shannon to tell her he was heading back to Antioch any day now.

How do I feel about that?

"How many people take *a whole week* to smile at someone after they first meet?"

Holman snagged her attention again.

Taylor wanted to snarl to leave her the hell alone so she could focus on what to tell the sergeant. She glared. "Really?"

"Just sayin'." His mouth twitched as if he was fighting a smile. Then he did smile, and looked like the kid he was. "See? It's not that hard. It actually takes more muscles to frown than it does to smile."

She rolled her eyes and looked back at her message.

They hadn't left the prison until almost four. It was just past five-thirty now. Shannon was probably done with court for the day, and she wouldn't be back in town until about eight.

Shannon.

She found herself wanting to be home. On her couch. Sitting with Shannon Crowley like she had a few nights ago.

God, where's my resolve?

Won't be home 'til late.

Taylor fired off the message and held her breath, then chided herself. She *wasn't* a school girl with a crush and she wasn't looking for a relationship—even a casual one. Needed to stick to her plan of *'no thanks'*.

She ignored the reminder in the back of her head that reminded her how Shannon made her feel. She liked it, and the three nights they'd spent together. The meals they'd shared.

Kisses they'd shared.

Dammit.

Her contradictory thoughts were enough to make her head spin. Since when had she been wishy-washy?

What time?

His answer was fast, distracting her from the chaos in her head.

Had to go to Texarkana. On the way back now, but it'll be after eight.

I can meet you at your place. I'll even bring cheesecake, if you like.

Deal. See you there.

She couldn't stop from smiling. More like beaming. Her heart skipped, and she felt lighter.

Taylor ordered her inner turmoil to hell. No matter what happened, it looked like she needed Shannon Crowley, at least for the night.

Or was it just the cheesecake?

She let out a low laugh, and her partner shot her a

wide-eyed stare.

"Wow," he whispered.

"Shut up, Holman."

"Hey, I'm all for whatever you're doing right now."

"How about you mind your own damn business?" She scowled.

"You got it." He held his hands up, but one corner of his mouth inched up.

"Hey, hands on the wheel. How about you just drive? Get us back at a decent hour, huh? Don't wreck my damn car, or make me regret letting you drive," she grumbled. Ignored the grin he wore, too.

Alec Holman hadn't known her long enough to earn the right to give her shit, even if he *had* saved her ass. At the holdup *and* with Joe Pompa.

"Got a hot date or something?" Now *he* was beaming.

Taylor opened her mouth to tell him to screw off, but he put his hand up again.

"No, wait. Lemme guess, that's in none-of-my-beeswax-territory, right?"

"Beeswax? What are you, five?"

Holman chuckled. "I like you, Agent Carrigan."

"I'd like to say the feeling's mutual..."

"Awww, c'mon. I saved you. Doesn't that get me *any* cool points?" His voice was light and he flashed another grin.

She shook her head. At least she hadn't honestly offended the guy. Come to think of it, she hadn't teased with a partner since—

No. Don't think of John.

Taylor sighed and closed her eyes.

When she met Holman's gaze, his smile was gone.

Great, she'd ruined his good mood, too.

"I said thank you, but I want you to know I really

mean it. Thanks for rushing in and saving the day at the holdup. I...uh, well, it could've gone bad."

He gave a curt nod, but his expression was sober, lacking the playfulness from moments before.

She hated to admit she hadn't minded the teasing. Thank God he hadn't told her he was just doing his job, either.

Somehow, she needed the idea that he gave a shit about her. That he wanted the trust he'd earned. "Thanks for today with Pompa, too. I appreciate how you handled things."

Holman was quiet, but he looked thoughtful. "You're welcome." His volume was low, as if he sensed she needed a gentle approach. He spared her a glance, and his blue eyes said, '*you and I are gonna be fine.*'

She blew out a breath and reclined into the headrest. Taylor couldn't say the words aloud, but she didn't disagree.

Chapter Sixteen

"I don't want to hear it, Eric." Cami's mouth was a hard line, but her green eyes, and the disappointment there—the pain he'd caused—just about massacred him.

Rowdy sighed and rubbed his hand over his newly shorn hair. Words escaped him. He couldn't tell her there was almost four hundred grand under her guest bed. Or that he'd been about to leave town with his brand-new-to-him pickup, taking half his money.

When he and his nephew had entered the apartment, he'd scooped up the letter he'd left on the kitchen counter. It couldn't be used today, but he didn't tear it up. Needed to get moving the first chance he could.

Tomorrow would be great.

He didn't regret picking Devon up from school. He regretted not being able to leave before his sister had gotten home.

Rowdy couldn't have disappointed the kid, either. Besides, he didn't have anyone to leave him with. He couldn't leave a six-year-old to fend for himself, even for a few hours. If something happened to Devon, and *he'd* been at fault... Yeah, he'd never get over it.

Besides, they'd had an awesome afternoon. Had gone to the park, then come home and played video games. It'd been...normal.

Rowdy had been right about Cami finding out he'd blown the job interview. It'd only been a matter of time. He was just glad she'd waited until the kid was tucked into bed to confront him.

Her expression had been stern all evening, all her smiles only for her son. When she'd looked his way, she'd been seething.

The dude must've called her, because Rowdy couldn't see her checking up on him. She trusted him. Or *had*, anyway.

"And why the hell did you shave your head?"

He cleared his throat. Words still wanted to play hide-and-seek. *Talk, dammit.* "Listen, I told you I needed to leave." Rowdy ignored her inquiry about his new hairstyle. Didn't matter—couldn't explain he was trying not to fit his known description.

His sister glared. Crossed her arms over her chest. Her mouth was that same flat line, and her eyes narrowed to slits.

He shook his head. "I told you I couldn't—"

"You didn't tell me. You *agreed.* So you just lied to me when you agreed to the job interview?" Cami barked.

Rowdy winced.

"You said you'd try." This was softer, but held accusation.

"I didn't. You just assu—"

"You fed me a line of bullshit to shut me up? That's what you did, Eric. Thanks a lot." The anger in her expression wavered and her mouth trembled.

Fuck. Please don't cry.

He couldn't take her tears.

"I can't stay," he croaked.

"Why?" The question came with misty eyes.

"C'mere."

She shook her head, but when he tugged her into his arms Cami didn't fight him. She slipped hers around him and squeezed almost too tightly.

Rowdy inhaled the clean scent of her hair—wild berries, mixed with the astringent hospital smell Cami complained she could never get rid of.

Closing his eyes, he rested his cheek on the crown of her head. Couldn't tell her everything, but he owed her something to make her understand. Something that might scare her into backing off. So he could get away. "Someone's after me. It's only a matter of time."

Her big green eyes were wide when she lifted her head. "Then go to the police."

"You know I can't. Every day I'm here, I put you and Devon in more danger. I have to go, Cam."

His sister shook her head and pounded her fist into his chest. "No. Stay here. You're safe here."

"I'm not. And neither are you. He *will* find me."

"The guy who shot you?"

"Yes, but I'm not the only one he shot. He *killed* four of my friends. One was a girl. He would hurt you without blinking. I *have* to go."

"Eric, what—"

"No more questions. I can't do this to you. It's too great a risk. I can't have anything happen to you, or Devon. You're my heart, both of you."

She blinked, but tears still fell.

Rowdy wiped them away, and kissed her forehead. "I can't thank you enough for what you've done for me. There's a black duffel under the guest bed—it's yours. You and Devon will want for nothi—"

"Stop. Just *stop*. I don't need your damn thanks." Her face hardened again, but this time because he'd insulted her. "You're family. You *do* for family. *You* taught me that. And I don't want your money." Her bottom lip wobbled and more tears wet her dark skin. "This sounds like a goodbye." The last sentence was so low Rowdy almost missed it.

He squeezed her tight and tried to smile, but his heart plummeted to his gut. "It is goodbye." He wanted to say so much more. Tell her he was sorry he was such an asshole. Sorry he'd brought danger to her door. Sorry he disappointed her. Sorry he couldn't stay in Phoenix and make a life. A life where he could see her all the time, and watch his nephew grow up. Even punch her good-for-nothing ex like the bastard deserved.

"I need to check your wounds, one more time." His sister sniffled and straightened her shoulders, finally getting it together like the strong woman she was. Cami didn't wipe her cheeks dry, but determination settled over her pretty face. She was all doctor now, but perhaps she had to be.

"I'm fine, because of you. All patched up. I love you, Camille." Rowdy's voice caught on the words he didn't say often, even to his sister.

She punched his chest again, a move reminiscent of when they were kids. "You're not supposed to use that as a goodbye, dammit."

A chuckle escaped his lips, unbidden. "Well, I won't say it at all, then." He rubbed his right pec. "Ow. Damn, girl, you have bony knuckles."

She flashed a tremulous smile. "Ass."

"Totally."

Their gazes collided and held. Rowdy's stomach dipped and he sucked in a breath.

"Who's this guy?" Cami whispered.

"Nobody you need to worry about, if I take off."

Her lips pursed all over, and she touched her cheek. "I don't want to hear a report on the news that my brother was killed." The last part of her statement shook, and she sniffled again.

"I know how to lay low. I'll be fine. You're the only one with the number to my phone. It's disposable. If—when—I get another, I'll call you. Promise. I'll keep in touch as much as I can."

She swallowed. Offered a curt nod that made him breathe a tad easier. "I don't like it."

"Cami—"

"But I understand."

"Thank you," Rowdy whispered. "I'm sorry I put you and Devon in danger."

"You didn't."

He prayed she was right, but didn't dare disagree aloud. "Keep the money. I'm serious. Pay off your school loans. Just be smart about how you spend it. You can't put it in the bank."

"How much?"

"Two hundred K."

Cami gasped. "Eric—"

"I'm leaving it. I'm serious. Do what you want, what you need to do with it."

Tears flowed freely again and Rowdy hugged her one more time, wiped her face then kissed her cheek.

She didn't say anything, which was Cami at her scariest.

"I need to go, Cam. It's not safe for me to even stay one more night. Tell Devon I love him, and I'll call you tomorrow when I get somewhere to lay low. First chance I get. Promise."

"Now?"

"Now."

Cami crushed her eyes shut, but she nodded.

Chapter Seventeen

Shannon had mixed feelings when he got to Taylor's apartment. He hesitated when he was about to knock on the door, but he shouldn't have. He'd told her he was on his way when he'd left the hotel, and the line at the bakery had been a mile long. It'd taken forever to get her favorite dessert.

He clutched the brown paper sack with two pieces of cheesecake inside. He'd gotten caramel sauce this time, and hoped she liked it.

How could he say goodbye?

He wanted—no, needed—to kiss her. At least hold her before he made his trek home.

Stop being pathetic. Antioch isn't that far away.

Shannon made a fist and raised it, shaking his head at himself.

The door swung open before he'd made a sound. He cursed and fought the urge to jump back.

"I was just about to call you. It's been forever since your last text." Taylor's beautiful eyes were wide, concerned.

He focused on her and forced himself to relax. "You were worried about me?"

She arched a fair eyebrow. "Not you. My dessert."

Refusing to give in to a laugh, he clutched his leather jacket over his heart. "Ouch. That hurts, Special Agent."

"Just get in here." A smile played at her lips and she tugged his wrist. Her expression was playful, yet unrepentant for her jibe. She pulled harder when he didn't move right away, and the paper bag crinkled.

Shannon regretted that her hand hadn't enclosed his bare skin. He wanted to feel her touch anywhere he could get it.

Taylor already had plates and two steaming mugs arranged on her coffee table, and he could smell the delicious tease of java, but her now-familiar scent was there too, just as delectable as his favorite drink.

He watched her unfold two paper napkins and set them by each small dish. God, he'd missed her over the last four days. It felt like weeks.

She stilled, and her eyes lifted from her task, meeting his. "I... I...missed you, too."

Shit. I said that out loud?

His heart skipped and he forced a breath. Commanded himself to calm and went for a nonchalant approach as he closed the distance between them. He set down the bag and slipped out of his jacket before draping it on a chair. Without a word, he drew her into his arms. He had to touch her.

She shocked him by sighing against his chest instead of pulling away. She didn't speak either, and she didn't wrap her arms around him, but somehow Taylor letting him hold her was enough for the moment.

Shannon closed his eyes and inhaled the floral perfume of her hair. It was still up, instead of down around her shoulders how he liked it, but that didn't matter right now either. "My trial's over," he whispered. "I'm leaving in the morning." He was supposed to have gone that night, but he'd called Nikki and told her he needed one more night in the hotel, and if he had to come out of pocket, that was okay, too. His boss's assistant had said not to worry about it. She'd said as long as she got the receipt, it'd be taken care of.

He'd report for work tomorrow evening, like normal. He was currently leading the seven p.m. to seven a.m. shift—but he only had a few weeks left, then he'd be back on the eight-hour rotation—afternoons, three to eleven. They switched shifts every three months. Chief liked a well-rounded crew, but it was killer on one's sleep schedule.

Right now, work didn't matter. Only Taylor did.

Shannon couldn't have left Dallas without seeing her.

"Did you win?" She lifted her head from his pec and met his gaze.

"What?"

"The trial."

Oh. Right.

He cleared his throat. "Yes. The scumbag got twenty years."

"Good."

"Won't bring the victim back."

"No, but her family has closure now." Taylor's words were soft and even, and she didn't look at him this time.

His gut clenched. *She* didn't have closure, because the guy who'd killed her fiancé was still out there. Shannon didn't have a chance with her—a *real* chance—until John Murray's killer was behind bars.

And maybe not even then.

He felt bad that she'd lost the guy, of course. Always had. But the selfish part of him, the part that wanted her more than he wanted his next breath, was pissed. Jealous. Helpless.

He should just go. Before he ticked her off, or pushed her. Or did something stupid, because she'd all but come out and said she couldn't handle what he wanted from her.

"Shannon?"

His name was full of concern.

He jolted, cursing the fact she'd no doubt felt his body jerk, since she was still tight against him. "Yeah, they have closure now, but it doesn't fix the hole in their hearts."

She nodded. "I know. You're thinking about your sister, aren't you?"

No, but it's a nice cover.

"I always do in these cases. Can't help it." It came out smooth, but turned his stomach even more. It wasn't exactly a lie—he *did* think of Sabrina when he arrested a drunk driver—but half-truths were just as bad as deceit. Shannon wasn't a liar, even if he couldn't admit he was grieving Taylor.

Get a grip. You haven't even said goodbye yet.

She slipped her arms around his middle and squeezed.

He wanted to crush the emotion that hit him square in the chest. She was comforting him because she thought he was mourning his sister, when in truth, he'd moved on from *that* pain years ago. Was still pissed when other families suffered the same type of loss, which was why he focused on taking drunken sleazes off the streets, but the agony of eleven years ago had faded to a dull ache. Seeing Cailey all the time, helping raise her had been healing— for him and his mom.

Guilt swirled when Shannon looked down at his FBI agent's strawberry-blonde locks, but his voice had taken a long drive. He couldn't tell her he was upset at the prospect of walking away from her. Or he was jealous because he couldn't compete with a ghost, and he wanted to spend the night in her bed instead of going back to his hotel room.

"Will cheesecake make you feel better?" Taylor wore her signature smirk.

He wanted to kiss it off her lips. "Sure." He made his mouth curve up in a smile, but he ached from the loss of her against him when she took a step back.

"I made coffee, too, but it might be cold now."

"Doesn't matter." He mumbled nonsense as he watched her take a seat and dig into the brown bag.

She was wearing a plain dark green tee with long sleeves, and those tight jeans he loved so much. Taylor didn't wear much makeup, and no jewelry, but the simple elegance she always carried herself with was present even in the way she served cheesecake.

"You gonna stand there all night, or come over here? I *will* eat both pieces." Her hazel gaze dared him, and a smile rippled her mouth, which of course made Shannon remember what she tasted like.

He jumped into gear, trying to shake off the way she enchanted him. He nodded, slipping onto the couch next to her. Thanked her when she handed him the small plate, but he had to suck back a groan when she licked her lips.

Don't watch her put it in her mouth.

Swallowing, he distracted himself by grabbing the coffee and taking a sip. Hot liquid made his tongue smart, but maybe that was for the best. Tried not to startle when the roof of his mouth burned.

Taylor threw him a sideways glance, as if she was reluctant to even look away from her dessert. "You okay?"

"Yeah, coffee's hot after all. Burned my tongue."

"Oh, bummer. I hate that. Hope the cool cheesecake helps. Love the caramel sauce, by the way."

Shannon smiled. "I'm glad."

She closed her eyes as she took a big bite. "God, this is good."

Her little moan shot heat to his cock and he made his eyes dart to the treat he had yet to tuck into. He just wanted to watch her.

She met his gaze and grinned. "This is awesome. I

always forget *just* how good Mario's is until I have sweets from there."

He couldn't stop staring, especially when she looked at him like that. "You have some..." He gestured to a fragment of cheesecake on the corner of her mouth.

Taylor put her plate on the table and reached for the napkin, but he stopped her.

"I'll get it." Shannon set his cheesecake down. Slid his hand around to the back of her neck and tugged her to him. Couldn't stop his lips from closing over hers. He tasted the dessert debris, licking the spot before running his tongue along the seam of her mouth.

She whimpered and leaned into him, opening for him. Her tongue tentatively met his.

He drew her to him, trying to keep things gentle.

She threw that out the window by climbing on his lap, kissing him with more pressure. Her thighs split on either side of his, and her bottom landed hard on his lap.

It didn't matter that they had layers of denim between them, his cock went granite at the contact and Shannon groaned into her mouth. He held her tighter, grappling for her shirt, tugging it out of her jeans and shooting his hands up her back.

Her skin seared him. Hot, smooth. Flawless.

His seeking fingers came into contact with her bra, and he wanted it gone. Wanted her breasts in his waiting hands with no encumbering fabric.

Against his better judgment, he forwent the clasp and dragged his hands around to the front, still under the cotton material of Taylor's T-shirt. He brushed her abs and ran his touch over her ribcage, inching up.

Shannon cupped her on the outside of her bra, fumbling his thumbs until he found the outline of her nipples and started to rub. It wasn't enough, so he pulled the bra away from her skin, flipping it out of his way.

The first touch of her tender flesh against his shot a bolt of lightning straight to his groin and made his balls ache. Her peaked nipples brushed his palms.

He kneaded her high, tight breasts. They weren't large, but they were perfect, filling his hands and making him crave more.

Taylor leaned back and broke their kiss.

He expected her to yell at him, but he gasped when she whipped her shirt and bra off. She didn't look as she flung the garments over her shoulder to the carpet of her living room floor.

Shannon didn't get a chance to take in her half-naked form, because she sealed her lips over his, pushing her tongue back into his mouth. There was a moan or two, and the heat of her body against his chest, the fabric of his button-down, was too much. Exquisite torture. They weren't skin-to-skin.

He pulled her to him, sliding his hands along her spine before teasing her nipples and eliciting the most enthralling sounds from her, which vibrated against his lips.

Taylor continued to kiss him until it stole his breath, and when he squeezed her breasts gently, she moaned and rocked in his lap, taking his mind to places it didn't need to go, at least not just yet.

He wanted to get her in bed first.

Shannon reluctantly released her, caressing the bare skin of her sides, then gripped her waist. "If you keep that up, I'm gonna come in my jeans." He pressed the words into her mouth, half amused, half serious.

His cock was throbbing and his balls were heavy, compressed against his crotch. His zipper had already taken a bite or two with Taylor's movements. He couldn't get more uncomfortable.

She pulled back and blinked. Her face was flushed a gorgeous pink up to her ears, making her freckles dance. Her lips were swollen and her eyes were hazy, lids at half-mast. The trail of her freckles didn't stop on her cheeks—they were strewn across her collarbone and shoulders, too.

He wanted to kiss and caress every one.

She was so gorgeous, it took what little remained of his ability to breathe. His chest was tight.

"Sorry," she whispered, but her mouth quirked.

"I'm not complainin', just would rather be naked before that happens." He smiled and leaned forward, nibbling on her chin before pressing another kiss to her lips.

Taylor froze on his lap. Crossed her arms and covered her bare breasts.

"What is it?" Shannon whispered, but he already *knew*. He should've shut his mouth and taken her to bed, so she wouldn't *think*. "Taylor, I want you. I burn for you." The truth tumbled out, and her eyes got wider with every word he spoke.

Passion dissipated from the beautiful hazel orbs. "Shan—"

"Stop thinking," he begged. "Just be with me."

She swallowed and he wanted to kiss her throat. She shook her head and her shoulders caved as she clutched herself, closing off her body despite her seat on his lap.

He reached for her, caressed her collarbone, but let his hand drop when she winced. That bit, but he tried to blink the hurt away.

This is my fault.

She'd told him where she was at.

"You want me, I can feel it," he whispered, then

cursed his mouth running away without his brain.

Her eyes flashed and Taylor backed away, awkwardly sliding off his lap without uncovering herself. "And you said you wouldn't push me. That we didn't have to label it."

Remorse hit his chest and spread out. "You're right. Taylor, I'm—" Shannon reached for her but she leaned away.

"You should probably go." This was hard, almost a bark. She made it to her feet, turned her back to him and pulled her shirt on.

His gut churned. He threw his head back into her plush couch for a moment, chiding himself. When he had the balls to look at his lovely FBI agent, her face screamed harshness, the thin line she'd made of her lips leaving no clues that they were kiss-swollen. "I don't want to leave like this. I'm going home. Antioch."

"No worries." Her demeanor belied the light phrase. Her frame held a slight tremor, but otherwise she was composed.

He wasn't foolish enough to touch her again. She'd probably shoot him in the ass—or the balls. Shannon had ruined everything.

Dammit.

"Thanks for dessert," Taylor said, in that same normal, even tone. No betrayal of emotion, like she hadn't just kissed his brains out and left him with blue balls the size of Texas.

Like his kisses and touches hadn't affected her physically. Like she didn't give a shit he was leaving town.

Like he meant nothing to her.

Hell, I guess I don't.

Too bad he didn't feel the same way.

Idiot.

"Welcome," he managed to croak. Stupid manners were automatic. Besides, if Taylor wouldn't betray her emotions, he didn't want to either.

She crossed the room and grabbed his brown leather jacket from the recliner. Held it out to him. "Have a safe drive back."

Shannon clenched his jaw. How could she be so smooth?

He was torn up inside, regret, desire and sorrow chewing him up. It was only a matter of time before all the mixed emotions would spit him out. Or, worse, come back for round two.

He sucked in a breath and stood taller. Shrugged his jacket on and met her gaze. "We're not done, Taylor Carrigan." He narrowed his eyes. Daring her.

Taylor fidgeted, but it was only a half-second before she schooled her expression. "I believe we are."

Shannon snorted and shook his head. He left her place without looking back, closing the door with a firm hand, just shy of a slam. "We'll see about that."

Chapter Eighteen

Planning had always been his thing, and making sure Rowdy Vargas got dead was no different. Since it wasn't just his old friend in the apartment, logic told Carter he was better off leaving the collateral damage at a whopping zero, so his mission would have to involve finesse.

Normally, he wouldn't give a shit who saw him or who ended up in a body bag, but he wasn't done in Phoenix, so he'd have to watch his ass. Being remembered enough to be described was the same as cops in general—a no-no.

This trip didn't include seeing any metal bars.

He wasn't worried. For a guy with a limp, he could do stealthy.

Carter had taken up a vigil outside the building for the last few days.

He'd seen Rowdy and the kid again—but only once, the night of the same afternoon he'd first driven by. He'd also spotted a pretty dark-skinned woman with hair just like the kid. Had to be the mother.

She'd come home alone that night, and gone back out, but the trip had been short, and they'd carried a few pizza boxes back inside the place. The female drove a silver Nissan, and often wore a white lab coat, like she was a doctor or scientist or something. Sometimes, she left at odd hours—really early or really late—and Carter had followed her to the university hospital twice.

He never saw his old buddy alone, or he could've taken care of him. Wasn't a baby killer, and he'd seen too much as a kid himself before he'd been taken away by

Child Protective Services, so he wasn't about to kill Rowdy in front of the kid.

Carter still had nightmares of his mom killing his dad. He'd only been six years old—a long-ass time ago. He might call himself a pussy about it, but he didn't want to traumatize another person like that.

Plus, he was curious as to who they were to Rowdy. It took a lot to hide a girl and son from their crew.

Had anyone known?

The guy *had* disappeared any time cops put heat on them, so Carter could only assume he'd come here, to Phoenix, to be with his family.

However, he'd seen the dude with women. *Fucking* women. A lot of them, so if this chick was his woman, he sure as hell hadn't been faithful to her. Not that Carter blamed the guy. Money tended to get pussy thrown at a man. When things had been good for their crew, they'd been *good*.

Speaking of dough, Carter's gut told him the black duffel he'd seen Rowdy carrying had cash in it. He'd had it in one hand, but it'd hung close to the ground, as if he'd really had to heft it. If it'd been heavy, maybe it was packed with enough to steal.

The POS old Ford truck wasn't in the parking lot. There was a detached three-level garage, but he doubted it was in there. When he'd seen Rowdy, he'd parked on the surface lot, like he couldn't get in the garage.

The woman's Nissan had left about thirty minutes earlier. Could only assume the kid was with her, despite the late hour. Or maybe Rowdy was with the kid in the apartment.

Or... Carter would get lucky and his old buddy would be alone inside.

If that was the case, it was game over. Problem

solved. Free money was the prize.

He'd watched the woman get the mail a few times, even knew where the right box was, in the wall to the left side of the front of the building, in a covered little alcove. The thing kind of looked like a block of mini lockers at a school.

Watching closely had given him her apartment number.

He hadn't located any secured areas of the building. He'd confirm when he went inside, and deal with it then. Carter had been putting off the B and E, but it was time. Tonight.

His first mission was recon, unless Rowdy really was alone. The guy had always kept his money under a bed in their hold place in LA, so he'd look there first. Would get revenge—which was what this was all about, of course.

Carter parked in the lot, like any other resident or visitor. Pocketed his keys and glanced around. Not a soul in sight, but it was late. He wouldn't know if he could get inside until he was at the double glass doors, but nerves tingled down his spine. He shook himself, growling lowly. Wasn't a coward.

Fitting his baseball cap tighter to his head, he kept his gaze low and his gait as smooth as he could.

Security cameras were on the corners of the building, so he could only assume there were some interior ones. He didn't want to make waves. Had to avoid his face being clearly recorded at all costs.

He'd be quick about this trip.

Just in and out to get the layout of things. Discover *who* he was dealing with, and maybe take care of Rowdy. See how much money was in there, too.

The main entrance wasn't locked. No keycards required or locks to pick.

Excellent.

Carter still hadn't seen another person. All to his favor. He pushed the doors and went in, carefully logging everything his eyes landed on.

The lobby was a pretty good size, with bronze-colored granite or marble floors and walls. It had a shiny finish that caught the florescent overhead light.

There was a desk to the left, but no one there. No chair either, as if it hadn't been used in some time. A closed door to the right was labeled *Stairs* on a black placard with white letters, complete with a stick figure.

Rowdy's woman's place was on the eighth floor, so *no thanks.* Carter wasn't hefting his bad leg up that many flights.

A large bulletin board was on the wall around the corner from what he sought—the elevators. His eyes scanned tacked papers—*lost dog, dresser for sale, babysitter available*—and the building's laminated fitness center schedule.

The *ding* didn't come fast enough after he'd pressed the up arrow, but he hurried on as soon as the doors opened and punched the button for the eighth floor. He was alone, and was pleased to discover that didn't change when he got to his destination.

Again, he scanned the hallway, but there wasn't a sound. At the end of the long expanse, there was a window with a small table and a green leafy plant at its center— more fancy hotel than apartment-buildingesque.

Carter made it to eight-hundred-eleven as quickly as his bum leg would carry him and popped his way through the lock without much effort, but made sure not to touch the metal with his bare fingers.

He *tsked.* Security here wasn't tight enough. Not that he should complain.

Carter pushed the door open and palmed his H & K. Waited two breaths before advancing—just in case he was surprising his dear old friend.

It was all dark and quiet.

He loosened his shoulders, but he didn't slip his gun away just yet. The place opened up to the left, with a sizable living room and a large flat-screen on the center of the wall. The furniture was dark and all matched, except for the red, green and blue brightly colored table and chairs in the corner shouting a kid lived there, too.

There was a formal dining room farther off to the left—with a large light wood table that sat eight. He assumed the kitchen was the room off the right of that, but he'd confirm in a moment.

A hallway was to his immediate right and had a nightlight plugged in near the floor, but it didn't illuminate much.

There were four doorways to explore.

He took a tour around the living room, examining all the pictures on the walls. Just the kid at various ages. None of the mom or Rowdy.

Carter slid back to the door and closed it silently. Yeah, having to open it back up in a hurry would be a bitch, but he couldn't risk leaving it ajar and have a concerned neighbor call the boys in blue.

He hit the hallway, where he assumed the bedrooms were. The first door on the left was a bathroom, so he didn't stay for a long look. The door next to that was open a crack, and he peeked inside.

It was a kid's room, all happy colors like in the living room, and with a poster of Superman on the wall. An old school one, with Christopher Reeve on it. On the opposite wall was the new version from the last few years, with Henry Cavill flying in a similar position. The bedding on the single bed was Superman-themed, too. Large red and blue letters spelled out *Devon* on the wall above the bed.

Carter left the room alone; doubted the money was there.

The door right across from the boy's room was closed. He slid his hand inside his jacket sleeve and turned the knob, cursing the fact he didn't have gloves. So much for being prepared.

It was decorated with all pinks and purples. Not a man's touch in sight, and the room was huge. The bed was big—a queen—at the center of the room, on a fancy four-poster frame. It was made up neatly, with a mountain of decorative pillows—all very girly colors—looking as if they'd been meticulously arranged.

Probably the master bedroom.

A woman's scent, something clean and citrusy, was in the air.

He inspected the place thoroughly, but didn't touch anything that would hold his prints.

There were framed landscapes on two of the walls, both rich pastel colors that complemented the pink and purple bedding and the dark purple overstuffed chair draped in clothing.

Hospital scrubs, a white coat like the one he'd seen the woman wearing, a few shirts and pants—the chair was about the only thing messy in the room.

Carter spun around and flipped the frilly bed-skirt up. The flashlight on his crappy burner cell told there wasn't a black duffel under there. Nothing but dust bunnies, their kids and grandkids, and a few shoe boxes.

He checked the walk-in closet. The damn thing was full to the brim of clothing—and it was color coded. Like a freaking rainbow on both sides.

His eyes swept up and down. Even the shoes on the

rack were in order—all the sneakers together, then boots, then high heels. A purple suitcase stood in one corner, and at a glance, he could tell all the clothes belonged to a woman. No male things hanging on either side.

But...

No black duffel.

Carter gave the attached bathroom a glance. The same scent was thick in the humid air, as if the woman had showered right before she'd left. Bottles were arranged by size all around the sink, next to toothpaste and a *single* purple-handled brush.

Maybe she's not your woman, huh, Rowdy? Whoever she is, she's a damn neat freak.

The last bedroom was at the end of the hallway, and he made a quick entry. It was small, like the kid's, and decorated sparsely. The bedding was a neutral tan, and the landscape on the wall matched the earth tones.

He hurried to the bed. It seemed like a double, smaller than the one in the master. Carter didn't need his flashlight. The light from a streetlamp shone through the open blinds, revealing the dark outline.

He dragged the bag out from under the bed, then flipped the nightstand lamp on.

The damn thing *was* heavy.

Carter slid his gun back into his waistband. The two zippers' screech cut through the air, but his wince melted away when the smell of money hit his nose. "Damn."

Definitely worth stealing.

Couldn't risk taking it out to count now, but going on what thirty grand had looked like in a similar bag—the money he'd borrowed from Bubba—there was *a lot* more than thirty K here.

He wanted to take it tonight. Visit Kai and tell him to go fuck himself. But he couldn't.

Carter didn't want Rowdy to know he'd been there. The guy wouldn't leave this kind of cash lying around, so he'd be back for it.

He'd continue to watch and make his move when he was ready. When the time was right.

When Rowdy least expected it.

He needed to get the hell out of here. Already been too long. Minutes felt like hours.

Carter slipped into the last room he needed to check—the kitchen. It was a galley style, but also had a small round breakfast table at the end of the sizable island. He turned the lights on and spotted the little nook in the corner on the counter. A mail sorter, full of lively little envelopes.

He pulled out the stack—sorted by size—and flipped through it. "Camille Bonner, huh?" So she wasn't Rowdy's wife, unless she hadn't taken his name.

Carter snapped a few pics with his phone and turned to go. His eyes grazed the refrigerator, and he froze.

Among the kid-art on display, a small magnetic dry-erase board had a note and a ten digit phone number. It'd been written by a neat hand in black ink.

Eric's new number.

Carter smiled.
Pay. Dirt.

Rowdy studied the shitty popcorn ceiling of the crappy roadside motel in Nowhere, Utah. He'd been on the road for a few days but it felt like a year.

He stopped when exhausted and only at seedy hotels with riff-raff like him—where not a lot of questions were asked. Where eyes were averted and people didn't want to be noticed or remembered.

They all politely ignored each other with the same hope—*you didn't see me. I didn't see you. It's all good.*

He'd ditched the Arizona plates on his truck when he'd crossed the border. Stolen some Utah ones at the first truck-stop he'd pulled in to. Cops tended to overlook in-state plates, zoning in on non-local ones, in his experience.

Sighing, he rolled over on the uncomfortable cheap mattress. It was a king, but *huge* didn't make up for lack of quality. Nothing like the bed at Cami's.

Rowdy doubted he'd be here all night. He'd paid cash for the room, so it wasn't like he had to check out, either. He couldn't sleep, even though he'd been lying in the same spot for over an hour. It wasn't late, before six p.m., and he'd wanted to crash after he'd stuffed his face with Burger King, but sleep *so* wasn't happening. He'd driven all day and should've been fatigued.

He was in northern Utah, and he could—would—be in Wyoming tomorrow, but he had nowhere specific to be, and wasn't *really* in a hurry. Just wanted to keep Cami and Devon safe by getting gone, even though his heart hurt more with every mile he drove away from Phoenix.

Rowdy didn't think Carter would look for him in a state that was sparsely populated and winter was still with a capital W, even though spring was right around the corner. Forecasts he'd caught at the previous craptacular roadside inn were pretty dire—blizzards and frigid temps.

He'd lived in the southwest over the course of his childhood, then California after becoming an adult, so he wasn't overly excited about snow, but he'd stop at a sporting goods store or something and get some winter gear.

Where could he go?

It was a delicate balance, really. He didn't want to run to a town so small he'd be spotlighted as *'you're not from around here,'* or land in a city too-big, either, with a lot of cops.

Shouting outside the thin walls made him jump, and he cursed. Rowdy flipped to his back and the bed creaked. Resisted the urge to reach for the gun he'd bought out of some thug's trunk before he'd left Phoenix. The serial number had been scraped off the Sig, but he didn't care about that, either. Was hoping to not have to use it.

He crept to the window and peeked around the smelly, crusty old drapes. He watched a scantily clad woman arguing with a man dressed way too nicely for this place.

Probably a working girl and her pimp.

An oversized meathead got out of a suped-up Escalade—which also stuck out like a sore thumb in the motel's small lot, with its huge chrome rims and mother-of-pearl finish to the ivory paintjob.

The guy's bulk screamed *bodyguard*. He was able to calm the woman, then the three got into that Caddy and took off.

His heart calmed and he screamed at himself for his paranoia, even if he had reason. Forcing a breath, then another, he retreated from the window, watching the dust fly when he returned the stiff fabric to its original position.

The sun was on its way to setting, the brightness around the edges of the curtains on the decline making the room dim.

There was no overhead lighting, only a lamp by the king-sized bed. The other lamp, on the table by the crappy TV—it wasn't even a flat-screen—didn't work, and he wasn't about to call what passed for a front desk to complain.

He didn't want to be here, but couldn't be where he wanted—with Cami and Devon.

Rowdy was done with the whole car-theft thing, but what the fuck was he supposed to do now? Be on the run for the rest of his life?

Maybe his sister was right, and when—if—the Carter thing blew over, he could go back to Phoenix and just live.

Then again, he had charges in several states—not to mention the whole fugitive from the FBI thing—so how long could he stay hidden in the open and stay out of prison?

I could always turn myself in.

He winced. Yeah, there was *that*.

Rowdy would even be safe behind bars—in theory.

What about his sister and nephew?

If he went to the authorities and Carter made a move on them, he wouldn't be able to act if he was locked up. Unless...

Could he sing like a bird and have his family protected in return?

He crushed his eyes shut as his heart took off like someone was chasing him. He was claustrophobic, truth be told. Of course, he'd been in and out of juvie, as well as a few stints in jail as an adult, and he wasn't a fan. Didn't want to walk willingly back to a small box, even if he deserved it for the crimes he'd committed.

Rowdy wasn't like Carter. He was a thief, not a murderer.

He'd have to mull it over. There was one guy he could call from the FBI, even if he didn't know where the dude was at the moment.

Last year, a fellow crew had been infiltrated and later busted. It'd turned out that their techy had been undercover FBI. Alex something. Alec?

Swallowing, he sucked in air, crushing his eyes shut, but Rowdy quickly refocused on mapping the water stains in the popcorn ceiling. One corner was puffed out, threatening to collapse into the room. Fragments of white already dusted the threadbare carpet, proving housekeeping was as sparse as the rest of the amenities at this place.

Had Carter-the-bastard not killed John, the fate of their crew would have been the same as Taz's.

Cami's and Devon's safety wouldn't be in question if he'd never turned up again.

Shit.

When he flipped backwards onto the mattress, the crappy bed creaked again, like the frame was going to refuse to support his weight.

He hadn't talked to Cami since the day before yesterday, so he could call her. Shouldn't wait until too much later in the day, either; he was unsure of her schedule this week.

Rowdy reached for his phone and dialed her number from memory. Wouldn't have the thing long, so he hadn't bothered with entering anything in the contacts.

"Hello?" Her greeting was breathless, as if she'd had to run to her cell.

"Hey, Cam."

"Eric. Thank God. I was starting to worry."

"I told you not to worry about me." He tried to keep his reminder light. Hide the stress inside him.

"Where are you? Wait... You're not going to tell me, anyway."

"I'm safe. Promise."

She didn't answer, but he heard a sniffle that made his gut clench.

"Hey, what're you crying for? I'm checking in like I said I would, and I'm not lying. I'm safe."

For now.

"Okay." The word was thick with tears.

"I miss you guys."

"We miss you, too."

"Cami..."

"Yeah?" his sister prompted when his hesitation stretched out.

"What if I turn myself in?"

There was silence for a good fifteen seconds. Rowdy clutched his phone tight and had to remind himself to breathe. His pulse thundered in his temples.

"For what, Eric?"

He laughed. Couldn't help it. "Cam, you don't think I came by all that money honestly, do you?"

She went quiet again, and seconds ticked away before he heard a big intake of air. "No. Half of me wants...needs...to know. But the other half...can't stand the idea of you being into something dangerous, let alone illegal."

"And I don't want to tell you." He wouldn't, no matter how she begged or prodded.

"And don't deny it's dangerous. You told me some asshole is after you, and you showed up on my doorstep with two infected GSWs."

"I'm not going to tell you anything."

Cami sighed. "Fine. Then why ask me? What do you care about what I think?" Irritation colored her words.

"Because I'm trying to talk myself into doing the right thing, which is something you're way more familiar with than me."

She laughed, but it was bitter.

Rowdy winced.

"Funny, when you think about it, since most of the time when we were kids, *you* were always telling *me* to do the right thing."

"Cami—"

"It would be okay."

His heart skipped. "What would?"

"If you did it. The right thing, I mean. Turned yourself in, or whatever. God knows we have the money for a good lawyer."

He snorted. "I guess. Unless the FBI confiscated it, which is likely. You'd have to hide it, and hide it good. But they'd still ask how you're paying said good lawyer. They'd find out."

"FBI?" she gasped. "It's that serious?"

Rowdy closed his eyes, banishing the picture of her wearing a disappointed expression when it popped in his head. She hadn't sounded anything but stunned. However, he knew his sister too well, even if he couldn't see her. When everything came out, she was going to be more than *disappointed*. Rightly so. "Yes," he admitted at a whisper.

"It doesn't matter."

"It doesn't?"

"No. I'll be there for you no matter what. You're my family."

Relief swirled around in his head and he bit his bottom lip to keep from crying like a little bitch. He didn't know what he wanted to do yet—what he *should* do—but at least he Cami had his back.

Chapter Nineteen

What the hell was I thinking? revolved in her head, taunting her as it had for *days.*

Taylor couldn't get her last encounter with Shannon out of her mind.

How his hands had felt on her bare skin, and how his kiss had tasted. How her body had been on fire—incendiary, from the inside out. She thought of him and dreamed of him, and no amount of miles run on the treadmill were helping.

Neither was her case, and work had always saved her before.

What was wrong this time?

She hadn't talked to him since that night, text or otherwise, and that was another kind of torture. Taylor didn't want to admit she missed him. Even worried whether he'd gotten home okay. She wouldn't reach out to him.

She'd been clear. They were done.

There was nothing else to say.

She was only glad she'd managed to *not* do something stupid that night. Something she would've regretted.

It'd taken all Taylor was made of to kick him out calmly. Faked her composure, fought the tremor that'd shot down her spine and ignored the screaming protest of her body when she'd put her shirt *on*, instead of ripping the rest of her clothes *off* and dragging him to her bed.

He'd made her burn for him, though she wouldn't have admitted it aloud, like Shannon had.

Telling him he was pressuring her had been a cop-out—mostly. She wanted him as much as he wanted her—was just scared shitless about it.

She wasn't ready for intimacy with a man, was she?

Her body sure as hell was.

Taylor growled and made a fist.

What happened to my self-control?

The guilt that assaulted her whenever she looked at John's picture made her want to vomit. Almost tempted her to take it off the entertainment center. That framed photo of the two of them was the last left on display in her apartment. The rest—along with all his things she couldn't bear to part with—were in the hall closet.

"Hey, Carrigan?" Holman's call from the doorway made her jump. Her partner had gone to a meeting with the analysts helping with their case.

She cursed and nearly missed ramming her knee into her desk. "What's up?"

"There's a call on line two. Vasquez, from LA."

"Thanks." Taylor grabbed the phone and hit the blinking line.

Holman might benefit from whatever info Eddie might have, so she pressed the speaker button, resting the handle back in its cradle.

"Carrigan."

"Hey, Tay."

She cringed at the detested nickname, and didn't miss her partner's smirk.

"I have news." The LA-based agent's voice was deep, with an urgent edge she wasn't used to.

She sat taller and exchanged a look with Holman. He settled on the corner of her desk. "Go ahead. Holman's here. You're on speaker."

Eddie took an audible breath and launched into a story that made Taylor's blood boil.

"What the hell? Are you serious?" Rage made her face hot and she bit back curses so she wouldn't scream even louder.

"I'm sorry, Tay. He didn't tell me until Carter Bennett left his place."

She growled and didn't spare Holman a glance, even though she could feel his stare. "Eddie, this is fucking serious."

Her partner stilled, and Eddie paused.

Yeah, she didn't say that word aloud too often.

Good thing they'd both noticed.

Holman slid to their office door and closed it.

Probably a good thing. Their fellow agents didn't need to see or overhear Taylor have a meltdown. She was close. Speaker phone wasn't always her friend.

"You're preaching to the choir. No worries, Bubba and I had words."

"Words? That doesn't cut it. That bastard was *staying* with him and he didn't think to give you the fucking heads up? I thought he was your CI? The reliable one? What the hell happened to *that*?"

"He says he didn't expect Bennett to up and leave, but I don't believe his ass. I'll get him to come clean, I'm working on it. Let you know. No worries."

She drummed her nails on her desk. Her head spun, her face seared—no doubt three shades of red. Damn good thing they were separated by fifteen hundred miles, because she wanted to strangle Special Agent Eddie Vasquez. "What the hell was he waiting for? What does *'working on it'* mean?"

Eddie laughed and it pissed her off even more. "I knew you couldn't help but take the bait."

"Bait? I swear to God, Ed—"

"Okay, take a breather. Sorry, I'll get to the point."

'Take a breather' was too close to *'calm down'* and made her ire rise even higher. Good thing for her colleague she was too angry to speak.

Her partner took one step toward her, but a glare stopped him in his tracks and he perched himself on the end of his chair, instead.

Smart man.

"Yeah, get to the point, Eddie," Holman muttered. He shook his blond head.

"The reason Bubba waited to call me is because Bennett was trying to set up a train hit, but it didn't pan out, according to him. He told me he wanted more evidence. Something solid before he called me, but I can smell the BS. He's hiding something, but I *will* get to the bottom of it. He fed me some shit that he was sorry, he knew he was wrong, but I know he's not sharing everything with the class. Don't worry, I'll find out what he knows or I'll haul him off to jail. Right now, I need him in play."

"Fuck that, Eddie!" Taylor made a fist. "Bennett was in his house! Arrest his ass now. Make him talk, or tell him you'll throw away the key!" Her voice rose with each word until she was shouting and her throat ached.

She didn't give a shit.

"Why didn't the train hit pan out?" her partner asked. *His* question was at a normal volume. He was calm, collected.

She forced a breath. If Holman could be calm, she should try. Didn't need word making it back to Baker that she'd lost it. Or that she wanted to go postal on a fellow FBI guy.

"Word's spread of Bennett killing off his crew, so no one will work with him. He even tried Grady O'Malley, according to Bubba."

"It must be bad, O'Malley's as scum as they come," Holman said. "Always out for a buck, no matter the risk."

"You know him?" Eddie asked what Taylor, too, wanted an answer to.

"Ran into him once or twice when I was under. None of the crew leaders like him much."

"Even thieves have honor," Eddie said.

She rolled her eyes. Her heartrate was starting to regulate. She whipped the little yellow, smiley-faced stress ball—compliments of Doc Wong—from her desk. Tried not to glare at Holman's snort. If he said anything, she'd kill him. "Why did Bennett leave?"

"Bubba won't say. My gut says he knows where, when and why. I have him by the balls. I *will* get an answer. Maybe it's something to do with Rowdy Vargas."

"Son of a bitch, that's the *last* thing I need!" Taylor gritted her teeth.

"Do you think Bennett found out Bubba's your CI?" Holman asked.

Her knee was bouncing a mile a minute of its own accord. She adjusted herself, settling on the edge of her seat, and squeezed the damn ball. Her palms were clammy. Her mind spun into chaos she couldn't make sense of. Demands she needed to make couldn't say. The answers she needed weren't there, anyway.

"Doubtful," Eddie was telling her partner. "No way he would've stuck around at Bubba's place if he did. As it is, Bubba says he wants to kill him now, too. Though, not sure I buy that."

"Why?" Taylor and Holman asked at the same time. She exchanged a glance with her partner.

His blue gaze was calm.

She sucked in a subtle breath and looked back at the phone.

"Bubba said Bennett relieved him of thirty grand on his way out, but he was too angry, it was too loud of a protest, if you know what I mean."

"Dammit," Holman muttered.

"Now the bastard has resources," she said.

"If it's true, I think Bubba gave him the dough. He's covering for him. It's not a million dollars, but it'll last him a little bit. More than get him to wherever he thinks Vargas is, if that's where he went," Eddie said.

Taylor could see him shaking his head in her mind, his dark hair flying, but him being annoyed with his CI didn't make her feel an ounce better. "Eddie, you'd better fucking fix this. Get that asshole in cuffs, today."

"I got it handled, Tay. Promise."

She scowled. Third time was a charm. "I told you not to call me that."

"I know."

He wasn't repentant. Sounded like he was grinning, actually, damn him.

"Why would he call you at all, if he's involved with Bennett in some way? Why let you know he was there if he's covering for him?" Holman asked, again in that unruffled tone. "If he hadn't said a word, we wouldn't know."

"Good damn question." The LA agent sighed. "Maybe he was afraid word would get back to me somehow, I dunno."

"You'd better find the fuck out. And call me the very *second* you do," Taylor barked. She hit the hang-up button without further word or apology. Glared at her partner.

Holman stared back, unaffected.

"If you tell me to breathe or something, I'm going to shoot you."

He chuckled but flashed his palms up in surrender.

"I wouldn't dare. I'm with you. This blows. I met Bubba a few times, and he's a convincing thug. No one could guess he's with Vasquez."

"Obviously he's not."

"I don't know about that. I think there's more to this, and Eddie'll get him to talk. He's good."

"This is bullshit." Taylor crushed the stress ball in both hands, fighting the urge to fling it across the room. "How's the search for the sister coming?"

Holman had been gone for a while before hollering that Eddie was on the phone. It'd taken every ounce of her self-control not to go after him as the minutes had ticked away. To let him handle it, and trust him to report back to her with any info they needed.

She didn't like relying on someone else. Needed to do it all herself. A part of her wanted Holman to know she *did* think he was a good investigator. She grudgingly had to admit they'd worked well together for the past few days.

He was her partner. Taylor didn't hate that idea anymore. Not all the way, anyway.

"They've ruled out New Mexico. Still looking in Arizona and Nevada. It's tough with only a guestimate at her years in state custody, no age and no last name. They didn't have any luck with using Vargas so far. I told them to assume Cami is short for Camille and look for both. All the spellings they can think of. We'll find her. Messing with kids' records is a bitch, too. Family Services, no matter the state, throws a confidentiality fit around a lot. They're fighting through it, though."

"What about prison records? If Vargas is a criminal, maybe it's all in the family?"

"Maybe, but Pompa said she wasn't."

"He didn't know much about her."

"True." Holman ran his hand through his short

locks.

She reclined in her chair and sighed. "I was hoping for more."

"Me too." He shook his head. "But we're a tad closer."

"Not close enough. If Bennett really did find Vargas, it's too late. We'll get the call about a body found."

Holman echoed her sigh and nodded. "I think so, too."

"Dammit. We need Vargas alive. I want to kill Eddie."

Amusement rippled across her partner's handsome face. "That wouldn't do any good."

She rolled her eyes, then glanced at the phone when her direct line rang.

It was Baker.

"Carrigan, come see me."

"Sure." She hung up and looked at Holman. "Be right back." Taylor didn't wait for his answer before heading out, but she left their office door open.

"You're off for the rest of the day, tomorrow, and this weekend. *Off.*"

Taylor hit her feet, her fists clenched at her sides. "The hell I am. I have to find Rowdy Vargas before Carter Bennett does."

"Holman will work on the case." Baker's tone brooked no argument. "*You* need some time away from it."

"Baker—"

"You remember the conversation we had the morning I paired you with Holman?"

She snapped her mouth shut. The word *ultimatum* danced around in her mind. No way would she acknowledge it aloud. "What is this about?" She forced the question out, chanting the word *calm* over and over.

"I heard about your little phone conference with Vasquez from the LA office."

Taylor cursed. Sank back into the chair she always sat in, on the left in front of her boss's desk.

"And before you rip your partner a new one, the info didn't come from Holman. I don't know how it's going with you two, since you don't tell me anything, but obviously the kid is loyal to you. Which I'm happy to see, by the way."

Of course he hadn't reported to Baker.

He's been with me the whole time, but Holman... Loyal to me?

Why?

Hadn't she been treating him like crap?

There'd been moments, like in the car on the way back from Texarkana, and the last few days in the office, where things were all right. More than all right.

"Working with Holman's okay," Taylor confessed.

Then cursed at the triumphant look on her boss's face.

"So, no issues with taking a few days off? Taking it easy for the weekend?" He smiled and intertwined his fingers, planting them on his desk.

"You know I have *issues* with that."

"Well, I'm glad to hear it."

Taylor blinked.

He was just going to pretend she hadn't spoken?

Baker's smile widened. "Have a good weekend. Get out of town."

Out of town?

Shannon's trial was over, and he was back home in Antioch, but Baker couldn't know about the sergeant.

"If you can take a breather, and next week goes okay, I'll even consider n*ot* shortening your work hours or benching you every weekend."

"Wait. Wha—?"

He threw a palm up. "I know you *heard* me when I told you I'd take you off this case. Everything is up to me. *My* call. Not yours."

Taylor growled. "No."

"Yes," he growled back.

"I thought Holman was—"

"You not working alone is the only reason you've survived the last two weeks with this case still in your custody."

"So this isn't about Holman?"

"No. It's about you, Carrigan. It's always been about you."

She narrowed her eyes. "I'm not doing this."

"There's nothing to be done. You're off until Monday. Three and a half days. End of story. Close the book, or you won't get to open it back up."

"Baker—"

"I'm done. Enjoy your afternoon. Go home. Get some lunch. Take a walk in the park. Go shopping. Get a dog. Anything but work. You're done for the day."

"Matthias, really—"

"The only thing you may say is, *'Thank you, Matthias.'* If it's anything else, you're off Monday, too."

Rage and defeat wrestled in her gut, then burned her throat on the way up. Her tongue weighed fifty pounds and her mouth was a desert. Taylor stood. Opened and closed her fists at her sides.

There were so many things she wanted to say, but Baker's gaze dared her.

She didn't want to lose another day of working, and

he was dead-serious. She didn't need a suspension in her work file, either. If she opened her mouth, she wouldn't be allowed to work next week. More than just the five hours left of her Thursday, and tomorrow.

Squaring her shoulders, and swearing she'd kill her boss if he showed one more ounce of satisfaction from her humiliation, Taylor forced a curt nod and turned on her heel.

No amounts of '*screw this*' was going to fix her problem. She was under Baker's thumb, and hated every second of it.

She left his office, trying not to stomp as if she was the spoiled child she felt like. Her cellphone dinged, and she dug it out of her pocket on automatic pilot, then froze in her tracks when she glanced at the message and noticed who it was from.

Been thinking about you.

Taylor's heart fluttered and she cursed it. She'd treated him like ass, kicked him out of her apartment, and he was texting her?

After days of no contact?

It didn't matter, because she'd been thinking about him, too.

Constantly.

Was the sergeant a glutton for punishment, or was she just the biggest idiot in Dallas?

She swallowed and clutched her phone so hard her hand ached. Closed her eyes for a second and considered not answering Shannon.

Then her thumbs flew over the letters.

What're you doing this weekend?

She didn't proofread her message, just hit *send* before she lost her nerve.

Chapter Twenty

"**Y**ou can put whatever gear you need in the back. Just make sure your clipboard is accessible." Shannon hefted his duty duffel into the back of the supervisor SUV he was driving for his last shift this week.

Then he was off for a long weekend, starting Friday, the next day. After a few long weeks of twelve-hour shifts, he was more than ready for a break. The week of the trial had hurt, not helped, and had just thrown his sleep schedule even more out-of-whack.

He waited for the rookie he was training to get her stuff and come around to the back of the vehicle. It was their first day together, but the new officer was in her second phase of training, and had come off the eight-hour rotation's midnight shift, which ran from eleven p.m. to seven a.m.

She'd go with him when Shannon went to second shift. Officer Russo was to be his charge for the next six weeks.

He wasn't supposed to work this morning, but the day sergeant had needed a favor, so Shannon had switched—and gained the long weekend as a perk. His trainee had joined him, like she would've if they'd reported at seven that evening instead.

"Sure, thanks." She put her gear next to his and smiled.

Shannon took one look at the excitement in her dark brown eyes and had to suck back a chuckle. He remembered those days well. She was nearly bouncing in her shitkickers.

Isabella Russo was tall, about five-foot-seven if he

had to guess, and gorgeous. Her dark hair was in a tight, clean ponytail, and her uniform crisp, not a thing out of place on her duty belt. The leather smelled new, untried—because it was. Raring to get in the SUV and hit the road.

New cops were always eager. Chomping at the bit to go, off to the next call—or adventure. That was how he'd seen calls when he was a baby cop, too.

Being edgy wasn't a problem, but caution was taught, not ingrained. Hopefully he could show her a thing or two. Small city or not, shit still happened in Antioch.

"Hey, Crowley!"

He looked up to see Detective Cole Lucas striding across the sally port from the back of the PD, a travel mug in his hand. He was dressed in jeans and a navy blue APD embroidered polo, his badge on his belt and his gun in a paddle holster. His dark hair was wind-mussed as his long legs ate the distance.

Shannon arched an eyebrow when Russo, still standing next to him, groaned and shook her head. "Something wrong, Lucas?" He glanced at his watch.

It wasn't even half past seven, and the detectives didn't usually roll in until after eight. The guy hadn't been at briefing he and his trainee had come from moments before.

Russo was gnawing on her bottom lip now, her discomfort palpable. She fidgeted at his side.

The detective threw out his hand. "Nah, nothing's wrong. Morning."

He shook the guy's hand. "Good deal. Morning. What's up?"

Lucas looked at Russo. "Morning, Bella." He grinned, flashing dimples.

"Officer Russo," the recruit muttered.

The detective looked at Shannon, obviously

unrepentant for the use of the young officer's nickname. "So, Crowley, just wanted to make sure Bella got settled in with you okay."

Where's the guy going with this?

Shannon arched an eyebrow and regarded him. "Yeah. We're about to take off. No calls yet, but maybe we'll go run some traffic."

"Detective, may I have a word with you?" Officer Russo's inquiry was clipped and her jaw tight.

"Ah...sure."

"If you'll excuse us, Sergeant," his recruit said.

Shannon nodded, and thumbed the SUV. "I'll just wait in the car. Take your time."

"Oh, it won't take time." Russo threw him a smile, then glared at the detective.

He climbed in the driver's seat and turned the engine over, but hit the down button for the window. To eavesdrop. Pulled out his notebook so it'd appear he was reviewing notes.

Russo kept her voice low, but it carried. They hadn't moved far from the unit. "Cole, you can't keep doing this. You're gonna make me a laughingstock."

"Just wanna make sure you're good."

Shannon watched from his peripheral vision.

Russo's body was pitched forward, and her hands were fists at her sides. "I'm a big girl now. I can handle myself."

The detective shifted from foot to foot. "I know. Just do me a favor and listen to Crowley. He's a good cop."

"Are you going to do this with *all* my training officers?" Her frustration was evident, and she shook her head.

"Probably."

Shannon bit back a chuckle.

Well, at least the guy's honest.

"Have a good day, Detective. I'm on patrol," Russo growled. She whirled and marched to the passenger side of the SUV. Got in and slammed the door for good measure. Then she glanced at Shannon, and her cheeks reddened.

He didn't want to offend her, so he held back his laugh and cleared his throat. "Ready?"

She nodded and reached for her seatbelt.

Shannon backed the SUV out of the spot, and returned Lucas' wave.

The detective hadn't moved.

Officer Russo didn't offer a gesture.

He snorted and they drove out of the back gate.

"Sorry." Her apology was low.

"No biggie. Sounds like he's just lookin' out for you."

"Oh, God. You heard." The recruit covered her face with both hands.

He could feel her mortification. Wanted to reassure her. "No worries, it won't go anywhere. Promise."

"Thanks." Russo sighed and leaned her head back into the headrest. Her cellphone chimed from her duty belt. "If that's Cole Lucas, I'm gonna kill him."

Shannon laughed, he couldn't help it. "Let's not, at least until you're off probation."

She smirked and glanced at the screen of her smartphone. "Well, that's a relief."

"Good news?"

"Andi, apologizing for Cole. Said she told him not to bug me, but he doesn't listen."

Andi was a detective, too. The only female on their detective squad, and Lucas' wife.

"So you know them both?"

Again, his recruit's cheeks pinkened. She was young,

and the blush made her seem even younger. "Yeah. I've known Andi for years. Since I was about seven. I used to babysit her son, Ethan. Well, then both boys, after she married Cole and they had Micah."

"Oh, okay. That's why he's a pain in the ass, then."

"Why?" She scrunched up her nose, still looking like the little girl she'd been not long ago.

"You're family, kid. Get used to it. APD is one big family, too."

"I wanna make my own way," she admitted.

"You will. I'm not worried about that."

"Unit three-oh-eight," the radio squawked, and Russo shot him an eager look.

Shannon threw his recruit a nod. "Go for it."

Russo grabbed the mic off its hook and pressed the button. "Three-oh-eight, go ahead."

"Disturbance downtown at the movie theater. Two hurt, medics asking for police assist."

"This early in the morning?" Shannon said, more to himself than Russo. He looked at her. "Tell her we're on our way."

The day took an arduous turn, but it wasn't because of his recruit. She was sharp and didn't need a lot of direction. She'd been with Sergeant Williams on mids for her first month and a half, and the guy was fantastic with cops fresh out of the academy.

It showed with Russo. She only asked questions when she needed to, and since she'd grown up in Antioch, she knew the geography.

All checkmarks in the positive column on her daily training log. The kid had the makings of a great cop. Shannon was proud to be a part of that. It was one of the reasons he never minded being an FTO.

Not all cops were effective field training officers, and the department was lucky to have a few go-to guys and gals on every shift.

Shannon had been trained by Lieutenant Chloe Stein, and they remained close, even years later. It was nice to have a positive impact on someone's career. He only hoped Russo saw him like that one day.

"Where do you wanna grab lunch?" he asked. They were behind schedule because of a bad car wreck they'd had to work most of the morning. Two little ones had been hurt—one badly—and that always got him right in the gut.

The stupid disturbance at the movie theater had happened when the owner had come in to restock the concessions and ended up finding a lover's tryst.

One of the managers, who had a key to the building, had spent the night there with her boyfriend.

The men had fought, and both had minor injuries, but the boyfriend had attacked one of the paramedics, too.

No doubt the manager was now out of a job, to boot.

Russo had handled herself impressively, yelling orders even before Shannon had said a word. When he'd complimented her afterward, she'd shrugged, grinned and said, "I'm Italian. Great at having a big mouth."

"Um, are you tired of Dixie's?" Russo asked, tugging him to the present.

"Nah, it works for me. I think Benton and Walton are there right now, too."

They met with their fellow officers for lunch at the Antioch mom and pop that'd been there forever, probably since Shannon's mom was a kid. It was run by the same family, including the matriarch, Marge herself, who was hollering orders and working the counter.

Conversation consisted of the other two officers

razzing Russo, since she was the rookie. Shannon took up for her once, reminding the younger cop, Joe Benton, he'd been in her shoes not too long ago, but the girl held her own after that.

They laughed and talked, and had the odd peace of no calls on the radio for the next forty-five minutes.

A flash of blondish hair caught Shannon's attention, and he zoned in on the cash register. A woman was picking up a takeout order, and even though her hair wasn't an exact match, his mind went straight to Taylor.

Damn, he'd been trying not to think about her. Was quite a feat, since he'd been dreaming of her every damn day since he'd been home.

Erotic dreams, built on their last night together. Dreams that went a hell of a lot further than they had. He'd only tasted her mouth then, but he'd seen and held her perfect breasts. His imagination had taken it from there, leaving her naked and writhing beneath him, screaming his name when she came.

"You all right, Sarge?" Russo asked.

Shannon fidgeted, forcing a nod. He suppressed a curse and sat straighter. Last thing he needed was a hard-on at work. Especially sitting next to a female recruit.

Three sets of eyes regarded him.

"Unit three-fifteen," one of the dispatchers called over the radio.

Walton answered, and Benton paid close attention.

Russo, too, was drawn to the dispatcher, and the spotlight was off Shannon.

Thank God. Saved by the call.

The partners departed to a theft report at the local pharmacy, and Shannon told them if they needed backup to give him and Russo a holler.

Too bad work didn't take his mind off Taylor

Carrigan.

"Sarge, I need to run to the restroom before we head out," Russo said.

"Go ahead. I'll take care of the check."

As soon as his trainee disappeared down the hallway toward the ladies' room, Shannon grabbed his cell out of the holster on his duty belt. He probably shouldn't, but he formed the message anyway.

Been thinking about you.

He kept it simple, but it didn't matter. Taylor probably wouldn't answer him. Shannon clipped his phone back and headed to the register.

"You know your money's no good here, Sarge," Marge chided.

"Ah, c'mon, I have a new one, let's show her the right way." He smiled and glanced over his shoulder to see Russo making her way toward the counter.

Marge chuckled. "It's the right way around here."

"Consider it a tip then."

The older woman smiled. "All right, hon, whatever you say."

He slid money on the counter and turned to join his recruit. His phone vibrated and he jumped.

Taylor had answered him?

No way, has to be someone else. Unless she's telling me off.

He tried to ignore the message until they got out to the patrol SUV, but he couldn't. His heart tripped and his fingers scrambled to his belt of their own accord.

Shannon read the message three times before it computed. Why would she want to know what he was doing over the weekend?

"You comin', Sarge?"

Russo made him jump. She had one hand on the car door.

"Gimme two seconds. Here, you drive." He tossed her the keys.

Her dark eyes widened and she squealed, making him laugh. "Sorry," she muttered, but grinned and hopped in the driver's seat.

He needed to get it together before he answered Taylor, then chided himself. Couldn't process that she'd actually answered him, let alone *what* she'd asked.

Off this weekend. Have something in mind?

He counted heartbeats until he had her answer.

Can I come see you?

Shannon blew out a breath as his heart took off. Stared at the screen, as if the words were in Chinese. Wanted to ask if she was playing a sick joke on him. Instead, he answered her.

Yes. I'm off at seven tonight, then have a long weekend, starting tomorrow.

Good. Me too. I can come into town tonight, if that's okay with you.

A small part of him wanted to fist pump, but he remembered where he was, and who just might be watching as Russo waited for him to come back to the SUV.

He looked back at his phone. Didn't want to seem too

eager to see a certain FBI agent. Questions zoomed through his head.

Why was Taylor, a self-proclaimed workaholic, taking three whole days off? Was her case over? Could that be the reason she hadn't contacted him?

Nah, not after the way she'd kicked him out.

Doesn't matter at the moment. Answer her.

He could ask all he wanted when she was *here*, in Antioch. Shannon was going to do his damnedest to get her into his arms, too.

Maybe his bed.

Fine with me. See you tonight, he texted.

He added his address so she could come straight to him, and left off what he'd really wanted to say, something like, '*can't wait to see you. I miss you.*'

Taylor Carrigan had told him they were done.

Guess we're seeing about that, after all, Special Agent.

Shannon smiled. Couldn't wait to show her *I-told-you-so.*

Chapter Twenty-One

O kay, so he was definitely in school-boy mode. Or, his anticipation was.

Shannon was antsy, pacing. His gaze darted back and forth from his watch to the clock on his living room wall.

Occasionally his cellphone got a turn, but he was looking for a missed call or text. No matter how stupid. The volume and vibrate were on high. He couldn't miss a thing.

She was driving, so she couldn't text. The delay made sense, right?

God, get over yourself.

Have a seat. Have a beer. Jack off.

His brain rejected the suggestions as he ticked them off. His feet wouldn't obey, or divert from the path he was wearing in his carpet.

Shannon could do something productive, like make dinner for her.

"Yes, I totally should do that." They hadn't really discussed the evening meal, but he didn't want to go out. Wanted to keep Taylor *in* his house. All to himself.

Unless she'd already eaten. It *was* getting late. He hadn't eaten since lunch, but he was too nervous, and the pacing was taking up his time.

Why didn't you ask her about dinner, dumbass?

His cellphone screamed and he jumped, then cursed himself, because the damn thing was in his hand.

Shannon glanced at the screen.

Not Taylor.

He swiped his thumb to answer. "Hey, Mom."

"Hey, baby. I need a favor." Her voice was rushed,

like she was in business mode.

In the background, he heard an announcement for a doctor somebody—that explained his mom's tone. She was at the hospital, where she'd been an OB nurse in Labor and Delivery since Shannon was a kid.

"Sure, anything for you."

"One of the many reasons I love you."

He could hear her smile, and laughed. "Love you, too."

"Cailey needs new softball gear and I'm working all weekend."

Oh.

He'd be busy this weekend, too. With Taylor. "When does she need it by?"

It was only Thursday, and no doubt his niece had school tomorrow. Maybe he could get away Sunday afternoon, but he didn't want to volunteer info.

"You know that kid, everything is immediate. Not sure if she actually has time or not. But I thought you were off weekends this rotation?"

"Well, I..." He couldn't exactly tell his mom he was hoping to spend the weekend in bed, wrapped around a sexy little FBI agent. If he could loosen Taylor up, that was.

"Do you have a date or something?"

Shannon chuckled. "Should I be insulted you sound so surprised?"

His mom laughed. "Sorry, son. It's been a while."

"Yeah, I know." It wasn't like he told her about his few-and-far-between casual sex exploits, either, but the woman who'd raised him was far from stupid.

"Well, as far as Cailey is concerned, no big deal. We'll figure it out."

"I'll text her and ask her deadline," he said.

"Oh, thanks. When do I get to meet this new woman?"

"I never actually confirmed or denied..."

Shannon's mom laughed again. "It's that new, huh?"

He smiled. She knew him too well. "Yeah, it is. Sorta. I mean, we went out a few times when I was in Dallas this last time, but yeah. New."

"Well, good luck."

"Thanks, Mom."

"Anytime. I love you."

Her last words resonated even after he'd hung up.

He sure needed *luck*.

Shannon didn't want Taylor to think he expected sex. Just seeing her, hanging with her and talking to her would be good enough for him—he'd missed her like hell throughout the days of no contact.

After their last encounter, his cock got hard at just the thought of her naked breasts and freckled skin. Keeping his hands to himself was going to be a challenge, to put it lightly. The way his heart was pattering, there was nothing *light* about his want for Taylor.

He needed to reach for his inner gentleman and talk to her. Find out why she'd asked to come see him. Ask why she wasn't working. Make sure she was really okay. Then, maybe, they could move things to the next level, but experience told him pushing her was bad news—the sure path to slammed doors and Taylor fleeing, which was the last thing he wanted for this weekend.

The sound of a car pulling into the driveway made him jump again. Shannon forced a deep breath and pocketed his cell.

Should he meet her on the porch or wait for her to knock?

He didn't want her to know how worked up he was.

Shannon was so indecisive about it; the *ding* of his doorbell solved the issue.

His whole body shuddered and he forced one foot in front of the other. Tried not to wrench the door open.

One look at the way she fidgeted on his porch and avoided looking at him right away made some of his anxiety melt off his shoulders.

She'd told him once that he calmed her, and he wanted to do that for her right now. Seemed like she needed that.

"Hi," he said.

Finally she glanced up. Taylor swallowed and he wanted to kiss her throat.

She was dressed for work—dark slacks and a matching blazer, with a light-colored shirt under it. A black leather belt cinched her tiny waist. The butt of her Glock was barely visible. No jacket, and it was chilly out.

"Hi," she returned. A ghost of a smile played at the corner of her mouth and Shannon wished it was a full one. Her breasts rose and fell, like she'd taken a deep breath.

"Wanna come in?"

"Oh, sure."

He regretted that she startled, and she didn't take his hand when he offered it. He pretended his heart didn't sink a little. "Are you hungry?" Shannon forced polite words out, which felt unnatural.

"I don't know."

He closed his front door and whirled around. Didn't miss that she was scanning his small foyer. Like she was cataloging everything. He hoped she wasn't looking for another exit. "You don't know?"

Taylor met his eyes. There was a slight tremor in her shoulders, but he didn't think she was cold. "Honestly, after the day I've had, I don't know a damn thing." Her mouth trembled, but she flattened it, pursing her lips.

Damn, he wanted to hold her. He slid forward slowly, not wanting to spook her. "Wanna talk about it?" He kept his offer soft.

She clenched her jaw and shook her head. "No. Rather forget it."

"Okay. How about we go in the kitchen and see what I can come up with? I didn't eat dinner."

Finally she smiled, but it was only a tiny one. "Sure."

"Do you want a beer?"

"Yeah, actually that sounds good."

"Let's get some food in you first. I'd hate for you to lose your head."

Taylor's slender shoulders loosened and she blew out a breath, then let go of a small laugh that shocked the hell out of him, but pleased him just as much.

"What's funny?" Shannon smiled, too.

"Not sure I believe you have innocent intentions."

Isn't that the truth?

God, he wanted to ask her if that was okay with her. Instead, he laughed. "Well, I told you no pressure, and that still stands."

Since you're not only speaking to me, but you're here, too.

She paused. Her eyes went misty, but she averted her gaze, and when she looked back at him, her pretty hazel orbs were clear of emotion. "Thanks," she whispered.

"Any time."

Should he apologize for their last encounter?

He wasn't sorry for the heated action between them, only for how it'd ended, and sorry he'd pushed her when he'd told her so many times he wouldn't.

Her current level of discomfort was reminiscent of the first night he'd shown up on her doorstep with the cheesecake from Mario's.

Shannon didn't like *awkward* when it came to him and Taylor. Weren't they were past all that?

Then again, she *had* ditched him when things got too hot for her to handle. So, maybe that was a setback after all.

Was it something they could come back from? Should he tell her he just wanted to be with her? The rest didn't matter. They could take this evening slowly, then tomorrow...

Would she really stick around all weekend?

He led her into his kitchen and sat her at the small breakfast table.

"Do you need help?" she asked. Taylor shifted on the chair, like she was torn between getting right back up and making herself comfortable.

"No, ma'am. My mom taught me not to put guests to work."

She smiled, fully this time, and it made his heart to skip.

She certainly looked lighter than she had when she'd appeared on his front porch.

Shannon poured her some iced tea after they'd settled on a frozen pizza.

Although she reached for the frosty beer bottle first.

Eating and talking was natural, and actually had him feeling some sense of normalcy with her. At the very least, back on the path they'd been on before things had ended badly that night.

She didn't tell him much about her crappy day, only that her boss had given her the weekend off.

He still hadn't touched her much. A brush of her hand here and there, but nothing like he wanted to. He was on edge...and so was his libido.

His dick got interested when she did...well, anything. When she licked her lips while she was eating, the little dart of her tongue made him have to adjust his jeans. When Taylor brought the beer bottle up for a drink, he couldn't look away from her mouth.

Shannon had a damn good imagination, and a perfect memory.

A bad combination.

Fantasies ran through his mind, and he needed to calm the hell down.

Now.

He jumped up to discard the round cardboard remnants of the pizza box and the paper plates they'd eaten on. "I'll just take care of these."

"Sure." Her cheeks were flushed pink from the alcohol, but Taylor had told him she didn't have much tolerance. Her shoulders were loose, but she still looked prim and proper in her work clothing, and her hair was up, with only one or two wavy flyaways.

He wanted to tug it out of its restraints and run his fingers through it.

She seemed as if she'd been able to relax.

Too bad that as she'd wound down, he'd wound *up*.

Shannon rinsed his cup out, watching the dark remainder of iced tea wash away. Needed his mind on something other than dragging her to his bedroom, stripping her down and showing her how much he'd missed her.

He glanced at the clock on the microwave. It was almost nine already. He put his glass in the dishwasher, then wiped his hands. His gut tightened when he faced her.

Taylor's gaze found his and she smiled.

His heart skipped. "Uh, want to watch a movie or

something?"

Geeze. What am I, seventeen?

"What about a tour of your house? This place is big. And nice. I love the décor." She gestured to his large kitchen, with its new appliances and dark granite countertops.

"The kitchen is new." The house had the feel of a mountain lodge that Shannon liked. "My mom helped. The house is old, built in the sixties. Little by little I've fixed it up. Hardwood in the foyer, new carpet in living room. New doors. It's kinda my weekend project."

"Ah, well you've done a good job."

"Thanks." He breathed a tad easier and pushed off the counter behind him. Talking about home improvement made him focus and think about something other than sex. "C'mon, let me show you around. Sorry you had to ask." He pointed out updates, showing her everything as they walked.

She didn't say much, just looked around, assessing, as if his house was a crime scene, which was so Taylor. She commented from time to time, but when she smiled, his heart sped up and Shannon's thoughts dipped back to the forbidden.

"Is this your niece?" She pointed to several framed pictures of Cailey in the hallway, at various ages.

"Yeah, that one's the new one." He indicated her latest school picture. "Eighth grade. I can't believe it."

"She's beautiful. Except for that blonde hair, she looks like you. It's those eyes."

Shannon chuckled. "Yeah. My mom has them too. Family trait, I guess."

"Gorgeous."

Their gazes collided.

He sucked in a breath because he wanted to hold her,

touch her. Kiss her. Couldn't even dig up a tease because she'd said he had gorgeous eyes.

Taylor broke the spell by looking away, but he didn't miss the rise and fall of her chest. It was faster than it had been.

She felt what he did, even if she didn't want to admit it.

He cleared his throat and reached for her hand. A jolt of energy shot up his arm and he entwined their fingers, trying not to pant. Shannon resisted the urge to yank her to him and crush his mouth over hers. He wanted to relive her taste.

She didn't pull away, and his belly flipped.

"Let me show you the rest of the house."

Chapter Twenty-Two

"This is the master... My bedroom."

She looked away as he gestured around the room and all Taylor could focus on was the king-sized bed that dominated the back wall.

The room was Spartan and masculine. The bed had four dark pillars fit for a king. There was a rifle rack on one wall, and a huge gun safe in the opposite corner of the room.

The dressers were mahogany and oversized, in-line with the lodgy-feel of his living room and kitchen. There wasn't a feminine touch in sight, but the place was to her taste. It had a homey, welcoming feel that appealed—probably too much so. Like coming in out of the cold.

Shannon had made this room the last stop on the tour of his four-bedroom home, as if it was some kind of test.

Why did I come here?

What did she want from him?

Taylor had made reservations at the hotel in town, an upscale four-story building called *The Covington*. She'd stayed there before, and the place was nice.

She should thank him for dinner and make her way there. Get some sleep and...

Then what?

She'd had a nice time with him so far, just like in Dallas. Had barely even thought about her stupid boss and her case.

Holman had promised to get in touch with her if something happened with Eddie and his idiot CI, even though that was against Baker's orders, showing he *was* loyal to her.

Her partner had told her to take the weekend to breathe, relax, and she hadn't been able to muster a growl at him when they'd parted ways.

Maybe she did need this weekend.

Need Shannon?

"Are you okay?" His whisper yanked her from her thoughts. Shannon swallowed, and his Adam's apple bobbed.

They stared at each other for several breaths, then she forced a nod.

He opened his arms and, instead of running the other way—like she should, Taylor entered his embrace.

She sighed and rested her forehead against his hard chest. Following him into this room—his *bedroom*—had been a bad idea, house tour or not.

Definitely against her better judgment, but she couldn't seem to protest.

Perhaps, being pulled into his arms had been inevitable.

Still, she didn't move away. Couldn't.

Shannon said nothing, just rubbed her back. Long, soothing strokes that made her want more.

She didn't do comfort. Didn't *need* comfort, but God that felt good. Almost as good as his lips moving over hers.

He hadn't kissed her today either, yet her body was loosening by the second. Thrumming for him. Needing. Wanting a hell of a lot more than just his large palm running over fabric.

A tremor slid down her spine and spread down her arms and legs. Warmth settled low in her belly, and an empty ache formed between her legs.

John.

No.

Taylor wasn't going there.

Not today.

Not tomorrow, either.

He isn't here.

He'll never be here again.

She needed to move on. She'd been with Shannon enough in Dallas to realize that, right? She'd already dealt with the guilt of kissing him, touching him, wanting him...

Hadn't she?

Shannon had told her he wanted her. Had begged her to stop thinking and just be with him. Could she do that?

Tell him she was...ready for that?

Am I?

Her chest burned, but she fought it. Pushed away the hurt and loss.

Emotion was *weak*.

Coming here, to Antioch, had been foolish. Maybe she'd known in the back of her mind that they'd end up here.

She crushed her eyes shut and squeezed Shannon's waist, tightening her grip until he felt more real. More *with* her. Had to swallow a few times.

His ministrations paused and she sensed his lips on the top of her head. "Taylor?" His whisper was warm against the waves of her hair.

She couldn't look up at him. Not when she felt so unstable. Taylor cleared her throat. "If I look at you, I'm going to kiss you."

Shannon laughed, a deep rumble she felt as well as heard. "That's a bad thing?"

"I shouldn't..." *want to.* She couldn't tell him that. It wasn't fair to him. Not this time.

"You shouldn't?" His confusion made Taylor lift her head.

His unusual whiskey-colored eyes darkened.

The desire she read there made her heart quicken.

"Kiss me if you want." He smirked, a sexy little dare she couldn't resist.

She pushed to her toes and pressed her mouth to his. Snaked her arms around his neck and tugged, needing to get closer.

He devoured her, sliding his tongue against hers, plastering her to his chest when he probed deeper, held her tighter, kissed her harder. Tingles shot up and down her body and heat enveloped her.

"God, I want you," Shannon panted between licks, nips and kisses.

Taylor moaned and snuggled into him. She crushed her lips to his again, answering him with her body, since—like in Dallas—she didn't have the guts to speak her desire.

He gripped her waist then slipped his hands to her bottom. Shannon squeezed and kneaded, rocking into her as his tongue dueled with hers. His erection rubbed her stomach with every forward motion and her sex pulsed in answer.

When he pushed her blazer off her shoulders, she let him, even straightened her arms so it could fall to the floor. He tugged her shirt from her pants, and Taylor let him do that, too.

Butterflies took flight from her stomach and clogged her throat. Her voice abandoned her, but it was just as well. She might order him to hurry up, or bark she could undress herself.

Wanting Shannon and having the guts to see it through were two different things. Her body needed him inside her.

What about her heart?

This wasn't about emotion, let alone love. It was

about need.

She told her worries to go to hell and kissed him when he reached for her. Holman and Baker had both told her to relax. So she *would.*

Shannon broke their lip-lock and cupped her face. "Are we on the same page?" His chest rose and fell as he struggled for normal breath.

Taylor nodded.

His amber gaze darted to her throat. "Are you sure?"

"Yes." The word was breathy.

He smiled and her heart flipped. "I told you in Dallas I wanted you, but I've pretty much wanted you from the first time I saw you. Even though Manning warned me about you. He said you were a piece of work." His thumb roved back and forth over her cheekbone and sent shivers darting all over.

She leaned into his touch and rested her hand over his. "I remember when you opened the door for me at that cop bar." Months that felt like years ago.

"Me too."

Their eyes stayed locked for two more breaths.

"Do you think Manning was right?" she whispered.

Shannon started unbuttoning her gray shirt. "Probably." He flashed a lopsided smile that faded as soon as it was born, but he didn't stop moving his fingers. "Does that bother you? What he thinks about you?"

Taylor's heart skipped for a reason other than the man undressing her. She shook her head. Jared Manning hated her—with good reason. It was a canyon she couldn't build a bridge over. She wasn't about to admit that—or the guilt about Pompa. Although, she hadn't had a nightmare in some time. Not since she'd interviewed Joe Pompa, and she didn't want to examine what that meant.

"It'd only bother me if *you* thought badly of me."

Truth.

She cared about what he thought about her. The notion bounced around in her brain. She tried not to fidget as his gaze came back to hers.

Shannon gathered her close, with her open blouse hanging off one shoulder.

Even through his shirt, she felt the heat of his body and craved more. Somehow she hated admitting that, even to herself.

He dipped down and kissed her collarbone, revving her up even more.

"I wouldn't be trying to get you naked if I thought badly of you."

"Don't try."

"No?"

"Do."

He smirked and shoved her shirt away in answer. It fell to the carpet at their feet. "You can put your gun on my trunk."

"Okay." She shivered, but it wasn't from the sudden air brushing her bare flesh.

Shannon's gaze devoured her as hungrily as his kiss did.

Taylor pushed the haze of passion away and reached for coherent thought. "That means a lot to me, you know."

Another truth.

"What?"

"That I have your respect."

"You have a lot more than my respect. I think you're a hell of an investigator. But I don't want to talk about that now."

It was her turn to smirk. "No?"

"Hell no. Get naked."

"You too, Sergeant."

His answering smile was easy and oh-so sexy.

She did some visual devouring of her own when Shannon tugged his tee off and tossed it to the floor. He was just as built as he felt through all that material. She gulped. She'd not gotten a chance to see any of this at her apartment, because she'd run away. Kicked him out.

Taylor shut down those thoughts and focused on him.

Here. Now.

His pecs were dusted with springy dark curls her fingers itched to touch. His six-pack was divided by a line of hair that disappeared into the waist of his jeans.

She wanted to trace it, then follow each defined line with her hands and tongue. Her body prickled and she jolted. Her nipples hardened.

There were two round puckered scars on his torso. Shannon had been shot.

Taylor had heard that before, but didn't want to pry for details. At least, not right now. She just wanted to be with him.

"What're you lookin' at?" he teased. "I don't see *naked* yet."

She blinked and heat kissed her cheeks. "I'd rather watch you," she confessed.

He paused, fingers on his zipper. "Yeah?"

"I like what I see," she whispered.

One corner of his mouth shot up and she wanted to lick him there.

"Special Agent, are you shy? That's not a word I'd have associated with you."

She cleared her throat and shook her head. "No. Carry on." Taylor covered her embarrassment by tugging on her ponytail holder. She rammed her fingers into her hair, pulling her waves loose and down, until they tickled her shoulders and back.

Sucking in a breath, she reached for the hooks on her bra and slipped it off. Her nipples tingled and she fought the urge to cover herself. Her self-confidence had packed bags and moved out, and it was ridiculous.

Shannon was about to see a lot more of her than bare boobs, which he'd seen and touched before.

She avoided his gaze, although she could feel his eyes on her. Undid her belt, slid her holster off, and shimmied out of her slacks, but left her plain black bikini panties on. She set her gun down where Shannon had indicated, at the end of his bed.

When she mustered the courage to look at her soon-to-be lover, he stood in nothing but light gray boxers about five feet away.

"You're gorgeous," he breathed.

Taylor made herself look at him as directly as he was her. Ignored the ludicrous shyness inching up from her gut. She hadn't been a virgin for a long time, so she needed to lose the sudden emotional baggage.

He closed the distance between them and settled his hands on her shoulders. "Are you okay? Still with me?"

She forced a nod. "Just... Been a while for me."

"For me, too." His expression was serious.

"Yeah?" she whispered.

His Adam's apple bobbed. "Yeah." His delectable mouth curved slightly. "I'm glad it's you."

"Me?"

"To end my drought."

A small laugh slipped out, surprising her. She should want to smack him, but she didn't. Taylor smiled. Her neck and her cheeks burned. "I'm glad it's you, too. For me."

Shannon cupped her cheek. "You're even more

beautiful when you smile, Special Agent."

She trembled until he pulled her into his arms. Coherence took a hike, but she didn't know what to say, anyway. She slid her arms around his neck and urged him down for a kiss.

It got heated in warp speed. He lifted her and they both groaned when their naked skin came together. She rubbed her breasts into him. His chest hair tickled, arousing her even more. Taylor's nipples hardened to the point of pain.

He slanted for a deeper kiss and hauled her closer, higher.

She wrapped her legs around him, her sex hitting his with a tease of friction that made her ache all over again. They were still separated by fabric, and it needed to go away.

Her thighs tremored with the effort to hold on to him, but she didn't have to maintain her grip. He laid her on his bed, following her down, resting in the cradle of her body, his pelvis against hers.

His kisses became torment as Shannon left her mouth to trail his lips over her chin, following her jawline and nibbling her earlobe. His hands roamed, cupping her, circling her nipples with his thumbs.

Taylor wiggled and writhed, demanding more without words.

He moved downward, lavishing licks and touches on her breasts.

She yelped when he sucked a nipple into the warmth of his mouth, and she buried her hands in his hair. It was soft, distracting her from what he was doing, because she needed to caress him, too.

He pushed her thighs wider, settling down, kissing and nipping her belly as he went. "You're perfect, your skin tastes made to eat," Shannon murmured. "Like I knew you'd be."

Taylor whimpered when he ran his fingertip inside the waistband of her panties but didn't pull them down.

He inhaled deeply, licking his lips. "You smell fantastic."

She wriggled and pushed at his shoulder. "You're a tease."

He grinned. The dimple in his right cheek was as appealing as he was. "I am?" He slid his hand inside her panties, his fingers brushing her swollen, ready flesh.

She groaned, but his touch was gone as quickly as it'd come. Her body screamed a protest and she tensed. "Noooooo."

"No?" Shannon arched a dark eyebrow. "In these situations, that's usually a bad word." He made like he would lift off her.

She growled and wrapped her legs around his torso. "Don't you go anywhere. Take my underwear off me and get inside me."

He bit his bottom lip as if it was the only way he could fight a smile. Lifted her panties away from her body, then stilled. "You sure?"

Taylor narrowed her eyes and lifted her hips—as much as she could with his weight on her. "Take them off."

He kissed her inner thigh. "If you insist."

"At this point, I don't care if you rip them off."

Laughter filled her ears. "That only works in the movies, or so I'm told."

She giggled—couldn't help it.

What is this man doing to me?

"Whatever works. While you're at it, take yours off, too."

"Yes, ma'am. I kinda like it when you're bossy."

Shannon wore a playful expression. He was even more gorgeous.

Taylor's heart skipped and her stomach fluttered.

Their eyes locked for a hundredth time and she had to swallow again when he grabbed her bikinis with both hands.

He was serious now—his face held an intensity that made her want him even more. Her temples throbbed with her roaring pulse.

Shannon didn't need help to slide the black cotton off one hip, then the other. He seemed as if he would tease, lowering them slowly, but after an audible intake of breath, her hot cop yanked them down and off.

Then stared at her.

Until she wiggled in his bed.

"Damn."

"Good damn?" She cursed her cracked insecurity. Taylor shouldn't care what he thought, but she did. Her body was leanly muscled, shouting her love of running. Because of her chosen form of exercise, her thighs were on the thick side. Muscle, of course, but what if Shannon—

"*Great* damn. You're beautiful." He reached up to tug on her earlobe. "I already told you that, Special Agent."

"Taylor," she whispered. "I don't like feeling distant from you." The words slipped out unbidden, and panic seized her.

Shannon was too quiet.

When she had the guts to glance back into his handsome face, he wore a soft smile. She read tenderness in those amber eyes. Her insides swarmed.

He hovered over her, taking her mouth with the same gentleness of that smile.

The kiss went on, melting into something

languorous and meaningful.

It scared the shit out of Taylor, as much as it made her scorch for him. She tried to control the flow of unwanted emotion and failed to shut it down. Her body ignored her mind's commands to move away from him, get up.

Get dressed.

Leave.

She'd made a reservation at *The Covington*, after all. She had a place to go.

Shannon started to rock, his boxer-clad erection grinding into her, distracting her from the chaos.

Physical demand asserted itself—she needed this. Needed him.

His movement wasn't enough.

She broke their kiss. "I want you and you're still not naked."

He caressed her cheek and flashed a grin, dimple and all. "I'll be right back. Condoms are in the bathroom." He popped up and she shivered, suddenly cold.

Taylor missed him with an intensity that didn't make sense. "Are they still good?" she called. "You said you were...um...having a drought."

Shannon came back to her laughing, holding up a blue plastic strip and waving it around. "They're still good. I checked the date on the box."

"And we need...six?" She arched an eyebrow.

His gaze burned when it landed on her. "Yes."

She sat up, cocking her head to one side. "We'll see. I haven't seen the goods just yet, let alone taken a ride."

Shock rolled over his expression. He threw his head back and chuckled.

She grinned. Weight lifted off her chest, but her heart sped into overdrive.

Shannon stalked to his bed. "I didn't know you had a sense of humor, sweets."

She pushed to her knees to meet him. Took the condoms and dropped them to his dark brown comforter. Taylor rested her hands on his hips, glaring at his boxers. "First of all, take these off." She tugged. "Secondly, don't tell anyone I don't always have a stick up my ass."

He smirked and slipped his arms around her, pulling her into his chest. His mouth landed hard on hers.

The same rush of desire hit, more intense as his pecs flattened her breasts and his large hands claimed her bare back.

Her *everything* somersaulted. Thoughts scattered and she pushed her tongue into his mouth.

Damn, the man can kiss.

She'd never been this overheated for someone. Combustible. Incendiary.

Taylor pushed her hands inside his boxers, caressing toned upper thighs on her way to the curve of his ass. It was toned, too. Firm, but his skin was soft.

Shannon flexed as she squeezed, and he leaned forward, kissing her harder.

She shoved his underwear down to his knees just as he pushed her backward, not giving her a choice but to land on his bed again.

His erection brushed her thigh and her sex answered with a rush of new warmth and a jolt of awareness for good measure. She was wet, overheated and wanting in a way she hadn't ever before. The ache made her feel empty.

He broke the seal of their mouths and his whiskey gaze bored into her. "I want to taste every inch of you, but...now...I need you." Shannon's movements were frantic as he tossed his boxers away. He snatched the strip of condoms, ripped the top one off with his teeth and leaned back.

Taylor stared, running her eyes up and down every inch of his glorious frame.

He knelt on the bed, perching his ass on his heels. His thighs were thick and tight, sparsely covered in dark hair. His erection jutted proudly, and watching him grip himself to roll the condom on did something to her insides.

His sac hung heavy and she wanted to cup him there, stroke his shaft.

He was *beyond* hot.

She opened her arms when he was done, needing to have him against her. Every inch of him over every inch of her.

Their gazes brushed when he descended, then slid a hand between them to join them. There was no hesitation—he filled her with one stroke.

Taylor gasped when he was seated deep inside. The feeling of fullness wasn't unusual—she'd had lovers before—but the perfection, the *rightness* marched her off to war between hauling him closer and shoving him away.

Nerves stole her voice and her breath. Her heart thundered when she felt Shannon's doing the same.

They were completely in sync, even their labored breaths.

"Are you all right?" His demand was strained.

He was holding back, and she hated it.

She wanted *everything* from Sergeant Shannon Michael Crowley.

"Move. I need you to move."

Shannon groaned and buried his face against her neck with the first thrust.

Pleasure jolted. She moaned, and lifted her ass to meet his second. Taylor wrapped her legs around his waist and tilted her hips to take him deeper.

She regretted the condom he wore. Regretted they weren't fully skin-to-skin, as dangerous as that could be, despite her birth control.

"God, Taylor." His breath was warm on her damp skin, and tremors made her hold him tighter. "You're tight. So beautiful…" His last word was a groan when she undulated, demanding more from him.

Shannon gave it to her, answering her every unspoken command as if he was inside her head as well as her body. He kissed and touched her into oblivion, shooting ecstasy all over her form as he moved in and out.

It was almost too much. Orgasm built and receded, teasing, hovering on the edge.

She moved with him, against him, until they were both covered in sweat and panting. Rhythm fell to the wayside but it didn't matter, because it was so good.

Taylor gasped when he pulled back only to slam forward again. Ecstasy sharpened, and her vision danced. Her head spun as the hard jar pitched her over the canyon. Her thighs quivered and her body tightened. She flexed her hands on his slippery biceps—needed to hold on to something.

He groaned and broke their latest kiss. His spine stiffened and he stilled above her. Shannon tilted his head back and whispered her name. His erection jerked inside her as he found release, too.

Shivers raced all over her body, aftershocks of passion that made hard swallow hard and pray for control.

"Taylor, Taylor." He repeated her name, a chant that told her Shannon was as affected by her as she was by him.

Was that good or bad?

She made herself look at him instead of averting her gaze like her cowardice demanded.

When he gazed down at her, he smiled. Then he kissed her until she clung to him, despite her post-climax boneless form.

Taylor had never experienced anything close to being with Shannon.

That's not right.

Is it?

He broke the kiss and pulled back. Concern darted across his handsome face. "What's wrong, sweets?"

"Nothing." She forced a small smile.

He slipped from her body and kissed her cheek. If he didn't believe her, he didn't say so. "Be right back. Gonna clean up. I'll get something for you, too." He headed to the bathroom.

His naked form was graceful...and delicious. Especially the curve of his perfect ass.

Shannon shut the door, and Taylor's gaze darted to the carpet, cataloging the locations of her clothes. Then she glanced at the clock on his nightstand.

Twenty after ten.

"I should go." Guilt threatened to overtake even before her whisper greeted her ears. She'd never checked in to the hotel. She'd have to pay for the room regardless.

She didn't want to leave.

If she stayed, she'd have sex with him again. Maybe tell him she was on birth control and that he could ditch the condoms.

She could be with him *completely.*

Taylor shivered. Dangerous thoughts. She blinked away sudden tears and swiped at her flushed face. Her hair was a tangled mess. Finger-combing did nothing to it, except shoot pain all over her scalp where she pulled. She gave up and covered her face with her hands. Forced one then another deep breath.

"What's wrong, Taylor?" Shannon's low voice was worried, but also an order.

She jolted and swallowed a yelp. Hadn't heard him come out of the bathroom, let alone cross the room.

He sat on the bed but didn't reach for her.

Should I be crushed or relieved?

"I should go." The blurt fell from her mouth and she sucked in air then held it.

He flexed his jaw and met her gaze dead-on. "I want you to stay, if I get a vote." His thigh brushed hers as he settled closer.

Temptation teased and her stomach flipped. Taylor studied his comforter. If she looked at him, she'd kiss him, just like she had earlier.

Strong but gentle hands cupped her jaw and tugged up, forcing her to meet his eyes. "What happened? Why're you retreating all of a sudden? Don't shut me out."

She shook her head.

He didn't release her. "Stay with me tonight. Relax with me. Let me hold you." Sincerity and yearning blanketed his expression. "I know you have nowhere to be until Monday."

Her heart stuttered. Her mind shouted *No*, warning her not to fall into that whiskey-colored gaze. To avoid looking at those full lips she already knew so well.

Taylor's heart told her head to go to hell. Couldn't even muster an emotional shutdown.

Shannon slipped an arm around her, but didn't pull her to him.

She closed the distance to his chest on her own, sliding her arms around him. Shuddered at the warmth of his body against hers, pretending she didn't feel so good in his embrace. When she felt his lips on her temple, her half-hearted resistance fell away.

How could he be so tender, but so hot?

"Yes," she whispered, kissing his pec.

"Yes?" he asked, hooking a fingertip under her chin and tilting up.

"I'll stay with you tonight." She couldn't speak for the rest of the weekend, and she wanted to curse him for knowing she was free until Monday.

His smile made her stomach dip, then dance to her toes.

Shannon claimed her mouth, and Taylor let him, moving in to his kiss and holding on to him with all her might.

Chapter Twenty-Three

Watching her sleep was bittersweet.

Shannon's chest was tight, and his heart thumped hard. He rubbed the spot, before forcing his hands back into his lap instead of giving in to the urge to touch her.

Thick waves of Taylor's strawberry-blonde hair were spread out on his pillow. She lay curled on her side, her knees up high under the blankets, as if she was trying to protect herself even in sleep.

She hadn't been leery of his touch when awake, but now...

Her position made him resist his desire to pull her into his arms. Or tuck her head under his chin and have her arms wrapped around him. He wanted to hold her just as closely. Show her there was reprieve from the evils of the world, from the bad guys they both chased.

When they were together.

Taylor still hadn't told him why she'd come to him, and he hadn't pushed her. She'd said she didn't want to talk about it, had only hinted at a bad day, and Shannon could give her that.

She'd given *him* so much more. Herself.

It'd been better than he could've imagined. The best sex he'd ever had. The second time, she'd told him she was on the pill and he could lose the condom, so he had.

It was probably pussyish of him, but he'd never felt closer to another human being than when he'd been inside her then. His breath had caught, his heart had threatened to beat out of his chest, and he'd just stared into those hazel eyes. Until she'd ordered him to move, just like their first time.

He'd known she was a spitfire, but not how much he'd enjoy her bossing him around in bed. It showed the desperation and desire she didn't—or couldn't—speak. For *him*.

Taylor faced him, his comforter up to her chin. Her pale lashes rested on high cheekbones and her breathing was quiet and even, suggesting deep sleep.

She was perfection, even if he felt the few inches that separated them as if they were miles.

He'd chased her. Now that he had her, he wasn't about to let her go.

Am I being an idiot?

Shannon couldn't compete with a dead guy, and it wasn't a secret she wasn't over her murdered FBI-agent fiancé.

He'd pursued her knowing that. Assuming that, as they got closer, she'd be able to move on.

Was he wrong?

Maybe.

He could only assume her hesitation tonight had everything to do with how she felt about John Murray, and nothing to do with him. It hadn't stopped him from kissing her. Touching her. Taking her.

His head told him to guard his heart. To be smart and not get sucked into those big eyes with their green and gold flecks. Or focus on candid moments when she said things that made his insides mush. Shannon's gut told him that Taylor never meant for those kinds of statements to slip out. Her pink cheeks and avoided gazes confirmed it.

His little FBI agent didn't like *vulnerable*. She was a hard-ass, and he admired her for it. Admired her drive to get the bad guys.

On the downside, was she so mired in work and grief

that she'd never open up? Never be able to show the world the real Taylor? A person he could already see.

His chest ached when she threw up her façade with him. He sighed and rammed his hand through his hair.

Shannon was in serious trouble.

He wanted Taylor Carrigan for keeps.

The feeling was most definitely *not* mutual.

How could they even make it work?

She lived and worked in Dallas. Her current case could take her out of town, from what she'd told him. Until she caught Carter Bennett, there was no telling how many more times Taylor would have to go away—sometimes for weeks at a time.

That he could deal with. It was work. He had similar responsibilities.

His life was in Antioch. He loved his APD family too much to consider leaving. Was a sergeant now. He'd worked his ass off for the promotion. Loved working with the guys and gals on his shift, and Chief was finally noticing him. Lieutenant in a few years was a real possibility.

Then... Cailey and his mom. He couldn't imagine not seeing that kid all the time. Mom wasn't a young woman anymore. She needed help with his niece. He had to stay close to them. After all, he'd bought his huge house with the intent of them living with him when his mom finally decided to retire.

Damn, he'd never imagined falling for a stuffy FBI agent who would jeopardize his plans, make him doubt his obligations.

Shannon's heart skipped.

Had he *fallen* for her?

Was he thinking about Taylor with his heart—not just his cock?

Yes.

Shit.

I love her.

His heart did a Texas Two Step against his ribs, then took a dive for his stomach. He'd fallen in love with a woman not many from his police department even liked. Not that he gave a shit about that.

His *guard-your-heart* plan had given him the finger. *I'm so screwed.*

No matter how hot she was in bed, no matter how she kissed him back, Taylor hadn't had sex with him thinking *relationship*, let alone *long-term*.

He was going to have a hell of a time convincing her otherwise, but he wasn't naïve to the fact it was *his* heart in the line of fire.

She'd shred it without so much as a glance over her shoulder if that was what his little FBI agent thought she had to do to protect herself.

Sure, he'd survive it.

Could Shannon let her walk away?

"Hell no." At least not without giving *them* a real shot.

Taylor stirred, sucking in air and stretching. She arched her back, pushing her bare breasts past the barrier of his dark brown comforter.

His cock shifted.

She blinked as she came around, rolling to her back and looking around as she oriented.

He cursed. Hadn't meant to wake her.

Shannon stilled, tensing in case she freaked out when she remembered where she was. What she'd done with him. The last thing he needed was a gun drawn on him when his wasn't close. The thought made him smirk.

"Shannon," she whispered when her eyes rested on

him.

"Yeah, sweets? I'm right here."

"So far away."

His stomach fluttered and he ordered himself not to get mired down by that soft smile and wistful tone. "I can fix that." He drew her sleep-warmed body to him, shivering at the *rightness* of holding her. Shannon settled back down, hyperaware of every inch of her naked form against his. He couldn't tell her a damn word of what was swirling around in his head.

Taylor snuggled close. Her breath tickled his neck as she sighed.

"I'm glad you stayed." He kissed the crown of her head, then rested his cheek on her soft hair.

"Me too." Her affirmation was muffled against him.

He rubbed her back, reveling in the feel of her supple skin under his fingertips. "What do you want to do tomorrow?"

"You." The word came out breathy.

Shannon chuckled. "Yeah?"

Taylor lifted her head and met his eyes. Her mouth rippled as if she swallowed a yawn. "Yeah. Just you."

A whole day in bed with her? Sign me up for that!

How about Saturday and Sunday, too?

If it wouldn't have dislodged her from his hold, he might've fist-pumped. "Pretty sure that could be arranged."

She smirked, then nestled back into his chest.

He kissed her head again and smiled. Shannon couldn't tell her how he felt about her, but he could damn sure use the weekend to show her.

Something's wrong.

Carter had been watching the apartment building for a week now. The problem was, he hadn't seen Rowdy since that first night with the kid.

Other than the huge bag of money, there was no sign of the bastard inside the apartment, either. No male clothing, or shoes, no signs. No brown F-150 in the lot, or the parking garage, either.

He'd rushed into the massive structure behind a resident who'd opened things with their keycard late one night before the arm had had a chance to come down. Had driven all the levels. He'd seen Camille Bonner's silver Altima in its assigned spot, which corresponded with her apartment number.

Damn, he'd have to go inside the place again.

Change his plans?

The day he'd done his recon, his fingers had itched to take that black bag and count the contents, but he'd left it alone because he hadn't been ready for anyone to know he'd been there.

Missing money would've been a sure sign to his old buddy someone had poked around, even if Rowdy or the woman couldn't put it together *who* had sticky fingers.

But now...

Where the hell are you, Rowdy Vargas?

Carter hated to think his observation efforts these days had been a waste. He wasn't ready for something drastic, like a snatch and grab. Sure, he wanted that money and he'd get it, but he still needed Rowdy to die, too.

How much cash was in that bag?

If nothing else, he needed to get back inside the apartment to count it. Rowdy had always been a hoarder when it came to money from their numerous jobs.

When everyone else burned through their cuts

partying, the guy always had some left, saved, hidden under his bed. He'd joked more than once that someone had to make sure they didn't starve.

Plus, the bastard had scored at least one of their former crewmates' dough when he'd escaped the LA house-turned-murder-house when Carter had gone postal on the traitors.

Had to be a lot of money. It was going to be his.

His cellphone dinged and he glanced at the screen. Only two people had the number of this current burner—Kai and Bubba.

It wasn't his friend in LA.

He curled his lip when he checked the message.

Meeting at the warehouse.

Carter's first instinct went something like, '*fuck off. I'm busy.*' He hadn't told anyone—least of all the asshole crew leader—about his new Phoenix mission.

He sucked in a calming breath and fired back a message asking when he needed to show up. Short and sweet, no smiley emoticon or some shit. Refused to kiss Kai's ass.

The response was quick.

Eight.

Well, at least the dickhead wasn't chatty. He didn't bother answering. Kai knew he'd show. Even if he didn't like what side his bread was currently buttered on...

Well, it's just for now.

He glanced at the time on his burner phone. It was only a few minutes after six. Good, he had almost two hours to get his shit done here, except that was limited, too.

The woman and kid weren't back home just yet, but the times she arrived varied.

Carter *definitely* needed to watch her more before he could make a significant move.

His second sweep of the apartment was as fast and stealthy as the first. The woman must be a neat freak, because nothing was out of place from when he'd been there before.

He looked in all the rooms again, even though there wasn't a real need. His steps were hurried when he went to the third bedroom. Like before, he made sure the money was still there. It was.

Carter whirled around and checked the closet, again confirming there was no sign of Rowdy. He pulled drawers out in the dresser—they were empty, as if ready for the next guest.

Hunkering down, he cursed when his leg gave a protest of the crouch and sent a jolt of agony up his thigh, skirting over his hip and making his spine burn. When he stood, his foot would likely quit on him and dump him on his ass. "Fuck," he whispered.

He could smell the money even before he tugged the duffel closer. The zipper was loud, like last time, but beckoned him. Unlike last time, he'd remembered latex gloves—go him.

Doing a complete count was probably too time-consuming to risk.

He shook his head and shot off a few more mental curses. Carter's gut shouted that the bastard wasn't around. Not staying in the apartment anyway.

Probably not in Phoenix anymore.

Why? No way he knew I found him.

He'd been careful. No one could've seen him

watching the apartment building. Rowdy sure as hell hadn't.

Dammit.

Had his old buddy slipped away from him again?

If the guy was gone, why was there a bag full of money here? Why would Rowdy leave that kind of stash behind? For safe keeping?

It could mean he'd be back. Right?

The sight of the bills distracted him from his tirade. It was mostly Benjamins, but there was a good mix of fifties, too. He made stacks and counted until he passed around forty grand, and the bag was still mostly full. It was deeper than it looked on the outside—no wonder it was heavy as fuck.

He glanced at the time on his phone. He'd been in the apartment for over ten minutes. "Time to go."

Carter dumped the money back in the bag and tugged on the two zippers. When he pushed it back under the bed, he made sure it was in the same position he'd found it.

It was definitely enough to steal. Was it enough to forgo the train hit, or did he need to be a greedy bastard?

He frowned. Should be smart—take Rowdy's stash and take off. Disappear.

Then he couldn't kill the bastard. Not if he had to track him all over again.

Wait... It wouldn't be hard this time.

He went back to the kitchen to check the stack of mail in the sorter. Different envelopes from what'd been there before, but still no clues as to Rowdy's whereabouts.

Carter stared at the refrigerator and that dry-erase board. Nothing had changed.

The phone number was the same.

He smiled. Slowly.

If Rowdy really was gone from Phoenix, there *was* one way to get him to come back.

Chapter Twenty-Four

Her foot slipped out from under her, and she squealed before she could even think, *oh shit*.

Something interrupted her doomed fall to the tile bathroom floor—a strong arm snaked around her naked waist.

"Easy there." His voice was breathless above the shell of her ear, but the tension in his solid forearm betrayed that.

Shannon had caught her.

Thank God.

Taylor couldn't speak. More accurately, she was afraid she'd squeak again. She sucked in air and let her body relax into his.

His chest hair teased her shoulder blades, and a quiver danced over her. Her lower belly warmed and her core answered with a begging throb.

His muscular thighs cradled her ass, the springy hair there tickling her skin, too. He didn't have an erection, but a wiggle or two could fix that.

"Are you okay?"

Shannon jolted her from the desire clogging her brain.

She nodded. Still couldn't talk.

"Are you sure?"

Taylor turned in his arms, sliding hers around his neck. Her heart still hadn't calmed—from the near fall, as well as arousal—so she rested her forehead against his right pec.

Baker had grounded her again—for the second weekend in a row—but this time he'd let her work all day Friday.

She hadn't argued when he'd called her in to break the news late yesterday, which had shocked them both.

The previous weekend with her sergeant *had* given her a moment to breathe—among other things. It'd been hard to leave him last Sunday to go back to Dallas.

In some ways, if she ignored her confusing, chaotic emotions, the sex-filled weekend had allowed her to recharge, so she could better focus on her case.

She was going to get Carter Bennett no matter what.

Eddie had called from LA and given Taylor and her partner the same line of bullshit about working on getting Bubba to talk, but at least the fellow agent had brought the bastard into the office. Locked him up in holding for as long as legally possible when that had failed. Had said he was handling things and would be in touch, soon.

Holman had texted this morning that he had a Saturday meeting with the analysts about Rowdy Vargas' sister, and Taylor was still waiting to hear if there was anything new or helpful.

She'd sought out Shannon's company and ended up in Antioch again. In his arms, in his bed. They'd had sex twice overnight, and she'd gotten up for an early run.

He'd offered a joint shower that would likely be steamy for reasons other than the water. Of course, she didn't have any *no* in her when it came to the sergeant.

His large, calloused hands made their way over her shoulders and down her back. Then up again, in soothing strokes, helping her breathe, helping her thundering pulse return to a normal rate, although she hadn't had the guts to ask him for that.

"You squeaked."

She whipped her head up, breaking the skin-to-skin contact. Mock-glared. "Somehow, I knew you'd give me shit about that."

When Shannon chuckled, she felt it rumble in his chest against her breasts. The vibration made her nipples peak.

"Sorry, sweets."

"Bullshit." The growled curse only made him grin.

Her stomach fluttered and her irritation slipped away, only half against her will. She melted into him, hiding a smile when he kissed her temple, then her forehead. The gentle press of his lips only made her want more.

"Thanks for catching me," she whispered.

"Always, sweets. Always."

She believed him. That scared the shit out of her.

Taylor sucked in a breath. "Water's gonna get cold." She cursed the shake in her words and couldn't look at him.

"Hey." Shannon's whisper made her jump. He guided her chin up, and she wanted to close her eyes, but didn't. "Are you really okay? What happened anyway?"

"I must've slipped on some water or something..." She tried to look down to confirm, but he hadn't released her. "I turned the shower on and backed up. I dunno."

"Be careful next time. You could've gotten hurt." The admonition was gentle, but the caring in his statements made her wince.

She should leave, instead of getting in the shower with him. She'd let him back her against the tile and take her, like he'd done in the very same shower last weekend.

"Hey, you're leaving me again. Stay with me." His gaze was imploring and the emotion she saw there sent her into an even wilder tailspin.

Taylor pushed it all way.

Stay in the here and now.

How he made her feel physically was unmatched.

Focus on that.

"I'm good. Let's get clean."

"Clean? Is that what this is all about? I thought it was about getting inside you."

Arousal roared again, and darted all over her before it settled low, making her sex ache. She flexed her hands on his biceps and had to smile when Shannon waggled his eyebrows.

Non-sexual, self-induced tension lifted and she was able to let go, relax a tad.

Breathe.

Because he'd lightened things, calmed her like he always did.

Taylor was about to let him rock her world.

She cleared her throat. "How about both?"

"If you insist." He chuckled.

She let him lift her into his arms. Wrapped her legs around his waist and moaned when his lips grazed her collarbone.

He stepped into the shower and the warm water cascaded around them. Shannon slid the glass door closed without releasing her or stopping his heated exploration of her skin with his mouth and tongue.

He pushed her backwards until the cool tile met her shoulders and caused a shiver.

Then his body was there, covering hers. His chest warmed her breasts, his erection was poised and ready against her sex, but he didn't join them yet.

The contradiction of the cool behind her and the warmth in front kicked her libido into overdrive. Steam and hot water carried her away.

Finally, he thrust inside her and they both groaned.

Taylor leaned her head back, resting it against the shower wall. She clung to Shannon, kissed him back, and just let go.

Taylor looked so freaking hot standing in his kitchen wearing only his black T-shirt. It fell mid-thigh, and her strawberry-blonde hair was free, down to the middle of her back. Bare feet, bare legs, had never been more appealing.

After their shower, air-drying her natural waves had forced them into tight curls. She was the total package, so beautiful it stole his breath and made his chest ache.

She was making coffee, and the fresh scent tickled his nose as it percolated. Even with the strong aroma of brewing beans, Shannon smelled *her*.

Fresh, clean and familiar. A mixture of his soap and something that was just Taylor.

His mouth went dry and his cock jumped. He'd had her in the shower but it wasn't enough. It'd never be enough.

He shouldn't have pulled jeans on. They were about to get too tight in a certain area.

"Want coffee?" She threw a smile over her shoulder and his heart skipped. The expression on her face was open and rare.

"I love your hair," Shannon blurted.

She arched a pale eyebrow and turned toward him. "Says anyone without naturally curly hair. I hate my curls. I usually brush and blow them out, unless I take time with the flat iron."

"You're speaking girl. I'm unfamiliar." He shook his head and flashed a grin.

Taylor laughed.

He paused, letting the sound ring in his head, and his heart. He had to swallow. Twice.

This was the side Taylor never showed the world. He was damn glad to be seeing it now.

The *real* Taylor Carrigan.

Shannon went to her in two strides and tugged her into his arms.

Her palms landed on his bare chest with a small slapping sound. Her lips parted on a *whoosh*.

As soon as their eyes locked, he dipped down and captured her mouth.

She kissed him back without hesitation, and he was lost.

He slid his hands down her back, cupping her ass, half over and half under the hem of the cotton of his tee. Already hard as granite, he rocked into her and she pressed right back, flattening her small, high breasts into his chest.

Shannon groaned and kissed her deeper, until their tongues merged and desperation took hold.

Taylor slid her hands over his shoulders and around his neck, shoving her fingers into his hair.

He lifted her to the edge of the counter, and she wrapped her legs around his waist, holding him tighter. He pushed up under the shirt, caressing her breasts, teasing her nipples into hard peaks with his thumbs, until she writhed under his touch. Dragging his hands down her belly, he stroked the soft skin below her navel, well on his way to her bare sex.

She broke their kiss and moaned into his ear. His FBI agent nipped his lobe, then nibbled his bottom lip, and spread kisses along his jaw.

Tremors ran down his spine. Shannon panted, trying to order himself to slow down, before he blew in his jeans. The zipper bit into his cock, begging for freedom.

Not long now, then he'd slide home—

"Uncle Shannon?"

Taylor's eyes darted somewhere over his shoulder. Then she froze in his arms. Her cheeks flamed all the way up to her ears. The passionate haze he'd seen in those hazel orbs was gone. They were wide, clear—and mortified.

He took a fortifying breath and ordered his dick to soften so he could face his niece. Shannon closed his eyes for a second before he could turn. He made sure his body blocked Taylor's. He hoped the island obstructed the view of his crotch.

His lover pushed at his shoulders until he stepped forward. Her bare feet slapped the tile floor but she stayed behind him.

He didn't spare her a glance. "Cailey, what're you doing here?" He cringed. Hadn't meant to snap a demand at her.

Knowing Cailey, she'd scream outrage at him instead of crying. At thirteen, one never really knew.

"Um..." Her brow furrowed. Confusion darted across her amber eyes. "Grandma's working today. She dropped me off. You're supposed to take me shopping."

Shit. That's today?

Shannon cleared his throat. His mom had asked him about taking Cailey *last* week, Taylor's first weekend with him.

Right.

He'd endured some Cailey-whining and Mom-nagging and had bought himself a week.

So...it *was* today.

Fan. Tas. Tic.

Cailey tried to peer around him and catch sight of Taylor. Then her gaze narrowed and she glared, perching both hands on her thin jean-clad hips. "You forgot. Didn't you?"

"Of course not."

"Right." Her ponytail flipped as she cocked her head to one side. She rolled her eyes. "I texted you." This was all accusation.

He fidgeted.

Taylor shifted behind him, too.

Shannon could feel her warm breath on his bare back, but she wasn't touching him. He half wished she was. "Sorry, kiddo, my phone's in the bedroom and I was—"

"Busy. Obvi." Her eyes were too knowing for a kid her age.

Tamping down his alarm at the fact his niece knew *exactly* what they'd been doing, he scrambled for words. "I was going to say, I was getting breakfast together."

"Right," Cailey said again. Amusement darted across her pretty face.

He sucked in a breath. Answering to his niece made him feel like he'd done something wrong. Like he was...well...*her* age. "This is Taylor." Shannon grabbed his FBI agent's hand and tugged her forward.

Taylor protested, pulling against him, but he didn't release her.

He didn't take a moment to laugh at her reaction—she'd just throttle him later. He focused on the curious look his niece wore.

Cailey's eyes darted up and down Taylor's petite frame, but the smile that curved her mouth was genuine. "Nice to meet you."

Thank God for Southern manners.

Taylor's expression said it was anything *but*, as far as his niece was concerned. She glared at him, cleared her throat and yanked the black tee down. Then she schooled her expression and offered Cailey a hand. "Nice to meet you, too. Heard a lot about you."

Shannon quashed the smile that hovered. He crossed his arms over his bare chest. He cared about these two females more than any others in the world—besides his mom, of course. What they thought of each other mattered.

Cailey grinned. "Haven't heard a word about you."

Damn kid.

He bit back a groan. "Cails, don't be a brat."

She narrowed her eyes at him and looked back at his lover. At least her smile was pleasant. "Are you going shopping with us?"

Taylor swallowed and shifted on her feet. "Uh…"

"You can, but no pressure," Shannon whispered. Wanted to take her hand, but didn't.

She didn't like comfort in general, and the show wouldn't be good in front of Cailey, even if innocent.

His stomach knotted while he waited for her to answer. He wanted her to say yes.

A day with both his girls might be just the thing they needed. To get closer. So she could see how important his niece was to him and move forward. With him.

With *them.*

"I need new softball stuff. I'm pitching this year. Season already started and I'm kinda behind." Cailey's pride was evident and Shannon threw her a smile.

He was proud of her, too. The kid was acing eighth grade and starred on the JV softball team. She was smart and getting prettier by the year. He'd be beating the boys away—in lieu of shooting them—any day now, and it scared the shit out of him. She already had a cellphone and was texting-crazy.

"Softball, huh? I played in high school," Taylor said.

"Cool!" His niece's face lit up. "What position did you play?"

His FBI agent's shoulders relaxed, but only an inch. She gave a slight smile as Cailey fired off questions about softball and she answered.

"I like her!" Cailey announced, grinning from ear to ear. She shot forward and patted his chest. "Don't screw it up, Uncle Shannon."

Shannon was caught between a laugh and an admonition. He glanced at Taylor.

Her cheeks were bright red again. "Uh, well..." She inched toward the hallway.

"Get a bowl of cereal or something, kiddo. We'll get dress—ready—and we can leave."

Cailey smirked. She hadn't missed his blunder. "I already ate. Meet you in the living room."

Taylor was too silent as they made their way back into his room.

"I'm sorry. I forgot I told my mom I'd take her. Mom got roped into working all the weekends this month." He shut the door and turned the lock. It gave a loud *click*. Not that Cailey would disturb them—it was more for his lover's comfort.

"It's fine." She turned her back to him to don her bra.

Shannon felt a canyon between them.

His gut clenched. He didn't like it. Wouldn't put up with it. Not when she'd been so hot in his arms minutes before.

He crossed the room and took over without a word, knocking her fingers away and fastening the small hooks. "Usually I'm taking this off you, not putting it on," he teased.

Taylor slipped away from him without so much as the smile he'd been going for. She popped her overnight bag on his bed, then tugged a folded red shirt out.

"Hey," he said.

"Hmm?"

"Taylor, don't do this."

She paused, the top still folded in her grip. Finally looked at him. "Do what?"

"If you don't want to go shopping with me and my niece, then don't. Like I said, no pressure. But don't freeze me out. Not after last night. And this morning. And...just now." Shannon offered a smile, hoping she'd relax. Be free with him like she had been before Cailey had busted in.

She closed her eyes. "I'm sorry," she whispered.

He gathered her to him, half expecting her to pull away, but she let him wrap his arms around her.

Taylor sighed into his chest. "I'm not good at this stuff." Her words were muffled against his skin.

Her breath tickled, and he tried to ignore the tremor that shimmied down his spine.

Shannon leaned back and cupped her face. "There's no good or bad. Just breathe. Hang out with me and the brat who already adores you."

She fidgeted, but didn't pull away. "Adores me?"

"Oh yeah. She loves softball. Expect her to talk your ear off about it, and brag about the catch of the season from last year."

"Of the game-winning variety?"

"You got it. Ninth inning, down two runs kinda thing."

Taylor smirked. "I have a few of those times."

"Good, you can swap stories." He brushed his lips over hers, but ended it before he could get swept away.

"No pressure?" The question was low and she looked lost.

He squeezed her into him. "No pressure, sweets. Just

me and a kid. A few hours."

"Okay. I can do that."

"There's the Taylor I know and lo—adore." Shannon cursed his almost slip. There was no way he could tell her how he felt about her and not have her not walk out on him.

The smile she flashed was sweet—and the last thing he'd expected.

Taylor pushed to her tiptoes and planted a loud kiss on his mouth that was over much too soon.

He went with it, caressing her cheek with his thumb after they parted.

Their eyes stayed locked for a moment.

"We'll have fun today," she whispered.

"Sure we will. She can be a brat, but she's a great kid. I love hanging with her."

"I hope I do, too." She slid from his embrace and took a deep breath. "No pressure."

"None, sweets. I promise."

Chapter Twenty-Five

*N*ever mind. This isn't a good idea.

The words died on her lips when the teenage girl's face lit up at the sight of them.

Shannon dropped her hand, looking at her, then at his niece. He ran his fingers through his thick dark hair and rubbed the back of his neck. His expression was uneasy, but only when he looked at her. The smile for his niece was natural.

Taylor tried not to fidget. She swallowed and made her lips curve up when the girl glanced at her.

No pressure.

Chanting Shannon's familiar reassurance did nothing.

He looked delicious in the dark gray T-shirt and light-colored jeans. The shirt hugged his pecs and biceps and the jeans outlined his thighs and the curve of his perfect ass. Not that those were appropriate thoughts with a kid in the room.

Cailey grabbed the remote and turned off the TV. She slid her arms around Shannon's waist. "I didn't hug you yet."

One corner of his mouth shot up as he embraced his niece and dropped a kiss on her blonde head. "Well thanks, kiddo. I missed it."

Taylor wanted to back away. The moment seemed...intimate, somehow.

She didn't belong.

Her lover sent a reassuring smile her way.

She wanted to shake her head and her gut tightened for some reason. The urge to bolt for the front door was almost overwhelming. She half-wished Holman would call and the case would demand her attention.

Should she check in with him about that meeting with the analysts?

They had to find Rowdy Vargas' sister, after all.

"Ready?" Cailey asked, practically bouncing with excitement. She turned to go, no doubt expecting them to follow. "I've never been shopping with Uncle Shannon's girlfriend before."

Taylor jolted.

Shannon shrugged when he threw her a glance, but his mouth twitched as if he was fighting a smile. He made no effort to correct his niece.

She couldn't, either. Her voice had disappeared.

Girlfriend implied *relationship*, and that wasn't what was going on between them.

Right?

It's just sex.

She had to tell herself that.

Ignored the answer that was too-quick—*it doesn't feel like just sex.*

Shannon reached for her hand and tugged. He kissed her knuckles before enfolding her fingers in his. Keeping her warm... Safe.

She sucked back a gasp. Needed to relax or she'd never get through this.

Jesus, what's wrong with me?

Taylor could force criminals—some really bad guys—to do whatever she needed them to. Cuff them. Arrest them. Manhandle them when necessary—even hold them at gunpoint—but she couldn't handle a shopping trip with a thirteen-year-old girl?

"Are you all right?" her lover whispered after he reminded his niece to buckle up and shut the back door to his truck.

She forced a nod. She'd have to be.

"Okay." He paused, staring. "Then..."

"What?"

"Why are you standing here? By the driver's side?"

"Oh." Heat burned her neck and she fought the urge to look down or jump fifty feet in the air. Taylor scrambled to the other side of the Toyota and wrenched the door open.

If he laughed at her, she'd kill him.

Cailey chattered away as soon as Shannon started to back down the long driveway. She talked about everything and nothing, making her uncle laugh along the way.

The more they interacted, the more discomfort clawed up from Taylor's gut. She tried to relax, but her spine was straight and her shoulders ached from bunching up. She sat as far away from Shannon as the bench seat would allow.

He slid a hand to her thigh and she jolted.

When their eyes met at a red light, she muttered an apology. She took a deep breath and told herself to chill out.

"Taylor..."

"I'm good," she said quickly.

Cailey had stopped talking.

She could feel the girl's gaze glued to them. Tried not to twitch. The warmth of Shannon's large hand seeped through her jeans. Her heart skipped, but his touch had the desired effect. She was able to calm. Breathe easier.

"Hey, Cails, why don't you regale Taylor with the tale of your epic save last season?" His amber eyes darted to the rearview mirror, then back to Taylor. He gave a half-smile that had her pulse stuttering again.

Taylor glanced at the kid in time to see the

excitement in her eyes. Her face came to life even before she'd said one word. She found herself smiling back; couldn't help it.

"It was epic! I am awesome."

Shannon chuckled and shook his head. "No ego, either."

"In the slightest," Taylor said.

Her lover grinned and squeezed her thigh like she'd made his day.

As his niece talked, she relaxed more and more. Listened to the eager youth, and laughed at the innocent enthusiasm Cailey exuded. She was so sweet and bubbly, but witty, too, and smart for her age.

She could see the girl's appeal, and as she watched, Taylor teetered from feeling like an outsider to being fully involved in their conversations. It wasn't like they tried to exclude her—quite the opposite—but from one moment to the next, alarm washed over her, as if she really was an unwelcome intruder.

Watching them interact was too real.

Their connection was too strong, more like father-to-daughter than uncle-to-niece. So normal. An ease of interaction and obvious affection that'd been absent in her own family.

Her staid and stoic father never would've teased her like Shannon teased Cailey. Never would've hugged her or kissed her forehead.

Never would've done a lot of things.

This kid meant the world to her lover. He'd told her that, but *seeing* it was different. Seeing it was…everything.

Shannon Crowley wasn't a good man.

He was a great one.

One that sent her emotions into havoc, and no amount of repeating her father's mantra helped. At. All.

He held Taylor's hand as they walked through the huge sporting goods store, and Cailey continued to prattle away, but like her uncle, the girl wouldn't allow her to be an observer.

Cailey asked her questions—and not just about softball. She wanted Taylor's opinion on the equipment she needed, other clothes she wanted, and acted as if she wanted to get to know her.

She didn't know how to take that. Or how she *wanted* to take it.

"Be right back, gonna try these on." She was breathless as she held up two long-sleeved shirts, one pink and one blue, with a similar screen-print on the front.

"You're not getting both!" Shannon called after her but his niece only flashed a grin and disappeared into the fitting room. "Brat will probably get her way."

Taylor laughed. "There's usually someone at fault when a child is spoiled."

"Hey, I don't spoil her!" His forced-protest came with a grin.

She smirked. "Right."

"She's not a bad kid."

"No, not at all. She's...a delight."

He fell silent, and his grin faded into a soft smile that did her insides in. Would've made her legs mush, too, if Taylor had let it.

Shannon was so handsome he took her breath. The word *'mine'* floated in her head, but she banished it.

"So..."

"So what?" She tried to make it a snap, but failed.

"Are you okay with all this?"

What's 'all this'? was on the tip of her tongue, but she was afraid of the answer.

"It's been a good day," Taylor whispered finally,

nodding.

Shannon grabbed her hand and pressed a kiss to her knuckles then squeezed her fingers. "I'm so glad to hear you say that."

Her tummy wobbled and she swallowed, fighting the urge to sway. Couldn't look away from his whiskey gaze, and that scared her to the marrow.

Rage boiled up from Carter's gut, and he saw red. He seethed from the inside out, panting for air. He read the text again, but all it did was make his hands shake more.

He let out a string of curses that would've made the foulest trucker proud, and he squeezed his cell in his palm in lieu of tossing it across his shitty hotel room. If it broke, he'd just have to go through the hassle of the next one set up. Had a bag full of new burner phones but was trying to make them last.

He let out the yell he was holding back then he screamed until his throat was raw.

Some of the anger dissipated, but he was still quaking from head to foot.

"Who does that fucker think he is?" Carter hollered at the walls. "Fuck you, Kai March!"

When he opened his eyes, the red receded slowly. He blinked to clear his vision and made himself breathe.

He was done with that fucker and his crew.

Rowdy's money would have to be enough.

He had most of Bubba's thirty grand left, too. If he disappeared, his Californian friend would just have to forgive him. Or he could wire it back when he got somewhere safe.

First he had shit to handle that didn't involve his ex-teammate or the big car fence.

Kai and his assholes had insulted him for the last time, and he was going to take care of it.

They thought they could throw him out of the train hit after all this time? After dealing with all their shit?

No. Fucking. Way.

He couldn't look at the asshole's text again, but it was burned into his memory.

You're out. We don't need you after all. The deal's off.

Carter had been strung along. Meeting after meeting, where no one had given a flying fuck about his opinion. The last meeting, ten times worse than the first. Had barely sat through it without answering the itch in his trigger finger.

Kai enjoyed ordering him around, having him at his beck and call. Screaming *'jump'* only to have him forced to ask 'how high?'

Now he'd been thrown out?

With only a few days left, and no reason given?

"Fuck that."

He yanked his jacket on and shoved his gun into his waistband.

Carter got in the jalopy and slammed the door. He dug around under the passenger seat and dragged out the box with ammo and extra mags for his H & K.

The magazines were already loaded, but he needed visual—no, physical—confirmation. He palmed two of the four, making sure that they were ready to go, like the one already loaded into his weapon. He always kept a bullet in the chamber, too.

The drive to the warehouse wasn't hurried. He stopped at all red lights and stop signs, and followed the various speed limits, too.

Couldn't risk getting pulled over—the police were still on the *no way* list. He'd never killed a cop, but if he had police interaction, he'd have no choice.

The farther he went, the more resolved he became to kill the whole crew. He'd root around their place, too. Take whatever money he could find. Hoped they'd all be home. Knowing Kai, there was probably another meeting, but this time he'd been excluded.

He didn't bother being quiet about his arrival. Pounded on the side door where he'd always entered the place.

It swung open, and Asshole Number One's—or was it Two, he couldn't keep them straight—eyes went wide. "What d'you—?"

Carter raised his gun and fired, putting his first bullet right between the guy's eyes. Blood spattered, and he blinked when it hit his face.

The body crumpled and he stepped over it.

The warehouse had soundproofing, according to Kai, so he pulled the door shut behind him. He'd contain this situation as much as he could.

Made his way down a winding hallway before he encountered anyone else.

The next two guys were in the living area, lying on the plush white area rug and playing a video game on the big screen like he hadn't just roasted their buddy.

It was a shooting game—fitting—but that might've been why they hadn't paid attention to the shot at the door. There was no way they *hadn't* heard it.

"What the fuck?" Another set of eyes widened when they noticed him.

Carter pulled the trigger and hit the guy on the right in the throat. Pretty *apropos*, since it was the bastard with the scary neck tat.

His body seized and he gargled, rolling over on the carpet. The other guy scrambled for the handgun on the table behind them, but Carter pulled his trigger and hit him in the back of the head before he got there.

The body collapsed, halfway on top of his buddy, his arm stretched out, only inches from the big Beretta.

Where were the rest of them?

He was three for three, direct kill hits, but it was still three loud gunshots.

A bullet whizzed by his head and he swore. Glass shattered from somewhere behind him.

So they know I'm here. Goodie.

Carter darted behind the massive TV. His leg gave a protest, but he ignored it and crouched down. A sore leg was better than *dead.*

He avoided a few more shots behind the big console, but it wasn't good cover. The TV had been hit, and shattered. He fired back, then stopped wasting his bullets and just listened. Needed to locate the rest of the crew and take care of business.

If memory served, Kai had a safe in his office. He'd head there next.

"Carter, I'm gonna kill your ass!" the crew leader yelled from somewhere to the left.

Not likely.

He didn't bother yelling back.

Someone darted in front of him on his way to cover.

Carter fired and the guy dropped. It was the blond computer tech.

Damn.

He felt a half-twinge of regret. The only one to not treat him like shit.

Guy wasn't dead. Started calling for help. For Kai to

save him.

Carter pushed off the floor and cursed at the pain in his leg. He shook it out and rounded the console, taking a shot to finish off Blondie.

His head listed to the right and blood leaked from his mouth. It'd already started to pool beneath his body, slowly creeping across the concrete on its way to the white carpet that was now a red sponge from the other two guys.

"You piece of fucking shit!" Kai fired rounds as he crossed the distance between them.

He dove and dodged, landing hard on his ass underneath the makeshift table they'd always had their meetings at. Chairs he bumped screeched backwards and one fell over. His hip and back throbbed, but he'd avoided getting shot. He grabbed the huge piece of wood and turned it upright in front of him.

Computers and the tech equipment hit the concrete with various thuds and shattering noises. The stacked milk-crates toppled and the plans for the heist floated to the floor.

Carter popped up and fired twice, but he didn't wait to see if he'd hit Kai.

The yell and clang of metal hitting the floor told him he had.

"You. Fucker." The over-pierced crew leader lay in a growing pool of his own blood, clutching his abdomen. He panted and couldn't sit up when he tried.

The blood was dark, almost black.

Good, he'd hit him in the liver.

His eyes darted to the gun, which'd slid about five feet from them, and the black-leather-clad asshole wasn't making an effort to retrieve it. Kai was too busy trying to keep his blood in his big body.

"What's the combination to your safe?"

"Fuck. You." The guy's spittle was red, indicating Carter had maybe nicked his lungs, too.

"Pretty sure it's a number, not a phrase." He smiled and raised his forty. "You can tell me, or I can get your sorry ass up and take you to your office with me."

Kai laughed and more red dribble and pink foam formed around his lips. "Do you think I'm afraid of you now?" he panted. His chest was heaving as he struggled for breath.

"Yeah, yeah, yeah." Carter gestured toward the office with his gun. "Just tell me what I need to know and I'll leave you...to rest."

"Fuck you, Bennett."

He rolled his eyes. "All I wanted was some dough. Only a few more days, then I would've been out of your life. So, really, you can take the blame for this...turn of events."

The asshole laughed again, and sputtered more blood. His head hit the ground and he rolled to his side, groaning. "Bubba...won't...like this. We go...way back."

"I'll apologize. The safe."

"It's open, you fucker." This was clearer than Kai's previous gasp. His eyes threw daggers at Carter.

"Thank you." He raised the H & K and pulled the trigger.

Kai's body jerked. More crimson spatter hit Carter's legs and shoes.

Shit.

It was going to take him hours to clean himself up.

He shook his head and looked down into the man's unseeing eyes. "Now you can rest." Carter made his way to the office.

The safe was about five feet tall, and about as wide. Kai hadn't lied—the heavy door was ajar.

He pulled it open and took a double take at the neatly stacked bills. There were guns and ammo, too. The first thing he grabbed was three boxes of forty caliber bullets. He shoved them, and all the money, into a red bag that'd been on the floor.

More for his cause. Good. Like Rowdy's money, he'd count it later.

When he got back to that apartment and had a little talk with Camille Bonner.

Chapter Twenty-Six

W yoming was balls-freezing cold, even though it was almost spring. Damn, he should've picked another state. The snow crunched under his brand new shitkickers as Rowdy made his way back to the little cabin he'd rented dirt-cheap.

The old woman who owned the place hadn't batted an eye when he'd paid for three months with cash, more than she'd asked, so he could be left alone.

She'd even directed him to the store where he'd gotten enough supplies—including a cord of firewood—to lie low for most of that pre-paid time.

He'd needed the wood, too. The cabin was old school with a *capital O*, with a wood-burning stove to heat the place.

The old woman had told him she'd always meant to get gas service installed, but the place was too remote and it was too expensive.

Its only *'luxury'* was indoor plumbing, but she'd cautioned him about pipes freezing. No gas, no hot water. She'd told Rowdy if he wanted a hot shower, he was welcome to come to her place, which was a few miles down the road.

No thanks.

He'd heat up water on the stove and make do.

If he managed to keep all his tender parts in the time he'd be there, he might consider paying for the install himself.

So far, the wood stove was adequately heating the two room building, though cooking food was a bitch.

The little general store even had burner phones, so

he'd bought one and slapped some minutes on it.

Luckily the phone worked at his new home, but he'd been warned by the old woman and the guy at the store that service could be spotty, especially when there was any kind of weather activity.

So far so good on the calls he'd made, though there'd only been two. He'd told Cami he was safe, but not where he was.

She'd begged to know more, but at least she hadn't sobbed. He'd even talked to Devon, and managed not to cry like a pussy when his nephew had wavered and the little guy had admitted missing him.

Rowdy missed them both, too.

He'd promised to check in at least once a week, and he'd stick to that. Didn't have anything better to do, after all.

Maybe he could take up hunting. God knew there were no cars for him to work on around here. Fixing and suping up cars—and stealing them—were about the only things he'd ever been good at, but he was done with all that.

He'd told his sister the truth. The crap with Carter aside, he'd been wanting out for some time. He'd just never had the balls to broach the subject with Joe.

Rowdy sucked in frigid Wyoming air and looked up at the bright sky. Snow had stopped falling, but more was due later that night.

He scanned the woods behind his new temporary home. No movement there now. He'd seen a rabbit or two the other day.

Rowdy whirled, looking at his truck, which was parked inside the small gated area around the cabin. His gaze followed the fence all the way down the long driveway. At least he'd see someone coming long before they got up to the cabin itself.

The gate and fences were made of rough logs and some of them needed attention. Maybe he could help the old lady with maintenance around the place. He needed to do something, or he'd go crazy.

He puffed out air to see his breath. His nose burned, it was so cold.

Damn.

The jacket he'd bought was down, and kept him warm, but his jeans weren't keeping his ass and thighs from freezing. The air moved right through the denim.

Maybe he should get a dog. He hadn't had one since he was a kid, and the general store had massive bags of dog food.

Rowdy wrenched the cabin door open and slid inside. The wood stove was going strong and the heat enveloped him.

The place already looked messy and lived-in; his stuff all over the place. He'd bought new clothes as well as bedding and supplies for living in what he considered close enough to be the Arctic.

He shed his jacket and hung it on the coat tree the old lady had given him.

An unfamiliar ring sounded and it took his brain a few seconds to catch up.

His new burner phone.

There was only one person with the number.

Rowdy dove to the end table right inside the room's door, next to the rustic couch. He hadn't taken his phone outside for his property recon.

The little table shook with the force, but he closed his fingers around the phone before the second ring ended with the barest glimpse at the screen.

"Cami, what's up?" His heart hammered when the

response wasn't immediate.

Something was wrong—he'd told her not to call unless it was an emergency.

"*Camille* is so much prettier than *'Cami'*, doncha think?"

The familiar voice froze Rowdy's blood. Tremors chased each other down his spine, and his heart plummeted to his gut and stayed there. "Where the fuck is my sister?"

The phone number on the caller-ID had been Cami's landline. In her apartment.

Carter laughed. "Mystery solved, thanks."

He swallowed and gripped the phone so tight his fingers burned, shooting pain over his knuckles. "If you hurt them, I'll kill you."

His former teammate's laugh was maniacal this time. "Oh, really? If you intended to face me, why've you been running from me for months?"

"I. Will. Fucking. Kill. You." His whole body began to shake. He was days—maybe more than a week with the snow—away from Phoenix.

Rowdy couldn't get back easily. There was no airport close to him, and he didn't have a valid ID to fly, not legally anyway.

Panic rose and took a bite.

Helpless.

"Oh, the way you greet an old friend, Eric."

"Fuck you, Carter."

"No thanks. But your sister, on the other hand... She's a hot little piece of ass. So, maybe. Definite possibility there."

"If you touch her—"

"And just who's gonna stop me? You're not in Phoenix anymore." The asshole's laughter filled the airway again, like Carter was having the time of his life. "Just *where* are you, my old friend?"

Rowdy sucked in a breath and hoped like hell the murderer hadn't heard him. How did Carter know he wasn't there anymore?

How the fuck had he found Cami?

"A doctor, huh? Handy to have one of those in the family. How come you been hiding her all these years?"

His head spun. He didn't have anything to say, so he didn't answer. He knew the dickhead well, and if he begged for Cami's life, Carter would kill her with a smile on his face.

What about Devon?

Would the bastard leave his nephew alone?

"Are you there, Rowdy? What's wrong? You're not very talkative." This had a pouty edge, like the sonofabitch was five.

"Where are you?" he managed to get out.

"What d'you mean? Didn't you recognize the phone number? I'm at Cami's place, of course." He sounded was bright, like he'd just shared the best news ever.

Rowdy crushed his eyes shut. "Where's my sister?" His voice broke.

Broken was pretty on par for how he was feeling, but he didn't need Carter Bennett to know how freaked the fuck out he was.

"Oh, no worries. Cami and me will have a fab evening when she gets home."

"No."

"Oh, yes, I have so much fun planned. Thanks for the dough, too. It took a long time to count. I had to make myself a sandwich." The fucker whistled. "I gotta say, two hundred thou, well, you're a very generous brother."

"I'm coming for you. I'm going to tear you limb from

limb. Cut your balls off and feed them to you."

Carter laughed again, as if Rowdy had delighted him. "Don't make promises you can't keep." His tone was the opposite of the previous glee, now deadly serious.

"Oh, I'll have no problem keeping it," he snarled.

"Bring it." The asshat took an audible breath. "We'll have a *blast* waiting for you." This was said in that light, happy tone he'd carried for most of the conversation.

Then the line went dead.

Rowdy dropped the phone and went to stomp it, but he stopped himself. This number was the only one Cami had.

The only way she could get a hold of him.

"Cami!" he shouted. He quickly dialed her cell. *Voicemail.* "Fuck!" The second and third call also went right to her recorded message.

"*You've reached Dr. Camille Bonner. I'm unavailable at the moment. If this is a medical emergency...*"

"Yeah, yeah, hurry." He gestured with his hand, as his sister droned on to call 9-1-1 and she'd return the call, even the "*Have a Blessed Day.*" His nerves pretty much had free rein over his body and Rowdy didn't give a fuck that he was alone and no one could see him.

The beep took forever and he sucked in another breath so he could talk. "Cami. Don't go home. Do. Not. Go. Home. Get Devon and get the fuck out of town. I mean it. Call me as soon as you get this, but please God, don't go—"

A loud *beep* cut him off and the phone hung up, like his message was too long.

He dialed her number again.

"*I'm sorry. The voicemail box for the person you're trying to call is full. Please try your call again later.*"

The phone went dead again.

"Fuuuuuuckk!" Rowdy jumped up and down since he couldn't shoot or stab something, as much as he pictured doing that very thing to Carter's smug face.

He glanced over his shoulder. It was almost six. If Cami was off rounds, she'd be on her way home after picking Devon up right now, which could be why she hadn't answered.

Rowdy dialed her number again, and when he got the same message, his eyes actually teared up.

Carter would get to his sister and he was too far away to act.

His nightmare was coming true.

It's all my fault.

He clenched his jaw until agony jolted up and down into his teeth.

Rowdy stared at his multifaceted reflection in the cracked mirror hanging outside the little cabin's bathroom.

There was only one thing he could do now.

Chapter Twenty-Seven

T he sun crested the horizon, and Taylor slowed her furious pace, breathing in the crisp April air so it burned her lungs and watered her eyes.

A glance at her watch told her it was barely seven.

She scanned the residential area that was so opposite to where she lived in downtown Dallas. Peaceful, not a car moving. Not even any people.

Road noise outside her apartment windows was the norm—Dallas never stopped, even on a Sunday morning.

Shannon liked to run in the morning, too. Last night, he'd told her they could go to the track at the high school, which was open to the public during certain hours.

I should've waited for him.

She just...couldn't.

Had to get out. Breathe.

This was her third weekend banned from work. Like last time, Baker had let her work all day Friday.

Her third weekend in Antioch. With Shannon. In his arms, in his bed.

Like the previous two weekends, she'd sought him out.

Taylor felt...everything, and it was killing her.

She'd had to get away from him, even for a little while. She'd head back to his place soon, where she'd snuck out of his bed over an hour ago.

She didn't know the total distance she'd run, but she'd pretty much memorized all the houses on his block—and the three surrounding it. She'd run the whole area three times.

The harder she'd thought—the harder she'd *felt*—the

faster Taylor had made her legs move, until her glutes were going to revolt. Or, worse, she'd tear a hamstring or a ligament in her knee.

Emotion is weak.

Her head spun. No matter how many times she repeated her father's favorite saying, her head rejected it now.

Get real, at least with yourself. It's not your head that has issues.

She slowed to a jog, avoiding Shannon's street one more time. She'd do another round of the street behind his, then head back.

Right?

No choice.

It wasn't like she could leave, with all her crap in his house. She'd left her keys inside intentionally, in case cowardice took too big of a bite to resist pulling an escape. The idea of heading back to Dallas *hurt* somehow.

He'd been asleep when she'd dug yoga pants and a running shirt that was supposed to help regulate her body temp from her bag.

She'd stared at his naked form with every article of clothing she'd pulled on.

Shannon had been lying on his side, his comforter half around him, and half over him. One powerful thigh had been exposed, and part of his fabulous ass visible.

His dark hair had been mussed, sticking up and out, a chaos that was contradictory to his peaceful sleep, but endearing. One muscular arm had been over the blanket, as if he'd been too warm with her beside him.

Taylor had forbidden herself from going around to the other side of the bed to see his face. Her feet had carried her there anyway, and she'd studied him, so gorgeous in repose it'd taken her breath.

She hadn't needed to touch him to feel him.

She could remember every second of their time together, and not just this weekend.

Every caress, every kiss. Every stroke of his body moving over hers.

It was soldered into her brain.

And it was a problem.

More than a problem.

She no longer saw John's deep brown eyes when she closed her own. Taylor saw amber ones.

It made her feel guilty as hell.

Rounding the corner, she took a deep breath that had nothing to do with physical exertion. Her body was pretty much warmed down. Her workout was done and she was at a walk now. Her legs and even her hips throbbed.

She stared down the street. Shannon's house was only three or four away now, yet her steps slowed even more.

Her renegade heart, on the other hand, flipped her off and sped up, as if she was still at a full run.

Figures.

A part of her wanted—needed—to see him. The other part wanted to say '*fuck it all*' and hotwire the Charger. Hightail it back to Dallas.

Heh, that'd be a great report.

"Why exactly did you hotwire your government-issue vehicle?" She could hear Baker in her head.

Taylor rolled her eyes.

She'd never been a fan of playing coward, and today wasn't an exception. She quickened her step. Made herself imagine walking back into Shannon's room. Even crawling back into his bed. Although, a shower first might be good—

Her cellphone rang and she jumped before she could mount the first step to his front porch. She actually screeched her startle aloud, then growled at herself.

Seriously?

Surprise washed over her when she glanced at the screen. It wasn't Shannon, whom she'd half-assumed it'd be.

"Hey, Holman, what's up?" she said by way of greeting.

"Oh, hey. I expected voicemail. I didn't wake you?"

Her partner's voice was familiar, pleasant, and helped her focus. For the time being, anyway.

"Nah, I was out for a run."

"Damn, you really never do take it easy, huh?"

Taylor paused. Yes, she did, if hot sex all night for the last two nights counted. Not like she'd explain that to Alec Holman.

"Carrigan?"

She jerked, then cursed herself for only the fifteenth time in the last hour. Maybe the non-answer had taken up too much time. "I'm here. What's wrong? You calling me on a Sunday before eight a.m., when Baker won't let me work, isn't good."

"Well, it's good and bad, actually. And you can definitely work."

"Yeah?"

"We got something. A *big* something. Rowdy Vargas called me."

Taylor blinked. Her mouth went dry. She couldn't have heard him right. Her heart slid into overdrive, and it had nothing to do with her lover. "Wh-wh-what?"

He chuckled. "Wow, I made you stutter. Never thought I'd see that, or hear it, as it were."

"Bite me. Details, now." Her command was hard and

she gestured with her hand, even though her partner couldn't see her.

"We can chat at the airport."

"Airport?"

"Yeah, we need to go to Phoenix. Can you meet me at DFW in about thirty-five?"

She did the math in her head. It would be an hour or more to get to Irving, where Dallas-Fort Worth Airport was. That was if she left this second. And Shannon... Her heart skipped. "Actually...I—"

"You're not in Dallas, are you?"

Taylor closed her eyes. She didn't want to know how much her partner knew about her weekend getaways. Nothing *she'd* told him, for damn sure. "No." The word came out in a whisper, and she cringed.

"No biggie. Get there when you can. Text you flight info. The Phoenix office is covering for us until we get there."

"What are we walking into?" Her gut clenched, as if anticipating the worst.

"Vargas told me where his sister is. Here's the kicker—Bennett's in Phoenix, too."

"Shit."

"I know. Be safe, see you soon."

"Not so fast, tell me everything. Now."

He laughed again. "I knew I wouldn't get away with knowing something you didn't."

She didn't rise to his barb. Her silence was cue enough for him to finish, and she didn't have to wait for her partner to get her up to speed.

Too bad what they knew didn't make her feel any better.

Holman ended the call and Taylor stared at the screen of her phone, then thumbed it clean, wiping away her face-print and the moisture from her sweat-damp hair.

Her heart thundered all over again. Bennett was finally in reach, they just had to find him. She swallowed, looking up when she heard the door close.

Shannon padded toward her, feet bare, wearing nothing but a pair of low-slung jeans that made her libido light up. He had a steaming mug in one hand and a smile on his handsome face. His dimple was on display, too.

She'd expected him to be cross with her for taking off, but his expression was open. Eager to see her, no admonition in sight.

Taylor wanted to run up the four steps and throw her arms around him. Press her mouth to his and beg him to take her back to bed. Apologize for leaving him. Make love to him again. Shower in his arms afterward, and whittle the day away enveloped in him.

Now she didn't have time. She legitimately had to go—work called, literally. She'd never been torn over work before, and didn't like the taste it left in her mouth.

She had to tell him, but didn't want to shatter that particular look on his face. Not before she kissed him one more time.

Taylor closed the distance between them and stood on tiptoes to press her mouth to Shannon's. It was a quick thing that made him grin when she pulled away, but that only washed pangs of regret over her whole body.

"Morning, sweets."

"It's too chilly out here for no shirt and no socks or shoes."

What the hell did I just say?

She shook emotion away when it hit her chest and resisted the urge to swipe at her cheeks when her vision blurred.

Tears? Really?

His chuckle broke off and he set his coffee mug on the thick porch railing. "Taylor, what's wrong?"

She averted her gaze.

Warm, calloused hands surrounded her cheeks, forcing her chin up. "I was going to tease you about not wanting to take advantage of the view..." His words trailed when their eyes locked.

Taylor managed a smirk. "I did enjoy the view...and the kiss."

The ghost of a smile curved his lips up. "Tell me what's wrong, sweets." Shannon whispered, but it was an order nonetheless.

That should have irritated her, but it didn't.

"Holman called. I have to go."

"Oh." His Adam's apple bobbed, but his gorgeous whiskey-colored eyes never left hers.

"To Phoenix, so I have to go right to DFW. He's gonna meet me."

"Wow. How long will you be gone?"

"I don't know." She wanted to say more, but what, she didn't know. Her body ached. "We...got a big break."

She wanted Bennett behind bars, but she didn't want to leave Shannon.

Even if that was stupid, because it wasn't forever.

Was it?

Taylor shouldn't tell him about her active investigation, but she'd already shared more than she should've, so the words tumbled out, giving her lover a brief version of what her partner had told her.

Shannon sighed and she couldn't help but notice the rise and fall of his muscled chest. "Well, do what you gotta do. Go get that asshole. Just...be safe."

It was her turn to swallow, and she cursed the rising

mix of feelings. He never pressured her, and this was no different, of course.

That made her feel worse, somehow.

She tugged free of his hold, but she couldn't back away from him like she should. Taylor shot forward and wrapped her arms around his middle. Buried her face against his bare chest and held on with all her might.

He laughed. "Hey, I need to breathe." He rubbed her back, like always. As if it was automatic on his part, but she didn't want to need his comfort.

She lifted her head and met his gaze.

I don't want to leave you.

Taylor couldn't say it.

"I'll be here when you get back," he whispered, as if he'd read her mind. "I'm only a phone call or a text away."

She smiled through her stupid, weak-as-shit tears. Weight lifted from her shoulders and chest at his carefree but sincere expression.

Maybe leaving wouldn't be so bad, if she had Shannon to come back to.

The phone rang the moment Taylor dragged her bag off the conveyer at baggage claim.

Holman was still waiting for his to come around.

She'd brought the clothing she'd had at Shannon's— it only included one work outfit, which she'd worn on Friday. Needed to find a hotel with laundry facilities or go buy some clothes. Wearing casual clothing to work might be okay with some FBI offices and bosses, but it was against her programming.

Her partner had given her shit about wearing jeans when they'd met up at the terminal, but a glare had snapped his mouth shut. It hadn't dispersed the twinkle in his blue eyes or his smartass smile, though.

She let the call go to voicemail—she'd check messages and get caught up when both she and Holman were situated.

The phone screamed her ringtone again.

"Geeze," she muttered and dug it out of her pocket. She answered without looking.

"Taylor." Eddie sounded breathless, urgent.

"What's wrong?"

"I called you a million times. Holman, too."

"We were on a plane to Phoenix."

Her partner joined her, rolling a small black suitcase behind him. He caught her eye then looked down at the screen of his cell.

"Good, you're there," Eddie said at the same time her partner exclaimed, "Shit!"

"Yeah. We just landed. Tell me what's wrong."

Holman was scanning whatever was on his phone. His eyes were wide and his shoulders tight.

It was bad news.

Of course.

"I got Bubba to talk."

Taylor's heart skipped. "Tell me."

"He 'fessed up that he sent Bennett to an old friend who runs a crew in that neck of the woods. Kai March. You know the name?"

"No, but keep talking."

"I sent two guys from the Phoenix office over to the address Bubba gave me. Evidently it's a huge warehouse on the outskirts of the city."

"And?"

Holman's phone rang, distracting her from her call.

Her partner answered and put it to his ear.

She tracked him as he started to pace. Unlike her, he

was dressed for work, in a navy suit.

The tailored jacket made his shoulders seem as wide as he was tall. His back was taut and his jaw clenched. He kept his volume low and listened more than he spoke.

Great. More bad news.

"They found a shitload of stolen cars inside, on display. It was definitely their home base," Eddie droned on.

Taylor tried to focus on her call, but she needed to be prepped for the bad news her partner was about to hit her with.

They made eye contact, then his gaze darted away.

"...five bodies."

She plugged back into Eddie's call. "What?"

"Five. Bodies. Kai March and his whole crew, evidently. Sound familiar?"

"Was Bennett there?" she asked, but knew the answer already.

We aren't that lucky.

"No. According to Bubba, and confirmed by plans found on scene, they were going to hit a train of Hummers, but it won't happen now, obviously."

"Dammit. He killed them all?"

"We surmise. They're over there now with the cavalry, and Crime Scene, Phoenix PD. There's no sign of Bennett now. Have you made contact with Crawford or Hamilton? They went to the warehouse."

"Not yet, you were my first call. I need to call the office and see what happened at the sister's apartment."

"No need," Holman said. He was off the phone, standing beside her.

"Eddie, touch base with you later."

"Okay, keep you posted with what else I can get from Bubba."

Taylor hit '*end*' and met her partner's eyes. His expression was tight, grim. She sucked in a breath and squared her shoulders. "Hit me."

"The sister's apartment was empty, but there were signs of a struggle."

"Shit."

"Vasquez briefed you about the warehouse?"

She nodded. "That's what your text was about?"

"That and the voicemails."

Taylor glanced at her phone. She had several missed calls and a few texts, too. "Shit, shit, shit. This isn't what I imagined."

Holman shrugged, but his mouth was still a hard line. "You want to meet Crawford and his partner at the warehouse, or Agents Avery and Townsend at the apartment?"

Chapter Twenty-Eight

t had been *days*.

Days that felt like weeks.

Taylor was going crazy. The sitting. Watching. *Waiting* was killing her.

She'd gone back out to the warehouse just to have another look while they waited for Rowdy Vargas to get to Phoenix.

Unfortunately, they had no choice but to let that bastard Carter Bennett dangle the whole damn FBI like a carrot on the end of a stick in front of an eager rabbit.

He didn't even know he was doing it, since he didn't know they were involved. That just made it worse.

Bennett kept calling Vargas' burner phone, but he was far from stupid, only using other throwaway phones that were virtually untraceable. So far it'd been three different numbers, according to Vargas. None had been repeated, so he either had some sort of number scrambler or an endless cache of phones.

Vargas had called her partner every time he'd received a call, but Bennett knew he was traveling and hadn't revealed his location just yet.

He promised he would the moment Vargas hit Phoenix. His endgame was still Vargas in a body bag, and as far as Bennett knew, things were going his way.

They'd had Vargas demand proof of life of Camille Bonner, and she was alive but scared.

Bennett didn't have her six-year-old son. He was safely with his father, which had been a happy accident, according to Vargas.

She'd just dropped the boy off for a visit the night Bennett had grabbed her. She'd fought him, but he'd overpowered her and taken her...somewhere.

The FBI was scrambling, searching everywhere, but hadn't had any luck on the location. They'd looked from seedy hotel to other apartments in the area—anywhere he might be. Bennett knew how to evade and hide, the bastard.

"Vargas is here," Holman called.

Taylor looked up from the computer she'd commandeered in the Phoenix office. She'd been filing a report about her observations at the warehouse.

Her partner had been in the conference room with four other agents, looking at the boards they had up regarding their case.

She tried to stay out of there unless they needed her. Photos of all the people Bennett had killed were posted—the ten they knew of, including John.

Taylor couldn't look into his dark eyes or see the smirk he'd worn in his FBI ID photo. He'd been so handsome, and he was...gone.

Shannon's not gone.

She startled. Shoved away the thought and cleared her throat, straightening her spine. "Is he coming up here?"

Holman nodded. "Should be pulling in any minute now. I'm going down to get him. Meet in the conference room in a few?"

"Sure."

"We're going to have him call Bennett and tell us where he's at. Bennett left a number on the last call. Then it's go-time."

Taylor nodded. "Sounds good."

Finally.

She logged off the computer and pushed back from the desk. Her cell dinged, catching her attention. She'd left it next to the desk phone, and would've likely walked out without it.

How are you today?

She read Shannon's message three times. Her stomach dipped and emotions clogged in her throat. They'd been in Phoenix a week.

Taylor *missed* him.

Dammit.

She pressed her thumb over his number and put the phone to her ear before she lost her nerve.

"Hey. I didn't expect you to call, but I'm glad you did." His familiar voice washed over her, but it was off somehow.

"You okay?"

"Exhausted. Almost done with seven p. to seven a. shift and I can't wait to get off. I'm whooped. Just crawled into bed."

She shut her mind down when it immediately inserted memories of his bed and them entwined in it. Her body warmed, and she squirmed on the end of the chair. "Oh. I'll let you go, then. Sorry."

"Taylor." Her name was all warning. "You can call me any time, any place. I thought we were past that?"

She sucked in a breath and closed her eyes for a split-second. "Okay," she whispered.

"Okay," Shannon echoed.

"I just needed to hear your voice." The truth tumbled out and she cursed.

"I'm glad."

Taylor could hear his smile, and couldn't help but smile back.

"Carrigan! We're ready!" one of the Phoenix agents

yelled from the conference room.

"Hey, I gotta go," she said.

"Are you running away from me?" Shannon was soft and serious, but somehow hesitant, too.

She was torn between doing just that—by hanging up on him—and reassuring him. "No, I promise." Reassurance won out. Her heart stuttered, and she stood so she wouldn't fidget. "We're going to get Bennett today. Or, I should say, we hope to." She wanted to tell him more, but people were waiting on her.

"Oh wow. Go. Get that bastard."

She smiled again. "I will."

"Taylor."

"Yeah?"

"Be safe. Come back to me."

Her breath caught, but she nodded. Then called herself an idiot because Shannon couldn't see her. "I will." Nerves flipped her belly and Taylor ended the call. She couldn't deal with an answer from him. Needed to keep her head in the game.

She pocketed her cell and headed to the conference room.

Carter laughed as he hung up one of his dozen activated burner phones. He tossed it on the table in the hotel room, against the wall.

Camille Bonner whimpered from the bed.

He threw her a look, then beamed. "Your brother'll be here shortly. Would you prefer I killed him in front of you, or not?"

Tears welled and spilled. She was really a stunner, with her mocha skin and vivid green eyes. Tall and slender, and her curly hair was tamed in a ponytail, but only because he'd been feeling generous that morning, and he'd let her freshen up.

He'd gagged her with a handkerchief. Hadn't wanted to, but she wouldn't quit screaming. Not even for a few moments when he offered her food. He'd made sure she sucked down water through a straw—couldn't have her passing out on him.

This was day five of their time together, and Carter was disappointed overall.

She hadn't warmed to him, and despite his threats to Rowdy, he wasn't a rapist. Besides, who wanted to have sex with someone bawling?

He wasn't into that shit. Of course, *she* didn't know that.

He'd felt her up for show, but her fear didn't get him hard.

"This will be over soon. As soon as your brother's dead I'll go, and you'll never hear from me again." Carter looked at his money, sitting on his bed in all its glory. Had close to half a million, including what he'd taken from Kai's warehouse.

Part of him said to forget Rowdy and move on.

The other part needed revenge for a betrayal that never should've happened.

"I'll even untie you," he told Camille.

She wiggled on the end of the bed and her eyes flashed.

He had a feeling, if her hands weren't tied behind her back, she would've flipped him off. Carter had tied her legs, too.

She'd kicked his bad leg in one of her two runaway attempts. Made his arm burn, too, because it'd taken a lot of strength to restrain her. Bitch was stronger than she looked.

"Look," he growled. "I haven't hurt you. I tried to feed you. Just sit pretty and do your part, and this'll be over soon."

Her emerald eyes shot daggers at him.

He paced the room, ignoring her. Rowdy had said he was in Phoenix. He'd be there soon. It would be over, and Carter would be on his way.

Things were going as planned.

Rowdy wasn't stupid enough to involve cops—he was a fugitive, too. Their car stealing exploits had left charges in several states, which is what'd involved the FBI in the first place.

Carter had watched the news; been stalking it really. They'd found the bodies in the warehouse, but the story was short, cryptic even. They didn't have a clue it was him.

The knock on the door made him jump. He pivoted and drew his forty. Pain bit back, shooting up his leg and into his hip at the fast movement, but he ignored it and crossed the room in three strides. Looked through the peephole and saw Rowdy standing there, bag of money in hand as instructed.

He darted to the window and discreetly scanned the parking lot, peeking around the thick drapes. No cars on this side of the building, except the crappy F-150 Rowdy was driving. He'd take that on his way out. The POS Bubba had given him was as far from the second floor hotel room as he could get it. Carter opened the door only a sliver. Enough for Rowdy to enter.

The guy dropped the bag as soon as he shut the door.

He aimed his H & K and Rowdy's hands shot up. "Weapons?" he demanded.

"No."

Rowdy Vargas looked like shit. He'd lost weight, his normally olive complexion was sallow, and his eyes were sunk-in. He wore a red baseball cap and his beard had to be a few days old, maybe more. His jeans were dark, as was his jacket.

The guy's gaze shot to the bed. "Cami," he breathed.

She whimpered and fidgeted, pulling against her bindings.

"It's going to be okay, Cami," Rowdy said.

"Sure it is." Carter kept his voice even. "You die, she lives, I leave."

Rowdy swallowed, making his Adam's apple bob. "As long as she lives, I'm fine with that."

Camille sobbed through her gag, and she sagged, half bent at the waist. She was shaking her head hard, making her ponytail fly.

"Let her go now." Rowdy had his palms high and flat. Begging.

"Kneel." Carter gestured with his gun.

His former teammate obeyed.

"I can't let her go yet. I want her to watch the show."

"C'mon, man, just let my sister go. You wanted me, you got me." He looked at Camille, then back at him.

Carter shook his head and flashed a smile. He raised his gun and took aim.

Chapter Twenty-Nine

"C'mon, man, just let my sister go." Rowdy Vargas' voice shook. "You wanted me, you got me."

She could hear it in stereo, in her ear, where the surveillance van had tapped his wire into her earwig, and through the thin door in front of them at the top of the stairs. She twitched and her hands shook.

Taylor opened and closed her fingers on the butt of her Glock, and gestured for the two Phoenix FBI agents to move to the right of the motel room door.

Holman was at her back, and they were all ready to go.

They had four more guys behind them, and four armored SWAT agents in front. The door didn't look like it'd need a battering ram, but the lead guy had one.

They'd insisted on going in first, but she and her partner were right on their asses.

"Carter, put the gun down and let's talk about this," Vargas urged.

"That's our signal," someone said.

The door split down the middle, wood shards flying among shouts of, "Federal Agents!"

Taylor rushed forward, Holman close behind.

The first gunshot made her ears ring, but return fire was quick.

She fired once when she saw Bennett, then ducked and looked for cover.

A body slammed into her before she was able to move forward, making her tumble backwards. She cracked her head on the doorway, and her vision swam as her body somersaulted.

Down she went, trying to catch herself, but her arms

flailed and concrete hit her back, knocking the breath from her lungs.

She landed on the top step, only because she was able to grab an iron rung with her left hand. Otherwise, she would've gone down the staircase. Her head hung over the edge.

Shouting surrounded her, but she couldn't make sense of it—or the searing pain in her right arm.

"Carrigan! Dammit, Carrigan, answer me!"

Holman's face was in triplicate. His fingers were in her hair. Probing, touching all over her head. Solid ground was under her again.

"What're you doing?" Taylor tried to yank away, but he wouldn't let go.

"Thank God! Does your head hurt?"

"No. My arm." She tried again to shake free, but her partner didn't release her.

Holman blew out a breath and helped her sit up. "Thank God the blood's not from your head. Someone call another ambulance! Carrigan's hit!"

An agent acknowledged her partner, but she couldn't tell who.

She let him manhandle her. Her head was fuzzy, and she couldn't see straight.

He pulled her backward, leaning her against the wall on the outside of the room's door.

Agents bustled back and forth, making the nearby staircase rattle.

White-hot agony burned from her biceps to shoulder, especially when Holman compressed her wound. "Fuck!" she breathed.

"Just hang on. I don't think it's as bad as it looks. But you've lost a lot of blood."

"You ever been shot before?"

"No."

"Remind me to tell you the same when you are, then."

Her partner smirked, and she could finally see just one of him.

Taylor hissed when he pushed on her arm again. "Bennett?" she panted.

"He's down, but alive. Dunno how many times he was hit, but I tackled him after he bowled into you. I'm guessing some of the blood on you is his."

She looked down. The front of her shirt was stained red, as were her slacks. "Dammit, I wanted to snap the cuffs on myself."

"I know you did, partner. But we got him. I'm glad you're okay. You scared the shit outta me. I thought for sure the blood was from your head, but you're not even cut."

"Hard head," she managed.

"You said it, not me."

She tried to glare, but her arm was demanding all her attention. Agony was her new state of being. It hurt so bad her teeth chattered, overriding the ache in her temples. Blood trickled down to her wrist. "Where's my gun?"

"Right here." Holman gestured with his head. The Glock rested on the concrete between them.

"Holster it for me, will you?"

He did, but admonished her to put pressure on her wound with her left hand.

Finally sirens wailed, interrupting the organized chaos of their little raid. Three PPD police cruisers pulled in behind the two ambulances.

"How long was I out?"

"A minute or so, probably. Felt like longer." Her partner's brow was drawn tight, his concern palpable.

"Vargas and his sister?" Taylor croaked. She couldn't see them among the moving figures.

"Fine. He threw himself over her and they took cover beside the bed. Bennett was shooting at us, not them. Vargas is still turning himself in, but we may need to make a few calls. Prosecutors need to know he cooperated."

"I'll handle it."

"Of course you will." Holman chuckled.

"Don't placate me."

"Never." The twinkle was back in his eyes.

If Taylor wasn't hurting so badly, she would've hit him, or told him off.

Thankfully the paramedics interrupted them and loaded her on a gurney, despite her protests, but when her partner told them he'd ride in the back next to her, she didn't argue.

Taylor's arm burned and she bit back a curse.

She *hated* hospitals, and she'd been awake for a few hours now. The minor surgery to get the bullet out had only lasted an hour. It hadn't done any damage to her bones—just torn flesh that hurt like a bitch.

The anesthesia was wearing off, and her arm throbbed from shoulder to elbow.

She didn't want more pain meds—a clear head was what she needed. Wasn't groggy at the moment, and they'd let her get dressed, although it was in FBI sweatpants and a loose tee her partner had brought.

Holman was holding up the wall next to her bed, worry etched in his expression. If he apologized one more time, she was totally going to kick his ass.

"What the hell's taking so long?" she grumbled.

The nurse had told them she was in the queue to be

discharged a good forty-five minutes before. They'd already kept her overnight, she couldn't take any more.

Her partner's gaze glued to her in two seconds flat.

Damn, his eyes are so blue.

Too bad she preferred amber.

She jolted and tried not to think about Shannon. Taylor had told him via text message she'd been shot—not a good plan. She'd been in the middle of doctors and nurses, about to get rushed into surgery yesterday—and in a hell of a lot of pain. Hadn't been able to respond, and Shannon had fired off worried texts, escalating with every non-answer. Not to mention the calls she hadn't answered. Hadn't been able to, but really hadn't *wanted* to, either.

Right before they'd wheeled her in, she'd thrust her phone at Holman and asked him to take care of it, but Taylor hadn't explained a damn thing. She'd just said, "Will you answer him?"

Her partner had obeyed, but now he knew she had someone in her life...

Her message history told her the two men had texted the whole time she'd been under, until she'd gotten to Recovery.

At least her sergeant had calmed, and knew she was fine.

His messages had started up first thing that morning, and Taylor had texted back herself, letting him know she was leaving the hospital soon. That day. If the doc didn't let her go, she'd walk. She was fine.

Shannon had said he'd been about to get on a plane. She'd smiled about that, but had shot him down quick. Told him she'd see him when she got home.

Why had it been so important for *him* to be the first to be told she'd been shot, priority over everyone else?

She bit back a wince that had nothing to do with her injury. There was no hiding Shannon's concern in the messages.

Holman would've put two and two together, even if he hadn't read the whole thread, but he'd had time. Taylor could only hope he hadn't been nosy enough to read *everything* between her and Shannon.

"Are you all right?" The demand made her look at her partner again. He was studying her in a way that had her squirming.

"Yes. I want out of here."

"Just—"

"Ms. Carrigan?" The young doctor who'd assisted in her surgery appeared inside her private room.

She'd already spoken to him that morning. He'd been the one to tell her she could be cut loose. Baker wanted them back in Dallas, but they had a few things to wrap up with the Phoenix office, too.

Holman straightened, hovering over the bed like he had to protect her.

Taylor cut off her instinctive glare. She should thank him for his concern, too, but it only irritated her. She cleared her throat. "Yes?"

"I'm sorry for the delay on your discharge, but there's a reason."

"Is everything okay?" her partner asked.

She threw him a glance and arched an eyebrow, then looked back at the doctor. Didn't chastise him.

He'd schooled his expression fast, like he knew he was butting in, and that was enough for her.

"Yes, but your bloodwork brought something to our attention." The doctor fidgeted in his scrubs, looking at Taylor then at Holman. "Do you want him to...?"

"He's my partner, it's fine. Is something wrong with

me?" Her heart skipped, but she tried to square her shoulders.

She *should* kick Holman out if she was about to get medical news, no matter the nature. It wasn't any of his business, and besides, she'd already put in an overshare with him finding out about Shannon. For some reason, she didn't want to face whatever it was alone. Would rather have her lover there, but she trusted her partner, too.

"No, ma'am. You're healthy, and as we talked about earlier, very lucky the bullet didn't do more damage to your biceps. No sign of concussion, either."

"Well, then—?" Holman said.

"You're pregnant."

Taylor blinked. "No." The denial was fast, but a whisper instead of the yell it should've been.

"Since you took a tumble when you were shot, we want to get an ultrasound to make sure the baby's okay. Make sure you're both fine."

"But I can't be—" She snapped her mouth shut and looked at her partner.

"I'm gonna step out," Holman said, but he didn't look uncomfortable about the bomb that'd just been dropped.

Panic clawed up her throat and a lump formed. Tears burned the corners of her eyes and she swallowed. Didn't try to speak. She forced a nod to her partner.

He squeezed her hand on his way out, and she wanted to hate that, but perhaps she needed the comfort.

The doctor went on, but the words just made her head spin. Didn't compute, like he was speaking another language.

I can't be pregnant.

She was on birth control.

Taylor just couldn't be...

"I'm on birth control," she blurted.

"Were you on antibiotics for any reason?"

"No." She shook her head for effect. As if it would change her...situation.

Pregnant?

No way. Just...

Hell no.

She started shaking. Head to toe. Wanted to clutch the blanket she'd shoved to the end of the narrow bed.

"I see that this is a shock to you."

That was putting it mildly, but she couldn't form words.

"Sometimes, a very small percentage of the time, birth control fails. Were you taking the pill as prescribed? Did you miss any?"

"No, I didn't miss," Taylor croaked.

"Well, let's start by checking you out right now, then you can think about options. We need to make sure your fall didn't cause any harm to you or the baby."

Baby.

The word jolted her all over.

She gripped the bed sheet so tight her knuckles whitened and ached.

No.

She'd never wanted kids. Never planned on them, even with John. She'd had him and the FBI, and that was enough. All she'd ever wanted.

This wasn't John's...baby.

It was Shannon's.

I can't do this.

Tears spilled. She tried to wipe them away, but she couldn't clear her vision. Cursed every one.

"I've put the orders in, Ms. Carrigan. Someone from

Radiology will come get you soon. Do you have any idea how far along you might be? Did you miss a period?"

"What?"

The doctor gently repeated his questions and heat burned her cheeks.

Get it together. Deal with this.

Taylor remembered the first weekend with Shannon. They'd only used a condom once. That was five weeks ago now.

So... It could've happened any of the times they were together. She'd been so busy she hadn't paid attention to her menstrual cycle.

She'd had cramps, but no bleeding. Hadn't stopped to worry about it. Her period had been wonky since she was a teen, despite the regulation birth control pills offered most of the time.

She cleared her throat and met the doctor's dark eyes. He was looking at her expectantly.

"Uh, no more than five weeks, I think."

"Okay, I'll note that. It helps us know what we're looking for." He repeated that Radiology would be with her shortly, then he was gone.

He'd been so placid and professional.

Two traits she'd always prided herself on. Too bad they weren't present right now.

Her world was turned upside down.

What the hell am I supposed to do now?

Chapter Thirty

Taylor took big, shuddering breaths and ordered herself to get it together.

She glanced over her shoulder to the building her doctor officed in, then back down at the little referral card in her hand. The clinic's name made it obvious as to what they did there.

The date and time, two weeks away, glared at her.

She needed to get back to work. Had some reports to file.

Baker had made her take a week off, and this was her first day back. Her boss hadn't sent her to Shrinkville this time. He'd told her it would be his call when she returned to work.

Her new *problem* had taken her attention away from the humiliation of getting knocked on her ass, not to mention shot, that day in Phoenix.

She'd chased Carter Bennett for months and months. Had craved justice for John, and, in the end, she hadn't been able to deliver it herself.

Not really. Holman had gotten him.

Bennett would live—he'd been shot once. When he recovered, he would go to trial, so her fiancé would get justice.

For that, she was grateful.

Their whole team had congratulated them on finally closing John's case.

Taylor hadn't told Baker about her pregnancy, and she didn't have plans to, either. She'd tell him she needed to take a few days' medical leave when the time came, and he wouldn't ask questions. Even if HIPAA allowed it, he wasn't the type.

Holman hadn't brought up what he'd heard.

She trusted him to keep it to himself, and he would.

Her phone dinged and she cringed. She knew who it was before she even looked at the screen. She didn't have time for Shannon.

Couldn't face *him*.

She hadn't talked to him, or answered his texts, in almost two weeks.

Are you home? Are you okay?

The same message, over and over again. He'd left a few voicemails, too.

Naturally, Shannon wanted to know what was going on. Things had been okay with them before Phoenix.

More than okay.

Taylor couldn't face that, any more than she wanted to face what was going on...inside her.

She crushed her eyes shut and clicked the button on the side of her cell to make the screen go dark. Then she pocketed it.

Her...medical condition wasn't any of Shannon's business, right?

It was her body. Her choice.

His baby.

Guilt jumped up and took a chunk out of her. The abortion appointment card burned the palm of her hand, so she shoved it in her pocket too. Touching it felt wrong.

She stumbled to the car and wrenched the door open. Wouldn't cry anymore.

Family meant everything to Shannon.

The day they'd taken his niece shopping felt like ages ago. Memories of his smile, his laugh, how his whole face had lit up when the kid had talked to him, laughed with him, and hugged him marched across her mind, making her guilt a million times worse.

He'd be a good father. In all the ways that counted, he already *was* a father.

Taylor *owed* him the news of the pregnancy, and her...plans. No amount of *'no, I can't have this baby'* was going to fix that. She *needed* to tell him.

But why?

Nothing was going to change her mind. She couldn't have this...*his*...child. It didn't figure into her plans, any more than her relationship with him did.

Tears clouded her vision and she wanted to punch something. Or scream.

She clutched the steering wheel until her fingers shot needles of agony into her knuckles.

What the fuck am I supposed to do?

Her headfuck wasn't Shannon's problem.

He was different. This wouldn't petrify him.

She could hear him in her head, see his beautiful eyes. He'd promise her that they'd deal with it.

Too bad they'd likely have different ideas of how to do that.

A sob threatened to break through her attempts to staunch her tears. Taylor's chest burned and no amount of forced air was fixing it.

Her phone blared from her pocket and she wanted to ignore it. Couldn't talk to him on the phone, especially when she couldn't stop bawling.

Surprise washed over her when she glanced at the screen and saw the Chicago area code.

She cleared her throat and swiped her thumb to answer the call. "Hello?" Taylor cringed; the word was a croak.

There was silence, and she almost repeated her greeting, but then he spoke.

"Taylor, are you well?"

"Yes, sir. How can I help you?" she asked her father.

"I haven't spoken with you in some time, so I thought I would check in. How are things?"

She inhaled through her nostrils and reached for the familiar, stiff formality that'd always ruled every interaction with her father. "Things are fine. Thank you for asking." Taylor didn't tell him she'd gotten shot and her arm still hurt like a bitch.

"That's good to hear." His gruffness washed over her, and she pictured him at his desk on base, where he ran the only Navy boot camp in the US, in Chicago. The place she'd grown up.

She'd been raised by this unfeeling man, who'd chastise her even today, if he knew she'd been crying in her car after scheduling an appointment to end her unplanned pregnancy.

Her mom had taken off when she was two, or so she'd been told. She didn't remember the woman, but pictures told Taylor they looked very much alike.

Maybe that was why her father had always kept her at a distance.

She glanced at the clock in her car. It was only half past nine, and he should be at work. Why was he calling her in the middle of his morning on a workday?

"Is everything all right, sir?"

"Yes."

Okay, well that didn't encourage conversation or questions, but that was just her father. "Are you working?"

"Yes. Are you?"

"I had...something to take care of this morning, but I'm headed in soon."

As soon as I can get my shit together.

Her father was quiet for a while—too quiet. "It's been some time since I've seen you."

Taylor sucked back a gasp to hide her surprise. This conversation was so unlike the ones she was used to from the man who'd raised her. "Yeah... I mean, yes, sir, it has been. Is everything all right?" she repeated.

"Yes. I was just thinking about you."

She blinked. Wanted to blurt, *'really, why?'* But she didn't.

She glanced at her reflection in the rearview mirror and winced at her puffy eyes. She'd have to do something about that before she got downtown. "Oh?"

"If it's possible, I'd like for you to come home for a visit."

Taylor's mouth went dry. She couldn't remember the last time she'd seen her father.

Two years? Three?

He'd never...requested her presence. Was he ill?

She didn't want to come out and ask.

"Ah. I have vacation time. I'll see what I can do."

"Good."

The very odd conversation with her father didn't last much longer.

Taylor stared at the dark screen of her cell when they disconnected.

What the hell? circled her mind a few times.

She couldn't help but think of her childhood, and it hurt. This man had raised her with stoic distance. Her clothing had always had to be impeccable. She'd only been permitted to speak when spoken to, and had always had to maintain good posture in his presence.

Everything had been like a rank to be achieved, including when she'd played softball—even in college, since it'd been a source of a scholarship. Grades lower than a B were unacceptable, and the honor roll had been expected.

He'd told her he'd been proud when she'd gone into the FBI, but Taylor hadn't *felt* it.

Her career choice was just one more thing her father could publicly declare to his colleagues. She was a centerpiece, not a person. If she'd failed, she would've been hidden from view. She knew it in her gut.

He was the reason she couldn't have a child.

She'd never put a child through that, and she didn't know anything different. She didn't know how to get close.

It doesn't have to be like that, though.

Her father's ways were so opposite of how things were with Shannon, and the way he interacted with his niece.

Shannon would be *nothing* like her own father.

The chaos of moments before her father's call seized her and sent her back into a tailspin she couldn't manage. Sweat broke out on her forehead and her lip.

Taylor panted to breathe, but couldn't get enough air down.

She cranked the car to life and hammered the window buttons. Put all four of them down and wanted to hang out of the driver's side like a dog. Her heart thundered as if it was protesting, too.

Breathe. In. Out. In. Out.

Voices caught her attention, and her eyes darted to the left.

A man, probably mid-thirties, held the hand of a small boy. His words didn't carry, but his tone did. He was reassuring the child, who couldn't be more than three or four.

The sounds of crying reached her, even though they

were feet away.

The man glanced around the parking lot, and stopped in an empty parking space, out of the way of potential traffic, but now they were closer. He knelt in front of the child and cupped his face. "It's gonna be okay, buddy. I know you don't feel good, but the doctor will help. I promise."

"Daddy..." The word broke on a sob.

Taylor watched, riveted.

He swept the child into his arms and patted his back. His voice was too low again, but the murmurs were no doubt comforting. Then they were gone, the father holding his son as they headed into the medical building.

The little boy had cuddled close, his head on the man's shoulder.

She couldn't move. Tears burned.

The exchange had been a private thing, Taylor the intruder.

She let her eyes slip closed. Leaned her head back on the headrest as confusion assaulted her.

Daddy.

Something she couldn't remember ever calling her father. Not even *Dad.*

He'd always been *sir.*

Her child wouldn't...

Taylor jolted and opened her eyes. There wouldn't be a child, so it didn't matter. She'd already made up her mind.

Right?

The appointment card beckoned, as if threatening to sear through her pocket, but she ignored it. She didn't want to look at the date. Couldn't bear to face the numbers that might make her resolve waver.

She screamed at herself some more about being

weak, despicable.

Taylor threw her shifter into gear and backed out of the parking spot.

She needed to get to the office—she had things to do.

Chapter Thirty-One

Pounding roused him, but Shannon had to fight a heavy veil of sleep to come around. The noise got louder as he threw his legs over the side of the bed.

"Shit." He dragged his hand down his face to clear his vision. Slapped the touch lamp on his nightstand but kept it on the lowest setting.

Thunder rumbled outside and rain struck his roof. Wind whistled, too. It was a wonder he'd been able to sleep.

He scanned for the nearest article of clothing—black basketball shorts—and yanked them on. Grabbed his Sig from his nightstand, too.

The frosted glass of his front door didn't reveal anything but shadows. Shannon slunk toward it, his gun at his thigh.

It was after midnight. A demanding visitor couldn't be good.

He opened the door and slid back, ready to raise his gun if he needed to.

Taylor stood on his porch, looking like a drowned rat. Her hair was plastered to her forehead and cheeks. Her clothing was so wet she was dripping on his welcome mat.

Lightning lit the sky above her head, and she shuddered. She rubbed her upper arm, probably where she'd been shot. "Do you always answer the door with a gun in your hand?"

"If I get a visitor this late, yes. What the hell's wrong?" He grabbed her wrist without giving her a chance to answer. "You're soaked. Get in here."

"I needed to see you."

Shannon paused.

She'd sounded unsure but her expression was typical Taylor—unreadable.

"At midnight? Why didn't you answer any of my texts?"

It'd been over two weeks. She hadn't answered his calls or voicemails, either.

"I... I'm sorry."

"Are you okay? How's your arm?"

"Yes. No. I don't know."

He studied her, but her pretty face gave nothing away.

"My arm's fine," she whispered.

Taylor shifted on her feet, but it was the shiver and chatter of her teeth that pushed Shannon into action.

"C'mon. Let's get you out of those wet clothes."

She didn't argue, but didn't come with him until he tugged her hand.

He left her at the end of his bed, put his gun down, and darted to the bathroom. Threw the cupboard door open and grabbed a big fluffy gray towel. It was new, part of a set his mother had insisted he needed.

Their eyes met when he came back into the room.

Taylor hadn't moved. She stood by the leather trunk, looking lost. Rainwater dripped down her hands from her blazer. Her strawberry-blonde hair was darker in color, and it'd already started to work into tight curls she'd complain about later.

Shannon set the towel down and pulled her out of the jacket.

Her pale blue button-down was just as wet, clinging to her body. Her nipples were hard and she trembled again.

He tore his gaze away from her breasts and started

to undo her buttons. "Why are you so wet? It's windy, but you're drenched. Didn't you park in the driveway?"

"I went for a walk."

"In a thunderstorm?"

"Had to clear my head." She looked down.

He bit back a sigh and cupped her cheeks. Tilted up so she'd have to look at him. "A walk in the rain. After midnight. What happened?"

"Nothing."

He wanted to chide her, but pushing Taylor never got him anywhere. Shannon needed her to want to open up to him. "Then what is it?" He studied her face.

"I just needed you."

His heart gave a little flutter he ignored. Didn't say anything, because he might be stupid enough to admit he loved her, then she'd shut down for sure. Would probably hightail it out of his house—especially after she'd ignored him for two weeks.

"I called you." This was low, an accusation.

He glanced at his cell, plugged into the charger on his nightstand. "I have it on '*do not disturb*'. Been having trouble sleeping since I came off midnights." He dropped a kiss on her damp forehead, and didn't like the cool temperature of her skin. Shannon redoubled his efforts in getting her shirt open and off.

She shrugged out of it and made no move to retrieve the material from where it'd fallen on the carpet. Her teeth chattered louder.

"Hold on, sweets, let me get the towel around you." When he turned back to her, Taylor had ditched the bra. He tried not to stare at her pink puckered nipples and dusky areolas.

The freckles on her shoulders drew his attention, too, and the ones on her collarbone. He wanted to spread kisses there, but it wasn't the time.

Blood was slowly sliding below the belt, and his cock twitched. Especially as she let him wrap the towel around her and shucked her dark slacks.

She stepped out of them, leaving them on the carpet next to her shirt. Shoes and socks were next. She left her plain blue bikini panties on, but it didn't matter.

Shannon had a great memory—and he'd missed her like hell. "Do you want to take a hot shower? It'll warm you better." He moved his hands up and down her arms outside the towel.

Taylor shook her head. "Shannon."

Her whisper was nearly his undoing.

He gathered her close, holding her quivering body to his chest, rubbing her back over the soft terry cloth material. "What couldn't wait until the morning?"

She shifted, her wet hair tickling his bare skin. "I..."

"You what, sweets?"

"Guess I missed you. I'm... I'm...sorry...about the last few weeks." The words were muffled against his chest, but he'd take it.

He leaned back and she looked up at him. Didn't smile, but the vulnerability in her hazel eyes flipped his stomach.

Shannon couldn't help himself—he dipped down and covered her mouth with his.

Taylor kissed him back, reaching up to put her arms around his neck. The towel slid to the floor. Now his hands were all over her, and they were skin-to-skin. She moaned as he deepened their kiss.

Tasting her was the same, only better. Their tongues dueled, until she entwined hers around his, plundering his mouth as much as he was hers.

He lifted her into his arms and walked them to the

bed.

She pulled him down on top of her, and he didn't fight it, lavishing kisses on her like he'd wanted to minutes before. Taylor wiggled closer, shoving her hands in his shorts, squeezing his ass and undulating into him. She was telling him she wanted it fast and hard, but that wasn't going to work.

He hadn't seen her in forever, and he wanted to make love to her, not give her a quick fuck. Then maybe she'd tell him what the hell was going on in that head of hers.

"Now, Shannon. Now."

Her demand slid down his spine, and his cock certainly agreed. Shannon fought against her urging, wanting to go slow, to show her what she meant to him.

Too bad Taylor's touches and kisses threw that right out the window, revving him up until he was about to explode.

"I want to worship you," he groaned.

"I need you inside me." She pulled on his arms.

They discarded his shorts and her panties, and Taylor threw herself into his chest, nestling into him. Her skin was too cold, too damp, but she wrapped her body around his, ignoring his concerns.

"You'll make me warm."

"I will," Shannon whispered.

She kissed him, pushing for dominance.

He ran his hand down her hip, palming her perfect ass. When she whimpered into their kiss and opened her legs, he got caught up in her urgency. He fumbled, but Shannon gripped his erection and joined them with one hard thrust.

Her legs slid around him as he drove forward, giving her what she wanted. He couldn't deny her—it was foolish to think he could.

He gave himself to Taylor, body, heart and soul.

It was just a shame he couldn't *tell* her that.

The shower was running when he woke, and the sun was streaming into his bedroom windows. Shannon stretched and smiled.

Last night had been *fantastic*.

Taylor was so hot when she came apart in his arms, and she had four—or was it five?—times.

He stood, arching his back like a cat. His muscles ached like he'd had a good workout, but then again, that was what good sex was like.

Shannon pulled on his black shorts and a gray tee. Didn't bother with socks, he'd have to shower. He could join her, hell, he wanted to, but she still hadn't told him why she'd shown up so late, so he'd let her be.

His little FBI agent loved her space. Maybe she'd talk to him when they ate.

He popped his head into the bathroom. "Hey, I'm going to make breakfast. Any special requests?"

"Oh, you're up. I didn't want to wake you."

"No worries, sweets."

Taylor slid the glass shower door open and their eyes met. "Did you sleep okay?"

She was so gorgeous it took his breath, like she did every damn time. "I did. I'm glad you came." Shannon smiled.

Her returning smile was small and hesitant. Something flashed through her eyes, but it was gone too fast for him to read. "Me too."

He told himself not to push her. "I'll start eggs and bacon. Coffee?"

"Yes, please." She gave him another smile.

He made himself leave the bathroom and allow Taylor her space. Took a few moments to gather her clothes, which were still scattered at the end of his bed. They were damp, too. He could throw them in the washer.

When he shook the blazer out, something that looked like a business card fluttered to the carpet. It was a little worse for the wear, mangled from being wet.

Shannon flipped it over and froze.

The words at the top were a tad smeared, but still legible.

A clinic, but not just any clinic. One known for performing abortions.

Taylor's name was written on the line below. It, too, showed signs of water damage—part of her last name was a blue blur.

The date was the upcoming Monday, and the time noted was nine a.m.

A cold flush rushed his body and he dropped her clothing. Blinking didn't fix what his eyes said was right there.

An abortion?

Taylor's pregnant.

Emotion caught in his throat. Shannon tried to swallow it away, but it didn't work.

The love of his life was carrying his child, and she didn't want it.

Was she going to tell him?

He stumbled from his bedroom, tripping over his feet and lurching into the doorframe. It took a bite of his shoulder, and pain radiated down to his wrist.

Shannon pushed off the wood, righting himself. He whirled, staring into the dim bedroom. Half of him wanted to rush in and confront her, but the other half told him to breathe through the shock, fury, and pain, to take a minute to gather his thoughts.

When he reached the kitchen, he started the coffee like he'd said he would. Shannon couldn't look away from the little white demon with tarnished blue ink, especially when he placed it on the dark granite countertop. It stood out in stark contrast, shouting for his attention.

The tempting aroma of his favorite roasted beans teased his senses, but he ignored it, slipping on to a bar stool and drumming his fingers on the counter. His heartrate increased with every *thump,* until it was in competition with the movements of his hand. His temples throbbed and his head spun.

He looked away from the appointment card when he heard her padding toward him. Covered the small white paper with a palm.

Taylor was wearing one of his T-shirts, nothing else, but he wasn't tempted. Her beauty *hurt* because this situation—if nothing else—proved she wasn't his.

Her smile faded when their eyes met. "Shannon, what's wrong?"

"Do you have something to tell me?"

She moved closer, the bar between them. "What?" The word sounded innocent enough, but the same *something* from the shower darted across her eyes.

"You tell me *what.*" He struggled to keep his sentence steady through the lump in his throat.

She was going to play coy, and wasn't that so Taylor?

It made the agony worse, until it spread down his chest. If she'd planned on telling him, she would've opened with it.

The truth of her deception sank his heart to his gut. "Shannon..."

He waited, but she said nothing more. Looked around, up and down, over her shoulder—anywhere but *at* him.

Shannon lifted his hand and shoved the appointment card toward her.

Taylor's eyes went wide and the color drained from her face.

Chapter Thirty-Two

I changed my mind.

The words were on her tongue, but the betrayal in Shannon's expression stole everything—coherent thought, the ability to speak, her breath.

Taylor wavered on her feet and gripped the edge of the bar in front of her so she wouldn't fall on her ass. Her injured arm smarted.

"Were you even going to tell me?" He pushed to his feet, stepping back from the island. Left the card on the dark granite.

Her eyes darted to it, as if it was spotlighted.

I came here to tell you.

Again, no sentences would form.

Taylor cleared her throat.

"I can't believe you. I just *can't*." Shannon shook his head and looked down, as if he needed a moment to gather himself.

"It's not what you think—"

"Then what *is* it, Taylor?" he barked, spitting her name like a curse. "You're pregnant, and the first thing you do is schedule an abortion?"

"I didn't—"

"I have a right to that baby, as much as you do." He pointed, but the speed he'd tossed his hand up made it more like a punch.

She winced. "Shannon, I..."

"You weren't even going to tell me, were you? You were just going to abort the baby like it was never there."

"I..." Every time she opened her mouth, he wouldn't listen. Taylor couldn't find the power in her gut to push anything out.

"I knew you could be cold, but this is a bit much, even for you, don'cha think?" He didn't pause, just kept talking, getting louder, walking as he shouted.

Foolish ideas of them actually trying to be a family dissipated with every harsh word Shannon lanced at her.

Her plan to tell him had been there last night—she'd just been trying to get her courage up. Then he'd held her, and she'd just...needed him.

She'd told herself it would all be okay in the morning. Shannon would help, he'd understand.

Taylor had canceled the appointment to end her pregnancy, but wasn't having any success telling him.

He wouldn't believe her anyway.

With every hurtful thing he spewed, she was torn open even more.

He paced the kitchen, the whole time keeping the bar between them as if he couldn't stand to get closer.

Like last night had never happened.

Why had she left the card in her pocket?

"I needed you, last night. So I could tell you today," she said. "I was going to tell you today, I swear."

"Hah! Right. You got caught, Special Agent Carrigan. What was last night? A goodbye fuck? Is that what you *needed*?"

Shock at his harsh words rolled over her, as if she'd taken a full-body dip in ice water. Tears burned the corners of her eyes, but she sure as hell wasn't going to give him that satisfaction. Taylor locked her jaw and met his eyes, battling back the hurt inside.

"I know you're not stupid enough to think I'd be *okay* with this. You had to know it would end us. So you needed what? To fuck me one last time?"

Agony shot through her like the bullet had her arm. "You've got this all wrong." What was a shout in her head left her mouth in a cracked whisper.

"No. You're what's *wrong*." Shannon rammed his hand through his thick, dark hair, and whipped the appointment card off the countertop. He flung it at her, but the thing helicoptered to the tile floor. "How could you be so damn selfish?"

He's right.

Taylor blanched. Her heart slid to her toes. She *had* been selfish. But she'd changed her mind.

She was petrified, but she wanted to try with him. Needed *him*.

She looked down.

Why can't I say anything? Say. Something.

"I fucking *love* you, Taylor. How could you ruin that? How could you want to kill *our baby*?"

Shock hit her square in the chest, like an ice bolt. Constriction took all her attention, made it hard to breathe. She sucked in air, but it didn't help.

Love?

Taylor couldn't deal with that.

He loved her, and she'd lost him on the same day.

As Shannon ranted more and paced, she tuned him out.

She watched his jerky movements as if she were a fly on the wall, especially when he attacked her character, name called. She put her hand over her mouth and sniffled.

Don't cry. Don't cry.

Taylor slipped from the kitchen, fleeing to his bedroom. Damp pants made her gasp when the material hit her skin, but she didn't pause.

She shoved her feet into her shoes and whipped her car keys from her pocket. Then she ran from Shannon's house without another word.

He made no move to stop her.

He'd known Taylor capable of a lot of things, but not this.

She'd really take the life of his unborn child?

Without a word to him?

What was he—chopped liver?

Selfish bitch.

Guilt bit at him for the disrespectful word his mom had raised him better than to call *any* woman, but his mind was blown.

Does she know me at all?

Shannon had thought he'd known *her.*

Being wrong had bite, too, because Taylor obviously didn't trust him enough to tell him the fucking truth, let alone be there for her.

He'd lost it when he'd seen the little appointment card for the abortion clinic. Seen red...and felt so much agony his chest had caved in.

How *could* she?

Sure, he'd flown off at the mouth, but who wouldn't have?

Remorse swirled up again, because of some of the things he'd said, and because he'd not really given Taylor a chance to say anything. She hadn't really tried, anyway.

Her mind was made up.

That was killing Shannon.

The perfect night he'd shared with her was shattered. Gone forever. He didn't want the good memory, or any of the others with her.

What Taylor intended, without consulting him, was worse than...*anything.*

"I guess I didn't know her after all."

"You say something, Sarge?" Brian McAuley asked. Like most evenings, he was running things at the local Antioch cop bar.

The place was an APD institution, but as far as the boys in blue were concerned, he was on his own tonight. Not a cop in the place. A little odd, but *Thank God.*

"Nope." He downed a shot of whiskey and slammed the glass on the bar. Then chased it with three gulps of beer. Finished the bottle off and tried not to think about how many he'd already had. "Gimme another."

The guy hesitated and Shannon glared until his bidding was done and he'd put a twenty on the counter. Told Brian to keep the change.

He ignored the bartender's concern—and Brian's muttering about him being cut off. He'd deal with it when the man had the balls to say it to his face.

A hot blonde chick at the end of the bar kept catching his eye, but he sure as hell wasn't in the mood. He sucked back his newest shot and ignored her. Gripped the new beer, too, with both hands, in true nursing form.

The chick wouldn't go away. Inched toward him, then away, and grabbed her cellphone from her tiny purse.

He finally caved and gave her a full onceover.

She was smokin' all right, sporting a short silver dress that stopped mid-thigh and was tight as hell over her perfect ass, hugging her waist and hips, but billowing out at the sleeves. It was low cut enough at the front to reveal some nice cleavage.

Still wasn't interested.

Shannon threw her a nod for what-the-hells, but instead of a returning smile, she looked concerned, then went back to texting—or whatever she was doing on her cell.

She looked relatively familiar to his alcohol-muddled brain, but he couldn't place her.

He sipped on the beer and his temples throbbed—he was more than halfway to the oblivion he sought. The next time he glanced over his shoulder, Hot Blonde was gone.

Shannon turned back to his frosty bottle. He didn't run the hot chick brigade, and he sure as hell wasn't in the market for anything. Not even a quick bathroom-stall fuck.

He wished Mark Rodriguez was still APD, but his buddy was in Dallas, and no way was he going to call him while said buddy was blissfully happy with his detective girlfriend.

"Jesus." He dragged his hand down his face and scratched the stubble he'd not bothered with.

"Crowley."

Someone familiar, but Shannon ignored him.

Until a large hand crashed down on his shoulder and he didn't have a choice but to find out who wanted his face smashed in.

He shoved the unwanted grip off and swiveled his bar stool around, glaring as hard as he could. His stomach pitched and his head spun, but he tried to focus on the surprise that washed over him. Even managed not reaching for the bar to steady himself when his world started to tilt. "Manning?"

The APD detective stood there, appraising him with narrowed eyes. His wife, Mel, stood arm-in-arm with Hot Blonde right behind him.

Manning sighed. "Carrigan worked you over, huh?"

'Fuck off' was his first instinct, but Shannon sucked it back and scowled. "Leave me alone."

"No can do, bud."

Bud?

They knew each other, sure. But they weren't close.

"Bri, some coffee, please."

Relief was written all over the tall redheaded man's face when he nodded, and did Jared Manning's bidding.

"Let's find a table, Crowley."

"No." Shannon turned back to the bar, and his beer.

"Shannon."

He paused at his first name.

"Last thing you need is for word to get back to Chief that you're piss drunk at *McAuley's*. Word to the wise—if you want to drink yourself under the table, do it at home."

I can't. I can only see her there.

"Fuck you, Manning." He heard the detective blow out a breath. "How'd you get stuck with my *rescue*, anyway?" he snapped.

"My wife's best friend. She called because she recognized you. Val also realized there weren't any other cops in here tonight. So you're the lucky winner who gets *yours truly* all to yourself."

Oh, goodie.

So that was why Hot Blonde looked familiar. He'd probably seen her at some APD family function.

"Come sit with me at the back table and sober up before I get you home."

The back table.

Unofficially designated for APD-only use.

Shannon groaned and turned to face his voluntold guardian angel. Didn't want help getting home, let alone to sober up.

If he wasn't drunk off his ass, he'd crash at his mom's, but there was no reason to bother her, or his too-curious niece, with Taylor's shit.

Besides, Taylor had already destroyed *his* image of her today—there was no reason for that to happen to

Cailey, too. Even if he didn't tell her *why*, his niece would be shattered that they weren't together anymore.

She idolized Taylor. Asked about her almost every day.

Manning kissed his wife where she still stood with her friend, and kept his voice low, but not so much Shannon couldn't hear him. "Don't wait up, baby. This'll take a while. Thanks for the call, Val. Can you take Mel home?"

"Sure." Hot Blonde grimaced and gestured to him. "I hope he doesn't hate me."

"*He* can hear you," Shannon drawled.

Hot Blonde had the decency to blush, visible even in the dim light of the bar. Too bad he wasn't in the market—she was gorgeous, and despite the tight clothing, she didn't come off as slutty.

"Don't be a dick because someone you don't even know gave a shit about you, Crowley," Manning growled.

He wanted to roll his eyes, but he just averted his gaze from the whole scene. Finished his beer, even though Brian McAuley glared from the coffee pot.

All too soon, the taller detective had ushered him to the back table and pushed a steaming mug in front of him.

He didn't thank him.

"You don't have to talk. Just drink that."

"Wasn't planning on either one. Hope you don't expect a thank you."

Manning was quiet—too quiet. He narrowed his dark eyes. "This isn't you, Crowley. You're not an asshole like me."

"Yeah, maybe I am. Maybe this is the real me."

"Bullshit." He shook his head.

Silence descended, and Shannon gave in to the coffee. He pulled the mug to him and took a sip. The bitterness played on his tongue, but he didn't want cream or sugar.

Bitter was pretty perfect for how he was feeling. Among other things.

"That bad, huh?" his coworker whispered.

"Thought you said I didn't have to talk," he quipped as he gripped the coffee cup with both hands. The warmth from the mug felt good on his palms.

"I thought you were bat-shit crazy when I heard you were involved with Carrigan. Then I thought, maybe you're just a misguided saint. Looks like it didn't matter, since she obviously fucked you over."

"*You* don't get to talk about her," Shannon snapped. Unwanted possessiveness and the need to protect Taylor rose up. He growled—at himself for his idiocy, and at Manning for his nerve. He brought the mug to his lips and forced a sip so he wouldn't deck the detective.

Are you serious right now?

Chiding himself didn't work.

Taylor had done something unforgivable, but he still loved her.

Dammit.

Manning's eyes widened. "Oh, shit. You've got it bad. Do you love her?"

"Mind your own damn business."

"God, you do, don't you?" the guy asked, his inquiry full of awe—or pity. His mouth was agape. "Jesus Christ. *Carrigan?* Of all the women—"

"Go to hell, Manning."

The detective blinked. "Sorry, dude." But he sure as hell didn't look repentant.

Shannon wanted to punch the look off his face. He gripped the mug until his knuckles ached. "None of it matters now."

"Damn, I really am sorry." Manning shook his head and rubbed the back of his neck. His discomfort was obvious, but nothing close to what *Shannon* was feeling right now.

"Yeah, me too. Just don't be a dick." He nursed the coffee, wishing it was a beer.

"Look, if you really love her, take a day or two to breathe, then go get her."

"Not an option. Not now. Not ever." He locked eyes with his coworker, daring him to ask what Taylor had done.

Manning didn't.

Smart guy.

Agony swept up from his gut with every passing moment as sobriety settled over him.

"If you say so," the guy whispered.

Shannon didn't answer him, just stared at the liquid that was as black as his heart.

Chapter Thirty-Three

Taylor's whole body shook as she left Baker's office. She'd left her boss in stunned silence.

Yeah, she'd never imagined having any conversation with him that included the words *'I'm pregnant'*, either. At least she'd had the floor with no arguments for a few minutes.

She'd explained she understood she'd be on desk duty until the baby came, but that wasn't going to be a problem now that her case was over. She could still handle all the rest of whatever Ross Catrone needed of her regarding Bennett—it was all paperwork, interviews and eventually testifying when the asshole was back on his feet and they could go to court. Texas wasn't the only state that wanted a piece of Bennett, but they were first up.

The bullet had nicked his spinal cord, so there was the question of whether he would walk again. Poetic justice for the car thief-turned-murderer.

She and Holman could attack their next case—but Taylor's pregnancy would leave her in the office for whatever came their way, anyway. Being stuck at her desk was going to be hard to swallow, but she didn't have a choice.

Baker hadn't said much about her little speech, except, "Okay," and nodded now and then. He approved of her plans. Hadn't said congrats or anything, but that was fine, too.

Holman was quiet when she returned to their office, but her partner was far from stupid. He was just waiting for her to speak.

She didn't feel like it. Got back to the report she was putting the finishing touches to for the prosecutor. Dove right in, scrolling to the top so she could proof it.

She had to work.

If she didn't, she'd fall apart, and that was unacceptable. It couldn't happen. Wasn't going to happen.

Not because emotion was weak.

Because emotion was *everything*, and Taylor was a hot mess.

Shannon's words resonated about her selfishness. Now that it'd been a few days, hurt and anger were there, too. He hadn't listened. He'd shut her down over and over, slicing into her with everything he could.

She was a badass, right?

Like everyone always considered her, but it'd been nowhere around that day. She'd shut down, and when she'd fled his house, Taylor had had to pull over around the corner since she hadn't been able to see. She'd cried so hard her gut had ached for the whole drive back to her very empty apartment.

She'd screamed and thrown things when she'd gotten home, including the framed picture of her and John that always lived on the entertainment center he'd set up.

That glass shattering had made the decisions she hadn't been able to before. She'd thrown away everything in her apartment that reminded her of fiancé, including the three or four video game systems she'd never bothered with after he'd died.

The two boxes of his things from the FBI office had gone into the dumpster—hadn't even opened one.

When she was done, she felt better...for about two seconds. Taylor might be over John, but she was far from over Shannon.

What was worse, she loved him.

She'd thrown herself on her bed and cried herself to

sleep.

Taylor had shown up at work on Monday after puking her guts out. According to the doctor, that was normal now—she was nine weeks.

Most likely, it'd be her new normal for the next few months, which was just perfect, because her whole life was vomit without Shannon.

She'd texted him, twice.

He hadn't answered.

"Hey, can you hand me that file, please?" she asked Holman. Taylor pointed to a casefile on his desk. Needed to check the evidence contents for comparison with the report she was about to submit.

He didn't say anything, but when she gripped the edge, he didn't let go.

"Hey," her partner whispered.

"What?"

"Should I say congratulations?"

She swallowed. Avoided his gaze. "If you want," she whispered. Her emotions were up and down, and it was too early to blame it on the baby.

A baby she was going to have alone now.

Taylor was scared shitless, but her actions were a deal-breaker for Shannon, so even though she'd changed her mind about things and wanted this baby, he didn't want *her*.

"What did your man say?"

She clenched her jaw. Tried not to fidget in her chair. If she spoke, she'd cry, and that *so* wasn't happening at work. She cleared her throat and tried. "That's not... I'm doing this alone."

Holman closed his eyes and his chest rose and fell as if he'd taken a breath.

She almost lost it. Swallowed a whimper and had to

look down. Noticed her shoe was untied, but it was hard to care.

"I'm so sorry, Taylor."

The use of her first name made her look up at him.

His face was a mask of concern, with his brows drawn tight. "That's such bullshit. Do you want me to go beat him up?"

Taylor snorted. The dose of amusement made her eyes burn less, but she shook her head. "No, it's okay. It's gonna be okay."

It's my fault, and I'll just have to get over him.

If she told herself that enough times, maybe it would sink in.

Maybe she'd start to believe it.

They stared at each other in silence for seconds that felt longer.

She wasn't even uncomfortable at the idea that this man cared about her. She trusted him. Liked him.

He was her partner.

"If you need anything, I mean anything, let me know. Okay?" Holman said finally.

She didn't want to shoot him down. *Alone* hurt too much. "Thanks, Alec."

He paused, then nodded, but he was wearing a small smile.

The phone rang, making them both jump.

Her partner grabbed it, and she couldn't help but watch him, the open folder on her lap. Taylor sucked in a breath and smiled a little.

Chapter Thirty-Four

Taylor turned the corner and pulled into the gas station on Main Street as soon as she hit the middle of Antioch.

She'd really pushed the Charger and should've stopped for fuel before now—the damn thing had gone past *E*, and was on fumes.

Her lower back ached, but she ignored it. She'd rub the spot when she got out of the car if it still bothered her. Hadn't slept well the night before. Or the one before that.

Combined with frequent car rides, and going up and down the stairs all the time at work, the soreness made sense, but it hadn't kept her from leaving Dallas to come here.

Nothing mattered but Antioch.

She'd just wanted—no, *needed*—to get there.

Taylor *had* to see Shannon and make things right.

She owed him a hell of a lot more than the no-contact thing over the past few months. Not that he'd tried to call or text her, but *she* should've reached out to him.

Cowardice had bitten her and clung, and the weeks had melted into months. She was running out of time.

Their baby would be here in less than six weeks.

She'd let him assume she'd gone through with the abortion and hadn't reached out, except for those two messages that'd gone unanswered a few days after he'd found the appointment card.

Selfish.

Taylor had no justification that mattered for not telling him. That was valid. That was forgivable.

Being without him was torture, an aching hole that'd

turned into a chasm eating at her from the inside out, despite the reserved happiness that'd worked its way into unmatched joy as her baby—*their baby*—had grown. Getting bigger at each sonogram.

The elation that the child was healthy and would be here soon was dimmed the whole time by the constant guilt that Shannon didn't know, and the agony that *she* was the one keeping him away because she couldn't own up to her feelings. Or let go of the need to do this herself, even though that wasn't good for her, the baby, or the man she loved.

And damn... She did love him. More than she'd thought possible. Too bad Taylor hadn't realized it until after she'd fled.

Holding on to the anger, the hurt, from the day he'd found the appointment card had been easier at first. A hell of a lot easier than embracing the real reason for her pain.

The confrontation was something she'd regret for the rest of her life. The things he'd said that day...

She hadn't even defended herself. Told him she wasn't going to the clinic.

Taylor winced and shut the car off.

It's all your fault, Taylor Marie Carrigan.

Could they even go back?

She wanted nothing more.

He was a good man. He'd *want* to be there. For her. With her. With *them*. Nothing mattered more to Shannon than family.

But...

She wasn't his family. Only their baby was. For all she knew, he wouldn't speak to her again.

He might not forgive her and take her back, but he had a right to know he'd be a father. Her sergeant would be happy, right?

Shannon would be angry she'd kept the pregnancy from him, but...

He still...loved her, right?

What if he doesn't?

He'd flung the words as an accusation, not a declaration. *"I fucking love you, Taylor. How could you ruin that? How could you want to kill our baby?"* would be burned into her consciousness for the rest of her life.

She shuddered and tried to push the memories away. Had to persevere.

What if Taylor's no-contact had made him think she'd written him off?

It would only make sense, especially since he thought their child would never be.

It's been months...

Afterward, during one of the half-a-million times she'd replayed the scene in her mind, she'd been able to process Shannon's shock.

He'd found that blasted appointment card, discovering she was pregnant in the worst way possible.

Tears stung her eyes—the wonderful side effect of pregnancy hormones. Taylor looked down at her rounded stomach. Tried to smile when her daughter kicked.

Shannon's daughter.

She sucked in a breath and rubbed the spot. "Get it together," she whispered aloud, and it helped.

Taylor could only go to him and say her piece. She'd tell him she loved him and apologize. Show him the latest sonogram and tell him that the baby was a girl. Tell him she wanted him back, she wanted to be a family and raise their daughter together, but if he couldn't forgive her, he could still have a relationship with their child.

Then...hope.

She'd leave the ball in his court.

Shannon *would* demand to be in his daughter's life. He just might not require *Taylor* the way she needed him to.

Pain crippled her heart and she had to breathe slowly to get air down.

Taylor stumbled on her way to put the pump's nozzle into the Charger. Had to brace herself on the back of the car. She'd almost dropped the handle.

The discomfort wasn't figurative. There was a sharp pain in her lower back, and another to her right side.

"Whoa, there, you okay?" An older gentleman from the pump next to hers grabbed her elbow. Steadied her.

She nodded and tried to breathe through the agony. "Thanks," she pushed out.

They looked down at the same time, and Taylor gasped. Blood covered her crotch and her upper thighs, soaking the denim.

"Ma'am..." the man said.

A stab daggered her lower back, and she cried out, bending over and grabbing her middle.

"Ma'am, when's your baby due? Do you want me to call your husband?" The man had a frantic edge that kicked up her heartbeat.

She hurt, but it didn't feel normal, like a contraction. Blood was steadily seeping downward, now coating her jeans almost to her knees. Her head spun, and she planted one palm to the end of the car and grasped the man's forearm with the other.

"Easy. I'm gonna call an ambulance."

"No... No... I'm fine."

"Damn, my phone's in my truck!" He looked torn as he held her up.

White-hot agony hit her and Taylor's knees buckled. No amount of scrambling was going to keep her on her feet. The pain spread from her spine and down, consuming her right side. Her hand slipped off the Charger.

The man seized her, which was the only thing that kept her off the ground. "Ma'am! Oh my God, that's a lot of blood." His brown eyes seemed to blur, and Taylor's head fell back.

"Hey, mister, is something wrong?" Another guy, but he sounded far away.

The guy screamed, "Call 9-1-1!" right as the world went black.

Shannon put down the barbells and scrambled to catch his cell as it vibrated its way across the magazines it was precariously perched on. He should probably clean that TV tray table off one of these days. It didn't belong in the garage, anyway.

He smiled when he glanced at the touch screen, then swiped his thumb across. "Hey, Mom."

"Shannon. You need to come to the hospital now," she said by way of greeting. She sounded urgent, on edge.

His heart slid to his gut and the good sweat he'd built up from his heavy workout in the garage chilled. "Cailey? Is she okay?"

"Not Cailey."

"What—"

"Just come down here, son."

"Mom, tell me what's going on. Is it you? What's wrong?"

There was a pause, but only for a split-second. "Taylor's here." The intensity in her familiar voice made him still on his workout bench.

Shannon was caught between giving a damn—his

stomach lurched—and hanging up, but a dismissal was too rude to put his mom through. He *was* a little curious, but...

"No, Mom," he managed through clenched teeth. His jaw smarted but he couldn't convince it to loosen.

No way was he about to let Taylor Carrigan drag him down again. His heart was far from healed, but he was trying to get over her. Little by little.

Yeah, that's working so well.

"Shannon. You don't understand."

"What don't I understand?" He'd not wanted to, but after their breakup, he'd told his mother the whole sordid affair, ending, of course, with Taylor ripping his heart into a million pieces because she was going to abort his baby.

All it had taken was his mother asking, *'What's wrong?'* one afternoon, and the whole damn thing had poured out.

He'd even cried a little, like a pussy.

She'd rubbed his back while he'd talked, and Shannon had tried to get his balls back, but he'd let her soothe him with her touch, like she had when he was little.

However, he hadn't liked his mom's take on things. She'd urged him to reach out to Taylor. She'd said they both needed to cool off, then they could heal together.

Mom had even said maybe the time wasn't right for the baby, reminded him it was Taylor's choice. That part had pissed him off. They might not have planned the pregnancy, but Shannon should've had a say.

His mother had even told him, if he loved Taylor, not to let her go.

Right. There are some things people can't move past.

He couldn't forgive her for making the important decision without him. No consideration that the baby was *his,* too. Even if it was a choice he never would've allowed. He didn't have a chance to fight for his child.

Shannon would regret that for the rest of his life.

What made him feel worse was he couldn't hate Taylor. He loved her too damn much.

Self-loathing hadn't fixed that, even as the months had gone by.

He hadn't answered her texts from a few days after he'd found the appointment card. Hadn't been able to, and time hadn't changed that.

"Shannon Michael Crowley, you listen to me, and you listen good. Get your ass down here. Now."

Jesus.

She'd broken out his full name, not to mention dropped a curse word, if only a mild one. He was doomed.

Shannon sighed, and pushed to his feet. "Tell me what I'm walking into, Mom." The cop in him needed that.

Again, his mom hesitated. "If I tell you, you have to promise me to breathe, and not drive recklessly. They'll both be fine, now. For a while, it was touch and go."

They?

"What're you talking about?"

"Taylor had the baby, but she was early. I was in the OR, so I couldn't call you until now, there wasn't time. It was an emergency C-section. Taylor collapsed at the gas station on Main Street. She was bleeding...hemorrhaging. Thank God there was a man there to help, and get the ambulance on the way. But...your daughter is strong, Shannon. She's small, but beautiful. Come for them." Her voice broke.

His strong mom's emotion broke *him* as much as the confusing words she'd said.

Nothing made sense.

Emergency... Operating room... Blood...

Standing had been worthless, because his legs quit on him and his ass hit the workout bench hard. It creaked a protest, and the thin padding did nothing for the new ache in his tailbone.

Baby?

"Wh—?" Shannon sputtered. His head spun, and his heart rushed into his ribcage from his gut, beating so hard it was going to pop out.

He couldn't breathe. His *everything* hurt.

White-hot agony spread disbelief all over his body.

"Taylor almost died, Shannon."

He had nothing.

Nothing would come out of his mouth. He took one painful breath, then another. "Mom—" he finally croaked.

"I know, baby. Just get down here. We'll sort it all out."

"Mom." He swallowed hard and blinked away the blurry vision.

No amount of screaming *Get it together* was working.

"Come meet your baby girl, and see her mama."

Chapter Thirty-Five

He shouldn't have promised his mom he wouldn't drive recklessly to get to the hospital, because his Tundra was in bat-out-of-hell territory, even though it wasn't more than a ten minute drive. Shannon did it in four, maybe five.

His heart was in his throat the whole time, and breath still didn't come easily. Hadn't taken time to change, either—they'd get him in black basketball shorts and the first muscle shirt he'd found in the garage to throw on. It was gray, and torn. Probably smelled like a sweaty workout, too.

A daughter.

His baby.

There was a whole lotta *'what the fuck?'* thrown in there for good measure.

Shannon swallowed.

He'd told Taylor he loved her.

His conscience coughed up *how* he'd told her. He'd flung the words, not professed them in a way she could've taken as sincere.

Couldn't blame her, really. It'd been a defensive move, to rub in her face that she'd never told him how *she* felt about him.

Shannon winced. Pretty cowardly, actually.

No way to tell the love of your life how you feel about her for the first time.

What was he supposed to do now?

"Get your ass in that building."

And make things right.

He couldn't say the latter part aloud, because he still

didn't know how the hell he was going to do it.

His anger had simmered to nothing some time ago, leaving him with regret and pain. He'd been dealing with that the best he could. But this...

I'm a father, after all.

Shannon should be steaming mad all over again. He wasn't. Maybe the adrenaline hadn't worn off yet.

What *did* he feel?

He was grateful she hadn't had an abortion...and he loved her.

It was too damn much at once.

He didn't even know what the hell to say, let alone what he *wanted*.

Shannon shook his head and slammed his truck door. He jogged into the hospital, ignoring the bite in the fall air. He should've grabbed a jacket. Or put on pants.

His mom met him by the elevator doors on the OB floor, and he almost lost it. He hugged her tight, grateful when she wrapped her arms around him and held him. Damn good thing, because his knees wanted to buckle. She was short, like Taylor, but strong enough to keep him on his feet for a few minutes.

"Are you okay?" she asked.

He released her and took a breath. "Yes. No. I don't freakin' know. It's a lot to process."

Empathy shone in her amber eyes. "I know. Let's sit and talk for a moment, then I'll take you to them."

"I don't know if I can see her, Mom," he blurted.

"Taylor or your daughter?"

Your daughter.

What a foreign phrase.

"Taylor. I just can't." His baby, on the other hand, Shannon wanted to see more than anything, as soon as he got the balls.

His mom took his hand and led him into a waiting room.

It was empty—thank God. The TV was on, the volume low, but he didn't pay attention to the screen. Chairs lined both walls, and there were a few end tables with scattered magazines. Against the wall, next to a Ficus tree, there was a crate of toys.

He collapsed into a chair next to his mother.

"Start with the baby, but Taylor wants to see you, honey. She asked for you when she came into the ER. Actually, that's why they called me. She kept saying your name over and over. They called up here to see if I was working. She's so beautiful, Shan. You did well. Your baby girl looks like you, though."

His mother's obvious pride and expression did nothing to stop his laugh. It had a bitter edge that made her glance at him in confusion, her brow furrowed.

"Mom, Taylor and I were done months ago. Yeah, she's gorgeous and at one time took my breath away, but what we had...it's just not going to happen again."

She shook her head and patted his hand. "You can't know that. A baby changes everything."

"Right. A baby she obviously didn't want me to know about."

"Shannon. Stop."

"Mom—"

"Listen to me."

The sharp edge to her voice snapped his mouth shut.

"She almost died today. Did you miss that, when I told you on the phone?"

Her eyes flashed with so much irritation, it made him gulp.

"You will *not* go in that room and break her heart. She asked for you for a damn good reason, and you're going to listen to her. She gave you a child today, so you *will* sit by her bedside and hold her hand. She had major surgery and she's on pain meds, but she wanted one thing. *You.*"

Shannon blinked. It had to be a record that his mom had cursed twice in one day—in the space of an hour, no less. His instinct was a resounding, *'yes ma'am,'* but his heart *hurt.*

He didn't know if he could. Wasn't about to repeat that to her. One tongue lashing was enough.

Thanks, Mom.

"What happened? Why did the baby come early? What put Taylor's life in danger?" His questions were soft, not much louder than a whisper, and his mom squeezed his hand.

"There was a tear in the placenta. It can be very dangerous, like in Taylor's case. She hemorrhaged. We're very lucky they both survived. They got her here quick, which saved them."

His chest tightened and his gut clenched. Not having her was one thing—at least she was out in the world somewhere—but to imagine Taylor truly gone, as in *dead,* made his whole body ache. Worse than just the broken heart. "I do need to see her."

A slow smile spread across his mother's full mouth and she patted his stubbled cheek. "Good. It's a start."

"She really asked for me?"

She nodded. "Over and over. Frantically. She calmed when I told her I was your mother, but she wanted you here. She kept begging me to tell you not to hate her."

Shannon had to look down to stave off the emotion rising up. Wasn't about to cry in front of his mom. Again. He couldn't take a moment to scream, either. Or punch something.

His mind spun in a chaos of *feeling*.

"I don't. Hate her, I mean. I love her." His voice cracked.

"I know, baby."

"Baby," he breathed. "I missed it. I missed her birth." He had to push words past the lump in his throat.

"You wouldn't have been allowed in anyway. It was bad. Taylor's pressure dropped, she lost so much blood we had to transfuse."

"If I was here, I would've freaked."

Again, his mom nodded. "I know. So not being able to call you until afterward was probably for the better. I was there, in the room the whole time. Doc Hayes got her stable as soon as he got the baby out. She's small, but not tiny, and she's breathing on her own. You're lucky. It was scary and Taylor was touch-and-go for longer than I like to see. But all is well now, and I have a new granddaughter!"

Shannon didn't know what to say, so he didn't try. Emotional rollercoasters had never been his thing. He studied his basketball shorts and noted the differences in his mom's hand, still entwined with his much larger one.

"I think she was headed to you, you know. If she hadn't collapsed, Taylor would've showed up at your house."

He laughed. "I still would've freaked." He managed to look into his mom's face.

"I know." She smiled. "Do you want to see your daughter?"

"Yes."

Tears flowed freely when his mom took him into the NICU.

His daughter was tiny, and perfect, and she *did* look like him, complete with a minuscule dimple in her right cheek.

The incubator made him feel a million miles from her—she was untouchable, instead of right in front of him. It highlighted her unbelievable fragility.

Shannon's mom slid her arm around his middle and squeezed, as if she could read his mind.

From all the neo-natal stories she'd told over the years, he knew he wouldn't be able to hold his baby, not yet anyway. He'd always felt bad for those parents his mom had talked about.

Now he *was* one; his minor regret for people he didn't know melted into something serious and personal. Pain, because he wanted to know his baby was okay, and all the monitors said she wasn't.

Emotion caught in his throat and he swiped at his face. "When can I hold her?"

"Not today, probably, but you can touch her." His mother's volume was low and solemn. She patted his lower back. "Go on. Talk to her. Touch her skin. She won't break. Let her know who you are."

He blinked tears away, sucked in a breath then sank into the chair Mom had pushed over. "Hi, baby girl." Shannon's statement shattered, so he cleared his throat. He stroked her arm.

Her skin was unbelievably soft. He lifted her tiny hand, and examined her little fingers, her nails.

The baby turned her face toward him and he almost lost it again. Her eyes were open and she shifted, lifting one of her little feet.

"I'm your daddy," he whispered, gripping that tiny foot and kissing the bottom of it. "How's she doing, Mom?" He looked over his shoulder to see his mother staring at them, a soft smile on her face.

"Okay for now. Don't let the monitors scare you.

They're standard and don't mean her prognosis is bad. We're keeping a close eye on her oxygen intake. It's good now, but if she needs help, we'll put her on the CPAP."

"She's beautiful," Shannon breathed, reaching out to caress her cap of downy dark hair.

"She is. Certainly looks like a Crowley." Her pride made him smile. "Keep touching her, baby. Talk to her. Let her know your voice. It'll help you connect since you can't hold her yet. Keep in mind, it'll be harder for Taylor. A lot of moms get very depressed they can't hold their babies. It's not a normal birth story. She'll need you. They both will."

"I love her. I love them both so damn much." His words were strained.

His mother rubbed his back and kissed his temple. "I know, honey. So you'll have to help them both, until you can bring her home."

Home?

Where the hell was *home* going to be for Taylor and his baby?

"When will that be?" he choked out.

"It depends on how she does."

He nodded because he didn't know what to say, and caressed his daughter's little leg.

"Doc Hayes will want to talk to you, too," Mom said. "Okay..."

Silence fell and Shannon watched and stroked the baby he'd thought would never be, until his heart was bursting with love for her...and her mother. "Mom, I need to see Taylor."

"I was hoping you'd say that."

He heard the smile in her voice.

Chapter Thirty-Six

Taylor came around slowly, and everything echoed. She blinked and tried to rub her eyes free of grit, but her hand smarted.

She gasped when she spotted an IV sticking out of it. The tape pulled against her skin, and she winced.

"Easy."

The familiar male jolted her.

Has to be a dream.

She needed to sit up. Movement was bad, because she *hurt*. It was a dull ache at the moment but—

Everything slammed into her at once—the gas station, the ambulance, Shannon's mom. The doctor telling her they needed to operate, *now*.

Wanting Shannon, and being told they couldn't wait for him.

"My baby!" Taylor cried. She tried to sit up. Agony assaulted her, radiating out from her middle, consuming her chest, but two strong hands pushed her back down, gently, until her shoulders touched the unfamiliar bed.

"Our baby is fine," Shannon whispered.

She met his eyes and burst into tears. "I'm so sorry." Moisture was hot on her cheeks and no amount of sucking in air was helping her regain composure.

Why is he here?

His mother had probably called him.

He'd come?

Probably for their daughter.

What if he hated her?

"I don't hate you."

Damn, she'd lost all control.

She was blubbering aloud?

Heat burned her neck and settled in her cheeks. Still couldn't stop *freaking* crying. "I'm so sorry, Shannon. So sorry," Taylor whispered through her gulps.

"Shhh," he soothed, pushing her hair out of her face. "We can talk about that later. Do you want to sit up?" His voice was soft, as if he thought she was going to break.

She wiped her eyes, and managed a nod.

Shannon pushed the button on the side of the bed until it inclined. He fluffed the pillow behind her and returned to his seat. The chair was pushed flush to the side of her bed, but he wasn't close enough.

"Are you hurting?"

Not physically.

"No. Where's our baby?" she whispered.

He caressed her cheek, which made her pulse speed up.

Unfortunately, the heart monitor gave her away in that regard.

When Taylor had the guts to look at Shannon, he wore a smirk. He was so handsome.

He'd finally cut his hair, and she found herself preferring it shaggy. His whiskey-colored eyes were the same, and the tenderness in his gaze made her long for him, but it confused her, too.

Am I seeing things?

"She's in the NICU, but she's a little trooper, she's breathing on her own. She's beautiful, Taylor. Just gorgeous. She weighs four and a half pounds, but she's doing well for being born at thirty-four weeks, or so my mom and Doc Hayes said." His expression, a mix of wistfulness and pride, made her heart skip. He looked...happy.

"Can I see her?" she managed, but it came out a half-stutter. "I need to see her. I didn't get to see her."

"The nurse told me they're running some tests, but I'm sure you can, in a little while. I'll go with you. Listen, Taylor—"

"Tests?" she demanded.

"Everything will be okay, I promise. It'll be a long road, but our daughter's strong. Here, I took pictures." Shannon handed her his phone.

Taylor held the cell like a lifeline, thumbing through six or seven pictures of their tiny baby girl. She had circular monitors stuck all over her little body, but she didn't look as bad as she'd feared.

She thumbed through the pictures several times, but the ache in her body was only relieved a little bit.

Her baby would be okay, but she still needed to see her with her own eyes.

Touch her.

Hold her.

Tears cascaded again when she looked at the last photo—a close up. The baby had Shannon's dark hair, his dimple, and definitely his nose.

"I'm so sorry," she blurted.

Shannon's expression softened. "I believe you, sweets."

Sweets?

Her bottom lip wobbled and she lost the battle to stave off more tears. She needed to touch him. Taylor reached for his hand.

Shannon didn't turn her away.

He entwined their fingers and kissed her knuckles. With his free hand, he wiped her tears away. "I owe you an apology. For the things I said that day."

She didn't know *what* to say, so she looked down. How could his need to apologize be stronger than hers?

She'd hidden the existence of their child.

And still... He'd returned to her side.

He leaned over and gently guided her chin up. "I'm sorry, Taylor, for the things I said to you. The rest we can talk about later."

She swallowed. "I'm not gonna fall apart."

"You almost died today." He stared hard. Like he was trying to figure out what to say next, or trying to read her mind.

When his gaze slid to her lips, Taylor squeezed his hand.

"Do you want to kiss me?" she whispered.

Shannon's Adam's apple bobbed. "I shouldn't."

"Shouldn't want to or shouldn't kiss me?" She tried not to wince.

Maybe he was only there because of the gravity of what'd happened.

Maybe the endearment meant nothing. Maybe the apology was a courtesy for the mother of one's child.

Maybe the look in his eyes didn't mean what she hoped it did.

"Both." He flashed a half-smile that revealed a touch of guilt.

She shouldn't have the capacity to think he was sexy at the moment, but she did.

Her *everything* hurt, and she was going to need pain meds soon, but perhaps she could relieve the ache in her chest regarding the man she loved.

"What if I wanted to kiss you?"

Shannon smiled, this time a full one that under normal circumstances would've made her insides wobble.

"And here I was, feeling like an asshole because of what you've been through today, and all I could think about was tasting your mouth."

"Not an asshole. C'mere."

He dipped down, painfully slowly, as if he really did think she was going to splinter into a million pieces, and brushed his lips against hers. He kept it short and chaste, until Taylor slipped her unencumbered hand to the back of his neck, and buried her fingers in his hair.

Then she opened for him, and their tongues dueled.

When he pulled away, she whimpered, not because he'd hurt her, but because she'd felt close to him again, as if no time had passed, and the duration of his lips on hers was too short.

She didn't want the kiss to end. Or for him to leave her side. Ever.

"Are you okay?" Shannon whispered against her mouth. He caressed her cheek and ran his other hand over her hair.

"Yes." Taylor kissed him once more before he leaned back. "Shannon, I—"

"Ah, you're awake. How're you doing, Mama?" A brunette nurse with a bright smile and royal blue scrubs swept into the room and destroyed the moment. She carried a pitcher of ice water, and set it on the bedside table.

She cursed. Had been about to tell Shannon she loved him. "I'm fine. I want to see my baby."

"Need pain meds?"

"In a bit, I want to see her first."

The nurse nodded and looked at Shannon. "How about you, Dad? You doin' all right?"

He swallowed and nodded, and took Taylor's hand again. "Can we see our daughter?"

"I'll check and be right back." Then she was gone.

"Dammit," Taylor whispered.

"What's wrong?" His demand was accompanied by knitted eyebrows and a squeeze of her fingertips.

"Nothing. She interrupted me. I love you."

Wow, way to blurt things.

Maybe the pain meds—or residual anesthesia—*were* muddling her brain.

Shannon was frozen. His beautiful eyes were wide and his mouth agape.

Is that bad?

Her heart thundered and she didn't even care that the monitor was giving her away again. She stared at the man she loved, the father of her baby. *Couldn't* look away.

He still had her hand in his.

That has to be a good thing, right?

Words fell out. "I was coming to your place today. Was gonna tell you everything and apologize. Tell you I want to be with you and raise our baby together. Marry you. I just didn't get a chance because...well, because of what happened. I'm so damn sorry for what I said and did, and I..." Taylor shook her head. "I don't know how to make it up to you. I just... I wanted you to know. You had a right to know. I was wrong. Selfish, like you said." She was babbling, and Shannon still hadn't moved. She swallowed. Sucked in air that only made her middle hurt worse. "I'm so relieved our baby is okay, and that you're—"

"Taylor."

"What?"

"Shut up."

She blinked. Her mouth snapped shut.

"I told you we'd talk about all this later," he growled.

"But—"

"I love you, too." Shannon kissed her again, this time without the gentleness he had moments before.

Taylor didn't care. She fused her mouth to his, clutching his gray muscle shirt with both hands, although she regretted that when her IV hand throbbed a protest.

He kissed her until her brains scrambled, and the heart monitor was fairly screaming.

When they parted, his eyes shot to the monitor, then back to hers, and they both laughed.

She flexed her hand, since she couldn't rub the soreness away.

"Are you all right? Was I too rough?"

She shook her head. "I love you."

Shannon smiled. "I love you, too. And yes."

"Yes?" She held her breath.

"Yes to everything, especially the marriage part. And the raising Lily together part."

"Lily?" Taylor gasped. She bit her bottom lip, but the damn tears had staked a claim again, clouding her vision and soaking her face.

"My mom suggested it. If you don't—"

"I love it. I really do. I didn't have a name picked out."

He cupped her cheeks, thumbing her tears away. Shannon kissed her forehead then pressed a tender kiss to her lips. "Mom'll love that. She went to get Cailey, I hope you don't mind. If it's too much for today—"

"It's not. They're family, right?"

His smile was slow and full, and his eyes were misty.

The nurse interrupted them again, but this time it didn't bother Taylor.

"Dr. Hayes says you can see her for a little bit."

Shannon kissed Taylor's knuckles and smiled again. "Let's go see our baby girl, sweets."

Her breath caught and she forced a nod, then sucked back some more tears. "Let's go see Lily."

About The Author

USA TODAY Bestselling, award winning author of historical and epic fantasy romance, as well as romantic suspense, C.A. loves to dabble in different genres. If it's a good story, she'll write it, no matter where it seems to fit!

She's a hopeless romantic and always will be.

Risking it all for Happily Ever After is what she lives by!

C.A. is originally from Ohio, but got to Texas as soon as she could. She's happily married and has a bachelor's degree in Criminal Justice.

She works with kids when she's not writing.

WEBSITE: http://www.caszarek.com

BLOG: http://www.caszarekwriter.blogspot.com/

TWITTER: https://twitter.com/caszarek

FACEBOOK: http://www.facebook.com/caszarek

INSTAGRAM: https://www.instagram.com/caszarek/

GOODREADS:https://www.goodreads.com/author/show/5815085.C_A_Szarek

NEWSLETTER SIGNUP: http://blogspot.us7.list-manage.com/subscribe?u=296abc5983ebc51c1d4d0972b&id=fb22ce93be

EMAIL: ca@caszarek.com

www.ingramcontent.com/pod-product-compliance
Lightning Source LLC
Chambersburg PA
CBHW031619180726
48284CB00005B/1614